THE FADING OF THE LIGHT

Cornwall, 1902. Edith Fairchild, deserted by her feckless husband Benedict eight years before, has established the thriving Spindrift artists' community by the sea and found deep and lasting love with Pascal. They have accepted that they cannot marry, but when Benedict returns unexpectedly to Spindrift House, all Edith and Pascal's secret hopes and dreams of a joyous life together are overturned.

Benedict's arrival shatters the peaceful and creative atmosphere of the close-knit community. When Edith will not allow him back into her bed, the conflict escalates and he sets in motion a chain of tragic events that reverberate down the years and threaten the happiness of the community forever . . .

THE ULVERSCROFT FOUNDATION
(registered UK charity number 264873)
was established in 1972 to provide funds for research, diagnosis and treatment of eye diseases. Examples of major projects funded by the Ulverscroft Foundation are:-

- The Children's Eye Unit at Moorfields Eye Hospital, London
- The Ulverscroft Children's Eye Unit at Great Ormond Street Hospital for Sick Children
- Funding research into eye diseases and treatment at the Department of Ophthalmology, University of Leicester
- The Ulverscroft Vision Research Group, Institute of Child Health
- Twin operating theatres at the Western Ophthalmic Hospital, London
- The Chair of Ophthalmology at the Royal Australian College of Ophthalmologists

You can help further the work of the Foundation by making a donation or leaving a legacy. Every contribution is gratefully received. If you would like to help support the Foundation or require further information, please contact:

THE ULVERSCROFT FOUNDATION
The Green, Bradgate Road, Anstey
Leicester LE7 7FU, England
Tel: (0116) 236 4325

website: www.ulverscroft-foundation.org.uk

CHARLOTTE BETTS

◆

THE FADING OF THE LIGHT

Complete and Unabridged

CHARNWOOD
Leicester

First published in Great Britain in 2021 by
Piatkus
an imprint of Little, Brown Book Group
London

First Charnwood Edition
published 2021
by arrangement with
Little, Brown Book Group
London

A catalogue record for this book is available
from the British Library.

ISBN 978–1–4448–4748–2

Published by
Ulverscroft Limited
Anstey, Leicestershire

Printed and bound in Great Britain by
TJ Books Ltd., Padstow, Cornwall
This book is printed on acid-free paper

For Julian and Lynn

1

June 1902

Spindrift House, Cornwall

Stars still glimmered as the rising sun began to paint the sky with streaks of apricot and gold. Up on the cliffs above the sea stood Spindrift House, its thick stone walls sheltering the sleeping community of the ten artists and five children that lived within.

As the stars faded in the brightening sky, a blackbird unfolded his wings in the great copper beech beside the house. He opened his yellow bill and trilled the first liquid notes of welcome to the dawn.

It was going to be a glorious summer's day.

★ ★ ★

Edith awoke to the sound of birdsong. Carefully untwining herself from Pascal's embrace, she slipped out of bed. She stood for a moment smiling down at his austere features, now softened in slumber and, in a rush of tenderness, bent to kiss his dark hair. His body remained curved around the warm hollow she'd left in the mattress. For a moment, she nearly slid back under the covers. But there was something she had to do.

1

Shrugging on her dressing gown, she ran barefoot upstairs to the studio on the second floor. She snatched up her sketchbook and rested it on the windowsill to catch the early light. Closing her eyes, she summoned those fleeting moments when she'd drifted between the dream world and consciousness, before the blackbird's song had woken her. Then she began to make swift pencil strokes.

A little while later, she let out a sigh of contentment. She'd captured her vision for a new painting before it evaporated like the morning mist. Lifting the sash, she leaned over the windowsill to breathe in the sea air and watch the seagulls wheeling overhead. After she'd spent several days cooped up in the studio with raindrops beading the windowpanes, the heavy showers had cleared. Beyond the undulating lawn and the grassy headland, the sapphire sea was calm again. It looked as if the weather was going to be fine for King Edward VII's Coronation celebrations later that week, after all.

Excitement bubbled within her. She couldn't wait to discuss her new painting with the others. The founder members of the Spindrift community had grown out of the friendships they'd made while they were students at the Slade School of Fine Art. Later, other artists joined them and the close-knit group provided each other not only with companionship and creative encouragement, but a buttress against difficult times.

Closing the window, Edith selected a primed canvas from a stack leaning against the wall.

Small encrustations of paint on the dusty boards impressed themselves on the soles of her bare feet, as if she were walking over crushed seashells down in the cove. Collecting together paints and brushes, she crammed them into her old carpetbag.

She heard a footstep and turned to see Pascal's lean figure in the doorway.

'I guessed I would find you here, *chérie*.' His brown eyes gleamed with amusement.

She ran into his arms and he slipped warm hands beneath her dressing gown and caressed her back through her thin nightgown. 'I had an idea for my next work,' she said.

He laughed. 'Didn't I say it would come to you once you stopped worrying about what to paint next?'

She rested her head against his chest. 'Whatever would I do without you, Pascal?'

'You will never have to do without me,' he said, combing his fingers through her black hair. 'Not ever. Now what is this masterpiece you will create?'

'It must have been the recent gales that made me dream about it,' she said. 'I'm going to paint the children flying their kites on a blustery day up on the headland. The sea will be in the background and clouds will be chasing each other across a blue sky. I can hardly wait to begin.'

'Very good but aren't your toes cold?'

She glanced down at her bare feet.

He nuzzled at her neck. 'You forget everything when you are working.'

3

'Except you.' She buried her face in his shoulder. Pascal was steadfast in both love and friendship. She'd known him for ten years and they'd been lovers for five, not counting that first time.

Quick footsteps clattered up the stairs. 'Mama? Where are you?'

Pascal released Edith as Pearl, her eight-year-old daughter, burst into the room.

'There you are, Mama! I came to look for you in your bedroom last night but you weren't there.' Her face was pink with indignation. 'I waited and waited and then fell asleep in your bed and when I woke up you *still* weren't there!'

Edith bit her lip and glanced at Pascal. Creeping along the corridor to his room at night was too risky now the children were older. It would have to stop. 'I had a marvellous idea for a painting,' she said. 'You shall be in it with your brothers and sister.'

'Shall I have a new dress?'

Edith shook her head. 'No, but we'll make you a lovely scarlet kite.' She ruffled her daughter's curls. 'It's time we were dressed, sweetheart. Will you help Hannah get the twins ready for school?'

Pearl scowled. 'They're *seven*, Mama. Can't they dress themselves without a nursemaid to help them?'

'Of course they can, but you know how they dawdle, and then you'd be late.'

Pascal held his hand out to Pearl. 'Come, *chérie*! We will see if your brothers and sister are awake.'

'Don't you think I should have a new dress,

4

Uncle Pascal, if I'm going to be in Mama's painting?' Pearl's hazel eyes and dazzling smile made her look uncannily like her father, Benedict. The father who had deserted Edith and four children seven years before.

Pearl's voice faded away as Pascal led her downstairs.

Edith shuddered. Remembering Benedict still upset her, not for his selfishness and unkindness or for their failed marriage that hung like an albatross around her neck, but for his part in the secret she loathed herself for never disclosing to anyone. Not even Pascal.

★ ★ ★

Spindrift House, formerly a working farm, adjoined a courtyard surrounded by once neglected outbuildings, now converted into studios and workshops with sleeping accommodation. One side of the courtyard was entirely taken up by a vast, ancient barn, the Spindrift Gallery, where the community sold their work in the summer season. Since the railway had been extended to Port Isaac, bringing increasing numbers of visitors to the area, the gallery and photographic studio were popular with holidaymakers seeking souvenirs of their seaside stay.

There had been such a press of customers there during the afternoon that Edith hadn't been able to enter the sales into the ledger. She had just enough time to do the books before the children returned from school. Two of her watercolour sketches of local scenes had sold, along with one of Clarissa's silver and sea glass pendants, a couple of Maude's printed silk scarves and a handful of Dora's Cornish wildflower postcards.

After she'd updated the ledger, she calculated how much was due to each artist. Even though the community had scraped together the funds to buy a substantial share of Spindrift House from Edith's husband five years before, they were still obliged to pay him rent, together with ten per cent of their sales. In addition, Benedict had coerced Edith into making another payment that the rest of the community, except for Pascal, knew nothing about. The hateful price to prevent him from selling his share of Spindrift House, or returning from London to live there, was three of her paintings every year. Himself an indifferent, if fashionable, portrait painter, Benedict sold her canvases, signed by himself and passed off as an alternative line of his own. In that way, he'd maintained his artistic reputation but it still made Edith sick to think of it. She'd had no choice, though, if she wanted him to stay away from Spindrift — and herself.

The bell on the gallery door jangled and Clarissa entered. Slender and flaxen-haired, she was one of Edith's closest friends and her daughter Lily was like a sister to Pearl.

'I've sold one of your pendants,' said Edith.

'The second one this week!' Clarissa held out a tray of bracelets and rings, many decorated with sea glass found in the cove. 'I've brought some new pieces for my display case,' she said. 'The children are waiting for you in the garden.

They're so excited about flying their kites. I'll lock up here, if you'd like to skip off a bit early?'

Feeling as if she'd been let out of school unexpectedly, Edith collected her sketchbook and pencils from under the counter and hurried off.

In the garden, she saw her children, together with Lily, chasing each other through the shrubbery, full of high spirits.

Pearl came running towards her. 'You've been *ages*, Mama!' She grabbed her mother's hand. 'We'd better hurry while it's still windy. I tried my kite in the garden but the strings got in a muddle.'

Pascal, sitting on the lawn untangling the ribbons and strings of the kite, glanced up at Edith with a rueful smile. 'I suspect we will spend a great deal of time undoing knots this afternoon. Ah, I have it!' Triumphantly, he lifted up the kite and shook the strings free.

Pearl hopped up and down. 'Come on then! Don't dawdle!'

'You,' said Edith, tugging one of Pearl's ringlets, 'are an impatient little madam. Now say thank you to Uncle Pascal.'

Pearl pressed a noisy kiss on his cheek.

The children, clutching their kites, raced off towards the garden gate, while Edith and Pascal followed at a more sedate pace.

'They're very excited,' she said. 'I hope there won't be tears before bedtime.'

'Fresh air and exercise will make them fall asleep quickly tonight.'

Edith slipped her hand into Pascal's. 'You're

7

always so good to my children.'

'I love them because they are a part of you.' He sighed. 'But still I wish we could make a child together. Sometimes I long for it so much my heart aches.'

Edith's heart ached, too.

He squeezed her hand. 'Don't look so unhappy, *mon amour*. You made me no false promises. I have always known that, for as long as Benedict lives, we cannot marry or have children together. Above all else, it is my joy to be loved by you.'

Her eyes smarted and she couldn't look at him. She had no secrets from Pascal except for the one huge one that ate away at her. And every single day she delayed telling him the truth, the harder it became. She knew she *must* tell him. But not now. Not yet.

Running on ahead, the children dashed through the garden gate and out onto the headland.

Pascal pulled on Edith's hand. 'Let's run, too!' Laughing, they sprinted through the garden and onto the clifftop.

The children were waiting for them beside the Bronze Age standing stone, hopping up and down with impatience.

Jasper, dark eyes squinting into the sun, gasped as a gust of wind caught a corner of his kite and flipped it up against his chest.

Pascal took it from him. 'I will help you.' He organised the children into a row with the wind at their backs. 'Hold the kite in your left hand and let the wind lift it, like this. That's it! Now

8

unwind the string a little at a time.' He handed over control of the kite to Jasper and went to assist Nell.

The breeze teased tendrils of Edith's hair from their confining pins and flicked them around her face. She caught her breath as, one by one, the kites flew up higher and higher. Overhead, in the blue, blue sky, a seagull circled slowly, as if investigating these strange, brightly coloured birds.

Pearl and Lily screamed with delight as the scarlet tails of their kites twisted and turned in the air.

Lucien was struggling to get his kite aloft so Edith helped him launch it. She squealed as the wind plucked it from her and it rose into the air, the string tugging at her hands as she unwound it from the spindle. Laughing, she tipped her face up to the sky. How wonderful it would be to soar silently through the air like that kite!

'Mama! May I hold it now?'

Reluctantly, she handed the spindle to Lucien. Her reward was to see the exultation on his face as the kite danced and swooped in the wind, the scarlet ribbons on its tail fluttering behind.

Lucien's twin, Nell, a sturdy little girl with black plaits and a gap-toothed smile, burst into tears when her kite plummeted to the ground.

Pascal ran to launch it again, guiding her hands until she had the feel of how to pay out the string steadily to keep the kite aloft.

Soon, all the children were managing with only a little help when needed.

Edith sat with her back against the sun-warmed standing stone and made lightning sketches. She captured the way Lucien braced his stocky little legs against the pull of the breeze and how the wind from the sea snatched the girls' hair ribbons and pinafore hems into the air. The red, green and yellow kites sang out against the intense blue of the sky.

An hour or so later, she had enough sketches and the children were tired. One at a time, the kites nose-dived to the ground.

'That was *such* fun, Mama,' said Pearl, the apples of her dimpled cheeks glowing.

'May we do this again?' asked Lily.

'Please?' pleaded Jasper.

'I'm sure we will,' said Edith, ruffling his hair.

Lucien pulled at her skirt. 'Mama, I'm starving!'

'So am I!' echoed Nell.

'Why don't you go home and see if tea is ready? Uncle Pascal and I will wind up the strings and bring the kites back.'

The children ran off and Edith and Pascal sat on the grass to disentangle the strings. At last the kites were stacked in a neat pile.

'Wasn't that perfect?' said Edith. The coarse grass prickled her bare ankles and the sun glowed on her cheeks. 'I felt like a carefree girl again.'

'Happy memories are made from days like this,' said Pascal. He wound one of her loosened curls around his finger. 'The children will never forget this afternoon with their *maman*.'

'They'll never forget you teaching them to fly their kites, either.' Edith was quiet for a moment. 'Sometimes, I think you're more of a father to them than I am a mother.'

Pascal turned up his palms and shrugged. 'You need to work, Edith. And not only to feed your children. You must paint, to nourish your soul.' He draped an arm around her shoulders. 'But perhaps the children need you to enjoy their company a little more often.'

She sighed. 'I'm always so fearful of not earning enough. Of not having enough commissions. Of not being good enough. The Spindrift Gallery is a useful sideline but even selling a hundred little watercolour sketches isn't as profitable as one decent commission.'

'Don't worry so much, *chérie*!'

'At least I can be happy that, this time, my urge to paint gave birth to the idea of flying kites with the children. We've all had a jolly time together and there are still the Coronation celebrations to look forward to.'

They ambled home, taking time to enjoy the sunshine.

Edith paused for a moment to look at Spindrift House. Built of Cornish stone and slate and clad with Virginia creeper, the spacious, sunlit rooms were comfortably welcoming. As always, there was the sound of the sea in the background — murmuring softly today, but sometimes roaring in anger. The very first time she'd seen Spindrift, as a bride ten years ago, she'd loved it. Despite all the troubles that followed, it continued to be a safe haven for herself and her friends.

Pascal placed a hand on her arm. 'You are daydreaming, *chérie*.'

11

She smiled. 'I was reflecting on how thankful I am to live here with everyone I most care about.'

As they were entering through the garden door, they could hear the children's laughter and excited chatter resounding through the hall.

'Isn't it heartwarming to hear them happy?' said Edith.

They followed the clamour to the dining room. The children had abandoned their half-finished plates of chocolate cake and were hunkered down in a circle.

'What's going on here?' asked Edith, raising her voice to be heard over the laughter and squeals of excitement.

Pearl stood up, her arms wrapped over her chest and a radiant smile on her face. 'Oh, Mama. Just look! This is Star. Isn't he adorable? He's a sheepdog.'

A pair of brown eyes surrounded by black and white fur peered at Edith from the safety of Pearl's arms. A puppy.

Then Lucien stood up, cradling another black and white pup. 'And this one is called Blue. Do you see, he has one blue eye! Mama, I've wanted a puppy for the whole of my life,' he said, reverently. Blue opened his mouth to yawn, showing a tiny pink tongue, and Lucien kissed his boot button nose. 'This the *best* thing that's ever, ever happened to me.'

'I don't know where you found them,' said Edith, hardening herself against the tugging of her heartstrings, 'but I've told you before that we don't have the time or the money to look after one dog properly, never mind two. I'm very sorry but you must take them back where they came from.'

Pearl burst into noisy tears and Lucien let out a moan.

'Mama, *please* . . . ' begged Jasper.

'You can't take our puppies away,' sobbed Pearl, 'they're not *yours*! They were a *present*.'

Edith looked to Pascal for support but he was motionless, staring grim-faced over her shoulder.

She turned around. An imposing figure in an impeccably tailored lounge suit and highly polished shoes had been standing unnoticed by Edith in a corner of the room. He carried an ebony cane, silk gloves and a smart felt hat. As he stepped forward, light from the window gleamed on his gold watch chain.

'Hello, Edith,' said her husband Benedict. There was a smile on his handsome face. 'I've come home.'

2

Edith stared at him, unable to speak for the tumult of her thoughts. He looked older, she thought, the once-firm skin slack around his jawline. He'd shaved off his beard but retained a neatly trimmed moustache.

Weeping noisily, Pearl buried her face in Star's neck. 'I love this puppy so much I'll simply die if I'm not allowed to keep him!'

'Pearl, stop that dreadful noise!' said Edith. 'We can't keep two puppies.'

Outraged, Pearl howled even louder, rolling on the floor with Star clutched in her arms. Lucien sobbed and hugged the other puppy, while Nell whimpered in sympathy.

'*Please* can we keep them, Mama?' begged Jasper.

'Oh, for goodness' sake!' said Edith. 'That puppy's had an accident. Take them into the scullery, right now!'

'But . . . '

'Do as you're told, Pearl,' said Benedict. He prodded Lucien with his silver-headed cane. 'Cut along, all of you. I want to talk to your mother.'

Pearl stopped crying and sat up, looking at him curiously. 'Will you tell her we must keep the puppies?'

He smiled. 'Of course you shall keep them!'

'Benedict!' said Edith.

He pinched Pearl's cheek. 'Go on, all of you, hop it!'

The children's chatter faded away as they carried the puppies down the passage. Then, in the distance, the kitchen door slammed.

Benedict shifted his weight from one highly polished shoe to the other and the floorboards squeaked in the sudden silence. 'Well,' he said, 'I guessed right then.'

Edith swallowed and glanced at Pascal, standing beside her. Was their world about to come crashing down? 'You guessed right about what?' she asked. Her voice didn't sound like her own and she cleared her throat.

'That I might not be a welcome visitor,' he said. 'I hoped the children, at least, would be pleased to see me if I bought them a suitable present.'

'Puppies are a most *unsuitable* present,' said Edith waspishly. 'Two more mouths to feed, goodness knows how much mess to clear up, and time I don't have to exercise them. You've put me in the painful position of telling the children they can't keep the puppies they already love.'

'The children will exercise them, Edith,' said Pascal.

She glanced at him, tight-lipped.

'Still here, old chap?' said Benedict. He took a step closer to Pascal and looked down at him from his superior height. 'I thought you'd have returned to France by now. I tell you what, why don't you go and see how the others are getting along? I want a private chat with my wife.'

Edith didn't have to look at Pascal to feel the

air around them crackle with his anger.

Straight-backed, he strode from the room. Pausing in the doorway, he made as if to close the door but then left it ajar. His footsteps clipped away down the passage.

A pulse throbbed in Edith's temple. 'What is it you want this time, Benedict?' She made a vain attempt to gather up her wind-blown hair and secure it in a bun with the few remaining pins.

'Leave it!' he said. 'With your hair loose, you look like the beautiful girl you were when we married.'

She twisted her tangled curls flat to her head, wincing when she jabbed her scalp with a hairpin.

He moved to the window and looked out at the garden. 'Do you remember the first time we came to Spindrift together?' His voice was low and seductive. 'I stopped the carriage before we reached the house, to show you our first glimpse of the sea. You were cross with me. I can't remember why but — '

'You don't remember?' A flash of rage made her snap. 'I was distressed because you'd betrayed me with Pascal's sister. On our honeymoon.'

'Ah, yes! Delphine.' A smile flickered across his lips. 'She was bored with that dreadful, pontificating husband of hers and so very eager for a little attention. But that was years ago, Edith.'

'And so many women ago.'

He ignored her comment. 'I can't tell you how often I've walked through Spindrift House in my

16

dreams.' Smiling, he glanced around the room. 'Nothing has changed here. There's something so comforting about it, isn't there? I've missed the soft air of Cornwall and the smell of the sea.' He turned to face her. 'But, most of all, I've missed you.' His hazel eyes were pensive. 'I've made many mistakes in life but perhaps my stupidest was leaving you.'

'Pretty words,' said Edith, 'but meaningless.' She squeezed her eyes shut, recalling their early married life. 'Once,' she said, 'I felt as if a light glowed within me whenever you were near. But what I thought was true love was merely infatuation for a man who turned out to be so much less than I'd believed. Deserting me was one thing but it was unforgivable of you to abandon our children.'

He dropped his gaze. 'Not one of my proudest moments.' Sighing, he said, 'I blame my mother. I could do no wrong in her eyes and was used to having whatever I wanted. And when I met you,' he glanced at her, 'I wanted you.'

If he'd hoped to soften her resistance to him, it wasn't working. 'But when you discovered the responsibilities that come with marriage,' she said, 'you threw my love away.'

'I've been thinking about that a lot. I've changed, Edith.'

She raised her eyebrows. 'Really?' She'd forgotten how his presence filled a room, pervading it with his unassailable confidence and the aroma of expensive hair pomade.

'I'm thirty-three. It's time for me to stop racketing about and look to the future. I want to be a father to my children,' he said, and smiled benignly. 'They're a fine bunch and you should be proud of them.'

'I am.'

'Pearl's a lively one, isn't she? And Jasper's grown into a handsome boy. It's the first time I've met the twins. They're, what, six years old?'

'Seven. And never even a birthday letter for any of them in all those years. They have no idea who you are.'

'I told them I was their papa.' He frowned. 'Did you never speak of me to them?'

'And say what?' She balled up her fists to still her shaking hands. 'That you couldn't bear to be in the same room with them? That they were nothing but an inconvenience to you? That you didn't care if they were hungry or cold and went shoeless while you enjoyed the high life in London?'

Benedict rubbed the back of his neck. 'I'll make it up to them. And I want to be a husband to you again.'

She recoiled, her pulse racing. How could she possibly have him back now that she loved Pascal? 'What makes you imagine I might want that?'

His eyes widened. 'You're my wife. You have a duty to me.'

'Duty! How *dare* you speak to me of duty?' She pressed a hand to her chest, feeling the pounding of her heart. Taking a deep breath, she said, 'Why have you really come here, Benedict, apart from to taunt me? Are you in debt again? You told me years ago that Cornwall bored you and you needed the excitement of London.'

Pulling reflectively at his moustache, he said, 'London is a little *too* exciting for me at the moment.'

'You're in trouble?'

'Whatever you think of my artistic talent, Edith, I've achieved a certain amount of success painting portraits of society hostesses.'

'And what about their husbands?' she asked.

'Painting rich old men never appealed to me.' His eyes glinted with amusement. 'Their delightful young wives, however, are an altogether different prospect.'

'No doubt.'

'Don't look so po-faced!'

'I'm as aware as anybody of your fondness for beautiful women.' She sighed. 'I suspect you flew a little too close to the flame for the husband of one of those beauties and he's making life difficult for you. Am I right?'

'The annoying thing is that the lovely Lucinda was as pure as the driven snow in the face of my attempts to seduce her. Despite what her jealous husband thought, I never touched her.' He shrugged. 'Not that I didn't try. Nevertheless, new commissions to paint a lady's portrait will be rarer than hen's teeth for me in London at the moment. Gossip spreads fast in the gentlemen's clubs.'

'So you've turned tail and fled?'

His lips twitched in irritation. 'Spindrift House is still my home, Edith. I know I've made some mistakes but I intend to make a fresh start.'

Nausea roiled in her stomach and she sat

19

down suddenly on a dining chair. 'At Spindrift House?' How could she ever be alone with Pascal if Benedict was under the same roof?

'Where else?'

She gripped the chenille tablecloth and twisted the tasselled edge tightly round her fingers. 'Anywhere in the world except here. You can't possibly believe you can walk back into my life after nearly eight years, as if you'd merely gone to the village to buy a newspaper?' Outwardly, she hoped she looked calm. Inside, she was filled with the utmost dread.

He spread out his hands, palms up. 'Look, I'm coming home, no matter what.' He gave the charming, false smile Edith remembered so well. 'I understand it may take you a little time to become used to my presence here again but I'm a different person now, I promise. Everything will be fine.'

If Benedict returned to Spindrift, nothing would be fine ever again. She had to make him go away. 'I'm different too,' she said. 'I'm not the bedazzled girl who fell in love with you. I'm a grown woman with a living to earn and four children to bring up by my own efforts.' She cocked her head at him. 'Or do you, at last, intend to carry out your duty to your wife and children and support us financially?'

His smile faded. 'As I explained, I'm a bit pressed for funds at the moment. And you appear to have everything under control.'

'Meaning you think you can continue to sponge off me?'

'That's a bit harsh, isn't it?'

20

Edith noticed that he had the grace to look uncomfortable. 'Is it? There's no room here for parasites meaning to live off the generosity of others. Let me explain how the Spindrift community works. We have only two full-time servants but we all pay a share of their wages and an allowance for our food. Everyone helps to grow vegetables and do certain household chores. We work in shifts to man the gallery between June and September. I collect the rents, a large proportion of which I send to you. Out of the remainder, I buy coal and arrange for any repairs to the house that we can't undertake ourselves. If you were allowed to return, you would be obliged to fit in with the community's rules.'

'Why should I?' He lifted his chin. 'Don't forget, I hold a sixty per cent share of this house.'

'Benedict, let me speak plainly.' Edith clasped her hands together to prevent herself from slapping his face. 'The community exists because we all work hard and respect each other. We've made ourselves into a family that certainly doesn't include you. If you force your presence upon us without embracing our ethics, you'll be held in the greatest contempt, which will be very uncomfortable for you.'

'You've become exceedingly hard, Edith.'

'If I have, you're the one who made me so.'

'But I haven't been here!'

'Exactly!'

He heaved a deep sigh. 'I expect it'll all work out.' His expression brightened. 'And it'll be fun to be part of an artists' community again. I'll

21

take my luggage upstairs and unpack.'

'Upstairs?' said Edith.

'To our room.'

'No!' She felt sick again. 'You are not sleeping in my room.'

'But you're my wife.'

'In name only! Look, Benedict, you've been paid handsomely to stay away from us. You placed me in a position where I had to compromise my principles and so I was forced to let you take some of my canvases, but I absolutely *will not* allow you back into my bed. Is that quite clear?'

He sighed heavily. 'Why make everything so difficult? I could insist on it, you know. Any court of law would back me on that.'

'Surely even you, Benedict, wouldn't stoop so low as to force yourself on me?'

'Edith . . . ' His voice was cajoling as he reached for her hand.

She snatched it away, folding her arms across her chest. 'I shall *never* forgive you for stealing my work, Benedict, but the worst thing of all was when you helped yourself to *Catching the Tide*. You knew that painting wasn't just an artistic breakthrough for me but doubly precious because it reminded me of an especially happy day playing pirates with the children. And then, to sign it yourself, have it accepted by the Royal Academy for their Summer Exhibition and brazenly claim the credit . . . ' She swallowed back bile at the memory. 'How *could* you do that?'

'I told you,' he said, 'I've changed. Let's give it

a little time then. You'll see.' His amused, complacent expression infuriated her.

'Make no mistake,' she said, 'if you insist on staying here, it's purely a business arrangement between us. Don't think, not for one single moment, that you'll ever talk yourself into my bed again. I shall discuss with the others if we can find a small room for you. Meanwhile, keep out of my hair and go and sit in the gazebo until we call you.'

Benedict's lips tightened. Before he could speak, Edith turned her back on him and hurried away. One thing she was already sure of: if Benedict couldn't be persuaded to leave, the equilibrium of the whole Spindrift community was at risk.

* * *

Pearl frowned as they all trooped out of the dining room. Mama's voice had sounded funny, as if she had a bad headache.

'I'm going to find Auntie Dora and tell her what's happened,' said Nell.

The rest of the children went to the kitchen. Mrs Rowe the cook glowered at them, hands on her narrow hips. 'You'd better get them dogs out of my kitchen,' she said. 'They'll have fleas, no doubt.'

'No, they haven't!' said Lucien.

'Please, Mrs Rowe,' said Jasper, 'may we have a drop of milk for Star and Blue? It's their first time away from their mother and they'll be hungry.'

23

The cook sighed. 'Take them in the scullery then.'

It wasn't long before Nell returned with Dora.

'Look what we've got!' said Pearl.

Dora's grey eyes softened and she picked up the smaller puppy from Jasper's lap. 'Isn't he sweet?' she cooed, stroking his velvety ears.

'Papa brought them for us,' said Lucien.

Dora stopped stroking the puppy and stared at him. 'What?'

'We were having tea when a man came into the dining room.'

Pearl picked up the other puppy and put it into Dora's arms. 'Aren't they adorable? The man said he was our papa and that he'd brought us a present.'

Dora pressed her fingers to her mouth. 'Papa?' The colour drained from her face, leaving her freckles looking like gingerbread crumbs scattered across her nose and cheeks.

Pearl nodded her head vigorously. 'I told him we don't have a papa. He said he really is our father but, a long time ago, he had to go away to find work.'

'He's come home to stay now,' said Jasper.

'My dear Lord!' murmured Dora. Absentmindedly, she tucked a wisp of sandy hair behind her ear.

Pearl stared at her. Dora never took the Lord's name in vain and wouldn't stand for anyone making a noise in church on Sunday.

'Where is he now?' she asked.

'In the dining room with Mama and Uncle Pascal,' said Jasper. As he said the words, the

24

scullery door opened and Pascal came in.

'Is it true?' asked Dora.

Pascal nodded his head. 'He sent me away so he could talk to his *wife* alone.'

'Hell's bells,' said Dora. 'Whatever does he want?'

'*Sans doute*, it will be something we don't want to give him.' Pascal rubbed at his eyes as if they were sore.

'We must make a bed for the puppies,' said Lucien. 'The velvet cushions from the drawing room are nice and soft.'

'Don't even think about using those lovely cushions, ducky,' said Dora.

Pearl knew she was cross because she only ever called them 'ducky' when she was annoyed. 'Please, dear Auntie Dora, can you find something else for them then?'

'I don't know what your mother will say.'

Pascal picked up Blue, who had started to chew his shoelaces. Sighing, he said, 'Shall we make them a home in the old pigsty?'

Nell gigged. 'They aren't piglets!'

'There's a wall around the sty so the puppies can't escape,' he said. 'Your mother may not allow you to keep them but we can make them comfortable for tonight.'

Pearl threw her arms around his waist. 'I know *you* can persuade Mama to let us keep them.'

'You know I never make promises I cannot keep.'

'Unlike some people,' muttered Dora. 'I'll go and find an old blanket. Lordy, whatever is going to happen to us all?' She walked out of the kitchen, shaking her head.

'Come on then, everyone!' said Pearl.

'You're so bossy!' complained Nell.

Pearl prised Star out of her sister's arms and they all set off for the courtyard.

'I'm so happy Papa is here,' Pearl said to Pascal. 'Some of the children at school said he went away because he didn't love me.'

Pascal gripped her shoulder. 'That was very cruel.'

'I cried.' She smiled up at him. 'But now I know they were wrong because Papa is here again and everything is going to be absolutely splendid.'

3

Dora took the egg basket and a bowl of kitchen scraps from Mrs Rowe and went to feed the chickens in the courtyard. The pony, dear old Ned, looked over the stable door and whickered at her as she passed. She stroked his velvety nose and gave him an apple core, then scattered the crusts and potato peelings, along with a few handfuls of grain, on the ground. The hens came pelting towards her from all corners of the yard, squabbling and pushing each other aside to peck at the scraps. Dora collected a basket of still-warm eggs, then went to the pigpen. The children were having a fine old time, bouncing a ball and squealing with glee when the puppies raced after it.

Pascal, aided or perhaps hindered by the young ones, had swept the pen clean. He put down his broom and came to stand beside Dora. 'At least the children are happy,' he said, his tone bitter.

'Poor Edith!' said Dora. 'She'll never be able to make them give up those puppies now. Benedict never did consider the consequences of his actions.'

'He knew *exactly* what would happen.'

Dora sniffed. 'There's bound to be trouble ahead if he comes to live at Spindrift again.'

'Do you think . . . ' Pascal hesitated.

'What?'

27

'Will Benedict stay? Might Edith give him another chance to be a true husband to her again?' He was gripping the top of the wall so hard his knuckles were white.

'Of course she won't want him back!' Dora glanced at Pascal and pitied his obvious unhappiness. Over the years, she'd gradually realised that he and Edith loved each other. Nothing was ever said and they didn't spoon over each other but their friendship was deep and lasting. Of course, Edith was already married to Benedict so if there was anything going on behind closed doors, Dora didn't want to know about it. It was enough for her that Edith was happy again and that Pascal loved the children.

'You've been such a good friend to her,' she said, 'and your friendship is far more important to her than anything she ever felt for Benedict.'

Pascal sighed. 'But Edith is always mindful of her duty.' He glanced over Dora's shoulder. 'Here she is.'

Edith's petite figure hurried across the courtyard towards them. 'We need to talk,' she said. Her face was chalk white.

'I heard the news,' said Dora.

Edith glanced at the children playing with the puppies. 'Not here.' Fleetingly, she brushed Pascal's hand with her fingers. 'Can we gather the whole community in the drawing room in ten minutes?'

'I'll find Augustus and Clarissa,' said Dora. 'Gilbert and Julian were in the vegetable garden a short while ago.'

Edith nodded. 'I'll tell Mabel and Maude.'

Dora found Augustus bent over his workbench soldering a copper bracelet. She waited while he plunged it into a bath of acid, where it sizzled and steamed.

He looked up at her, his gold-rimmed glasses perched on the end of his nose. 'You look worried,' he said. He fished the bracelet out of the bowl with tongs and laid it on the bench.

'I am,' said Dora.

The workshop door opened and Clarissa came in. 'What is it?' she asked, catching sight of Dora's expression.

'Benedict's back.'

Clarissa's blue eyes widened. 'What! I thought we'd rid ourselves of that feckless waster years ago. What does he want?'

'He's come back to Spindrift. For good.'

'But we paid him to stay away,' said Augustus.

'Well, he's back,' said Dora. 'And, since he's the major shareholder of Spindrift House, I don't see how we can force him to leave. Edith wants us in the drawing room in a few minutes to discuss it. Augustus, would you find Wilfred? I'm going to tell Gilbert and Julian.'

A short while later, everyone convened in the drawing room.

When Edith had brought them all up to date, a horrified silence gripped the room. The elderly spinster sisters Mabel and Maude Ainsley clutched at each other's hands for support.

'How can he possibly think you'd want him back?' said Wilfred.

'It's the very last thing I want,' said Edith. She

looked down at the floor. 'And there's another thing.'

'What?' asked Dora.

Her friend's eyes were bright with unshed tears and her cheeks flushed. 'He wants to move back into my bedroom.'

Dora heard Pascal's breath catch in his throat.

'Of course, I've told him he can't,' Edith said, 'but he has the law on his side. And,' she glanced at Pascal, 'when he realises he can't sweet talk me, he may become spiteful.'

'Is there no way we can get rid of him?' asked Julian.

'We certainly shan't make him welcome,' said Clarissa.

'Where *will* he sleep?' asked Pascal.

'I can't imagine he'd allow himself to be banished to the last unconverted stable,' said Clarissa. 'And no doubt he's in debt again and wouldn't have the money to make it habitable.'

'I may have to make up a bed for myself in the studio,' said Edith, chewing her lip.

'No!' said Dora. 'You can't!'

'Don't you *dare* let him push you out of your room!' said Clarissa.

After some discussion, Wilfred agreed to share Augustus's double room so that Benedict could have Wilfred's single room.

'That's generous of you,' said Edith. 'It would be a great relief to me.'

'But Benedict must pay for Wilfred's room,' said Clarissa.

'I suspect he's spent all his money,' said Edith. Her face brightened. 'We could deduct it from

30

the rent money we give him.'

'Benedict grows bored very easily,' said Dora. 'Surely he won't stay for long?'

'I pray you're right,' said Edith. 'I suppose that depends on where and when he finds his next source of income.'

Clarissa linked her arm through Edith's. 'I'll come with you while you tell him. I don't imagine you want to be alone with him?'

Edith shook her head and they went outside.

Pascal watched them walk across the lawn. 'Everything will change,' he murmured, glancing up as a dark cloud hid the sun.

Dora sighed. And not for the better, she thought.

★ ★ ★

Storm clouds were brewing when Edith and Clarissa went into the garden to find Benedict.

'For years I've buried my head in the sand to avoid contemplating the awful possibility that he might return,' said Edith. 'I was devastated when he left but I soon discovered that, apart from money worries, the children and I were far better off without him.'

Clarissa gave her a sideways glance. 'Pascal must be especially distressed about Benedict trying to weasel his way back into the marital bed.'

Edith came to an abrupt standstill. 'What do you mean?'

'Benedict is an intruder into the very special friendship you have with Pascal, isn't he?'

31

Clarissa linked her arm with her friend's. 'Don't worry, your secret is perfectly safe. I'd never do anything to betray either you or Pascal.'

A little of the tightness in Edith's stomach loosened. 'How long have you known?'

Clarissa shrugged. 'Years. Pascal is the husband you should always have had,' she said. 'If you've found happiness with him, I can only be thrilled for you. You're both perfectly discreet. If I didn't know you so well, I'd never have guessed.'

'But you've never said anything to me. Or to Dora?'

'The three of us have supported each other through thick and thin over the years, but dear Dora is such an innocent she'd be uncomfortable with the knowledge so I'd never tell her.' Clarissa's half-smile was enigmatic. 'Besides, we're all entitled to keep our secrets, good and bad, aren't we?'

Edith glanced at her, wondering if she had also guessed her friend's other long-held secret. But what secrets did Clarissa have, apart from that of Lily's paternity? She'd never disclosed that to anyone.

'You and Pascal must be careful, though,' said Clarissa. 'There has always been one set of standards for men and a completely different set for women. If Benedict suspects you two have an intimate relationship, or if you should become pregnant, he'd have clear grounds to prove you an unfit mother. You might lose the children and find yourself without a home.'

'Do you think I don't know that?' Edith

pressed a hand to her chest as a wave of panic rose within her. 'But I can't have him back in my bed. I simply can't!'

'Nor shall you!' Clarissa squeezed Edith's arm. 'But you have to be firm. Even Benedict, for all his faults, is unlikely to insist on his conjugal rights if you don't want his attentions. I'm sure he'd prefer to look elsewhere for a woman who'd fall on her back for him with no effort at all on his part.'

Once, that thought would have wounded Edith deeply but now it could only be a relief.

'It's a difficult situation for Pascal,' said Clarissa. 'He'll need your reassurance and love while Benedict is here.'

'It hurts me to see Pascal upset and anxious.' Edith sighed. 'I haven't had time to speak to him alone yet.'

'Then I suggest that you do, as soon as possible.'

They climbed the hillock to the gazebo and found Benedict dozing on the bench inside, his long legs stretched out in front of him and his chin upon his chest. His coat and waistcoat were unbuttoned and Edith couldn't help noticing that years of good living had given him a paunch.

Clarissa glanced at her with a mischievous smile and prodded Benedict's broad shoulder.

He started and reared to his feet. 'Clarissa!' He held his arms wide. 'How delightful to see you!'

If she hadn't been so upset, Edith might have laughed at how smartly her friend stepped

33

backwards to avoid his embrace.

'I wish I could say the same,' Clarissa said, her voice cool. 'Have you run out of people to leech off in London?'

Benedict's smile faltered and his arms dropped to his sides. 'You always were a tease, Clarissa! Has Edith been telling tales out of school about me?'

'She doesn't need to; I know you too well. We've found you a room. Augustus and Wilfred have kindly agreed to share.'

Benedict raised his eyebrows at Edith. 'So you really mean to push me out into the cold?'

'You'll be perfectly comfortable,' she said. 'It has a view towards the harbour.'

He shrugged. 'As you wish.' He winked at Clarissa. 'In any case, I daresay it won't be for too long.'

'So you're leaving soon, then?' she said.

'Not at all. I'm home for good.'

'What a shame!'

He examined his perfectly manicured finger-nails. 'Look, I know I didn't behave well a few years ago and I'm sorry for that. I'm determined to make it up to my wife now.'

'You can never make up for those lost years, Benedict,' Edith sighed. 'You'd better come into the house. I'll find some clean sheets for you to put on the bed.'

'Me? Can't the maid do it?'

'I told you, we all have household duties and making our own bed is one of them. You're not in a smart London house now. Until fairly recently we couldn't afford any servants at all.'

Benedict remained silent as they walked back to the house.

When they arrived at his new bedroom, Wilfred was packing the last of his possessions into a portmanteau.

'Good to see you again,' said Benedict.

Wilfred acknowledged this with a curt nod. 'I'm finished,' he said, snapping the case shut and carrying it from the room.

Benedict sat on the bed and bounced up and down on the mattress. 'It's a poky little place but I shall be reasonably comfortable here.' The corners of his eyes crinkled as he smiled lazily up at Edith. 'For the time being anyway.'

'I'll fetch the sheets,' she said.

Clarissa followed her into the corridor. 'I really need to go back to the workshop,' she said. 'Will you be all right if I leave you with him?'

'Yes, of course.' Edith retreated to the linen cupboard and found a set of sheets and pillowcases. One of the sheets was perilously thin but it couldn't be helped. If Benedict wanted fine linen on his bed, he could jolly well buy it himself.

When she returned, he was staring out of the window at the view of the harbour in the distance. 'Dinner is at eight,' she said, 'after the children are in bed.' Making her escape before he could attempt to engage her in conversation, she hurried upstairs to the studio to find Pascal.

He glanced at her from his easel and there was such apprehension in his eyes that she felt even more wretched. She ran to him.

He opened his arms and pulled her to his

chest, resting his chin on her head while he murmured endearments. They stayed locked together for a long time, taking comfort in each other's presence.

'Would you like me to leave Spindrift now Benedict is back?' he asked. He pressed a finger to her lips as she opened her mouth to protest. 'He is still your husband. If you decide you must give him another chance, I shall understand.'

'I can feel your heart beating against mine,' she whispered. 'Benedict will *never* come between us. You know that it's you I love, now and forever.'

'Now and forever,' he echoed. He wound his fingers through her hair and she clung to him, tears escaping from under her eyelashes.

'As long as you still love me, that is all I ask.' He kissed her forehead. 'But we must be very careful if we want to be alone together.'

Grateful for his understanding, she said, 'I've made it plain to Benedict that I'll never be a wife to him again.' She sighed. 'Unfortunately, he thinks it's only a matter of time before he wins me around.'

Pascal shrugged. 'I wish from the bottom of my heart that we could declare our love openly but we must be satisfied with what we have. There is little we can do except wait until he grows weary of us all.'

'It was so unfair of him to bring puppies for the children,' said Edith. 'How could they resist thinking well of him after a present like that? And now I shall be Wicked Mama if I send them away.'

Pascal stroked her cheek. 'When I was a boy, my dog Maxim and I had many adventures together. Perhaps you should allow the puppies to stay?'

'I suppose you're right. Lucien has asked me for a pet again and again.' She pressed her fingers to her temples. 'I don't know how to look after dogs.'

'But I do.'

She gave him a grateful smile. 'I must tuck the children into bed. Come with me and we'll tell them the good news.'

Jasper and Lucien were still running around in their nightshirts but Lily, Pearl and Nell were all sitting in bed in the room they shared. Pascal called the boys and they raced into the girls' room and jumped onto Pearl's bed.

'Auntie Dora has already read us a story,' said Nell.

'Good because I want to talk to you all.' Edith's heart warmed at the sight of the five little faces turned towards her. 'I've decided to let you keep Star and Blue,' she said, 'but you must promise me . . . '

Her words were drowned by Pearl's and Lily's squeals of joy.

Lucien smothered her cheeks in kisses and Jasper did a handstand.

'Quiet!' she shouted over the hullabaloo. At last there was sufficient peace for her to be heard. 'You can thank Uncle Pascal,' she said, and glanced at him with a wry smile. 'He tells me you've all promised to look after the puppies. They must be walked twice a day, even if it's

37

raining, and they will sleep outside. Is that clear?'

The children nodded their heads earnestly.

'Now you must have a good night's sleep,' said Pascal, 'to be ready to start training Star and Blue after school tomorrow.'

Obediently, the girls wriggled under the covers and Edith kissed them good night.

Pascal blew them a kiss. 'Good night, Jasper and Lucien,' he said. 'Lily, I'll tell your mother you are waiting for her to tuck you in.'

Edith herded the boys into their room.

'Won't the puppies be frightened all on their own outside tonight, Mama?' Lucien's face was taut with worry.

'They'll cuddle up together and be perfectly happy,' she said as she tucked them in. 'Now sleep tight, mind the bugs don't bite!'

Oh, Lord, she thought, as she closed the bedroom door behind her. Suppose the puppies had fleas? Sighing, she went downstairs.

4

Evening sunshine streamed through the dining-room windows, illuminating Wilfred's murals of voluptuous, semi-clad ladies reclining on silken cushions and attended by cherubs.

Dora placed a vase of roses in the centre of the table and then began to set out the cutlery. She paused while she deliberated. Benedict's arrival meant squeezing in an eleventh chair and it was going to be uncomfortably squashed.

The door opened a crack and Mabel and Maude peered through it. Their long noses, lanky figures and slow and deliberate way of walking always reminded Dora of a pair of amiable storks. They'd dressed for dinner by adorning their usual homespun dresses with vibrant silk shawls and embroidered slippers of their own making.

'May we help?' asked Mabel.

Dora sighed. 'I was wondering how to set the table with an extra place. I think we must seat all the ladies on one side since we take up less room than the men.'

'Whilst I'm sure we'd all prefer to observe the social niceties of the correct placement of ladies and gentlemen at the dinner table,' said Maude, 'in this instance, it can't be helped.'

'I'm a little nervous of meeting Edith's husband,' said Mabel. 'I've not heard anything good about him.'

'You'll probably find him perfectly charming,' said Dora, 'at least, on first acquaintance. But never forget the cruel way he treated her and the children.'

Gilbert's booming voice resounded down the passage and he entered the dining room accompanied by most of the others.

Edith arrived a moment later and silently collected the napkins from the sideboard and placed them beside each place setting.

'We'll have to embroider a napkin ring for Benedict,' said Maude.

'Perhaps he won't stay long enough to need one,' said Dora hopefully.

Maude coughed and made a face at her.

Benedict, sleek and broad-shouldered in his city suit, was standing in the doorway.

Dora blushed, wondering if he'd heard her comment, and made herself unnecessarily busy straightening the knives.

'Good evening to you all,' he said. 'Dora, how lovely to see you again!' He smiled warmly at Maude and Mabel. 'Someone, please introduce me to these two lovely ladies.'

Dora left Clarissa to perform the introductions. She listened to Benedict flattering the two spinsters, admiring their scarves and expressing his admiration for their skill when he learned that they'd designed and printed them themselves.

'Sit here, Benedict,' Dora said, 'between Julian and Wilfred.' She saw him glance at the head of the table, where Gilbert had already taken up residence, and then at Pascal who sat in his usual place at the other end. Benedict shrugged and sat on the chair she'd indicated.

Clarissa fetched bowls of boiled potatoes, carrots and beans from the kitchen. Hannah carried in a large cheese and onion pie and placed it on the table before Edith, who served it.

'All the vegetables are from the kitchen garden,' said Gilbert. Dora noticed he still had earth under his fingernails.

'How very resourceful of you all,' Benedict said, frowning at his pie. 'It looks very appetising but did Cook forget to add the meat?'

'We have meat only when we can afford it,' said Dora, smiling to herself at his crestfallen expression.

He ignored her and turned to Julian. 'Tell me about yourself and how you came to join this happy community.'

Julian, tall and distinguished-looking with silver streaks in his brown hair, pursed his lips, as if reluctant to speak. 'I'm a photographer,' he said.

Benedict nodded encouragingly. 'Go on.'

'The holidaymakers keep me busy in the summer and then there are weddings, christenings and so on,' said Julian. 'My real interest is artistic photography. I write and illustrate articles about that for magazines and newspapers.'

Benedict looked sceptical. 'How can you make artistic photographs? Surely, what you see before you is the image that appears in the photograph?'

'It isn't as simple as that,' said Julian, a gleam

of enthusiasm lightening his expression. 'It's possible to modify the image with different filters and chemical processes. And I'll arrange a background setting with props.'

'How fascinating!' said Benedict. He turned to Gilbert. 'And how did you come to be here?'

Dora stabbed at a lump of potato. She could hardly bear to watch Benedict smarming his way into the other men's good graces. No doubt he was set on making allies to undermine anything Edith might have said about him.

Gilbert, a big bear of a man, dabbed at his bushy red beard with a napkin. 'I taught English for many years but, after my wife died, decided it was time for me to do what I'd always wanted.'

'And what is that?'

'My uncle was a carver mason,' said Gilbert. 'He created stone embellishments for churches, libraries and banks. As a boy I used to watch him take a piece of cold, hard marble or a lump of limestone and turn it this way and that before picking up his chisel. 'You need to let the stone speak to you, my boy,' he always used to say. He'd chip away at it until, bit by bit, some fantastical figure or an intricate bas-relief emerged.' Gilbert shook his shaggy head. 'Seemed like magic to me. Still does! Uncle offered me an apprenticeship but my mother wanted better for me. She didn't like the idea of her son getting his hands dirty.'

'So you became a teacher to please your mother?' said Benedict.

'It was no hardship. I'd always enjoyed the beauty of the English language.' Gilbert laughed.

'Though, when I finally went back to my uncle, cap in hand, he said he'd never heard of such an old apprentice. He was nigh-on seventy himself.'

Benedict leaned back in his chair and turned to Clarissa. 'You're still making your little trinkets?'

She took a leisurely drink of water before she answered him. 'Augustus and I sell our handcrafted jewellery to a number of prestigious shops in London and Truro, as well as through the Spindrift Gallery.'

'Who could have imagined that a gently brought up young lady such as yourself could ever become a successful businesswoman?'

There was a sardonic twist to the corners of Benedict's mouth and, when Dora saw the glint in Clarissa's eye, she knew she wouldn't let it rest there.

'You might be surprised what mere females are able to achieve by means of hard work, Benedict,' Clarissa said. 'And what about you? We know your financial success has been largely due to the funds you threatened us into sending you, but why don't you tell us about your artistic achievements? Assuming, of course, that there are any?'

A muscle flickered in Benedict's jaw. 'Quite apart from my rightful due of the rents from Spindrift House, I've had many artistic triumphs. There are my portraits, of course, but I've made a name for myself with a small but significant number of canvases depicting bucolic scenes set in the French countryside. You remember that idyllic holiday we shared in France together?'

43

Edith caught her breath and her fork clattered to the floor.

'You mean your honeymoon with Edith?' said Clarissa.

Benedict smiled. 'Ah, happy days! And then, for the past few years, I've moved in aristocratic circles and painted the portraits of many society beauties . . .'

'I wasn't enquiring about your conquests but about your artistic successes,' said Clarissa.

'One and the same, my dear Clarissa,' Benedict drawled. He pushed away his half-eaten plate of pie and leaned back in his chair. 'Pascal,' he said, 'do tell me what you've been doing with yourself over the past few years? Still dabbling with different styles of painting?'

Pascal's face bore no trace of his usual good humour. 'My seascapes continue to sell very well. There are two galleries in Paris and one in Truro that regularly sell my work.'

'Do you not feel homesick for your homeland?'

Shrugging, he said, 'Cornwall is agreeable. There is much to inspire me here.'

Dora glanced at Edith, who listened to the conversation without taking part. She'd barely touched her dinner either, a sure sign she was upset. And why wouldn't she be? Here was Benedict, perfectly at ease while he lorded it over them exactly as if he were still the master of the house. She sighed. Of course, in some ways, that was exactly what he was.

Hannah pushed open the door and cleared the plates with a great deal of noisy clatter but at least that stopped Benedict holding the floor.

Gilbert began a new conversation with Augustus and Wilfred, while Maude and Mabel bickered amicably over the relative merits of Art Nouveau and the Arts and Crafts movement.

Hannah returned from the kitchen with a large treacle sponge and a jug of custard and Dora noticed Benedict was happy enough to have seconds of that, even if the cheese and onion pie hadn't been the fancy fare he was used to.

Finally, dinner was over.

'I shall stroll down to the cove and enjoy a quiet smoke,' said Benedict. 'Would any of you care to join me?'

'You forget, Benedict,' said Edith, 'there's still the drying up to be done. You're on the rota with Mabel and Augustus this evening.'

He accepted that with surprising equanimity. 'Then I shall postpone my stroll until my duties are concluded.' He offered his arm to Mabel with a small bow. 'May I escort you into the scullery, Miss Ainsley? And perhaps you will initiate me into the mysteries of the drying up cloth?'

'Oh!' Mabel stood up in a flutter of silk. 'I should be delighted.'

Benedict led her away, followed by Augustus.

'But he's perfectly charming!' said Maude.

'Didn't I tell you?' said Dora.

'And so handsome, too!'

'All I can say,' said Dora, wrinkling her nose, 'is that you shouldn't forget: handsome is as handsome does.'

★ ★ ★

The next morning, late for breakfast, Dora hurried downstairs. The children sat at a small table in the corner of the dining room, making their usual clamour. Hannah was attempting to keep her charges in some kind of order as they reached over each other for the bread, spilled their milk and smeared jam on their clean clothes.

'What a racket!' said Dora. They were never quiet, bless their little cotton socks, but they brought such life to Spindrift. She took her usual place beside Edith and Clarissa. 'I suppose everyone else has finished breakfast and started work?'

Clarissa, her flaxen hair swept up into soft coils, passed Dora the tureen of porridge. 'Did you oversleep?'

Feeling dishevelled beside her friend's easy elegance, Dora tucked an escaping strand of sandy hair back into her bun. 'I was working on my new book until the small hours and then I couldn't sleep for being cross with Benedict for coming back.' She scraped the congealed remains of the porridge into her bowl and sprinkled it with brown sugar.

'It appears he's overslept,' said Clarissa, 'so at least we haven't had to face him over the breakfast table this morning.'

Edith poured Dora some tea.

'It doesn't look as if you slept well either,' she said, noticing dark circles under her friend's eyes.

'Every time I tried to I saw his complacent smile,' said Edith. She glanced at the children and murmured, 'I couldn't forget him telling me so confidently that I'd 'come round' and want him back in my bed.' She shuddered. 'What is wrong with him that he never understands how much distress he causes to others by his selfishness?'

'It was ever thus with Benedict,' said Clarissa.

Edith left the table and went to kiss the children. 'Work hard at school today,' she said. 'Hannah, I haven't forgotten it's your afternoon off and I'll walk them home this afternoon.'

'Come along, children,' said the maid. 'Time to wash your sticky fingers!' She hurried the protesting children away.

Clarissa dabbed her mouth with her napkin. 'I must go to the workshop.' She left the dining room with Edith.

Dora finished her porridge and poured herself a second cup of tea. It was cold and she grimaced as she sipped it.

'Good morning, Dora.' Benedict strolled into the dining room and sat down at the head of the table. He frowned at the sight of the thin crust remaining on the breadboard.

'The porridge has all gone, too,' said Dora. She bit the insides of her cheeks to stop herself from laughing at his aggrieved expression and pushed the pot of cold tea towards him. 'You need to rise earlier if you want breakfast.' She didn't wait for his reply but left the dining room.

Half an hour later she'd set up her easel in the gazebo and was working on an illustration for her latest story, *Princess Elowen and the Piskie*. She was rinsing her paintbrush when Wilfred sauntered across the lawn towards her, the breeze ruffling his fair hair. They'd become best friends at the Slade. Theirs was an unlikely friendship; a scholarship girl from a working-class family and the young man who'd led a privileged, if stifled, life with his widowed mother.

'I'm looking for Augustus,' said Wilfred, walking up the gazebo steps. As always, his artist's smock was perfectly starched and his red silk neckerchief neatly tied. There had never been anything remotely romantic about Dora's friendship with Wilfred but he spent so much time with Augustus lately that, sometimes, she felt quite jealous.

'Isn't he in the workshop with Clarissa?' asked Dora.

Wilfred shook his head. 'Anyway, I'm off to take my turn manning the gallery. Let's hope the sun brings out the holidaymakers to buy their souvenirs.' He plucked a crimson rose from the climber that scrambled over the gazebo and tucked it into one of the buttonholes of his painting smock. Peering at her work on the easel, he said, 'It's Lily!'

'Her spun-silver hair and delicate features make her the perfect princess for a fairy tale, don't you think?'

'Absolutely. And your piskie has a wonderfully mischievous face, peeping out from behind that tree.'

'My publishers commissioned me to create illustrations similar to Arthur Rackham's in *The Fairy Tales of the Brothers Grimm*. They're ever

48

so popular,' said Dora, 'but I told them I won't mimic Rackham's work but must be allowed develop my own style.'

'You've achieved that,' said Wilfred. 'Your watercolour work is beautifully delicate but the pen and ink makes a good contrast. How many illustrations shall you make?'

'Three colour plates and ten black and white for each book. I'm writing three stories to begin with for the piskie series.'

Wilfred whistled. 'That's going to keep you in pin money for a while.'

She couldn't help grinning. 'I've come a long way from working in a biscuit factory. Even five years ago I couldn't have begun to imagine how successful my *Theodora the Pirate Queen* series would become.'

He squeezed her hand. 'You always did hide your light under a bushel.'

'My first publisher's advance came at exactly the right time, didn't it?' She shivered, despite the warmth of the sunshine. 'If we hadn't raised enough money between us to buy our share of Spindrift House, I can't imagine where we'd all be now.'

'Scattered to the four winds, no doubt,' said Wilfred. 'That would have been a tragedy because the community has become our family, hasn't it?'

Dora picked up her brush again. 'Except for Benedict. It made me sick to see him wheedling his way into Maude and Mabel's good graces last night.'

'But then,' said Wilfred, 'we were all taken in

by Benedict's hollow charm, once upon a time, weren't we? I'd better get on.' He lifted a languid hand and loped off down the steps.

Dora continued painting, thinking about what Wilfred had said. He'd hit the nail on the head; the community had grown into a family that, in many cases, was more dear to them than their own flesh and blood.

She sent up a prayer of thanks for that every day.

5

Edith had forced herself to stop brooding over Benedict's return, for a while anyway, and had finally begun to concentrate on her work again. She was on the cliff, working on her new canvas, when she remembered the time. If she didn't hurry, she was going to be late collecting the children from school. Cursing under her breath, she hastily packed up her easel and paints and carried them back to Spindrift. She deposited them in the gazebo with Dora for safekeeping before hurrying back over the clifftop for the fifteen-minute walk down to Port Isaac.

The Penrose children passed her as she reached the outskirts of the village, already on their way home to Cliff House on the other side of the cove from Spindrift. Their nursemaid didn't respond to Edith's nodded greeting but hurried her charges on, clearly warned by her employer that they were to have nothing to do with the Spindrift community. Edith sighed. There had been a dreadful scandal some years before when Hugh Penrose's father died and left Spindrift House to his mistress, Benedict's aunt Hester. She had died of a broken heart a few days afterwards, in turn leaving Spindrift House to her nephew. Hugh believed he had a moral claim to the property and the Penroses nursed a long-standing grudge against Benedict and the whole community.

The steep and narrow village streets were decked out with bunting and banners in preparation for Edward VII's Coronation. A vast bonfire had been built on the Platt, the open space behind the harbour foreshore. Edith sprinted past the Golden Lion inn and up Fore Street towards the school. Children, happy to have escaped the confinement of the classroom, already chased each other through the streets or huddled in front gardens playing pitch and toss.

Edith's children, together with Lily and young Tom Mellyn, were playing hopscotch outside the school railings, watched by Tom's mother, Tamara. Polcarrow, the Mellyns' farm, ran alongside Spindrift House and they were always friendly, having no time for the Penroses' tittle-tattle.

'Don't run, Edith!' called Tamara. 'They're all quite safe.'

'Mama!' Nell held up her face to be kissed.

'Did you have a good day, sweetheart?' Nell nodded and slipped her hand into her mother's. 'Thank you for minding them, Tamara,' said Edith. There was a stitch in her side and she pressed one hand against it to knead it away.

'Don't tell me, you were painting and forgot the time?' There was an understanding smile on Tamara's face.

'I'm afraid so.' Edith grimaced at the paint stains on her fingers.

'Don't you worry! There's been many a time I've been churning the butter and lost myself in a dream. My ma used to call me Dolly Daydream.'

Edith called to the children. 'Time to go!'

Pearl ran to hug her mother and then raced off along the street with Lily. The rest of the children gambolled around them.

Tamara walked home beside Edith. 'Have you heard the news?' she asked. 'The Coronation has been postponed.'

'Postponed?' Edith came to a standstill.

'The King had to have an emergency operation on his stomach.'

'How dreadful! And three days before Coronation Day, too. He will recover, won't he?'

Tamara shrugged. 'I hope so but all the visiting heads of state will have their plans upset.'

Edith glanced up at a banner proclaiming *God Bless our King and Queen* hung across the harbour fish cellars. 'What about all the preparations?'

'The headmaster came to speak to us after the class was dismissed. There's still to be a public holiday tomorrow. The children's tea party and the old folk's lunch have to go ahead to avoid waste but the processions, military bands and the bonfire are cancelled.'

'Anyway, I don't suppose we'll feel like celebrating if the King is in danger,' said Edith.

When they reached the Platt, Edith saw that Jasper and Tom had gone onto the beach and were paddling. 'Lucien, will you go and fetch the boys, please?'

He skipped off, followed as usual by Nell.

Pearl and Lily sprinted after them, squealing with glee and chasing each other around the now redundant bonfire.

'We'd better fetch them ourselves,' said

Tamara. 'They forget all about us once we're out of sight.'

'I ought to work,' said Edith, 'and the afternoon will be gone if we don't get home soon.'

'There's always tomorrow.' Tamara smiled as she watched the children enjoying themselves. 'One day you'll look up from that easel of yours to find they've grown up and left you. You'll be sorry then if you haven't made time for them.'

Perhaps it was only her hovering anxiety over Benedict that made Edith sensitive to Tamara's comment but a tiny shiver of unease ran down her back. Her own mother had never had time for her and she'd be miserable if her children thought the same about her. 'You're right,' she said. 'Let's go down to the beach.'

Lucien and Nell were lying on their stomachs, staring intently into a rock pool and dabbling their hands in the water.

'Mama!' said Lucien. His green eyes, so like her own, sparkled. 'There's a snake-locks anemone.'

'All I can see is seaweed.'

'Look at its tentacles! They're green with purple tips.'

Edith peered into the pool again. 'So they are.'

'And you can see the prawns' insides through their shells,' said Nell, her plaits trailing in the water.

'It's a whole little world down in that pool, isn't it?' said Edith.

'Magical,' said Lucien, his expression rapt.

Edith caught Tamara's eye and smiled. 'I suppose we could stay a little longer.'

They sat on the rocks while the children paddled, had seaweed fights, chased seagulls, clambered over coils of rope and generally got in the way of the fishermen mending their nets.

'I love it here,' said Edith. The land rose sharply to either side of the harbour, the village's narrow streets lined with whitewashed and slate-stone cottages. A verdant, rolling landscape was visible behind and the whole delightful picture was extended beneath the wide Cornish sky.

'I often played here with my friends when I was a girl,' said Tamara. 'Life was so happy and free then.'

'That joyful freedom is what I want for my children,' said Edith. 'My sister and I were mostly confined to the nursery with Nanny.'

'What a shame!' Tamara chewed at her thumbnail and then said, 'Edith, I hope you don't mind me asking but, while we were waiting for you, Pearl mentioned her father has returned to Spindrift?'

Edith nodded, her stomach clenching at the thought. She'd never spoken of it to anyone in the village, though Jenifry Penrose was given to murmuring to her friends after Sunday services about 'the goings-on and loose morals of the Spindrift community', just within Edith's ear-shot.

Tamara frowned. 'Forgive me, perhaps it's only village gossip, but didn't your husband move to London some years ago?'

'Seven years ago. I never imagined he'd return.'

'That's a long time to be apart.' Tamara hesitated and then said, 'Are you happy about it?'

Edith could hardly say it made her want to scream and rage at her powerlessness to make him leave. 'Unfortunately, we're not suited,' she said.

'How awful!'

Tamara's voice was so sympathetic that Edith found herself explaining further. 'I married Benedict before I really knew him.' She remembered what a god-like figure he had appeared to her then. 'He dazzled and flattered me and I wanted desperately to leave home. Marriage offered me the way.'

Then Jasper, dripping with seawater and crusted with sand, came running towards them. 'Mama, I'm hungry. Shall we go home for tea?' He shook his head releasing a shower of sand.

'You're always hungry,' said Edith.

'Just like Tom,' said Tamara. 'They have hollow legs at this age. Every time I turn around, I swear he's grown another inch.'

Edith attempted a smile. 'Jasper, put your shoes on and fetch the others.'

A little while later, as they all trooped off the beach, Edith felt the back of her neck prickle. She glanced around and recognised a young, dark-haired woman leaning out of an upstairs window in the Golden Lion, watching her. Tamsyn Pengelly. Years before, she'd been Benedict's model, until Edith had caught them canoodling together. Benedict had never needed much encouragement where women were concerned, but, in Edith's opinion, she'd never met a more insolently flirtatious vixen in her life than Tamsyn Pengelly.

★ ★ ★

Two days later, Edith and her friends walked to the church of St Endellion, followed by Maude and Mabel driving the pony and trap. Instead of the planned service of Thanksgiving for the Coronation, there was to be an intercessional service to pray for the King's return to health.

Thankfully, Benedict hadn't asked to accompany them. During the sermon, Edith leaned back against the pew and soaked up the church's tranquil atmosphere. Benedict's shocking arrival had agitated Pascal quite as much as herself and, glancing at his face, it saddened her to see new lines of strain around his eyes. Her husband had betrayed her so many times but Pascal had loved and supported her for years, asking nothing except her love in return.

A flood of memories washed over her as she remembered Benedict's first betrayal. It was on their honeymoon, ten years before, that she'd discovered him *in flagrante delicto* with Pascal's sister, Delphine. Grief-stricken, she'd fled from the scene but Pascal had found her and she'd clung to him, utterly distraught. Then, out of the blue, desire had ignited between them with the intensity of a flaming torch. Afterwards, Edith had been so ashamed, she barely spoke to him for years.

It had taken her a long time to learn to trust a man again but Pascal had earned that trust.

Now, however vulnerable it made her feel, she must reassure him of her love by completely opening her heart to him. She had to confess to him the secret she'd never told anyone, the fact that Jasper was his son, the result of that first, emotionally charged coupling.

As if he felt her gaze upon him, Pascal turned his head and gave her a smile so full of love that she yearned to reach out and touch him.

Then the sermon came to an end and the congregation rose for the next hymn.

Edith held the hymn book in front of her like a shield. She should have told Pascal the truth a long time ago but, when she'd realised she was carrying his child, she'd barely known him. To safeguard the baby, she'd had no choice but to allow Benedict to assume Jasper was his own and to do her very best to mend their shattered marriage. So she kept her secret, terrified Pascal would guess the truth and that Benedict would find out. Then Pascal had left Spindrift and didn't return until after Benedict had deserted her. Over the following years, they fell in love but, until now, the time had never seemed right for Edith to tell him the secret he had an absolute right to know.

As the congregation knelt for the final prayer, she resolved to reveal the truth as soon as they were able to be alone together.

★ ★ ★

After they returned from church, Dora collected a basket from the pantry and went to the kitchen

58

garden. Gilbert had lost no time changing out of his Sunday best and was already hoeing between the rows of onions.

'What can I take to the kitchen today?' asked Dora.

Gilbert pushed his cap to the back of his head and wiped his forehead with a none-too-clean handkerchief. 'There's strawberries and some peas. A lettuce or two . . . and you might find some asparagus.'

Dora picked the last of the ripe berries and went to cut the lettuces.

Later, her basket overflowing with produce, she called out a goodbye to Gilbert and closed the kitchen garden gate behind her.

In the courtyard, she waved at Wilfred and Augustus, who were talking together outside the jewellery workshop. They didn't see her and there was something so intent about their conversation that she didn't like to interrupt them.

Passing the old cart shed, now converted into Julian's photographic studio, she glanced in through the window and stopped suddenly.

Julian was speaking to Clarissa, holding her by her shoulders. Her head was bowed and there was an expression of such torment on Julian's face that it made Dora catch her breath.

But then Clarissa touched his cheek and he pressed his lips to her palm.

Slowly, she tipped up her face and Julian bent his head to kiss her.

Dora backed hastily away, disturbed to have witnessed such a private moment. Clarissa kept herself to herself as far as men were concerned. At least, she had ever since she'd given birth to Lily out of wedlock. She'd never disclosed her lover's name, saying only that he was married and the affair had been a dreadful mistake. Dora returned to the house, feeling strangely down in the dumps.

It wasn't until later that she worked out why seeing Julian kiss Clarissa had made her melancholy. She was envious. Although she'd never wanted to give up her independence to marry and become subject to a man's selfish whims, her precious freedom came at a high price. She sighed, imagining for a moment how absolutely heavenly it would be to have someone special to love her above all others.

★ ★ ★

Later that afternoon, Dora, Edith and Clarissa accompanied the children to the village for their Coronation tea party.

Clarissa, unusually animated, swung Lily's hand as they ambled along the coast path, chattering about the forthcoming tea party.

Dora glanced at Edith, who by contrast was wrapped up in her own thoughts. 'Is everything all right?' she murmured.

'Yes, of course.' Edith forced a smile.

Dora guessed she was anxious about Benedict's return.

Down on the Platt, trestle tables had been set up in readiness for the party.

Tamara Mellyn was talking to some of the

other mothers. She waved and came to join them. 'It's in the newspapers that the King is making excellent progress,' she said.

'That's wonderful news!' said Dora.

'Now that there's something to celebrate,' said Tamara, 'there's going to be a brass band after all.'

The Reverend George and the headmaster welcomed the guests. The schoolmistress chivvied the children into their seats, boys on one side of the trestles and girls on the other, and bid them put on the crepe-paper hats they'd made at school. The Reverend said grace and then the children fell upon the feast of egg sandwiches, sausage rolls, saffron buns and fairy cakes sprinkled with hundreds and thousands. The vicar's wife and the church organist presided over the hot-water urn, dispensing tea.

Dora and her friends collected their teacups and carried them to a trestle table set up for the mothers. They were soon chatting with Tamara and the other women, mostly speculating as to when the delayed Coronation would take place.

Clarissa spoke to Dora in an undertone. 'I do believe Jenifry Penrose is trying to stir up trouble for us again.'

Hugh Penrose's wife was frowning as she spoke with the vicar's wife, shooting glances over her shoulder at the Spindrift party.

'Well, really!' said Dora. 'We haven't done anything to make her get her bloomers in a twist this time.'

'Unless she's heard Benedict is back,' said Clarissa. 'Jenifry has nothing better to do with her time than gossip. I've always thought she and her awful husband deserve each other.

'I can't bear the thought of any more conflict in that quarter,' said Edith.

'I've never cared for Jenifry Penrose,' said Tamara. 'She loved to stir up trouble even when we were at school together.'

The brass band started up, drowning out any further conversation. After tea, there were three-legged and egg-and-spoon races for the children, with a winner's prize of a jigsaw portrait of the soon-to-be King and Queen.

When it was time to go home, Edith, Dora and Clarissa thanked the headmaster and the Reverend George for hosting the party. His wife, a firm friend of Jenifry Penrose, looked on with pursed lips. She'd never approved of the Spindrift community.

The children waved goodbye to their school friends and the Spindrift party set off up the hill.

Tamara and Tom fell into step beside them. 'I'm coming to the Spindrift Gallery tomorrow,' said Tamara. 'I'm looking for a present for Mother's birthday and your gallery is such a treasure trove.'

'Perhaps I can help you choose something?' said Dora. 'And why don't you stay for a cup of tea afterwards?'

Tamara smiled. 'I'd like that. I'm fascinated by your community. It must be such fun to share a house with others who are as interested in the arts as you are?'

Dora nodded. 'But it's good to have friends outside the community, too.' She sighed. 'Some of the so-called better sort in the village — like the Penroses — disapprove of us. But we're all hard-working artists and Spindrift really isn't the hotbed of depravity that Jenifry Penrose seems to imagine.'

Tamara laughed. 'How *very* disappointing!' she said.

6

Outside, a summer storm raged and Edith was too unsettled to sleep. Knowing Benedict was under the same roof as herself still unnerved her and there was no question of slipping along the corridor to seek comfort, never mind pleasure, in Pascal's arms. Apart from that, her mind churned, planning how she was going to tell him that he was Jasper's father.

She winced as the darkness was split by a brilliant flash of light, followed by a thunderous eruption that threatened to shake the slates from the roof.

Moments later, the door handle rattled and she sat bolt upright, every nerve vibrating. She'd turned the key in the lock when she came to bed, fearful that Benedict would try his luck.

'Mama! I'm frightened!'

Letting out her breath in relief, she called out, 'I'm coming!'

A moment later a flash of lightning illuminated three small figures in their nightgowns cowering in the doorway.

'I'm frightened of the dark!' said Pearl.

'I'm not!' said Jasper. 'But Nell was crying and Lily went to find Auntie Clarissa.'

'Thunder won't hurt you,' Edith said. 'My nanny always used to tell me it was God rearranging his bookcase and dropping his books on the floor of Heaven.'

There was another flash of lightning and Jasper laughed. 'God must have knocked over his lamp, too!'

'I don't like it!' Nell clung to Edith's knees.

'Come and cuddle up with me for a while, sweetheart.'

The children didn't need a second bidding and all three of them jumped into her bed.

'Mama, do you think Papa is frightened?' said Pearl. 'Should we go and see?'

'He'll be asleep.' Edith sighed. It certainly wouldn't occur to Benedict that his children might be frightened of the storm and need reassurance.

'Will you sing the frog song to us, Mama?' begged Nell.

'If you promise to go back to sleep afterwards.' Edith began to croon 'A Frog He Would A-wooing Go' and the children joined in with the chorus.

Nell rested her head on Edith's breast and in only a moment fell asleep. Jasper yawned widely as she started the sixth verse for the second time, his eyelids closing by the end of it. He was warm and heavy against her as she finished the song.

' 'Heigh-ho! says Anthony Rowley',' murmured Pearl.

Torrents of rain lashed against the windows and thunder rumbled continuously. In the distance the angry sea roared and pounded against the rocks. Edith listened to her children's sleeping breaths and was overwhelmed with love for them. It was impossible for her to understand how Benedict could have abandoned them when they were so small and vulnerable. A deep and terrible fear that his selfishness and lack of responsibility might hurt them again made her hug them even tighter. 'I promise to keep you all safe, my darlings,' she whispered.

A dazzling light momentarily lit up the sky, followed by another great crash of thunder that made her jump. If Lucien had been startled awake, he'd be afraid to find himself alone. Gently, Edith extricated herself from the tangle of sleeping children. Sliding her feet into slippers, she wrapped herself in her shawl. She peeped out into the shadowy corridor and, finding it deserted, lit the oil lamp on the landing table and padded along to the boys' bedroom. The sheet on Jasper's bed was thrown back but the bedding on Lucien's bed entirely covered his sleeping form.

She pulled back the sheet a little and leaned forward to kiss the top of his head. The woolly lamb Dora had knitted for him when he was a baby lay on the pillow. Dragging back the covers, she revealed another pillow. 'Lucien?' Perhaps he'd been frightened by the thunder and hidden somewhere. She looked under the bed but there were only shoes and dust bunnies. She searched under Jasper's bed and opened the wardrobe door. Nothing.

Hurrying into the corridor, she looked into the lavatory. He wasn't there. Anxious now, she ran back to the girls' bedroom but it was deserted. In the corridor again, she stood still and listened but there was only the booming thunder and the

66

thudding of her heart. She glanced at the door to Benedict's bedroom and then crept past it along to Pascal's room. There was a glimmer of light under the door and she slipped inside.

'Edith!' He was sitting up in bed with a book open on his knee. 'Is it wise to come to me tonight?'

'I can't find Lucien! I looked under his bed and in the wardrobe. The rest of the children are asleep in my bed . . . '

'Have you looked downstairs?'

She shook her head, unease shivering down her back.

'Do not worry, we will find him.' Pascal pulled on his dressing gown and opened the door, taking care to be quiet. Glancing into the corridor, he beckoned her forward.

They crept downstairs, avoiding the fourth step that always creaked, and hurried through the rooms opening cupboards and looking behind the furniture and curtains.

In the kitchen, Edith checked the pantry and then put the lamp on the table. 'He's not here! What if someone crept in and took him?'

'Shh!' Pascal caught her by her elbows. '*Reste calme*, Edith! You must think. Was he happy when he went to bed?'

'Perfectly. You saw him, too.' She nibbled at her thumbnail while she thought. 'I peeped in to see him again before I retired and he was fast asleep then.' She frowned. 'At least, I thought he was. When I looked under his covers just now, they'd been arranged over his pillow to make it look as if he was sleeping there.'

'I wonder . . .' Pascal hurried through to the scullery.

Edith followed and watched him go to the candle cupboard.

'One of the storm lanterns is missing,' he said. He lit a candle stub and put it inside a lantern. 'I shall search outside.' Fetching a mackintosh from the back lobby, he buckled it up.

'Surely Lucien would never go outside in a storm like this!'

Pascal shrugged. 'He isn't here but I have a thought as to where he might be.'

'Where?'

'Let me look. If I don't find him, we will wake the rest of the household to help us search.' The key was in the back door but it was unlocked. A blast of wind snatched the door and banged it against the wall. 'Wait here!' He stepped outside into the darkness.

Edith watched the glimmer of the lantern as he crossed the courtyard. Then it disappeared. Shifting from foot to foot, she stared into the night. Teeming rain splashed up from the ground. Was that a glimmer of light she saw? A flash of lightning dazzled her and when her vision cleared the light had disappeared. She couldn't bear to do nothing but wait. Kicking off her slippers, she thrust her feet into the first pair of wellingtons she could find, pulled her shawl over her hair and ran outside.

She gasped as the full force of the wind hit her. Rain hammered down upon her head and shoulders. Her cotton nightgown was drenched in seconds but the wavering lamplight was ahead of her and she ran towards it, sloshing through the puddles. An oblong of light appeared and she saw that it was a doorway. The pigsty. She ducked her head and stepped inside.

Pascal lifted up his lantern and smiled at her. 'Look!'

Lucien lay curled up on the floor in a corner of the sty, fast asleep with both puppies hugged to his chest. A rivulet of water ran down the wall from beneath a slipped roof slate and pooled on the floor beside them.

'I should have guessed he'd be here,' said Edith. She pressed a hand to her heart, relief making her knees tremble.

'He is very brave,' said Pascal. 'Few seven-year-olds would go outside, alone in the dark, during a storm.' Gently, he removed the puppies from Lucien's arms and lifted the boy from the floor.

'We'd better bring them all into the house,' said Edith. She gathered up the puppies in their blanket. Their little bodies were warm and soft against her rain-soaked nightgown.

Edith felt a rush of love for Pascal when he tenderly tucked the sleeping child beneath his mackintosh. 'Bring the lantern,' he said. 'Ready?'

She nodded.

Heads bowed, they launched themselves through the doorway and out into the pelting rain. They burst into the house through the scullery door.

Lucien woke up in a panic, clutching at Pascal. 'Where are Blue and Star?'

'Here,' said Edith, shaking wet hair out of her

eyes. She pulled back the blanket and Star licked her cheek. Blue looked up at her with trusting eyes and her misgivings about keeping the puppies softened.

Lucien nestled back into Pascal's arms.

'I'll carry him up to bed,' said Pascal.

Edith toed off her rubber boots and settled the puppies on their blanket in a corner. She filled a dish with water and placed it on the floor beside them. In the kitchen, she rubbed her dripping hair with a towel, then followed Pascal upstairs.

In the boys' bedroom, he sat on the edge of Lucien's bed, talking quietly to him.

Edith placed the lamp on the chest of drawers and tucked the blankets around her son's shoulders.

'May I have Star and Blue up here with me, Mama?' he asked.

'Not in your bedroom,' Edith said.

'But they'll be crying for me!'

'I will go and make sure they are comfortable,' said Pascal, 'but you must go to sleep now, *mon petit.*' He patted the boy's cheek then turned to Edith, an appreciative smile in his eyes. 'And you must change into dry clothes and go to bed or you will catch a cold.'

Glancing down at her sodden nightgown, she saw how it clung to the curves of her body, calling attention to her nakedness beneath. 'It's the middle of the night and we should both be tucked up in bed, shouldn't we?' She looked at him, her expression innocent.

Pascal let out a low growl of laughter. '*Coquette!* I shall go and see to the puppies.'

'G'night, Uncle Pascal.' Lucien closed his eyes.

Edith listened to the rumbling thunder while she stroked Lucien's forehead until he fell asleep. Picking up the lamp, she crept from the room.

She was closing the door when a pair of arms slid around her waist from behind. 'Pascal!' she gasped. 'I nearly dropped the lamp!' She turned around and reeled back.

Benedict's face reflected her shock. 'You thought I was Pascal? Were you expecting him to embrace you?'

'I thought he'd . . . No, of course not!' Edith set the lamp down on the landing table to avoid meeting his searching gaze. 'Lucien was missing. He'd gone to the pigsty to sleep with those dratted puppies you brought. Pascal helped me to find him.'

'You went out in the dark in a storm with Pascal, in a state of undress?' Benedict's gaze raked up and down her body.

Edith folded her arms across her chest. 'I was too anxious about Lucien to delay and put on a raincoat.'

Benedict frowned. 'Aren't you aware that rain has rendered your nightdress transparent? Did you not think it improper to display your, it must be said, considerable charms, so freely to Pascal?'

'I'm aware that I'm cold and tired and want my bed.' She pushed past him but he caught her by the elbow.

Smiling, he said, 'Perhaps I should come with you and warm you up? I am your husband, after all.' He pulled her so close she could feel his breath on her cheek.

Uneasy, she leaned back but he didn't release his grip. 'Let go of me!'

'You can't blame me for wanting you when you're in my arms, practically naked,' he whispered. 'Any red-blooded man would feel the same.' He kissed her neck. She struggled to break free but he only held her tighter. 'Edith!' he cajoled. 'It's been so long.'

'Let me go!' Her voice was shrill with fear.

A shadow flickered at the edge of her vision and, all of a sudden, Benedict released her.

He staggered and fell backwards against the wall. 'What the hell . . .'

Then Pascal was beside her. 'Did he hurt you?'

She shook her head.

Benedict regained his balance and glowered at Pascal. 'What do you think you're playing at, shoving me like that?'

'Edith asked you to release her,' said Pascal, standing his ground. 'She asked you twice.'

'And what business is it of yours?' demanded Benedict.

'For Heaven's sake,' said Edith. 'Lower your voice, Benedict! You'll wake the children.'

'I won't be fobbed off,' he said, and looked Pascal up and down. 'You're altogether too friendly with Edith. What's going on between you two?'

'I merely prevented you from forcing yourself upon her. You frightened her.'

'Nonsense! And what gives *you* the right to tell

72

me how I should behave to Edith?' He became very still, his gaze boring into Pascal. 'Are you having an affair with my wife?'

Edith froze.

Pascal sighed. 'We shall go downstairs to the kitchen where we can talk without waking the household. Edith, perhaps you would care to change into dry clothes? We will wait here for you.'

Shivering, she hurried to her room. If Benedict had a mind to it, she'd never see her children again. A sob of panic rose up in her throat. It was unthinkable and she must not, could not, let that happen.

She put on a dry nightgown and tied the belt of her dressing gown with trembling fingers. Taking a deep breath, she went to join Pascal and Benedict.

They filed down to the kitchen in silence and Pascal shut the door firmly behind them.

'Right,' said Benedict. 'I shall ask you again, Pascal. Are you having an affair with my wife?'

'Perhaps you should ask Edith?' he said, mildly.

Benedict thumped his fist on the door. 'I'm asking you, dammit!'

'And I will not be intimidated by a man such as you.' Pascal folded his arms and stared back at him challengingly.

Edith swallowed. This had to stop. She must show Benedict she wouldn't be bullied. She braced herself for the onslaught. 'So what if I *am* having an affair?' she said, lifting her chin and looking him straight in the eye. She heard his indrawn breath and saw Pascal's eyes widen in surprise.

'You admit it?'

She sat down at the kitchen table, afraid her legs would collapse beneath her. 'Did you really imagine I would spend the rest of my life living like a nun after you deserted me? Pascal came to my rescue when I thought my world had ended. He's supported and cared for me and the children ever since. He's been more of a husband to me than you ever were.' She'd burned her boats now and there was nothing for it but to fight her corner.

Stepping closer, Benedict planted his fists on the table and loomed over her. He fixed her with a hostile gaze. 'Then I shall divorce you.'

'No,' she said. 'You won't.' She sounded calm but, inside, she was quaking with a mixture of rage and terror. 'You may wish to be rid of me, just as I long to be rid of you, but you won't divorce me.'

Pascal sat down beside her and she gathered courage from the touch of his knee against hers under the table.

'What makes you think that?' Benedict's eyes blazed.

'Of course you won't,' Edith said, her voice as cold as a midwinter day. 'For a start, divorce is only for the exceedingly rich and well connected. *You* certainly couldn't afford it.' She laughed. 'Unless you're under the misapprehension that I might pay for it? I'm sorry to disappoint you but you've already squeezed me dry.'

'As a self-confessed adulteress, you'll never see

74

your children again,' hissed Benedict. 'Every court in the land will be behind me when I throw you out into the street.'

A red tide of mingled fury and fear rose in Edith's breast. 'You cannot prove any adultery on my part.'

'Really?' Benedict sneered at her. 'Don't tell me your friends don't know what's going on beneath their noses?'

Edith forced herself to remain calm. 'By all means, do ask them.' A tremor of panic made her grip her hands together but then Pascal's knee pressed against hers again and she steadied. Apart from Clarissa, she didn't know if the community were fully aware of her relationship with Pascal. She hoped, even if they were, that they were as loyal to her as she believed. Otherwise she was done for.

'Are you quite sure about that?' he said. 'It's in their interest to support me, the main share-holder of Spindrift House. They were eating out of my hand at dinner this evening.'

She gave a snort of derision. 'Hardly!' she said. 'They were laughing behind your back at you.'

His lips thinned. 'I could force you to leave Spindrift.'

She shrugged. 'And what would you do with four children, without me to look after them?'

'I've told you, I intend to be part of their lives now.'

'But for how long?' she said. 'I can't see you wiping their noses or reading them bedtime stories. And surely even you wouldn't send them to an orphanage? Can you imagine what your mother would think of that?'

'They have a nursemaid.'

'But I'm the one who pays her to care for the children while I'm working,' said Edith. 'Don't forget, the community and I own a sizeable proportion of Spindrift and, if you forced me to leave, you can be sure the others would follow. You'd be waving goodbye to all the money we send you every month. And, of course,' she forced a laugh, 'then we might sell our share to Hugh Penrose. He's always wanted to get his hands on Spindrift House.'

Benedict frowned. 'I might sell him my share first.'

Edith raised her eyebrows. 'And kill the Golden Goose? When you've frittered away the proceeds of the house sale in a year or two, what will you live on then? You'll have *nothing* left, except your so-called talent.'

Rain teemed down the windowpanes and a crack of thunder resounded through the tense silence.

Benedict chewed at his thumbnail.

Every nerve in Edith's body jangled while she waited to see what he would do.

'You're still my wife,' he said at last, 'though you bring shame on me and our children by your adultery.'

'Not as much as you bring on yourself when you cheat and lie and tomcat around with almost every woman you meet.' Edith sighed. 'Look, Benedict, you tired of me long ago. You don't really want to be a husband to me again. Marriage and children are all far too much effort

76

for you. Be honest with yourself: you've only returned to Spindrift because you've run out of other options.'

There was a scratching from behind the scullery door and the puppies started to whine.

Edith rubbed her eyes. 'I'm exhausted and there are three children in my bed so I'm unlikely to get much sleep tonight. You brought the puppies here, Benedict, so you can settle them.'

'Go to bed, Edith,' murmured Pascal. 'I will lock the back door.'

Standing up, she smiled at him gratefully before turning to her husband again. 'No one wants you here,' she said, 'least of all me. If you must stay then, for your own comfort, it would be advisable for you to make some effort to pull your weight in the community.'

He regarded her with silent animosity and Edith left the room wondering how he would take revenge on her for tonight's revelation.

7

By the following afternoon, the storm had blown itself out and the sun shone. Pearl, Lily and Nell skipped through the girls' playground to where Dora was waiting for them at the school gates.

'Where's Hannah?' asked Pearl.

'She was busy turning out the larder so I said I'd walk you home,' said Dora. 'Jasper and Lucien have already run on ahead.'

Lily tugged at Dora's arm. 'How are the puppies?'

'The naughty little things had me running around all day cleaning up after them. My publisher's chasing me for the illustrations for my book and I haven't had a minute to myself.'

Pearl didn't think Dora was really cross but, to be on the safe side, hugged her. 'Is Papa at home?'

'Pearl told everyone at school that her father has come back,' said Lily, 'but some of the girls don't believe it.'

'I hate Adela Penrose!' Pearl scowled.

'I do, too,' said Nell.

'Do you think *my* papa will come home one day, Auntie Dora?' asked Lily.

'Sometimes,' said Dora, 'it's best not to wish for the moon. You might find it's made of mouldy cheese.'

Lily looked at Pearl and frowned. 'What's she talking about?' she whispered.

Pearl rolled her eyes and tapped her temple.

Both girls burst into giggles.

'Race you home!' said Pearl. She ran like the wind, laughing when her hair ribbon fell out, leaving her curls bouncing down her back. There was a strange feeling inside her, as if she were a pan of milk about to boil over. She just knew everything was going to be more exciting now Papa was home.

A little later, Pearl and Lily reached the headland and saw Edith was there, working at her easel.

Pearl threw herself on the grass at her mother's feet, panting for breath. Lily fell in a heap beside her.

'Did you both have a good day?' asked Edith. She didn't look up from her canvas but frowned at it with her brush poised.

Pearl went to look at the painting. She sniffed at the familiar smell of the paint. She always found it rather comforting, perhaps because it reminded her of Mama. 'Which one is me?'

Edith nodded. 'That's you flying the scarlet kite. Lily has the yellow one. I haven't added the others yet. Pascal will be over here, helping Nell and Lucien. Jasper and Tom will be by the standing stone.'

'It's going to be a lovely picture.'

Dora, hair escaping from her bun, hurried up to them, pulling Nell by the hand.

'Jasper and Lucien sprinted past on their way home a few minutes ago,' said Edith.

'The little monkeys ran off.' Dora pushed wisps of hair off her flushed face.

Edith turned her attention back to her canvas again and Pearl pulled at her skirt. 'Where's my papa?'

A fly landed on Edith's wrist and she swatted at it irritably. 'When I last saw him he was fast asleep on a rug under the beech tree.'

'I'll go and find him, then.'

'Pearl . . . ' Edith opened her mouth and then closed it again.

'Yes?'

'Nothing. That is, he might be busy. Don't be upset if he doesn't want to talk.'

Pearl laughed. 'He can't be busy if he's sleeping, can he?'

Edith glanced at Dora and shrugged.

'Come on then,' said Dora, 'let's leave your ma in peace to finish her work.'

★ ★ ★

After tea, the children went into the courtyard with Pascal, where he showed them how to make the puppies walk on a lead.

'Me first!' said Pearl, snatching Star's lead from his hand. 'It looks easy.'

'Why must you always go first, Pearl?' complained Jasper.

'You can take Blue,' said Pascal, handing him the other lead. 'Pearl, please remember your manners.'

It wasn't as easy as she had thought. Star ran around her, making excited little yips and tripping her over. She glowered at Jasper, who was walking more slowly with Blue by his side.

80

Then Lucien walked Star round the courtyard and persuaded him to sit.

'Very good, Lucien!' said Pascal.

Pearl saw Benedict standing outside the gallery. She handed Star's lead to Lily and ran to see him.

'Did you see me training Star?' she asked.

'I was watching Pascal ordering you all around,' he said. 'I don't know how you stand it. It's not his place to talk to you as if he were your father.'

'Sometimes he is rather bossy,' said Pearl. She saw her father's scowl lift at her comment and, hoping to please him further, said, 'It's really very annoying when he keeps telling me what to do.'

Benedict cracked his knuckles. 'Well, I'm your real father and I'm home now. I'm going down to the cove. Do you want to come?'

Pearl glanced back at the others. Pascal was still talking to Lucien. She nodded vigorously and slipped her hand into her father's. 'I'm so happy you've come,' she said, as they walked over the lawn.

He looked a little surprised but then he smiled. 'You're a funny little thing but at least someone is pleased to see me back at Spindrift.'

'You will stay, won't you, Papa?'

'Your mother and Pascal don't want me here. They were really nasty to me and I'm afraid your mother's a very bad wife.'

Pearl thought about that. She'd never thought of her mama being anyone's wife and she wasn't unkind. Still, she wanted to be friends with Papa.

'I'll be your friend, if you like?'

He looked at her consideringly. 'I could do with an ally in the enemy camp. I'd be very sad if your mother and Pascal forced me leave Spindrift. And you of course.'

Pearl tightened her grip on his hand. 'I won't let them!'

'I'd forgotten what a sharp tongue Clarissa has,' he said, 'and Dora looked at me this morning as if I were something the cat brought in.'

Pearl giggled. 'We haven't got a cat!'

'Perhaps we should get one?'

'Can we really?'

Benedict pinched her cheek. 'One thing at a time, poppet.'

They went through the gate at the end of the garden and onto the headland.

'There's Mama,' said Pearl, waving at her, but Edith was too intent on her painting to see.

'She's still working, then?'

'Mama is always working. Sometimes she doesn't notice me for *days*.'

'It used to be the same for me and I can't see that changing now.' Benedict sighed. 'I could do with some congenial company. I'll go down to the Golden Lion until dinner's ready, though whether you can call an onion pie a proper dinner, is debatable. You run on back to the house now.'

'But you said we'd go down to the cove together!'

'Another time.'

Pearl stamped her foot. 'No! You promised

we'd have a walk. I'll come to the Golden Lion with you, then.'

'Little girls can't go inside.'

'Then I'll wait for you outside.'

Benedict laughed and tugged one of her ringlets. 'You're an imperious little madam, aren't you? Come on then.'

Pearl skipped along beside him, unable to match his long strides as he marched along the coastal path. She chattered about school and her plans to set up a stall to sell lemonade to the summer visitors when they came to see the gallery or to have their photographs taken by Julian. Sometimes her papa laughed at her comments and that made her feel all warm inside.

They entered the village and strolled past the harbour towards the Golden Lion.

'Tell you what,' said Benedict, 'you go and sit on the beach and I'll bring you a drink. What'll you have?'

Pearl frowned. She wanted something grown up. She remembered Dora telling her about the time she'd been to a public house when she'd visited her family in London. 'I'd like a port and lemon, please.'

Her father stared at her and then threw back his head and roared with laughter. 'Well, why shouldn't the little lady have a port and lemon?' He walked off towards the public house, still chuckling.

Pearl wandered down to the beach, picking her way over stones and clumps of stinking bladderwrack. She poked a dead crab with her toe and said hello to two old fishermen sitting on an upturned boat while they smoked their pipes.

After a while Benedict returned. He handed Pearl a pretty pink drink. 'Keep the glass safe and I'll return it to the bar later.'

Pearl sipped it. It was sweet with a funny aftertaste a bit like cough mixture.

'Stay here on the beach,' said Benedict, 'until I come for you.'

She sat on a rock and finished the port and lemon. It made her head swim and she felt a bit sick.

The sea was as calm as a mill pond and the early-evening sun twinkled on the water. Placing her shoes and the empty glass on a flat bit of rock, she trotted down to the water's edge to paddle.

She was wriggling her toes in the shallows when a shout came from behind her.

Two of the village boys came racing across the stony beach to skim pieces of broken slate over the sea. Pearl gathered up slate stones in her pinafore and began to hurl them over the water.

One of the boys came to stand beside her. 'You're doing it wrong,' he said.

'Show me then.' She held out one of her pieces of slate and watched him carefully when he threw it with a flick of his wrist. After several attempts, Pearl managed to make one of the stones bounce twice. She cheered and jumped up and down.

The boy laughed. 'Got to go in for my tea now,' he said, and ran off to join his friends.

The jumping had made Pearl feel sick again

and rather dizzy. Half-heartedly, she threw a few more stones but none of them bounced so she went back to the rock to put on her shoes. She looked towards the Golden Lion but there was no sign of her father. Picking up her empty glass, she walked over the beach to the Platt. How long did it take him to finish one drink? She stared at the outside of the inn but the windows were too high up for her to peer inside.

Pearl walked along Fore Street to the main entrance of the Golden Lion and hovered outside for a while but there was no sign of her papa.

The door opened and three men came out, laughing and smoking as they set off along Fore Street. The door stayed open.

Pearl sidled up to it and looked inside. There was a dark passage in front of her and a lot of chatter coming from an open door at the end. There was an unpleasantly strong smell of beer and tobacco smoke. She didn't like it. Her stomach lurched and she wondered for a moment if she was going to be ill. Swallowing hard, she crept down the passage and peeped into the room beyond. It was full of men but then she spied her father, leaning on the bar talking to a lady with dark hair.

'What are you doing here?'

Pearl spun around, her heart thumping. An angry-looking man was glaring at her.

'I brought this glass back,' she stammered.

The man snatched it from her. 'No children are allowed on these premises. Now get along with you before I lose my licence.'

Pearl ran.

She hurried back to the beach and sat down on the stone bench by the fish cellars. Bored, she counted the seagulls.

Ages later, the sun had dipped towards the horizon. The fishermen had finished their pipes and were ambling up the beach.

'Time you went home, missy,' said one of them as they passed her.

The lower edge of the sun disappeared into the sea, sinking lower and lower until it was submerged, taking the light with it. Still her father didn't come. Pearl glanced back at the Golden Lion. The windows glowed with lamplight. What was Papa doing in there that took so long? A cool breeze stirred her hair and she crossed her arms, shivering. At home, Hannah would be looking for her by now to make her clean her teeth before bed. Her stomach churned uneasily and she leaned back against the wall and closed her eyes.

It was dark when her father shook her awake.

'Time to go home,' he said.

'You were away so long, Papa.'

'Was I? I didn't notice.' He tugged at one of her curls. 'I was having a fine time catching up with old friends.' He set off in the direction of Spindrift.

Pearl hurried after him, watching her step on the cobbles and glad of the light that now spilled from the village houses. By the time they were on the coast path she'd fallen some way behind Benedict. She kept stumbling because there was only a little moonlight to show her the way.

'Papa, wait for me!'

He stopped and turned to watch her. 'Hurry up!'

'Hold my hand then,' she said. 'My legs aren't as long as yours and my tummy aches.'

His hand engulfed hers. It felt warm and comforting.

At last they reached Spindrift and Benedict led Pearl inside. She was so tired she could have wept and the horrible sick feeling wouldn't go away.

Her mother ran down the stairs. 'Pearl! Where have you been? I was worried to death. Pascal and Julian have gone down to the cove to search for you.'

'I was with Papa at the Golden Lion,' she said.

'The Golden Lion?' Edith put her hands on her hips. 'What on earth were you thinking of, Benedict?'

'I merely went to look for some more congenial company, since there is none to be found here,' he protested. 'The child followed me.'

'Papa bought me a port and lemon,' said Pearl.

'Benedict, how *could* you?'

'Mama,' said Pearl, her voice wavering, 'I don't feel well.' And then she was sick, all over her papa's shiny shoes.

8

July 1902

Edith had tried to find a quiet hour when she might be alone with Pascal to confess her secret to him but, so far, she'd been thwarted at every turn. She'd planned to accompany him on his trip to a gallery in Truro to deliver some paintings but Lucien had caught a summer cold and she'd been needed in the sickroom. Inevitably, Nell caught it too and neither twin was well enough for school for several days. Twice, she'd tried to speak to Pascal in the garden but Benedict had taken to prowling around, furtively watching her. Pascal lost his temper and they almost came to blows when Benedict was discovered eavesdropping outside the studio door. Fretful and unable to concentrate on her work, Edith knew she must make the opportunity to talk to Pascal before the children finished school for the summer holidays. They'd never have a moment alone then and she might have to wait until September.

★　★　★

'I shall take my paints and walk along the coast path towards Kellan Head today,' said Pascal at breakfast, a few days later.

Edith determined to give Benedict the slip and follow Pascal so they could talk in private.

'Tamara Mellyn told me she'd seen dolphins swimming near Kellan Head the other day,' said Dora.

'I have seen them a few times already this year,' said Pascal, his face lit by a smile. 'I love to watch them leaping out of the waves.'

Hannah bustled in and herded the children together ready to walk them to school. As the noisy group was leaving the dining room, Benedict sauntered through the door clutching a handful of letters.

Pearl ran up to him and hugged him. 'Good morning, Papa. Don't forget you promised to come down to the cove with me after school,' she said.

'I'm looking forward to that.' He patted her head. 'Off you go now, all of you! And behave yourselves at school.'

Edith was uneasy. Pearl's hero worship of her father hadn't been at all tarnished by his neglect of her on their previous outing and, without accepting any blame, he'd readily forgiven her for the unfortunate incident with his shoes. Edith didn't trust Benedict's jovial manner and guessed he was making the effort to befriend his daughter only because it suited him for some purpose or other.

'The postman was early today,' said Benedict, once the children had left. He scrutinised each of the envelopes he held before distributing them. 'The writing is so poorly formed on this one for you, Edith, I can only imagine it's a tradesman's

89

bill. And here are several missives to Clarissa from London. Orders for your little trinkets, I imagine?'

'Indeed,' she said. 'Have you had any commissions recently, Benedict? I haven't seen any evidence at all of you working since you imposed your presence upon us.'

Ignoring her, he held up the next envelope to study the stamp. 'French.' His lip curled in disdain and he dropped it onto Pascal's plate of toast and marmalade. 'Isn't it about time you went to visit your family, Pascal? Better still, why don't you stay there? I don't care to have foreigners living in my house.'

Edith's temper flared and she opened her mouth to protest but Dora caught her eye and shook her head slightly.

'Stow it, Benedict!' said Wilfred. 'There's no need to be offensive. Quite apart from your lack of courtesy to my cousin, we're all part-owners of the house, including Pascal.'

Keeping his face expressionless, Pascal picked up the envelope and used his napkin to wipe off the toast crumbs and sticky smears of marmalade. He opened the letter and began to read it.

Edith noticed the rigid set of his jaw as he scanned the words. She ached to go to him but that would only inflame matters further.

Dora broke the uncomfortable silence by chatting nervously to Wilfred about his plans for the day.

Hacking a slice of bread off the loaf, Benedict spread it thickly with butter.

'If you're going to be so greedy,' said Clarissa,

'we'll have to deduct a greater percentage of the rent money from you to cover the additional costs.'

'Damn you, Clarissa!' Benedict stared at her with hostility. 'No wonder Lily's father deserted you rather than marry such a harpy.'

Clarissa flinched but before Edith could come to her defence, Pascal screwed up his letter and shoved it in his pocket, eyebrows drawn together in a frown.

'Oh, dear,' said Benedict, 'it looks as if the Frenchman's had some bad news.' He smiled. 'Perhaps the Paris galleries he boasted about don't want his little daubs anymore? If he spent more time painting instead of sniffing around my wife he might do better.'

Goaded, Edith banged her fist on the table, making the teaspoons rattle. 'You might do better, Benedict, if you spent more time working and less trying to stir up trouble!'

Pascal scraped back his chair and reared to his feet. He strode around the table and stood over Benedict, his fists clenched. 'You are nothing but a filthy piece of scum, a despoiler of women, and unworthy to utter Edith's name.'

Benedict tried to rise but Pascal shoved him back onto the chair and then left the room without a word.

'Benedict, you really are one of the most loathsome men I've ever met,' said Clarissa. Patches of scarlet burned in her cheeks.

'What?' said Benedict, his eyes wide and innocent. 'What did I say to make him have such a childish tantrum?' Scowling, he punched the palm of his other hand. 'I should have gone after him and taught him a lesson he'd never forget.'

Silently, Dora and Wilfred left the table.

'Oh, for God's sake!' Benedict ran his hand through his hair. 'Can't anyone here take a joke?'

Clarissa stood up, pointedly ignoring him. 'Shall we go, Edith?'

Seething with resentment, Edith followed her from the room, feeling Benedict's baleful stare boring into her back.

★ ★ ★

Half an hour later, Edith was hurrying along the coast path towards Port Quinn. She'd last seen Benedict stretched out on the sofa in the drawing room, smoking one of his foul-smelling cigarettes, and had taken the opportunity to slip away.

She pushed him out of her mind to concentrate on what she was going to say to Pascal. He wanted a child of his own and revealing the truth about Jasper was the most precious gift she could give him. He might be annoyed with her for not telling him sooner but, surely, he'd soon forget that in his delight on discovering that the boy he already loved was his son? Of course, Pascal would have to keep the secret, too, especially now Benedict was living at Spindrift. If he learned the truth, even though he might disown Jasper, he'd make sure Edith was separated from her other children. She quailed at the thought.

At last she caught sight of Pascal. He'd set up

his easel beside the path further ahead, facing towards Kellan Head. She slowed her pace, suddenly nervous. As she drew closer, she saw he hadn't started work but was staring morosely out to sea, his hands in his pockets.

'Pascal!' she called. The wind buffeted her skirts and teased her hair.

Impassively, he watched her as she hastened towards him.

'Thank you for defending me this morning,' she said. 'Benedict was absolutely vile.'

Pascal shrugged. 'Nothing changes there.' The brim of his hat was pulled low on his forehead and his eyes were dark and unreadable below the wide brim. 'What can I do for you, Edith?'

His distant manner unnerved her. 'I came to see if you were all right.' She'd temporarily forgotten the words she'd so carefully planned. 'You had a letter. I wondered, was it bad news?' He nodded and his expression was so bleak she ran to him.

He pulled her into his arms and rested his chin on her head. 'I am so ashamed of what has happened, I hardly know how to tell you the truth.'

She looked up at him. 'Ashamed?' Uneasy again, she said, 'Please, tell me. Whatever it is.'

He hesitated and then said, 'The letter was from my sister. Delphine says Édouard's health is failing. He has a tumour in his stomach and she expects to be a widow within the year.'

'But that is very sad for her.'

'She is shocked. And she has bad dreams imagining how terrible it would be for Gabrielle

93

if her *maman* were to die also.'

'All mothers worry that they might die before their children have grown up,' said Edith. 'I know I do.'

Pascal rubbed the heels of his hands into his eye sockets. 'Delphine has confided in me that Édouard is not Gabrielle's father. She has charged me with the heavy responsibility, in the event of her own untimely death, of telling Gabrielle the identity of her blood father so that she may seek him out. And the shameful thing is . . .'

Pressing her fingers to her mouth, Edith said, 'God in Heaven! It's Benedict, isn't it?'

Pascal nodded. 'I am so sorry, Edith.'

She stared at the sea, so blue and sparkling in the sunshine. 'After I caught them together that time, when I heard later on that Delphine had had a child, I wondered if it might have been Benedict's but I couldn't bear to think about it.'

'I have never ceased to be ashamed of my sister for her affair with your husband. And now, to find she deceived Édouard by pretending another man's child was his . . . ' Pascal's lips twisted in disgust. 'That is an unforgivable betrayal.'

Edith caught her breath. She despised Delphine but what she'd done was no worse than Edith's own action in allowing Benedict to assume he was Jasper's father. 'I expect she was frightened of the consequences and didn't know what else to do.'

Pascal stared at her in astonishment. 'That you, of all people, should excuse her! There *is* no

94

excuse. None at all.' His voice rose in anger. 'I disown her as my sister. She is deceitful and dishonourable. And now I am in an impossible position. Édouard should know the truth but he and my parents would be destroyed if I exposed Delphine's treachery. Though, God knows, she deserves it!'

Edith's heart began to pound. How could she ever tell him she'd made the same decision as Delphine to hide her own unplanned pregnancy? His views were so uncompromising that he'd be sure to be disgusted by her. Her palms prickled and she wiped them on her skirt. Pascal meant everything to her and her heart quailed at the possibility of losing his love.

'Edith?' His voice was soft now. 'I'm sorry. You have turned so pale.' He lifted her limp hand to his lips. 'This is a shocking discovery for you. Sit here on the grass for a while and, when you have recovered, I'll take you home.'

'You're so kind to me,' she murmured, 'but I'll be all right. You stay here. Running into Benedict is the last thing you need now.'

A few minutes later, she pressed a Judas kiss on his cheek and set off home.

Despair weighted every step she took. She'd wanted so much to be open and honest with Pascal but, if she was to keep his love, she must continue to carry the heavy burden of her deceit.

9

King Edward VII made a good recovery after his operation and was finally crowned on 9 August. The Spindrift children all had a part to play in the Port Isaac British Empire Pageant, each one costumed to represent a different country. Nell tripped over her sari and had to be removed from the procession, bloody-kneed and howling. Pearl, dressed as Britannia in a feathered helmet, waved regally to the peasants as she passed through the streets on a flower-bedecked wagon.

In the evening, the community went to the village bonfire party on the Platt and Edith was inspired to create a painting to commemorate the occasion.

Benedict celebrated the event by becoming embarrassingly drunk with his new drinking cronies from the Golden Lion and fell flat on his face beside the fire.

Jasper ran to help him to his feet. 'You've had too much to drink, Papa,' he said.

Benedict flailed his arms, knocking the boy to the ground. 'Gerroff me, you priggish little brat! What did I do to deserve a useless son like you? Get outta my sight!'

White-faced, Jasper stood up.

Edith, conscious of the villagers' avid glances, stepped in to rescue him. She led Jasper away

96

and looked back over her shoulder at Benedict. 'You should be ashamed of yourself!' she hissed.

Unrepentant, he didn't return to Spindrift until the following evening when he'd slept it off.

Over the ensuing weeks, he rubbed almost every member of the community up the wrong way at one time or another, except for Pearl. When Edith had first met Benedict he'd been handsome and charismatic but now it was hard not to feel contempt for his sullen manners and unkempt appearance. If he wasn't drinking in the Golden Lion or the Dolphin, he usually passed his time alone in the garden or the drawing room at Spindrift, slouched over a cigarette with a bottle in his hand. At every possible opportunity, he made cutting remarks to Edith but she refused to rise to his bait; it would only worsen the general unease if there was outright warfare between them. She was extremely relieved when he began to eat his evening meals at the Golden Lion.

★　★　★

One hot afternoon at the end of August, Edith crossed the courtyard towards the gallery. She carried *Children Flying Kites* in her arms, intending to hang the canvas as the centrepiece of her display of work.

Pearl, sitting at a table outside the gallery, waved at her. 'I've sold ten glasses of lemonade today!'

'Well done!'

97

'Have you seen Papa?' asked Pearl. 'I promised to save him some.'

'I think he went into the village.' It disturbed Edith that Pearl was so beguiled by her father. It disturbed her even more that, flattered by her admiration, Benedict encouraged her to follow him around and treated her with a careless charm. Edith hoped he wouldn't hurt Pearl's feelings when, as was inevitable, he grew bored with an eight year old's adoration.

Pearl looked up at Edith from under her eyelashes. 'Mama,' she said, 'have you been kissing Uncle Pascal?'

The canvas almost slipped from Edith's grasp. 'Whatever do you mean?'

'Papa asked me to tell him if I saw Uncle Pascal kissing you or coming into your bedroom at night. He said it was to be our little secret. I told him I hadn't seen Pascal doing that.'

'I should think not, indeed!' Edith was outraged that Benedict should stoop so low as to use their daughter to spy on her.

'And he said he'd give me a penny if I refused to do whatever you asked me to do.'

'That was very wrong of him, trying to set us against each other!' Edith crouched down before Pearl. 'Thank you for telling me the truth, sweetheart. You know you must always tell me the truth?'

Pearl nodded solemnly and her arms crept around her mother's neck.

Edith kissed her nose. 'Will you save me some lemonade, too?'

Pearl filled a glass and handed it to her. 'It

costs a penny. It's for the Spindrift coal fund for the winter.'

Edith laughed. 'How very enterprising of you!'

'I don't want to be as cold as I was last winter and you always say we have to work together.'

'Indeed we do. Remind me at teatime to give you the penny.' Edith drained her glass. 'Delicious!' She lifted up the canvas again. 'I'd better go and hang this canvas now.'

Pearl waved as her mother walked towards the gallery.

Julian burst out of the gallery. He turned back to give a jaunty wave to Clarissa before striding off towards his studio, whistling as he went.

She was standing before her jewellery display cabinet, staring at the contents, when Edith joined her.

'No customers?' said Edith.

Slowly, Clarissa turned towards her. 'Sorry. Did you say something?'

'I asked if we'd had any customers.'

Clarissa looked about her with a distracted air.

'Are you all right?' asked Edith. 'You look utterly preoccupied.'

'I'm fine.' Clarissa drew a deep breath and gave a luminous smile. 'Really, absolutely fine. It's just there's something I need to think about.' She unlocked the glass case and began to rearrange a tray of bracelets.

Edith shrugged and lifted down several of the smaller paintings from her display to make a space for *Children Flying Kites*. She adjusted it until it was level, then stood back to study it. A little *frisson* of excitement ran through her.

Though it was too late in the year to submit the canvas for the Royal Academy's Summer Exhibition, it would be a suitable entry for the following year.

Clarissa came to look. 'You've really caught the feeling of that sunny blustery day, Edith. It's full of movement and the colours are so vivid.' She went closer to peer at the figures. 'Look at Lily and Pearl, hair flying in the wind!'

'It's a joyous painting, isn't it?'

'Joyous,' repeated Clarissa. 'That's exactly the word.' Her pale blue eyes shone. 'It's time we all had more joy in our lives, isn't it?'

Edith nodded. 'The atmosphere here since Benedict returned has been dreadful.'

'I'm afraid you made it worse for yourself by admitting to him that you and Pascal love each other.'

'I was angry,' said Edith, 'and needed to demonstrate that I refused to give in to his threats. Nevertheless, I daren't allow him to find any proof that we're actually lovers.'

Clarissa hugged her. 'Well, we must lift your spirits. While the weather is still so good, why don't we have a picnic in the cove this evening?'

Edith smiled, though she knew it would take more than a picnic to take her mind off her problems.

'The gallery's been quiet today,' said Clarissa. 'Could you manage alone here if I muster the troops and help prepare the picnic?'

'I'll close early if there are no more customers,' said Edith.

'Splendid!' Clarissa frowned. 'I must speak to

100

Lily, too,' she murmured. Distracted again, she left the gallery.

Edith picked up a feather duster and set to work.

* * *

At five o'clock, she locked the gallery and returned to the house. The kitchen was fragrant with the aroma of baking and Clarissa was laughing at something Julian had said. Dora and Maude chattered while they buttered sandwiches. Mrs Rowe was lifting a batch of rock cakes from the oven and Julian was helping Lily and Pearl to polish apples. Gilbert, taking up far too much space and full of noisy good humour, packed bottles of ginger beer into a wicker basket. A fierce growling came from under the table where Lucien and Nell were playing tug of war with Star and Blue and a length of rope.

'How can I help?' said Edith.

'Take them dogs out of my kitchen!' said Mrs Rowe. She wiped perspiration from her forehead with the back of her hand. 'Begging your pardon, Mrs Fairchild, but it's like a lunatic asylum at full moon in here.'

'Go on, Twins!' said Edith. 'Outside!'

As the twins and the puppies left, Augustus and Wilfred came through the back door.

'Mackerel, fresh from the fishing boat,' said Wilfred. 'We'll cook them over a fire on the beach.'

'Benedict was at the harbourside, waiting for the Golden Lion to open,' said Augustus.

101

'I hope he doesn't disturb us again tonight, coming in late, singing bawdy songs and dropping his boots down the stairs,' grumbled Dora.

'Has anyone seen Pascal and Jasper?' asked Edith.

'They returned from their sketching expedition,' said Julian, 'and went down to the beach to light the fire.'

At last the baskets were packed and everyone trooped down to the cove. They trudged over the sand and set up camp near the rocks.

The cooling, onshore breeze carried a seaweed smell and sparked the fire into brisk flames. Pascal watched over Jasper while he fed it with driftwood.

Mabel and Maude shrieked in alarm when the puppies chased each other over the picnic rugs, scattering sand in their wake.

The men and boys played a boisterous game of rounders on the hard sand where the tide had retreated. Pearl, Lily and Nell splashed along the water's edge, throwing a ball for the puppies.

Edith and Clarissa set out the picnic on a gingham tablecloth laid over a flat rock, while Dora cooked the mackerel over the fire. When all was ready, Edith called the others to the feast by banging a spoon on a tin plate.

'I'm starving!' said Lucien. 'Can I have an extra piece of fish?'

'No, you can't, Sunny Jim,' said Dora. 'Don't think I haven't noticed you slipping little treats under the table to the puppies.'

'But they're growing boys!' wheedled Lucien.

'Get along with you now,' said Dora. 'Go and sit with the other children and perhaps we'll see if there are any scraps later.'

Pascal and Edith sat with their plates on their knees, the late-afternoon sunshine warm on their faces. 'Benedict is not here to spoil our picnic,' said Pascal.

Edith grimaced. 'Thankfully not,' she said. 'I can't understand why he doesn't leave Spindrift. He can't have drunk away *all* of the rent money we give him. I'm sure he only stays to spite me.'

'And me,' said Pascal. 'I can see in his eyes that he is looking all the time for an excuse to fight me.' He trailed his finger along her wrist. 'And I miss you,' he whispered.

'I miss you, too.' She wanted to hold his hand but there were too many people nearby.

'Perhaps we could go away for a while?' he murmured.

'I daren't,' said Edith. 'Not now. He's waiting for an opportunity to prove we're lovers. If he finds it, who knows what he'll do then? Even if it did mean he'd have to assume all responsibility for the children.'

Silently, Pascal picked at his fish.

'How was your sketching expedition with Jasper?' asked Edith.

Pascal's expression brightened. 'He has a great deal of talent for his nine years and is so quick to learn. Some of my happiest moments are when we are drawing or painting together. He is the son I wish I had.' He gathered a handful of sand in his palm and let it filter through his fingers.

The sadness in his voice made Edith want to

weep. She looked out to sea while his words reverberated in her head. Somehow, she would have to tell him the truth eventually. Perhaps his uncompromising attitude to Delphine in passing off Gabrielle as her husband's child would soften over time and Pascal would understand why Edith had followed a similar course of action.

'You're dreaming again!' he said to her.

Edith blinked and returned to the present. 'Sorry.'

'Benedict saw Jasper with me in the village this afternoon,' he said. 'He accused me of stealing his son's affections.'

'That's ridiculous!' said Edith. 'You saw how unkind he was to the boy at the Coronation celebrations. He's been far too busy flattering Pearl and bribing her to disobey me at every turn, to take any notice of Jasper. Or the twins, come to that.' All at once, Edith wasn't hungry anymore.

They sat in silence, watching the children paddling in the sea.

Julian had brought his camera to record the picnic. Mabel and Maude laughingly protested when he took their photograph, smiling into the sunlight. Lily, a small replica of her elegant mother, sat at Clarissa's side, their flaxen hair stirred by the sea breeze as the image was captured forever. Edith leaned away from Pascal when Julian set up his camera and tripod before them, making sure nothing in their pose would betray the intimacy of their relationship.

Julian asked everyone to gather together for a group photograph. Once the shutter had clicked, he cleared his throat. 'I have an announcement to make,' he said, and held out his hands to Clarissa and Lily. 'My dear friends, it's my very great privilege to tell you that, earlier today, Clarissa did me the honour of agreeing to be my wife.'

Gilbert let out a resounding cheer and there was a chorus of squeals of pleasure and good wishes. This was followed by applause and catcalls when Julian kissed Clarissa on the lips and then lifted Lily into his arms.

Edith glanced at Pascal. 'I'm so happy for them,' she said, tears in her eyes. 'Don't they make a handsome couple?'

'But I do so wish it was us,' Pascal murmured.

Julian had brought Champagne to celebrate the engagement and the children shrieked when the corks popped. 'I proposed weeks ago,' he said, 'but it was only this afternoon that Clarissa accepted. I'm the happiest man alive.'

Hugging Clarissa, Edith said, 'Now I understand why you were preoccupied when I came to the gallery this afternoon.'

Julian clapped Pascal on the back. 'Will you be my groomsman?'

'I would be honoured.' Smiling, he shook Julian's hand vigorously.

There were more games of rounders and then, when the sun began to streak the sky with orange and gold, Dora sat the children in a circle on the sand and told them the story of Princess Elowen and the Piskie.

Meanwhile, the adults packed up the remains of the picnic and, as the sun set, they all climbed the cliff steps back to Spindrift.

After the children were in bed, the adults congregated in the drawing room to finish the Champagne.

Edith watched Julian and Clarissa holding hands on the sofa, their eyes shining with love, and tried not to be jealous of their happiness.

Wilfred teased Julian, asking him what had taken him so long to propose, when Edith heard the floor creaking in her bedroom above. She sighed. One of the children must have clambered into her bed again. She slipped away from the party and went upstairs.

In the corridor she saw a pile of clothes on the carpet outside her bedroom door. Her clothes. As she watched, a pair of shoes and her hairbrush sailed in an arc through the open doorway and landed on the carpet. The little devils were rooting through her wardrobe! She shouted, 'What do you children think you're doing . . . ' And then she froze.

Tamsyn Pengelly stood in the doorway in nothing but her chemise and drawers, hands on hips and sloe-dark eyes glittering in triumph.

Over Tamsyn's shoulder, Benedict lay on Edith's rumpled bed with his arms behind his head, laughing.

Bare-chested, he sat up and then came to wrap his arms around Tamsyn's slender waist. 'Ah, Edith,' he said. 'From now on, you're to sleep in the cramped little room formerly consigned to me. As you can see, Tamsyn and I have reclaimed the master bedroom that is rightfully mine.'

10

The following morning, naked except for the sheet twisted around her thighs, Tamsyn yawned and stretched. Benedict lay beside her, one outflung arm resting on her hip. She studied his handsome face while he slept, almost having to pinch herself that she was there beside him, in the master bedroom at Spindrift House, no less.

Over the years she'd known a lot of men but Benedict Fairchild was different. He was a gentleman. She was only a girl when he chose her to be his artist's model. She'd really fancied him and been quite cut up when, after they'd had a run in with his wife, he'd left Cornwall for London. Then, one evening a couple of months ago, she'd been pulling pints in the Golden Lion when he'd appeared out of the blue. He'd looked her up and down, very slowly, and smiled at her with an invitation in his come-to-bed eyes. She'd melted inside. He told her he'd missed her and it must have been true because he'd been there, in the bar, every single day since.

And yesterday he'd asked her to move into Spindrift House with him. She'd been knocked sideways. Never, in all her dreams, could she have imagined such a thing.

'But what about your wife?' she'd said.

'Don't worry about her!' He'd scowled. 'She's been living in sin with that Frenchman for years.

Why do you think I left Cornwall in the first place?'

'But wouldn't it be tricky? I wouldn't stand for it if you were *my* husband.'

'Edith's had everything her own way for far too long. You'll be my wife in everything but name and we'll stand firm together.' He'd laughed uproariously then. 'And won't she hate that!'

Tamsyn chuckled to herself. Her Aunt Nessa Rowe would hate it too. She had been the cook at Spindrift for the last couple of years and gave herself airs and graces. Looking down her pointy nose at Tamsyn, she'd warned her to keep her hand on her ha'penny or she'd end up with a little bundle of trouble.

Anyways, the previous evening, while the Spindrift lot were down in the cove, Benedict had led Tamsyn into the silent house. She'd had second thoughts then but he'd pushed her against the wall and kissed her until she was breathless. He took her upstairs and gave her a good seeing to on Edith's bed. Afterwards, he'd egged her on to throw all his wife's things out of the room and laughed like the Devil while she did it.

And then Edith had turned up. By God, she was a cold-hearted bitch!

Tamsyn, all fired up for a slanging match, had tossed her hair and leaned back into Benedict's arms so that they blocked the bedroom doorway.

Edith had given her a withering look, just as if she was something nasty stuck to the bottom of her shoe. 'I can see you're both spoiling for a fight,' she'd said, 'but I'm not prepared to risk distressing the children by making an undignified scene in the presence of this little hussy, Benedict. We'll discuss it tomorrow.'

Edith had walked away then looking as if she had a poker up her backside and, somehow, the fun had gone out of it all.

Tamsyn sighed. Still, Benedict had told her she was the mistress here now. He wanted nothing more to do with Edith but he'd explained he couldn't get rid of her, not unless he caught her having it off with the Frenchman.

Beside her, Benedict rolled over and his puffing breaths made Tamsyn giggle. Poor lamb; he'd quite wore hisself out last night. She stroked his hair, liking the silky feel of it.

Tamsyn's belly rumbled. They hadn't had any dinner and she was famished. She blew on Benedict's cheek, hoping he'd wake up. She didn't fancy going downstairs by herself to look for breakfast. Not yet, anyways. Not until Benedict had spoken to Edith and put everyone right that Tamsyn was the new mistress of the house. And then she'd ring the bell and tell Aunt Nessa to fetch her breakfast in bed.

★   ★   ★

Edith had breakfast with the children the following morning before Hannah walked them to school. Pascal was still seething after the previous night's shocking turn of events and Edith was anxious he'd come to blows with Benedict and make it all worse. She suggested it

109

might be better if he went off in the pony and trap to collect an order of artist's materials from the supplier in Truro and, his face like thunder, he left without another word.

Edith and Clarissa went down the cliff steps to the cove and walked arm-in-arm along the tideline, their skirts billowing in the breeze.

'At least the fresh air's lifting my headache,' said Edith. 'I barely slept last night. Rage made my heart race and my mind churn with vengeful plans to throw Tamsyn and Benedict over the cliff.'

'That seems perfectly reasonable in the circumstances,' said Clarissa.

'I'm sick with dread at the prospect of facing him this morning. I'm sure he only brought Tamsyn into the house to punish me.'

'Of course he did!' Clarissa squeezed Edith's hand. 'You've shown him you won't be browbeaten and you must continue to stand firm.'

Edith sighed. 'That's easy to say but if I tell him to send Tamsyn away, he'll only laugh at me. The awful truth is, he has a right to be here and I have no legal redress.'

'You need to show him you have sharp teeth! There must be something in his heinous past that gives you a hold over him?'

'I can't think of . . . ' Edith hesitated. Perhaps she might threaten to expose his deceit at taking the credit for her painting that he'd exhibited at the Royal Academy?

'What is it?' asked Clarissa.

'There is a matter he wouldn't wish to be

110

known. The trouble is, to expose it might bring censure on my head, too.'

'How intriguing!' said Clarissa. 'I shan't ask you to tell me about it, unless you choose to, in which case I shall be all ears. There is another tack you might try. Benedict assumes you'll be angry and will beg him to send Tamsyn away. So don't.'

Edith frowned. 'I see,' she said after a moment. 'Because he won't be expecting that and it'll take the wind out of his sails?'

'Exactly! I can't imagine he will want that little trollop underfoot for very long. Perhaps you might set some rules? You could confine them to certain parts of the house. I know the rest of the community will stand firm behind you on that.'

'I could try,' said Edith, doubt in her voice.

'You must be resolute or he'll grind you underfoot forever.'

Edith gave a wan smile. 'Over the years, we've weathered some heavy storms together, haven't we?'

'And many of them caused by Benedict.'

They reached the rocks at the end of the cove and turned back.

'I'm so delighted you and Julian are to be married,' said Edith. 'He's a good man and obviously adores you.'

'I know. It's taken me years to overcome my mistrust of men. My father . . . ' Her voice trailed away.

'I know he was very unkind to you.'

'Unkind!' Clarissa snorted with laughter. 'He nearly destroyed me. Julian has been as patient

111

as a saint and almost restored my faith in mankind. And Lily loves him or I wouldn't have contemplated marrying him.' She bent down to pick up a pearly shell from the sand. 'Actually, there's something I wanted to ask you. Julian would like to bring his son to live with us. Would you mind?'

'Not at all. The few times I've met Will I thought he was very well behaved.'

'His grandmother is seventy now and she shouldn't have to bring up an eleven-year-old boy. Naturally, Julian's very grateful to her but Will needs a father's influence. Perhaps Julian can toughen him up a bit.'

Edith jumped and retreated as a wave foamed over her shoes. 'The tide's turning,' she said.

'There's something else,' said Clarissa. 'There isn't room for us and two children in the loft over the photographic studio. We wondered about looking for a cottage in the village but neither of us want to move from Spindrift. We wondered if we might rent the coach house?'

'But it's semi-derelict!'

'If we renovated it, perhaps we might negotiate a rent-free period?'

'That's an excellent plan.'

'Then we'll arrange the wedding for after the work is finished.'

'I never thought I'd see you succumb to matrimony.'

Clarissa shook her head in wonder. 'Neither did I but now I've finally made the decision, I can hardly wait!'

They climbed the cliff steps and, at the top,

Clarissa said, 'I'll go and tell Julian the good news.' She hugged Edith. 'Good luck with Benedict.'

Edith returned to the house with lagging steps. Pascal had offered to stay with her while she confronted her husband but that wouldn't have ended well. She knew she mustn't show any weakness or lose her temper with him but her natural instincts made her want to hurl insults and rage at him.

As she walked into the hall, she heard his voice coming from the dining room. She stopped outside the half-open door and breathed deeply for a moment before stepping inside.

Gilbert glanced up from his scrambled eggs. 'Morning, Edith.'

Tamsyn was sitting beside Benedict as bold as brass and he studiously ignored Edith. He draped his arm around Tamsyn's shoulders and continued his conversation with Wilfred and Augustus. Waving his toast and marmalade in the air, he said, 'I disagree. It's entirely appropriate for me to return, not only to my home, but also to my muse.' He pressed his lips to Tamsyn's cheek. She turned her face and lingeringly kissed his mouth.

Maude and Mabel, their porridge untouched, stared at the couple, their faces frozen in matching grimaces of distaste.

Tamsyn stretched like a cat. Her dark hair was loose and she showed an altogether unseemly expanse of bosom for the breakfast table.

'I must protest!' There were hectic spots of pink on Mabel's cheeks. 'Such conduct! And at the breakfast table . . . '

'Disgraceful!' tutted Maude. 'It's untenable to be exposed to such lewd behaviour.'

'Tamsyn has inspired me to paint again,' said Benedict. 'I shall set to work straight after breakfast.'

'There are some things we must discuss first,' said Edith. She heard the slight tremor in her voice and cleared her throat.

'Oh?' He raised his eyebrows. 'I don't think there's anything important that you and I have to say to each other.'

'Nevertheless,' she persisted, 'I shall speak to you and I'd prefer to do so in private.'

He sighed. 'If there's something you *must* say then say it now.'

'If you insist.' Heat flushed through her body. 'Your behaviour in bringing your . . . ' she paused ' . . . your *model* into Spindrift is deeply offensive,' she said in clipped tones, 'and the manner in which you dispossessed me of my bedroom contemptible.'

'Ooh!' said Tamsyn. 'Hark at her! Hoity-toity!'

Benedict nudged her sharply in the ribs.

Edith pointedly ignored the interruption. 'For many years Spindrift has been a happy place but since you returned, Benedict, it has ceased to be so.'

'Hear, hear!' said Gilbert, crunching noisily into a piece of toast.

'Indeed,' said Wilfred, delicately blotting his lips with his napkin, 'the friendship I once felt for you has been sorely tried and is unlikely ever to flower again.'

114

Benedict cast a look of extreme loathing at Wilfred. 'That's rich, coming from the cousin of the man who has seduced my wife.'

Gilbert frowned. 'What are you blathering about, man? Edith and Pascal are great friends but . . . '

'She actually admitted it!' Benedict's eyes gleamed with triumph.

'Utter nonsense!' said Maude, in tones that brooked no argument.

'A more hostile and judgmental group of . . . '

Edith held up her hand. 'Benedict, let me finish. It's an entirely different situation since you brought Tamsyn into our home. You're setting an appalling example to the children.'

'Not only is bringing your mistress to Spindrift a grossly provocative and inappropriate act,' said Wilfred, 'but it threatens to disturb the serenity the community requires. If we're unable to work in a harmonious atmosphere, we may choose to leave.'

'And for the reasons we've already discussed, I don't suppose that's what you really want, is it, Benedict?' said Edith. 'It seems we're *all* obliged to adapt to new circumstances so as to minimise unpleasantness and disruption. Therefore, I agree it's a sensible arrangement for you and Tamsyn to have the master bedroom.'

Benedict's mouth fell open.

'Furthermore,' she said, 'you shall have your old studio. In addition, you and Tamsyn will have the sitting room for your sole use. Mrs Rowe will provide meals to you both, the cost of which will be deducted monthly from the rents you receive.

You will eat them at the table in your sitting room. You will not be permitted to use the drawing room.'

'You're banishing us?' said Benedict. He gave a bark of incredulous laughter.

Edith sighed. 'I'm doing my best to find a solution to making day-to-day living tolerable for all of us, including you. You've already stated you take no pleasure in the community's company.'

'And, God knows, we take none in yours,' said Gilbert.

Edith tapped her fingernails on the table. 'Where was I? Oh, yes. *If* you take your turn in manning the gallery in the summer months, you'll be provided with an area on which to display your work for sale. I think you must agree this is a fair arrangement?'

Tamsyn nudged Benedict with her elbow. 'Go on!' she said. 'Tell 'em!'

'Tell them what?'

'You know.' She fiddled with his shirt button, looking up at him through her eyelashes. 'Tell 'em that I'm the mistress of Spindrift now.'

Wilfred barely suppressed a snort of laughter. 'Madam,' he said, 'you are sorely mistaken if you believe weaselling your way into this house qualifies you to be any more than the mistress, the *current* mistress, of Benedict's bed.'

Tamsyn shot him a glance of such glowering hatred that Edith almost smiled. She still had to expose her own inglorious deed. 'Now that the living arrangements are clear, Benedict,' she said, 'I'm giving you notice that I shall no longer allow you to browbeat me into providing you with any

116

more of my work for you to pass off and sell as your own.'

'What? That's monstrous!' said Augustus.

Wilfred pushed back his chair and stood up. 'Edith, tell me it isn't true! How could you?'

'I'm horribly ashamed of it,' she said, 'and I always hoped none of you would ever know, but my work was the only thing I had left to bargain with. I *had* to stop Benedict coming back to live here or selling his share of Spindrift to Hugh Penrose.'

'The man is a damned cad! An absolute sewer!' White-faced, Wilfred sat down again.

'No need for *you* to be ashamed, Edith,' said Gilbert. His lips curled in disgust as he glanced at Benedict. 'How many canvases has he stolen from you?'

'Three a year, ever since he deserted me,' she said. 'That is, twenty-four, plus several he stole and sold before I realised what he was doing.'

Maude pressed a hand to her breast and Mabel passed her a vial of smelling salts.

Benedict slammed his hand down on the table. 'Stop condemning me, all of you! It was a business arrangement and Edith willingly agreed to it.'

'You threatened to put me and the children out onto the street, Benedict,' she said, 'leaving me no choice but to agree. But now you've returned to Spindrift, you've broken our agreement and you'll have no more of my work.'

'I need the money.' He shrugged. 'Or I *will* have to sell my share of Spindrift.'

'Don't threaten me!' she said. 'Besides, we've

had that conversation already. Spindrift is your last asset, Benedict. If you sell it and spend the money, you have nothing. You've already fallen foul of your rich patrons in London and, I promise you, once I make it known throughout the art world that you coerced me into providing you with my work, you'll be discredited. You will never have another commission again.'

He leaned threateningly over her. 'I'll see you and that bloody Frenchman thrown out of Spindrift!'

Edith wiped his spittle off her cheek.

Gilbert lurched to his feet. 'Step away from her!'

Benedict glanced up at the formidable figure and stilled.

'If you attempt to have me removed from Spindrift,' said Edith, 'I shall go to the Royal Academy and tell them that the painting they displayed five years ago, entitled *Catching the Tide*, was my work. I still have all my preparatory sketches.'

'You colluded with me for your own reasons, Edith,' said Benedict. 'You never made any complaints five years ago so I hardly think the Royal Academy would be interested now.'

She leaned towards him, rigid with fury. 'You *stole* it from me and passed it off as your own.'

'You bastard!' yelled Gilbert.

Tamsyn screamed as Gilbert, three inches taller than Benedict and a good deal brawnier, hoisted him from his chair and manhandled him from the room.

There was a loud crash in the hall and a yelp

as the front door banged open.

Gilbert returned a few moments later, brushing his meaty hands together.

'What've you done to my Benedict?' shrieked Tamsyn. She flew at Gilbert, pummelling his chest.

He caught her by her wrists. 'He's in the garden, nursing his grievances. From now on, you'd better keep to your own rooms, you little hussy, or I'll throw you out too.' With a penetrating glare at her, he thrust her away.

Tamsyn scuttled out of the room, casting a frightened glance over her shoulder.

Edith let out a shuddering sigh. At least that was one of her painful secrets out in the open and her friends hadn't condemned her. 'I think,' she said, 'we need a fresh pot of coffee.'

'Preferably as hot as Hell and black as sin,' said Gilbert.

11

November 1902

Dora was staring out of the dining-room window at the persistent rain when the postman pushed open the front gate. She hurried to open the door.

He tipped his cap and handed her two letters, slightly damp. 'One for you today, Miss Cox.'

Dora didn't recognise the handwriting. Curious, she slit the envelope and extracted a stiff white card engraved with black copperplate. An invitation from her publishers, Pettigrew and Alleyn, to a Christmas sherry party. She wouldn't go; it was such a palaver going up to London and it wasn't as if she knew any of the other authors.

The second letter was for Edith and Dora took it upstairs to the studio. She was worried about her friend, who'd become increasingly quiet during the three months since Benedict had moved that shameless little madam into Spindrift. It had been vexing for all of them but, for Edith, it was downright insulting. Although Tamsyn was meant to stay in her own rooms, she always seemed to be skulking about in the hall or loitering in the kitchen, watching everyone and making cheeky remarks. Edith was working even harder than usual, ignoring Benedict and Tamsyn's vulgar behaviour, but the strain was telling. Pascal was unhappy, too. All the light had gone out of his face and he often took himself off with his easel from early in the morning until dark.

Climbing the stairs to the studios, Dora heard raucous laughter and thundering footfalls from above. She pinched her lips together at the sound of Tamsyn's ear-splitting squeals of laughter. It sounded as if there was slap and tickle going on behind the closed door of Benedict's studio. Again.

Dora found Edith working at her easel beside the window.

'A letter for you,' said Dora. Edith continued to work without looking up. 'Edith?' After a moment, Dora touched her lightly on the arm.

Edith jumped and turned to face her.

'Are you all right?'

Edith smiled. 'Sorry. Did you say something?' She pulled cotton wool from her ears. 'This is the only way I can get anything done with that racket going on next door.'

'It's shocking,' said Dora, shaking her head as yet another shriek emanated from the neighbouring studio.

'They only do it to provoke a reaction from me.'

Dora handed her the letter.

She opened it and clicked her tongue in annoyance. 'After all these years, the tenant from Woodland Cottage is leaving. I shall have to advertise for a new one.'

Dora moved closer to the easel to look at Edith's work. Lively and colourful, it depicted Wilfred, Augustus, Julian and Clarissa reclining on a tartan rug in dappled sunshine under the copper beech.

'I made the watercolour sketches back in the summer,' said Edith. She picked up a photograph from among the scattered papers on her work table. 'Julian took this for me. Now the summer's over, it's such a useful *aide memoire* of the setting and the tonal values.'

'It's foul weather for working outside,' said Dora. 'Not that Pascal cares. I saw him setting off at first light again with his easel.'

'Benedict's continual insults and attempts to draw him into a fight are very wearing. Pascal wants to be as far away from him as possible. He takes a giant umbrella to keep the rain off the canvas and wears that disreputable old mackintosh and battered hat with the big brim.' Edith sighed. 'I suppose, if I'm looking for a silver lining, Pascal's black mood has resulted in some magnificently dark and stormy seascapes.'

'He deserves every bit of his success,' said Dora. 'Unlike *some* I could mention.' She nodded her head meaningfully at the studio wall.

'Pascal has been such a source of strength to me over the years,' said Edith, 'and I refuse to stop being friends with him simply to please Benedict.'

Dora didn't want to know if Edith and Pascal were having an affair but she wouldn't blame them if they were. Everyone needed an extra-special friend; she knew that as well as anyone. Since her sister Annie had left Spindrift, her loneliness had grown more acute. Sometimes, she felt quite wretched.

Another strident peal of laughter resounded from next-door and she put her hands over her ears. 'Let's leave them to their carryings on without the benefit of an audience and go down for elevenses.'

Clarissa, Julian and Augustus were already in the dining room, drinking coffee and eating shortbread.

'It's impossible to think in the studio,' said Dora. 'Benedict and Tamsyn are making a beastly disturbance, chasing each other around.'

'Tamsyn's vulgar behaviour is rubbing off on Benedict,' said Clarissa, making a *moue* of distaste.

Edith shuddered. 'Talk about something else. Tell me about progress on the coach house. I saw the builders have finished repairing the roof.'

'Just in time before the weather turned,' said Julian. 'It won't be long before it's ready for us to move in.'

Clarissa talked about the furniture she'd ordered and the curtain fabric she'd chosen. She reached out for Julian's hand, her eyes shining. 'The first of the banns will be read this Sunday. I shall be Mrs Julian Clemens in time for Christmas.'

Julian lifted her fingers to his lips and kissed them.

Dora added her best wishes to the general congratulations, keeping a smile pasted on her face. She was so pleased for Clarissa and Julian, really she was, but seeing their glowing happiness made her own heart ache with emptiness. She finished her coffee and retreated upstairs to fetch her sketchbook.

She stopped dead along the upstairs corridor when she saw Benedict and Tamsyn entwined together in the open doorway of their room. Benedict released the girl and disappeared inside.

The front of Tamsyn's blouse was undone and she stared pertly at Dora, making no attempt to cover herself. 'What're you lookin' at?'

Heat rose to Dora's throat and cheeks. 'You ought to be ashamed of yourself, showing your bosom like that, you cheeky little baggage!'

Tamsyn laughed. 'Jealous, you are,' she said. 'A dough-faced old spinster like you will never get a man.'

'I don't want a man! And I certainly don't want one like Benedict.' Her fingers twitched with the effort of not slapping Tamsyn's face.

'Dried up old crow!' Tamsyn flounced into the bedroom and slammed the door behind her.

Dora stared at the door, her heart pounding. Tamsyn's catty remark had made her gloomy mood even worse.

She crept to the lonely sanctuary of her bedroom and sat on the bed with her head in her hands. Edith and Clarissa had been her closest friends for years but they had their own concerns and less time for Dora these days. All at once, she was overcome by homesickness but it was more the idea than the reality of home that she missed. After so many years living apart, she had little in common with her family now. Her last visit to the back-to-back terrace in Lambeth had been awkward for them all. Her sister Annie was the only one who understood how much Dora's horizons had opened up and changed her from the girl she'd once been.

Dora put a hand in her pocket and took out the invitation card. She was due to deliver her latest batch of illustrations to her publishers. Perhaps, instead of posting them, she ought to grasp the opportunity and stay with Annie in London? Why, she might even buy herself something nice to wear and be brave enough to go to the party.

★　★　★

Two weeks later Dora knocked on the door of a red-brick terraced house in Kennington. Annie opened it and Dora flew into her arms.

Soon, the sisters sat at the kitchen table, chatting over a pot of tea about the time when Annie had lived at Spindrift, helping Dora to manage the house and look after the children.

'Where's my little nephew then?' Dora asked.

'Sam's having a nap,' said Annie, moving the clothes horse draped with damp washing a little further from the fire. 'He's teething and fretful.'

'Poor little mite!'

'Do you remember when the twins were teething?' Annie smiled, her freckled face so dear and familiar to Dora. 'There was always one of 'em awake and screaming. Exhausting times those were! I count myself lucky, though, that I had the chance to practise on someone else's babies. I don't worry about Sam as much as I might have without that. Not to mention that one baby is so much easier than five little ones.'

'They were exhausting times, weren't they?'

Dora smiled fondly, remembering. 'I miss them in some ways. I felt needed then.'

'But you can have too much of a good thing. John and I have agreed we'll have three babies and that's that. Rents are too high and a carpenter's pay won't go far if we end up with seven or eight.'

'That's all very well, Annie,' said Dora, 'but you'll have as many babies as the Good Lord sees fit to send you.'

Annie poured the tea and set a cup down in front of her sister. 'There are ways to stop you having too many.'

'Keeping your legs crossed works well, so I've heard.'

'That's no way to keep your husband happy, though.' Annie's cheeks grew pink and she tucked a wisp of her sandy hair back into her bun. 'John's married sister put me right on what to do and I use a sponge tied on a ribbon while John takes . . . ' she leaned forward and whispered ' . . . *precautions*. It's called a French letter.'

'I've heard rumours about such things,' said Dora, 'but aren't they for a — *you know* — certain kind of woman? And is it right to go against God's will?'

'Better than having too many children to feed or being so worn out you die in childbed!' said Annie tartly. 'I've often thought about poor Edith having four children so close together. Those twins were nearly the death of her.'

Dora shuddered at the memory. 'And our ma was always so tired and looked so old before her time.'

'Exactly,' said Annie. 'I'm not going to let that happen to me. Now tell me, how is everyone at Spindrift? I could hardly credit it when you wrote to say Benedict moved his mistress in to the house.'

Dora brought her sister up to date with all the news and finished by saying, 'So I had to get away for a while. I couldn't stand the atmosphere. Besides,' she patted Annie's hand, 'I've really missed you.'

'We had some good times, didn't we?' said Annie.

'We did and now I've plans for us to have a lovely day out together. I'm going up to the West End tomorrow to buy something to wear to my publisher's sherry party.'

'Ooh, hark at you!' Annie laughed. 'Now my sister's a famous author she's gone all posh.'

'Get away with you! But I'd like you to help me find something smart. I'll treat you to lunch somewhere nice and we can give Sam an airing in the park. What do you think?'

'It'll be like a holiday! Wait 'til I tell John — he'll be ever so jealous!'

★ ★ ★

Four days later, Dora arrived outside her publisher's offices, carrying her portfolio of illustrations for Mr Pettigrew. Dusk was falling and she stood on the pavement for a moment, looking up uncertainly at the imposing facade of the building. Light glowed from within and she wondered if she was brave enough to go to the

127

party. After all, no one would miss her if she turned tail and ran back to Annie. Shivering, she pulled her cape more tightly around her shoulders.

There was a constant stream of horse-drawn traffic and Dora watched two men cross the road and walk into the building, soon followed by another with a lady on his arm. Still undecided about entering, Dora smoothed down the elegantly draped skirt of the forest green costume she'd bought for the occasion. It was the most expensive item of clothing she'd ever owned but, when she looked in the mirror, she hardly recognised herself as the modish lady who looked back at her. The puffed sleeves and cleverly draped bodice, worn with a new corset, gave her the fashionable pouter-pigeon silhouette. Annie had helped her to pin up her curly, red-blonde hair into a puffy bun and then placed the new hat at a rakish angle over the top. She'd adjusted the ostrich feathers then clapped her hands together. 'My, don't you look the business!'

Now, Dora stood up straight and lifted her chin. She'd come this far and it would be cowardly to bottle out. After all, it wasn't the first time she'd been to Pettigrew and Alleyn's offices. Before she had time to change her mind, she dashed over the road, taking care to avoid soiling her shoes in the heaps of horse dung. She nearly jumped out of her skin when a hansom cab hurtled by, missing her by an inch. Her pulse still racing, she pushed open the entrance door to the offices and went inside.

A clerk sitting at a desk in the hall ticked her name off a list. 'Fourth floor, Miss Cox.'

She stopped on the third floor to catch her breath. Subdued chatter and genteel laughter drifted down the stairwell.

On the fourth-floor landing, a maid took her cape and directed her to the boardroom, where sherry was being served.

Mr Pettigrew, short and rotund with a neat white beard and moustache, came forward to greet her. 'My dear Miss Cox! How delightful that you have come all the way from the wilds of Cornwall to grace us with your presence.'

Blushing, she said, 'I've brought the illustrations for *Princess Elowen and the Piskie*, as promised.'

Mr Pettigrew took the brown-paper package from her. 'As efficient as ever, Miss Cox! Now, do allow me to find you a glass of sherry.'

About twenty people, mostly men, were gathered in small, chattering groups. Mr Pettigrew introduced Dora to two young authors and then excused himself to take her illustrations into his office.

Dora pretended an interest in the other two guests' discussion of *The Hound of the Baskervilles* that she didn't feel, since she didn't much care for Sherlock Holmes's arrogance. The two men, whose names she'd already forgotten, took not the slightest notice of her. After a while, she drifted away.

A maid offered Dora a tray of titbits and she selected a cucumber sandwich and a sliver of ham rolled around a pallid spear of tinned

129

asparagus. She sipped her sherry, uneasily eyeing the other guests. They all seemed to know each other and she wished she hadn't come.

The boardroom walls were lined with shelves, displaying the publisher's latest books. She examined several volumes, covering subjects such as household management, gardening, illustrated history books and children's stories. Surprised and delighted, she saw that the reprinted edition of her first book *The Adventures of Theodora the Pirate Queen* was prominently displayed.

'Miss Cox?'

Dora turned to find a tall, fair-haired woman smiling at her.

'Yes?'

'Forgive me, I should have waited for Mr Pettigrew to introduce us but he has been cornered by an angry young man who is arguing with him over the title for his next book and I simply couldn't wait. I am Ursula Hoffman.' Her palm was warm and lightly callused when she took Dora's hand and shook it briskly.

'Are you one of Mr Pettigrew's authors?' asked Dora.

'Indeed, yes.' Miss Hoffman, a spinster for she wore no wedding ring, appeared to be in her late thirties. She lifted one of the books from the display and held it out to Dora with a smile. Her eyes were a pale blue and as clear as spring water in her lightly suntanned face.

Dora leafed through the pages of the book, titled *A Year in an English Garden*. 'I like the lists of what needs to be done in the garden each

130

month,' she said. 'And the photographs and illustrations are attractive.' Privately, she thought the watercolours insipid.

Ursula Hoffman shrugged. 'They suffice but I hope for something better for my next book.' She leaned towards Dora. 'And that is why I particularly wished to speak to you. You see, when I last met with Mr Pettigrew, I noticed an illustration from your wonderful Cornish Piskie series, hanging on the wall.'

'I was flattered when he asked if he might frame it and hang it in his office,' said Dora. Miss Hoffman had a slight accent that she couldn't quite place.

'My attention was particularly caught by your excellent rendering of the bindweed climbing up a tree trunk and I said to Mr Pettigrew, 'That is the illustrator I want for my next book. The bindweed looks alive.' And then,' said Miss Hoffman, 'Mr Pettigrew told me that you started your career with illustrations of plants and other natural forms.'

'I sold several wildflower and seashore illustrations to *Nature Review*,' said Dora, 'but it was hard to make a decent living from them.'

'So you chose to write children's stories instead?'

'It wasn't quite that straightforward.' Miss Hoffman's expression was interested so Dora continued. 'For over ten years I've lived within an artists' community. My dear friend, Edith is a very talented painter but after we moved into Spindrift House she gave birth to four children within the space of two years.'

Miss Hoffman frowned. 'Is this possible?'

'The last two were twins,' said Dora, 'and by the time they were born, Edith's husband had deserted her. So I set aside my artistic dreams and looked after her babies for a few years so that she could earn a living with her painting.'

'But what a sacrifice for you!'

Dora shook her head. 'I love the children with all my heart and the sacrifice was worth it when Edith had one of her paintings hung in the Royal Academy. I used to make up bedtime stories for the children and paint illustrations to go with them. Then Edith showed the stories to Mr Pettigrew and he offered to publish them.'

'And your books have been a very great success ever since!' Miss Hoffman laughed, her eyes twinkling. 'Don't pull that modest expression! You know it's true.'

'Well, I suppose it is.' Dora patted her cheeks, feeling the rising heat of her blush.

'My selfish question,' said Miss Hoffman, 'is this, my dear Miss Cox. Would you have time, amongst your other commitments, to illustrate my new book?'

'That rather depends on Mr Pettigrew,' said Dora. 'I've finished illustrating *Princess Elowen and the Piskie* but there are to be other stories in the series. We haven't yet discussed how soon he wants them.'

'I wouldn't need the illustrations straight away,' said Miss Hoffman. 'You see, my next book will be called *A Year in the Potager* and I can't begin to write it until I've found a suitable garden for the setting.'

'What is a *potager*?' asked Dora.

'It's a French name for an ornamental vegetable garden. It's beautiful as well as providing food for the table. Ideally, it would be a walled garden where I can make my own little world and the owner would allow me complete control over design and planting.' She sighed. 'So far, such a paradise has eluded me.'

'How extraordinary!' Dora smiled broadly. 'I may have the answer to your difficulty. It's not my decision alone but I think you should come and meet the Spindrift community and see our walled vegetable garden.'

Miss Hoffman grasped Dora's hands. 'My dear Miss Cox, I am not a superstitious person but I have the strangest feeling that Fate has brought us together.'

A warm glow of elation was expanding right under Dora's breastbone. 'I do believe, Miss Hoffman, that I agree with you.'

12

December 1902

It was Clarissa and Julian's wedding day and Edith and the children waited outside the church of St Endellion in the pale December sunshine. Lucien and Nell were racing beetles along the churchyard wall while Pearl and Lily twirled around showing off the frills on their brides-maids' frocks until they became giddy.

Edith caught Pearl as she lurched towards a puddle. 'Careful!' she scolded. 'You'll make your pretty dress dirty.'

Julian's son Will, who'd arrived at Spindrift the previous day, stood stiffly beside Edith watching the other children, his expression unreadable behind his spectacles. She'd tried to engage him in conversation but he remained monosyllabic almost to the point of rudeness.

Jasper, keeping watch in the lane, called out, 'They're here!' and the pony and trap, decorated with swathes of tulle and rosettes of white ribbons, rolled into view.

The children cheered and waved.

Augustus slowed the pony to a standstill and tied Ned's reins to the church gate. Then he assisted Clarissa down from the trap.

'You look beautiful,' Edith told her.

Clarissa wore a cream cloak trimmed with swan's down over an ivory silk gown with guipure lace at the neck and hem and mother-of-pearl buttons. Her flaxen hair was loosely twisted into a chignon and decorated with roses. 'I'm not making a mistake, am I?' she whispered. Her hands trembled so much that her posy of white roses shook. Her complexion was as pale as alabaster.

'Of course not!' said Edith. 'You're perfect for each other.'

Clarissa nodded. 'Last-minute nerves, I suppose.'

Lily came to kiss her mother and then Edith marshalled the children into a crocodile behind the bride and gave them their final instructions.

Augustus, who was to give the bride away, took her arm.

A few moments later, Edith slipped into a front pew beside Dora. 'Clarissa has arrived,' she whispered. Her eyes were drawn to Pascal, so elegant in formal clothes, as he waited beside Julian at the altar.

Clarissa's aunt Minnie sat on Dora's other side, the only member of the bride's family who'd been invited. The wedding party consisted of the Spindrift community and a sprinkling of villagers. Tamara Mellyn had come with her husband Walter and son Tom. Clarissa and Julian had felt obliged to send an invitation to Benedict, though they drew the line at asking Tamsyn, but, to their relief, had received no response.

The organ heralded the entrance of the bride on Augustus's arm. Edith smiled at the children, who looked angelic as they followed the bridal procession. Julian turned to watch Clarissa walk up the aisle and tears prickled Edith's eyes at the love and awe in his expression.

The Reverend George began the ceremony.

Augustus gave Clarissa away and then Pascal stepped forward to hand Julian the wedding ring. After that, he came to sit beside Edith. His expression was solemn but his arm pressed comfortingly against hers while they listened to the bride and groom's responses.

Edith remembered her own wedding to Benedict. The only good thing to have come out of that misbegotten alliance had been her children. She'd entered into marriage with such high expectations but it had been a terrible mistake almost from the start. It seemed as if she and Pascal would suffer for it the rest of their days.

Pascal stirred beside her. He glanced at her with such longing that she yearned to lean against him. 'I wish with all my heart that we were the ones standing at the altar,' he whispered.

She nodded, the ache in her breast growing as she held back tears.

Dora made no such attempt to stem her own tears and blew her nose noisily into her handkerchief.

After the ceremony, the bride and groom climbed into the trap, followed by Lily and Will. Julian kissed his bride and a cheer went up from the guests.

Clarissa's face glowed with happiness and Edith was relieved her former nerves appeared to have evaporated.

The guests threw handfuls of rice at the happy couple as Julian picked up the reins and flicked Ned into a trot. The children chased after the trap as it rolled away down the lane and the chattering wedding party set off behind it.

Clarissa's aunt Minnie walked with Edith and Pascal. 'I can't think why Clarissa waited so long to marry,' she said. 'I knew she and Julian were right for each other years ago.' She shook her head. 'My niece can be very obstinate sometimes.'

'Julian will be a perfect stepfather to Lily,' said Edith. 'He's known her since she was small and she already thinks of him as a father.'

'It will be more difficult for Will, I think,' said Pascal. 'Living at Spindrift will be very different from being with his *grandmère*.'

'We'll all do our best to make him welcome,' said Edith. 'Jasper's only a couple of years younger so perhaps they'll become friends.'

'Both are quiet and sensitive boys,' said Pascal.

The wedding party arrived at Spindrift and hurried into the courtyard behind the house. Edith caught sight of a movement at one of the upstairs windows and saw Tamsyn's face pressed against the glass, watching the comings and goings. She moved back sharply when she saw Edith staring at her.

Clarissa, Julian and their two children waited inside the gallery to receive the guests. A small ensemble of musicians hired from Wadebridge were playing. Braziers set in the corners of the barn had been lit the previous night and evergreen garlands and candle-lit chandeliers created from cartwheels were suspended from the beams of the soaring roof. Polished silver and crystal glasses gleamed on trestle tables dressed with starched linen. Vast bunches of whitewashed twigs were decorated with brightly wrapped sweets that twinkled like jewels.

When it was Edith's turn to greet the bride and groom, Clarissa hugged her with tears in her eyes. 'You've turned the barn into a fairyland for us. It's so beautiful!'

Pascal kissed Clarissa on both cheeks and shook Julian's hand. 'Congratulations, *mon ami*. I wish you every happiness.'

Gilbert, tall and with a powerful voice, had been appointed master of ceremonies. Once all the guests were inside the gallery and the barn doors closed to keep out the draughts, he escorted the bride and groom to the long table displaying the cold collation. Wreaths of ivy surrounded platters of game pies, sausage rolls, vol-au-vents and Scotch eggs. The Mellyns had provided a gigantic home-cured ham, glistening with treacle glaze and studded with cloves. There were dressed salads, vegetables in aspic, bowls of nuts and shivering jellies. Crusty loaves, whole cheeses and fresh butter vied for space with tiered plates of meringues and macaroons. The centrepiece was a magnificent wedding cake decorated with tiny replicas of Clarissa and Julian on the top, moulded from sugar paste.

'What a feast!' said Tamara Mellyn.

'It is rather wonderful, isn't it?' said Edith 'Dora, Mabel, Maude and myself were baking and making jellies until the small hours last night and Mrs Rowe has surpassed herself with the cake.'

Clarissa and Julian took their seats at the top table and Gilbert called out to the other guests to help themselves to the feast. Then he offered his arm to Clarissa's aunt Minnie. 'Dear lady,' he said, 'may I have the honour of leading you to the table?'

Edith caught Pascal's eye and smiled. 'It was something of a surprise this morning to see Gilbert, dust-free and so smart in his morning suit, even if it does reek of mothballs.'

Pearl and Lily chattered excitedly together as they filled their plates at the buffet but Edith couldn't help noticing Will watching his new stepsister with wary eyes. She whispered to Jasper, 'Look after Will, won't you? It must all be a bit strange for him.'

Before long, everyone was seated and enjoying the delicious wedding breakfast. Edith was pleased to note that Will and Jasper sat together at the children's table. Nell and Lucien had disappeared to let the dogs out into the garden.

Wilfred opened bottles of Champagne and the musicians fell silent when Gilbert called for a toast.

Augustus, standing in as father of the bride, spoke of his respect for Clarissa as his business partner and thanked her aunt Minnie for providing the wine.

Aunt Minnie rose to her feet. 'It's unusual for a woman to make a wedding speech,' she said, 'but as Clarissa's aunt, I wanted to say how delighted I am that Clarissa and Julian are joined together in matrimony and to give my blessing to their union. For many years I despaired because my niece rejected all thoughts of marriage but now I know that she was simply waiting for the right man.' She smiled at Julian. 'And now she has found him. Please, raise your glasses to Clarissa and Julian.'

'Clarissa and Julian!' chorused the guests.

Next Gilbert called upon Pascal to say a few words.

He rose to his feet. 'I believe that, as Julian's groomsman, it is my duty to tell you scandalous stories about him . . . ' Wilfred and Augustus let out a loud cheer and Pascal gave them an exaggerated frown. 'However, I am pleased to inform you that I am unable to do so. If Julian has behaved badly in any way, I have no evidence of it. Instead, I commend him to you as a loyal and hard-working friend, worthy of his beautiful new wife and their children. Please raise your glasses to Mr and Mrs Clemens and to Will and Lily. May you always be happy.'

Julian stood up and made the appropriate response, thanking those who had helped to make the reception a success. He stopped in mid-speech when the barn door creaked open.

Benedict strolled in with Tamsyn on his arm. 'I apologise if we're a little late,' he said in ringing tones.

Edith felt the smile fade from her face. She prayed they weren't going to make a scene.

Tamsyn, tricked up in a shiny ochre-yellow dress and matching hat, faltered and took a step back at the sight of all the faces staring at them.

Benedict frowned at her and pulled her to his side.

Pushing out her chest, Tamsyn stared brazenly back at Edith.

'Congratulations, Clarissa and Julian!' said Benedict, smiling benignly. 'I'm not in favour of marriage myself but I wish you better luck with your wife, Julian, than I had with mine.'

Edith flushed and glanced at Pascal, whose jaw tightened.

Benedict waved his hand airily at Julian. 'Sorry, old man, did I interrupt you? Carry on and take no notice of us.'

Tamsyn giggled nervously as Benedict led her to the buffet table and the two of them chatted loudly as they piled their plates with delicacies.

Edith saw that Clarissa was white-faced while Julian manfully struggled on with his speech.

The instant he finished, Gilbert was on his feet proposing another toast.

Benedict called for Champagne. 'Can't have a toast without a drink in our hands, can we?'

Augustus, clearly annoyed, took them each a glass to avoid further disturbance.

After the toast, the guests spoke to each other in hushed voices. Gilbert hurried over to speak to the musicians and they struck up a waltz.

Julian led Clarissa onto the floor for their first dance as a married couple. They circled around in each other's arms, gazes locked.

'Don't they make a perfect couple?' Edith whispered to Dora.

Her eyes glistened. 'How wonderful to be loved like that.'

At the end of the dance, Gilbert led Clarissa's aunt onto the floor and Wilfred came to ask Dora to dance with him.

'I wish to dance with you, Edith,' murmured Pascal, 'but Benedict is glowering at us and I won't risk any unpleasantness, for Clarissa and Julian's sake.'

'Perhaps he'd stop watching us if you danced with Mabel or Maude?' she said.

He nodded and went to speak to them.

Benedict guided Tamsyn to the dance floor, holding her indecently close. As they passed Edith, he called out to her, 'It seems you're a wallflower. Has your paramour deserted you?' He pulled a mock-tragic grimace.

Tamsyn gave a throaty chuckle and reached up to kiss him full on the mouth.

Edith, her face aflame, turned away. A red mist rose up to cloud her vision and her hands shook with the effort of preventing herself from slapping their gloating faces. Benedict *knew* he still had the might of the law behind him to dictate her future, as a mere female, whereas he could escape retribution and flaunt his mistress without any consequences. The happy atmosphere of Clarissa and Julian's wedding had been ruined for Edith. Hatred burned within her breast.

13

It was early in the new year when Pascal, his face strained, came to find Edith in the studio.

'I have received a letter from my mother,' he said. 'My father has suffered a heart attack and is very sick. He asks for me.'

'Oh, Pascal!' Edith put her arms around him.

'I feel bad I haven't seen him for so long. If anything should happen . . . ' Pascal's voice trailed away.

'You must go to him,' she said. That was the right thing to do, she knew without question, but she would be bereft during his absence.

He gnawed at his thumbnail. 'I'm worried to leave while Benedict is so uncivil to you.'

'Don't think about that,' she said, resolutely pushing her anxiety away and smiling reassuringly.

He kissed her forehead. 'You are very understanding, *mon amour*. Then I shall leave tomorrow but I would be so much happier if you would come with me.'

'I cannot leave the children.' Her voice dropped. 'And if I brought them with me, Benedict would follow and snatch them back to spite me.' Dread clamped itself around her heart as she imagined losing her babies.

'I love your children too much to steal you

143

away and risk condemning them to their father's care. Or rather, lack of care.' His nostrils flared in anger. 'How can one respect a man who would deny his children a loving mother, purely to satisfy his own spitefulness?' He sighed. 'Edith, I have been thinking . . . Perhaps I should stay away for several weeks?'

'Several weeks! But why?'

'If you make Benedict believe I have left because we no longer care for each other, perhaps then he will stop watching us. And Pearl must believe that too, since she is close to her father.'

Edith gripped the studio windowsill and swallowed hard to dispel the nauseous feeling in her stomach. Focusing her gaze on the paint-splattered floor, she named the colours in her mind — alizarin crimson, cobalt, ultramarine, chrome yellow, madder — until she'd fought back her tears. 'For how long?' she murmured.

'I cannot say. Even if Papa recovers, I should spend some time with Maman.' He pulled a face. 'Though I wish I did not have to see Delphine, after what she has done.'

Edith glanced away, remembering how distressed she'd been by Pascal's angry and unforgiving attitude towards his sister. 'Will you write to me?' she murmured

'Of course I will.' Wearily, he rubbed his palm over his face. 'But if we wish to give the impression we have parted, too many letters may alert him to the lie.'

'I can't bear to be separated from you but you know I'll always love you,' said Edith, her voice trembling. Pascal held her tight, stroking her hair and murmuring words of endearment.

Edith heard heavy footfalls, then the sound of Tamsyn's shrill voice and Benedict's deeper tones as they came up the stairs. Pascal released Edith and made a hasty retreat to the other side of the studio.

Benedict stepped through the open doorway with Tamsyn behind him. They watched Edith and Pascal with avid curiosity.

Eventually, Edith looked up from her easel. 'Yes? Is there something, Benedict?'

He shot a suspicious glance at Pascal. 'You're working indoors today?'

Pascal shrugged. 'As you see. And you, yet again, are *not* working?'

Benedict glowered and stepped heavily back through the doorway onto Tamsyn's foot. She yelped and Edith heard her grumbling until Benedict slammed the door of his studio behind him.

★ ★ ★

A few days later Edith picked up the post as it dropped through the letterbox. It was too soon for a letter from Pascal but there were two letters for her and one for Dora. She carried them into the dining room and joined Clarissa and Dora for elevenses.

Dora pounced upon her envelope, scanned the contents and gave a wide smile. 'You remember I wrote to Ursula Hoffman?' she said. 'Well, she's accepted our invitation to stay and she's coming next month!'

145

'I'm pleased for you,' said Edith. 'I know you liked her and I'll be interested to hear her ideas for the vegetable garden. We could certainly do with another pair of hands to maintain it.'

'If her *potager* idea is anything like the Potager du Roi at Versailles,' said Clarissa, 'then it'll need an army of gardeners.'

Edith put aside the coal merchant's bill and opened the second envelope. It was a response to her newspaper advertisement seeking a replacement tenant for Woodland Cottage.

'Listen to this,' she said, putting down her coffee cup. 'It's from a Reverend Algernon Musgrave. He's a retired clergyman and is writing an epic biblical poem — *a sure and moral guide to man's salvation, second only in importance to the Holy Scriptures.*'

'How modest!' said Clarissa.

'He requires a secluded location where he will be undisturbed for a few months. He asks that nothing be left in the property except the most essential items of furniture since he will be bringing his own books and cannot bear other people's knick-knacks. I shall write to him by return,' said Edith.

'Are there many knick-knacks in Woodland Cottage?' asked Dora.

Edith shrugged. 'I've never been there. The land agent found the last tenant before I dispensed with his services to save money. If you remember, Woodland Cottage was the secret love nest where Benedict's aunt Hester used to meet her lover.'

'Hugh Penrose's father, Jago,' said Clarissa.

'And what an upset that affair caused!'

Edith sighed. 'Oh. Lord! I suppose I shall have to go to the cottage and see what's there.'

'Why don't I come and help you?' said Dora.

★ ★ ★

The following morning was bright and clear with a hard frost. Edith and Dora took the pony and trap and packed a picnic basket as well as cleaning materials. Edith, glad of her woollen scarf and the tartan rug over their knees, drove Ned briskly along the lanes.

'You're very quiet, Edith,' said Dora. 'Is it because Pascal has gone away? I was surprised when he upped and left so suddenly.' She gave her friend a sharp glance. 'You didn't quarrel with him, did you?'

Edith shook head. 'But it would be good if Benedict thought I had,' she said. The urge to share the truth with Dora was too strong to be ignored. 'Confidentially, Pascal returned to France because his father's had a heart attack.'

'The poor thing!' Dora pursed her lips. 'But Pascal said he was going to Montmartre to study new styles in art. Why didn't he tell us the truth?'

'Benedict is so jealous of my friendship with him that he never stops spying on us, trying to find proof we're having an affair. It's become an unbearable strain.'

'But when Pascal returns, won't Benedict start spying on you all over again?'

Edith sighed. 'I can only hope he'll have gone away by then.'

147

'Or he'll realise it's untrue. It's wickedly unfair of Benedict to be jealous of you being friends with Pascal when he's brought his own mistress into the house.'

'He never could bear to be thwarted,' murmured Edith, guilty at deceiving her friend with a half-truth.

Before long, they turned through a gateway into a copse. The frosted trees shimmered in the pale sunlight and a narrow track through the brambles led to a clearing with a small stone cottage set at its centre. To one side was a well under a thatched roof and an open store stacked with firewood.

'How delightful!' said Edith. 'It's like Hansel and Gretel's cottage.'

Dora laughed. 'I must draw it for one of my fairy tales.'

They released Ned from the shafts of the trap and tied his reins to a tree.

Edith unlocked the low door of the cottage. Inside, was a living room with a beamed ceiling and an inglenook fireplace that took up much of one wall. A faded rag rug lay before the hearth, with well-worn leather armchairs to either side. Paintings hung on the walls and there was a bookcase with glazed doors. Despite the cottage's charm, it was bitterly cold and smelled damp.

Shivering, Dora rubbed her hands together. 'There's kindling and logs in the inglenook,' she said. 'I'll set a fire.'

A copper kettle hung from a hook and Edith went into the lean-to scullery to search for a bucket. A larder revealed a forgotten loaf of bread, now gnawed and green with mould. Mice had left their calling cards all over the slate shelves. Grimacing, she found a bucket under the sink and scooped up the mouldy bread.

Outside, behind the cottage was a privy and the remains of the kitchen bonfire, where Edith disposed of the bread. She cranked a worn wooden handle to draw water from the well, filled the horse trough for Ned and carried the brimming bucket back into the cottage.

Dora set the kettle to boil while Edith found the soap and scrubbing brush. They packed the books, several of them badly foxed by damp, into a box then lifted the framed watercolours from the walls.

'Look,' said Edith, 'there are two different styles; some are signed H. Tremayne and others J. Penrose. These must have been painted by Hester and Jago.' She wondered how often those star-crossed lovers had been able to meet secretly at Woodland Cottage.

'The paintings are surprisingly good,' said Dora.

Edith lifted up a view of gently undulating hills. 'This one is charming. Benedict once told me it was his aunt who encouraged him to paint when he was a boy.'

'Might I take it to hang in my bedroom?' asked Dora. 'It would be pretty on the wall above the spare bed for when Ursula comes to stay.'

'I'm pleased to find a home for it,' said Edith.

Upstairs, the bedroom was low-ceilinged with sprigged muslin curtains at the dormer window.

A brass bedstead covered by a faded patchwork quilt dominated the room, which was sparsely furnished with a wardrobe and a washstand.

'It's a pretty room,' Edith said, imagining for a moment all the lovers' trysts that had taken place there. 'But I imagine Hester and Jago's meetings would have held an undertone of sadness.'

'Forbidden love must always be painful, don't you think?' said Dora.

Edith turned away to hide her anguish at the thought of Pascal so far away. Her heart ached that a love that was so right and true could not be openly displayed. Perhaps Benedict's aunt and her lover had felt the same?

Inside the wardrobe, there was clean bed linen on the shelves with lavender bags tucked neatly between the sheets to keep them sweet. The hanging rail was empty but there was a heavy wooden box at the bottom of the cupboard. Edith lifted the lid, painted with a wreath of flowers, and saw some folded clothing and shawls. 'We'd better take this away, too,' she said.

They loaded the boxes and paintings into the trap and then scrubbed out the larder and swept the floors. When they'd finished, they toasted their stockinged feet by the fire and ate their picnic of sandwiches, Madeira cake and apples.

Afterwards, Dora doused the fire while Edith tidied away the remains of their lunch. 'We'd better hurry,' she said. 'It'll be dark before long.'

Later, as Ned trotted through the lanes, Edith wondered what Pascal was doing. His absence was like a sore tooth; she couldn't stop thinking

about it and the pain of it brought tears to her
eyes.

★ ★ ★

Standing in the draughty hall, Tamsyn listened to
the silence. Faintly, she could hear the sound of
the grandfather clock ticking on the landing
upstairs. It depressed her, ticking her life away
like that. She'd thought everything was going to
change for the better when Benedict told her he
wanted her to come and live with him but it
hadn't turned out like that. And now he'd gone
out somewhere, again, and refused to take her
with him.

Bored, she wandered into the kitchen. At least
it was warm there, unlike the rest of the draughty
old house. She sat on the table swinging her legs
and watching her aunt Nessa peeling a mound of
carrots and turnips.

'If you'm nothing better to do, you can lend a
hand,' said the cook.

'I'm not your scullery maid,' said Tamsyn.
''Sides, I'll be off to the Golden Lion soon.' At
first, she'd been surprised Benedict had expected
her to go on working but now she was glad of it.
She looked forward to her shifts in the bar these
days. They relieved her boredom and there was
always someone friendly to chat to, not like the
stuck-up lot at Spindrift.

'You'm want to watch yourself, my girl,' said
Nessa. 'Got ideas above your station, you have,
like your ma. And look where that got her!'

'Wasn't her fault she died!'

151

'She wouldn't have, if she hadn't been so free with herself after your pa passed over.' Nessa chopped the carrots fast and furious and threw them in the stockpot. She pointed her knife at Tamsyn. 'And when she got herself in the family way and it turned out her fancy man was already married, drinking all the gin in the world and throwing herself downstairs wasn't the answer, neither.'

'It was an accident!'

'Breaking her neck might have been an accident but the rest of it wasn't.' Nessa filled the pan with water and thumped it on the range where it hissed and spat. She rested her knuckles on her hips and gave her niece a hard stare. 'Gave my brother the runaround, did your ma. Can't say I was sorry when she passed. Saved the rest of our family a whole heap of shame and trouble.'

'If you hadn't all been so mean to her, she'd never have died!' Tamsyn sniffed. 'I was only fourteen and Lord knows what would have happened to me if old Curnow hadn't taken me on to work in the bar.'

'I offered you a home but you laughed in my face.'

'You didn't really want me.'

'I was afeared you'd go the same way.' The seething soup rose to the top of the pan and Nessa shoved it off the heat. 'Looks as if I were right, too. It's not decent you living here, with him.'

'My Benedict's a gentleman and he's the master of Spindrift House, so you want to be careful how you speak to me! I could have you out of here in two shakes of a lamb's tail.'

'Don't you threaten me, my girl! As for Benedict Fairchild being a gentleman, you've got that wrong. No gentleman would have brought his whore into the same house as his wife.'

Tamsyn gasped. 'I'm not . . .'

''Course you are. And there's not a soul in this house, including me, who doesn't despise you for it. I'll thank you not to tell any of them you're my niece. Wouldn't do me any good at all.'

'Anyway,' said Tamsyn, 'Benedict asked me to complain to you about the fried eggs at breakfast. They were hard. Please don't let it happen again.'

Nessa laughed. 'Sends you to do his dirty business, does he? Let me tell you, he's no right to complain because he isn't the one who pays my wages. Now why don't you get out of my kitchen and leave me to get on with the dinner?'

Tamsyn stared at her aunt's back as she stirred the soup. Slowly, she slid off the table and sauntered out of the room. She refused to let Aunt Nessa think she'd had the last word.

In the hall, Tamsyn paused and listened. That damned clock on the landing was still ticking her life away.

'What are you doing here?'

Tamsyn jumped when she saw Dora had come out of the drawing room. 'What's it to you?'

'You know you're not to go sneaking about,' said Dora. 'You must stay in your own rooms. If I catch you listening at doors again, you'll be sorry.'

'Oh, yes?' Tamsyn tossed her hair. 'What'll you do about it?'

Dora lifted her chin and stared back at her. 'Perhaps you'll find yourself locked in the privy until you know your place.'

Tamsyn pushed her aside. 'You don't frighten me.' She put her nose in the air and went into the sitting room. She slammed the door behind her and leaned against it, her heart racing while she listened to Dora's footsteps walking away. She'd imagined that once Edith had left, the others would come round. But Edith hadn't left. Benedict really hated her and had said it would be fun to teach her a lesson. Somehow, though, that snooty cow always seemed to have the last word. Even worse, she was a handsome woman and, sometimes, Tamsyn wondered if Benedict didn't still fancy her.

Slumping down onto the sofa, Tamsyn closed her eyes. She always seemed to be worn out these days. A few minutes' shut-eye was all she needed and then she must hurry or she'd be late for work. Her shawl lay on the arm of the sofa and she pulled it around her shoulders. Two minutes later, she was fast asleep.

14

Dora straightened the new watercolour on the wall above the spare bed and hummed to herself while she gave her room a final flick of the duster. She'd searched through the entire linen cupboard to find sheets that weren't too thin or darned and looked out one of the best towels to fold neatly onto the end of the eiderdown. Hands on her hips, she surveyed the room. Fresh soap on the washbasin, sprigs of yellow forsythia in a vase on the dressing table and the rag rug had been hung on the washing line and beaten. Everything looked nice and neat and she hoped Miss Hoffman would be comfortable. She nodded in satisfaction and closed the door behind her before going downstairs to the kitchen.

Passing the dining-room door, she heard the children's voices raised in noisy chatter while they had their tea. Pearl, as usual, was making her opinion known at the top of her voice and one of the puppies was barking. Hannah ought to know better than to let the dogs in the dining room.

She opened the kitchen door and hesitated when she saw Tamsyn sprawled in the rocking chair by the range, warming her feet on the fender with her skirt up to her knees. There was

155

a plate of cooked crab on her lap and she was sucking the meat out of one of the claws. She gave Dora a bold look, making no attempt to straighten her skirt.

Ignoring her, Dora said, 'Hello, Mrs Rowe.'

The cook sat at the kitchen table, jointing rabbits for the evening's stew. She looked up, wiping her hands on a cloth.

'Is there any last-minute shopping you need from the village for tonight's dinner?' asked Dora. 'I'll take the trap out shortly to collect my guest from the station.'

'I have everything, thank you, miss,' said Mrs Rowe. 'There's a nice bread and butter pudding in the larder just waiting to go in the oven. Extra currants, like you asked for.'

'I'm sure it will be lovely,' said Dora, hoping the dumplings for the stew wouldn't be as stodgy as last time.

Tamsyn tore a leg off the crab and noisily cracked it open.

Mrs Rowe glanced at her with pursed lips.

Dora went to make sure the sitting room was tidy. She straightened a pile of books and puffed up the cushions. Miss Hoffman would likely want some tea when she arrived. The train journey from London was always tiring, despite sitting down all day.

Outside in the hall, a door slammed and footsteps clattered across the floor, followed by a rhythmic knocking sound.

Curious, Dora went to investigate.

Will, Julian's son, stood with his forehead against the wall, kicking the skirting board.

'What are you doing, Will?' asked Dora. 'You'll scuff the paintwork.'

He stopped kicking. 'Don't care,' he muttered.

'Well, I do. Now tell me what's the matter.'

'Those awful little children . . . '

'What have they done?' Will's face was scarlet and Dora could see he was trying not to cry. He put her in mind of her younger brother Alfie and she knew Will wouldn't appreciate it if she hugged him. 'Tell me,' she coaxed, 'and perhaps I can help.'

Will shuffled his feet. 'I never wanted to come here but Grandmother said I must.'

'You're missing your grandma?'

He nodded, mouth twisted with the effort of holding back tears. 'And Father likes Lily more than me. He pretends to like me, but he's only being polite.'

'It's a big change for you, leaving your grandma, but I know for a fact your father loves you,' said Dora. Poor little blighter, he was homesick. 'You haven't lived together for such a long time it's bound to take a while for you to be easy with each other.'

'Lily's completely spoiled!' burst out Will. 'She hates me and Pearl gangs up with her to say horrible things. I don't have any friends at the new school and they tease me because I wear spectacles. And it's always so *noisy* at Spindrift; the children never stop shouting and I don't want to play their stupid games.'

'They can be very loud,' said Dora. 'I like a bit of peace and quiet myself sometimes. Don't you have a bedroom of your own in your new home?'

Will shrugged. 'Father doesn't like me being in there on my own all day. And Lily taps on the wall when I'm in bed.'

'She's probably trying to be friendly.'

He gave her a look of such scorn that Dora changed tack. 'How about if I found you a corner where you could go and read without being disturbed if the others get too much for you?'

He looked up at her. 'I'd like that.'

'You're a couple of years older than Jasper but he's a quiet boy, too. He's grown up for his years and you could do worse than make friends with him. He's shy, though, and probably looks up to you because you're older so you'd have to make the first move.'

Will nodded and the scarlet flush on his cheeks began to recede.

'I have to collect a friend from the station now,' said Dora. 'Perhaps you'd like to come with me? We'll take the trap and I'll teach you how to drive it.'

'Would you?' His face lit up.

'Go and put on your coat and muffler and I'll see you in the stables in ten minutes. Oh, and tell your father where you're going.'

'I will.' He hurried away.

Dora sighed. She'd been looking forward to seeing Miss Hoffman again and didn't really want that awkward child to accompany her. But then she remembered his woebegone face and chided herself for being selfish.

A short while later they were bowling along in the trap. Dora was wearing her second-best hat and Will, a fiercely determined expression on his face, was holding Ned's reins.

'You're doing very well,' she said and was rewarded with a smile. The poor boy simply needed a bit more time to settle in. She'd have a quiet word with Julian and Clarissa.

Dora took over the reins again as they approached the station at Port Isaac Road. They drew up outside and she tied the trap to the metal railings. There was an odd fluttery feeling of excitement in her chest. She and Miss Hoffman had exchanged several letters over the past couple of months and already she felt as if they were friends, but what if things felt different when they met for the second time?

A plume of steam appeared, approaching along the railway line.

'Will you look after Ned and the trap while I go and meet my friend?' she asked. Will nodded and Dora hurried off.

Half a dozen people were waiting on the platform, looking up the railway line as the train clanked into view with a great hissing of brakes.

Dora peered through the billowing steam and saw two men deep in conversation descend from the train, followed by a woman with a small boy. A few other passengers alighted, slamming the train doors behind them but none of them were Miss Hoffman. The guard let out a piercing whistle and Dora's stomach turned over in disappointment. Had her friend missed the train or simply decided not to come?

And then she glimpsed her, a lean figure in a

159

sensible navy coat, striding energetically down the platform. Dora waved, her heart lifting.

'My dear Miss Cox!' Miss Hoffman dropped her portmanteau and shook Dora's hand, her aquamarine eyes sparkling. 'I feared the train would leave with me still on board. A gallant old gentleman offered to lift my bag down from the luggage rack but it was too heavy and he struggled with it.'

'I'm so glad you're here,' said Dora. 'I wondered if you'd changed your mind.'

'How could I? I have been looking forward to this visit for weeks.'

Dora picked up Miss Hoffman's portmanteau and they chatted about the train journey while they walked out of the station.

Will was standing beside Ned, fondling the pony's ears when they arrived at the trap.

'And who do we have here?' asked Miss Hoffman.

'This is Will Clemens,' said Dora. 'He's learning to drive the trap and making a pretty good fist of it, too.' She smiled at him. 'Before long we'll be able to send him on all the Spindrift errands.'

Rather pink about the ears, Will shook hands with Miss Hoffman. 'Shall I put the bag in the trap, Aunt Dora?'

'Thank you, Will.' Dora was delighted the boy seemed to have lost his sulkiness and had, finally, addressed her by name. 'We'd better hurry back,' she said, 'it's growing dark.'

It was dusk when they arrived at Spindrift House. Will drove into the courtyard, with a little guidance from Dora, and came to a stop outside Ned's stable.

Julian came out of his studio and hurried towards them. 'Dora, I'll see to Ned while you take our guest inside.' He greeted Miss Hoffman and clapped his hand on Will's shoulder. 'It's good to see you're making yourself useful, son.'

Dora was pleased to see the boy's smile. 'Shall we go inside, Miss Hoffman?'

'What a shame it's too dark now to see the garden,' she said.

'We shall see it at first light,' said Dora, 'and you shall spend as much time looking at it as you wish.' She bit her lip. 'I do hope it won't disappoint.'

'Your description leads me to believe it will be exactly what I am looking for,' said Miss Hoffman. 'And if it is not,' she shrugged, 'I shall have had a few pleasurable days with my new friend.'

Dora smiled and they went into the house and drank tea by the drawing-room fire.

'Everyone is working now,' said Dora, 'but you'll meet them at supper tonight.'

'Will you tell me a little about each person?' asked Miss Hoffman. 'It will be hard to remember their names if I am to meet so many all at once.'

Dora gave her a potted history of each member of the community, including brief details of how Benedict had brought Tamsyn into the house.

Miss Hoffman pressed her fingers to her mouth. 'That is unpardonable. And I suppose

161

there is nothing Mrs Fairchild can do to make either of them go away?'

Dora shook her head. 'I don't care to gossip but I thought I ought to warn you of the situation here in case you meet Benedict.' She changed the subject. 'I'll show you our room now, Miss Hoffman, and you can unpack before supper.'

'I wish you would call me Ursula,' she said. 'I'm quite sure we're set to become fast friends, aren't you?'

'I am!' Dora beamed. 'It's very strange but I've felt that since we first met.'

★ ★ ★

Later that evening, the community congregated in the dining room. Dora watched her friends closely as they were introduced to Ursula and was relieved to see that they all seemed to like her.

'We're very informal here,' said Clarissa, 'and all use first names.'

'I am so interested to hear about your community,' said Ursula. 'Not everyone wants to live alone and I'm curious to hear if this situation works well for you.'

'We're like a family,' said Edith, 'but a family formed through choice rather than fate.' She gave a wry smile. 'Like any family, there are times when there are petty frustrations and quarrels but we're held together by respect and a genuine affection for each other.'

'Do you have a family, Ursula?' asked Augustus.

'Yes, indeed, though I haven't lived at home for a long while. My father came to England from Germany some forty years ago to teach history. Soon afterwards he met and married my English mother.'

'And Dora told us that you plan to write an illustrated book about growing vegetables,' said Gilbert.

Ursula nodded. 'For several years I lived at Stansfield Hall in Surrey. Lady Violet Stansfield was an old school pal of mine and when she married, the garden at the Hall was very neglected. Together, we redesigned it and worked with her gardeners to lay it out to the new plan. I oversaw the planting. Once it was finished, Violet invited me to stay while I wrote *A Year in an English Garden.*'

'And now you're looking for a walled garden for your new project?' said Gilbert.

'I intend to design a productive and ornamental vegetable garden known as a *potager*. Then I shall write a book following the seasons of the gardening year.'

'We already grow most of our own vegetables,' said Edith, 'but the idea of a decorative vegetable plot is appealing.' She smiled. 'After all, we are artists.'

'As William Morris said, we should have nothing in our houses that we do not know to be useful or believe to be beautiful,' said Ursula. 'That must apply to gardens, too, don't you think?'

'Absolutely,' said Edith.

Ursula studied the murals on the dining-room

163

walls. 'These are very eye-catching. Who was the artist?'

Wilfred held up his hand. 'I confess it was I.'

'Bravo,' said Ursula. 'Are murals your usual line of work?'

'I illustrate periodicals but, now and again, I have a commission to decorate a house. I'll be invited to stay for a while and embellish my host's favourite rooms.'

'Do your clients usually ask for scenes such as these?' Ursula indicated the voluptuous, semi-naked ladies reclining upon silken cushions with attendant winged cherubs.

'The murals selected for reception rooms are generally more restrained. Vistas of Italian gardens, Greek temples or oriental landscapes, you know the kind of thing. The master bedroom, however, is often, shall we say, more *flamboyant*.' His eyes gleamed with amusement. 'Occasionally, I've been asked to paint naked ladies surrounding a mirrored ceiling.'

Ursula laughed and Dora listened to her bantering with Wilfred. It made her happy to see them becoming friends.

After a convivial evening, Dora and Ursula retired upstairs.

'I hope you don't mind sharing with me,' said Dora. 'I wondered if I should put you in Pascal's room since he's in France at the moment but it's full of his things and . . .'

'I shall like to share with you,' said Ursula.

Dora hummed to herself while she folded her clothes and cleaned her teeth.

'We'd better get to sleep. It will be an early

start tomorrow,' said Ursula.

'Shall I put out the light?'

'Please do.'

Dora lay quietly, her thoughts drifting and full of plans for Ursula's visit. After they'd looked at the walled garden, she'd show her some of the botanical illustrations in her portfolio. Perhaps they'd go down to the cove and walk beside the sea. She yawned.

'Are you still awake?' whispered Ursula.

'I am.'

'Good night, my dear.'

'See you in the morning,' murmured Dora. She lay smiling into the dark, listening to Ursula's breathing slow as she fell asleep.

15

Pearl tiptoed across the studio to watch Edith painting. She often played that game, to see how close she could get before her mother noticed her. The tip of Mama's tongue was between her lips as she concentrated, using her finest brush to add a dab of white to the crest of a wave. Pearl breathed in the comforting scent of linseed oil. Her mother's clothes always smelled of it, though her skin was perfumed with roses or violets.

Edith narrowed her eyes, took a sudden step back to study her work and trod on Pearl's toe. She whirled around, alarm making her eyes wide. Fanning her fingers against her chest, she said, 'Pearl! Don't creep up on me like that. I thought it was your father.'

'I wanted to see your painting of the cove. Is that man on the beach Uncle Pascal, looking at the sea?'

Edith nodded, her face sad.

'Why did he go away? Is it because he doesn't like Papa?'

'He went to visit his family and he wants to work in Paris for a while.'

'But he will come back?'

Rubbing her eyes as if she was tired, Mama said, 'Perhaps.'

'Uncle Pascal always made time to talk to me when you were too busy,' said Pearl.

Edith blew her nose and didn't answer straight away. 'Sweetheart, I need to work now. Would you go and play with the other children for a while? Or find Hannah.'

'Lily's gone into Wadebridge with Auntie Clarissa and Hannah's dusting and doing the fires.'

'Why don't you see how Auntie Dora and her friend are getting on in the garden?'

Pearl stuck out her bottom lip. 'You never have time to play with me, do you?'

'You know I have to work, Pearl, otherwise there'll be no food for the table and no coal for the fires.'

'Papa told me to run along, too. He was smoking in the sitting room but he was having a rest and told me to leave him alone.' She huffed out her breath. 'Nobody wants me!'

'That's not true, sweetheart.'

Pearl ran out of the studio and didn't turn back when she heard her mother calling after her. Perhaps that would make her take more notice next time.

The twins were hunkered down on the floor amongst their wooden blocks, building a maze. Nell glanced up. 'We're going to let Lucien's beetles play in here.'

'Beetles don't play, silly!' scoffed Pearl. 'And they're sure to escape out of the gaps and run off all over the place.'

'We're too busy with our work to talk,' said Lucien, 'but you can help if you like.'

Pearl didn't fancy playing with the twins; they always made her feel like an outsider. Most of the time they didn't even need to speak to each other to know what they were going to do next. She lifted her head and sniffed. Mrs Rowe must be baking. The twins didn't look up as she wandered away along the passage to the kitchen.

Mrs Rowe was drinking tea at the table with Tamsyn. It looked as if they'd been having an argument because Tamsyn was crying and Mrs Rowe had on her cross face. There were three loaves of bread and a rack of cooling biscuits on the table. The smell was irresistible.

'What are you after, Miss Pearl?' asked Mrs Rowe. 'As if I didn't know.'

'Please may I have one?' Pearl couldn't take her eyes off the biscuits. They were studded with currants and sparkling with sugar.

'Just one or you'll spoil your lunch. Then run along and let me have my sit-down in peace.' Mrs Rowe sighed. 'Wouldn't that be nice?' she muttered.

Pearl took a biscuit and ate it in silence, savouring the delicious sweetness of it. Tamsyn sat on the opposite side of the table with her head in her hands, sniffing. Her black hair was knotted and unbrushed, as if she'd come down to the kitchen straight out of bed. Mrs Rowe's lips were in a thin line and she had red spots of colour in her cheeks.

A vast stockpot was bubbling away on the range and Pearl thought she ought to break the angry silence. 'What are you cooking, Mrs Rowe?'

'I'm boiling an ox tongue for your supper.' She sighed. 'I suppose I'd better get on and skim the

168

scum off the cooking liquor.'

Tamsyn groaned and ran from the kitchen.

Mrs Rowe wiped her face with the palm of her hand. 'Get along with you now, Miss Pearl. I'm busy.'

Obediently, she slid off her chair. She waited until Mrs Rowe had her back turned and was skimming disgusting, smelly froth off the pan and then snatched up another biscuit and slid it into her pinafore pocket. 'Thank you for the biscuit,' she called, hurrying out of the kitchen.

In the back lobby, Pearl changed her shoes and put on her coat. It was cold outside and she hadn't gone more than a few steps when she saw Tamsyn leaning over with her hands on her knees, staring at the ground.

'What you looking at?' she said, turning her face towards Pearl. She had a long string of dribble hanging from her mouth.

'You've been ill again.'

'Get away from me!' Tamsyn retched and vomit spattered on the ground.

Pearl wrinkled her nose. She would have fetched Tamsyn a glass of water but she wouldn't bother now she'd been so rude. She trotted through the courtyard and towards the kitchen garden. The gate in the wall was open and she went inside. Auntie Dora and Miss Hoffman were over by the compost heap, turning it with a fork and examining it as if it was actually interesting.

Pearl skipped along the gravel path towards them. 'I saw a horrible thing,' she said, important with news.

'And what was that, child?' said Miss Hoffman.

'Tamsyn was being sick outside the back door.'

'How very unpleasant,' said Dora. 'Perhaps she ate something that had gone off.'

'*And* she was sick the other morning,' said Pearl. 'I was waiting outside the lavvy and she was in there for ages.'

Dora dropped the garden fork. 'Are you sure?'

'Of course I am.'

'Oh, Lord,' murmured Dora. 'I do believe that's upset the apple cart!'

Miss Hoffman pulled a face and nodded her head towards the child.

'Pearl,' said Dora, 'Tom has come to play with Jasper. They've gone down to the cove if you want to go and find them?'

'I'd rather stay with you.'

'All right, dear, but we're talking about the design of the vegetable garden and you might not find it very interesting.'

Pearl folded her arms and shrugged.

'Tell me more about how you'd arrange the vegetable beds, Ursula,' said Dora.

'I imagine a central feature, a wooden obelisk perhaps, with a climbing rose or runner beans.' She pointed to the centre of the kitchen garden where presently a few Brussel sprouts clung to some withered stalks. 'And then a network of paths making a geometric pattern for the beds. We'll have a box hedge in a circle around the obelisk. Traditionally, all the beds would be edged with box or lavender but, in the short term, we may have to manage with chives or other herbs.'

Pearl sighed. Their conversation was boring. She walked away, scuffing up dead leaves on the path as she went. Glancing over her shoulder, she saw that Dora and Ursula hadn't noticed she'd gone. She wandered through the garden and onto the headland. A cold wind tugged her hair, reminding her of last summer when her mother had taken her there with the other children to fly their kites. They'd had such fun although, even then, Mama had gone to sit by the standing stone to make sketches of them all. That was also the special day when her papa came home, bringing Star and Blue as a present.

Pearl walked to the cliff edge and looked down to the cove. The wind made her eyes water and she couldn't see Jasper and Tom. Disappointed, she was about to turn away when she saw Blue and Star having a tug of war with a clump of seaweed down by the rocks. Then the boys came out of the cave.

Clinging to the frayed rope handrail, Pearl ran down the cliff steps and across the sand. The boys waved their arms as she ran towards them.

'What are you doing?' she asked, slightly out of breath.

'We've been in the smugglers' cave,' said Jasper, 'looking for a tunnel.'

Tom's nose was cherry red with cold. 'Pa says smugglers built hundreds of tunnels so they could bring in the brandy from the ships. They hid the barrels in caves until the excise men had gone.'

'They couldn't have dug through all that rock, silly!' said Pearl. 'It's far too hard.'

171

'Yes, they did!' said Tom indignantly. 'Cornish-men are miners and Pa says there's a tunnel from the cellar of the Golden Lion out to the sea.'

'Did you find it?' asked Pearl.

'It's too dark to see properly without a lantern,' said Jasper, 'but there's a crack in the rock at the back that might be one.'

'Can I see?' Pearl followed the boys inside the cave. It grew narrower towards the back and the shadows made it feel as if it was pressing down on her. It was cold and smelled of fish and dead things. She rested her hand on a wide ledge and snatched it back when she touched something wet and slimy.

Outside, the puppies began to bark. Jasper, followed by Tom, hurried to see what was happening.

Pearl shivered when they momentarily blocked out the light as they ran through the mouth of the cave. She followed slowly, taking care not to step in the puddles left by high tide.

On the beach, Blue and Star were bounding through the surf, barking excitedly as they played with a black Labrador. Two boys and a girl were talking to Jasper and Tom by the water's edge, while throwing a rubber ball for the dogs.

It wasn't until Pearl drew closer that she recognised the other children as Noel, Timmy and Adela Penrose. Cliff House had private steps down to the cove but the Penroses usually kept their distance from the Spindrift community.

The boys ran off to climb over the rocks.

Pearl stood a few feet away from Adela. In the

172

past, the other girl hadn't always been kind to her at school, saying nasty things because Pearl's father didn't live with her.

Adela threw the ball again and laughed when Star fetched it back with the other two dogs prancing around them. 'Aren't they just the sweetest little puppies?' she said. 'I've never seen a dog with one blue eye before. How old are they?'

Pearl was surprised she seemed so friendly. 'Six months,' she said. 'The one with the blue eye is called Blue and the other is Star. You see the white star on his head?'

'My dog's called Bertie,' said Adela.

'He's very handsome,' said Pearl, thinking that if she sucked up to Adela perhaps she wouldn't be so unkind at school. 'My papa gave me Blue and Star as a present.'

Adela frowned. 'That was kind of him.' She threw the ball back into the waves and the dogs raced after it. 'Mother always told me your father was a bad man and I wasn't to talk to anyone from Spindrift House.'

'Well, that wasn't very nice, was it?' Pearl kicked at a piece of seaweed with the toe of her boot. 'Mama has always told us to keep away from your family, too. Our parents had an argument before I was born and now they never speak. I don't know why.'

'Mother says your father stole Spindrift House from my father,' says Adela.

'My papa wouldn't steal a house!'

Adela looked uncertain. 'We never lived in your house so I don't really understand. My parents don't like it if I ask questions.'

'Grown-ups don't know everything, do they?' said Pearl scornfully. 'And they never listen to their children and are always too busy to talk to you.'

'My father ignores me,' said Adela. 'I think he only likes boys.'

'That's so unfair!'

'And my brothers don't always want me tagging along behind them. I often wish I had a sister to play with.'

'I have a sister but Nell hardly ever plays with me,' said Pearl. 'She only wants to be with her twin. Lily is more like a sister to me.' She glanced at Adela. 'We could meet here in the cove sometimes, if you want? The dogs need exercise every day. We could make an obstacle course for them and train them to run races.'

Adela nodded. 'We don't have to tell our parents *everything*, do we?'

'It will be our secret.' Pearl looked over at the rocks where the four boys were in a huddle, head to head. 'Why *shouldn't* we all be friends, if we want to?'

Then the dogs came running out of the sea and shook themselves dry, splattering them with seawater and sand.

Pearl and Adela shrieked and ran away from the dogs, who thought it was a game and chased them until they collapsed in a heap on the sand, laughing themselves into hiccoughs.

16

When the evening's allocation of coal had collapsed into ashes, Edith said good night to the others. On her way up to bed, she peeped into the girls' bedroom. Lamplight from the corridor spilled across the empty bed where Lily used to sleep. It felt strange without her, now that she'd gone to live in the coach house with Clarissa and Julian. Nell slept in a tight ball like a dormouse while Pearl stretched out like a starfish, her dark ringlets spread over the pillow. Edith sighed. Her eldest daughter was going to break hearts when she was older and her beauty and headstrong character were bound to cause tussles between them. She kissed the girls' foreheads and straightened their eiderdowns against the chill of the bedroom air.

Next door in the boys' room, Jasper was asleep under the covers and Lucien had both puppies curled up on the end of his bed. Edith had capitulated to his tearful pleas and allowed the pups to sleep in a basket in the corner of the room but, frequently, she'd find them all together. She'd given up protesting and accepted that Star and Blue were members of the family now.

A small sob came from under Jasper's eiderdown and Edith crept into the room and pulled back his covers enough to see his face. 'I didn't know you were awake! What is it, sweetheart?' she asked.

Jasper's arms crept around her neck. 'When is Uncle Pascal coming home? I miss him.'

Edith, her heart aching, lay down on the narrow bed beside him. 'He'll write soon, I'm sure.'

'But *when*? I want him to help me with my painting again. It was Papa who made him go away, wasn't it?'

Edith hesitated. She didn't want to lie to Jasper and compromised on a half-truth. 'Uncle Pascal wants to stay with his family for a while. On his way home to us, he's going to visit the Paris galleries to see what is fashionable in the art world. He'll tell you about it when he returns. And wouldn't it be marvellous if he could place some of his canvases in the Paris galleries?'

Jasper buried his face in the curve of Edith's neck. 'But I still hate Papa and that horrible Tamsyn. Papa's always saying rude things about Uncle Pascal.'

'You mustn't take any notice. Your father is a little jealous of your friendship with Uncle Pascal, that's all.' Edith smoothed the dark hair off his forehead. 'Go to sleep now and I'll stay beside you for a while.'

She heard the murmur of Dora and Ursula's voices as they passed along the corridor on their way to bed and, soon afterwards, the heavier tread of Wilfred and Augustus's footsteps.

Gradually, Jasper's breath became deep and

even and Edith kissed him softly and went to her own room. She undressed and sat on the end of the bed with her head in her hands. Edith missed Pascal's quiet presence as desperately as Jasper did but there was nothing to be done about it.

It was no good, she couldn't sleep. She'd fetch her book from the drawing room and make herself a hot drink.

She was in the kitchen, sipping her cocoa, when she heard the front door slam and then the sound of Benedict and Tamsyn's voices. Tamsyn must have been working at the Golden Lion and Benedict frequently spent his evenings there before walking her back to Spindrift House.

Edith finished her cocoa and waited for them to go upstairs but they were still talking. She lurked in the kitchen passage but it seemed they'd gone into their sitting room. Creeping into the hall, she noticed the door was ajar. She'd decided to tiptoe past but then heard raised voices.

'It's not *my* fault!' wailed Tamsyn.

'God damn you, woman, that's the last bloody thing we need!' said Benedict.

Edith took a step back. She didn't want them to find her apparently eavesdropping.

'It's your baby, too, Benedict!'

'I should bloody well hope it is.'

Edith cupped her hand over her mouth. Frozen to the spot, a shock wave rippled through her. Not another illegitimate baby!

'Don't you *dare* throw me out!' said Tamsyn, breaking into noisy sobs. 'I've nowhere to go and I'd be shamed. You oughta marry me now.'

'No chance,' said Benedict. 'You know I can't — and I never did promise you marriage.'

'You *promised* me you'd be careful.' Her voice rose shrilly. 'You said you knew how to stop me having a baby.'

'For Christ's sake, don't cry, Tamsyn. I can't stand it and your eyes will swell up and make you ugly. Come here!'

There was silence for a long while except for muffled sobs.

Edith was plucking up courage to slip past the door when Benedict chuckled.

'On the positive side,' he said, 'this will annoy the hell out of Edith. She's already looking more sour-faced every day since her Frenchman upped and left. You'll have to go on working, though. There'll be another mouth to feed.'

Tamsyn sniffed loudly. 'You're not going to throw me out then?'

There was a pause before Benedict said, 'Not if you behave yourself.'

Tamsyn gave a soft laugh. 'You said you liked it when I was wanton. And another thing,' she said, 'we don't have to be careful no more.'

'How right you are,' murmured Benedict. 'I'm going to take you to bed, you little strumpet.'

Edith backed away as fast as she could, just in time to retreat into the drawing room. She peeped from behind the door and saw them going up the stairs. Benedict, his arm around a giggling Tamsyn, was squeezing her buttock.

They stopped to kiss on the turn of the stairs and Tamsyn laughed throatily. 'Come to bed and show me how much you love me then.'

Shivering in the cold, Edith waited until she heard their bedroom door close before going into the hall. She turned down the oil lamp until it flickered and went out.

★ ★ ★

The following morning, Edith overslept and went downstairs late. Clarissa and Dora were lingering over their breakfast.

'Where's Ursula?' asked Edith.

'Outside talking to Gilbert,' said Dora. 'She says the walled garden is perfect for her needs. I waited to catch you so I could ask if she may stay with us for the next year or two? She'll pay her way, of course.'

'Ursula would be an excellent addition to our community,' said Edith. 'As long as the others are happy, she can move in as soon as she likes.'

Dora beamed. 'We'll ask them at suppertime, then.'

Clarissa poured Edith a cup of tea. 'I should go to work. Augustus will be wondering where I am.'

'Before you go,' said Edith, 'there's something I must tell you.' She could hardly bear to say the words. 'I overheard Tamsyn telling Benedict she's pregnant.'

Clarissa glanced at Dora.

'Dearie me!' said Dora. 'I suspected as much and mentioned it to Clarissa only moments ago. Pearl saw Tamsyn being sick yesterday and said she'd been ill the other morning, too. I couldn't help wondering but didn't want to worry you about it, if it wasn't true.'

'I suppose it was inevitable,' said Clarissa, 'but it's a ghastly situation, especially for you, Edith.'

'It's hateful. I don't love Benedict and haven't done for years,' she said, 'but when I heard Tamsyn say she was pregnant, it was like a slap in the face.' The news, after hearing that Delphine's daughter was also one of his bastards, was doubly shocking. 'And then there are the children to consider. It's dreadful enough that their father's mistress lives here, without her producing an illegitimate half-sibling.' She covered her face momentarily. 'It's bound to reflect badly on them at school. And what will they say about us in the village?'

'No doubt Jenifry Penrose will be delighted to point out to everyone who will listen that we're all depraved for allowing such a thing to happen,' said Clarissa.

'Benedict can't be bothered with children,' said Dora. 'Perhaps this baby is the kick up the backside he needs to get rid of Tamsyn?'

'I'm not so sure,' said Edith. 'I overheard him say that the best thing about it was that it would annoy the hell out of me. And then he took her off to bed.'

'What a beast!' Dora thumped her cup down, slopping tea on the cloth. 'And I'm sorry for the poor baby. Imagine having such useless parents as Tamsyn and Benedict!'

'You're more charitable than I,' said Clarissa. 'I hope Tamsyn runs away and has her baby elsewhere. Perhaps Benedict will return to London then.' She drained her cup. 'Tamsyn's rather stolen my thunder,' she said. 'There's something I have to tell you.'

Dora gripped her wrist. 'Don't tell me *you* have some happy news?'

Clarissa nodded, her eyes shining.

Edith and Dora both leaped up from the table to hug her.

'How marvellous!' said Dora.

'Absolutely wonderful!' said Edith.

'Julian is beyond thrilled but we haven't told Lily and Will yet,' said Clarissa. A worried frown creased her forehead. 'I hope beyond anything that the baby will unite us into a proper family. I confess, I hadn't imagined it would be so difficult. Will isn't happy and turns his back on me whenever I try to make him feel welcome.'

'He misses his grandma,' said Dora, 'but he'll settle down eventually.'

'I hope so,' said Clarissa. She gave a wan smile. 'If we go on at this rate, soon there'll be more children in the Spindrift community than adults!'

Edith laughed dutifully at Clarissa's little joke. Of course, it was wonderful news about her baby but all she could think of was that it would make Pascal yearn even more for a child of his own.

★　★　★

Later that afternoon, Edith turned away from her easel with a sigh. She found it impossible to concentrate for worrying if the children would be shunned at school when the news of Tamsyn's baby was common knowledge in the village. She

181

covered her palette to stop the paint drying out and went downstairs.

Stopping only to put on her coat, she hurried into the garden and out onto the headland. The Atlantic was steel grey, topped with white-crested waves that raced each other into the cove. The low thunder of the sea called to her and she climbed down the cliff steps.

Head down into the cold wind, she walked along the waterline, picking her way around clumps of bladderwrack and driftwood. Lost in thought, she barely noticed the waves crashing onto the sand and flecking her clothing with spume. She didn't look up until she reached the end of the cove and came to an abrupt halt at the sight of a figure sitting on the rocks. Backing away, she walked in the opposite direction. The very last person she wanted to meet was Benedict.

She hadn't gone far when she heard him calling to her.

'Edith, wait!' His footsteps crunched across the wet sand behind her.

Unable to avoid the inevitable, she stopped.

'Edith, I need to speak to you.'

Turning to face him, she folded her arms and waited.

'There's something I must tell you.' He raked his hair with his fingers and licked his lips.

'Well?' she said.

'It's a bit awkward.' His eyes were puffy, as if he hadn't slept well.

Edith sighed. 'If you're trying to tell me Tamsyn's expecting, I already know. I was in the

182

hall when she told you.'

His gaze slid away from her. 'I didn't plan it, Edith.'

'Nevertheless, your actions, yet again, were entirely without regard for the almost inevitable result.'

'It was a mistake! I don't love Tamsyn and I wish now that she'd never come here.' He looked out to sea and sighed heavily. 'When I returned to Spindrift, I really wanted to make a go of our marriage again. It hurt me that you wouldn't even try.'

'I can't imagine why you ever imagined I might subject myself to such torture again.'

'You're so sharp with me! Now your Frenchman's left, if I send Tamsyn away, will you let me be a good husband to you and a father to our children?'

Anger boiled up inside her. 'You will never be a good husband. If you cared for me even a tiny bit, you would not have brought your mistress into Spindrift House, expressly to humiliate me. And as for being a good father — that's laughable. You have *no* regard at all for the deleterious effect of Tamsyn's presence upon our children. You've already brought shame upon the Spindrift community that can only worsen once her condition becomes apparent.'

He snatched hold of her sleeve, a belligerent glint in his eye. 'You're such a hypocrite! What about *your* affair with Pascal?'

Unable to meet his eyes while she lied to him, Edith pulled herself free and set off along the beach again. 'What affair?' she said. 'I only said that to make you leave me alone. You can spy on us as much as you like but you'll never find proof of something that doesn't exist.'

17

July 1903

Pascal had been away for six months and Edith walked regularly into the village to collect his letters from the post office. She forced herself to wait to read the latest one until she arrived back at Spindrift, where she hurried through the garden gate and into the gazebo.

Mon amour,
Your letter is folded inside my pocket,
close to my heart. I have saved them all
and re-read them when the pain of our
separation grows too strong.
Papa is growing better at last and I
spend my days reading to him or painting
while he rests. I long to return to you but
must remain a while longer because now
Édouard is failing. Maman assists Delphine
in the sickroom so I mind Gabrielle after
school. I try not to let the anger and disap-
pointment I feel at my sister's deceit
influence my relations with her daughter.
As for your news, I am happy for dear
Dora that her friendship with Ursula
brings her such pleasure and I look for-
ward to seeing the vegetable garden
transformed into a place of fruitful beauty.
Clarissa must be nearing her time now and

I hope the summer heat is not too troubling for her. Julian will be anticipating his new child with great joy but I wonder if we can believe Benedict is as joyful about the impending birth of Tamsyn's baby? It is no surprise he finds her less attractive as she grows closer to her confinement but it was unkind of him to tell her so. It pains me to remember his lack of care and concern for you before the birth of your babies and I fear this most precious gift of fatherhood is wasted on him.

I cannot believe Benedict is all at once a reformed father and agree with you it is a matter of concern that he is making an effort to befriend your children. Pearl especially craves to be noticed by him. I fear she will be wretched if he ceases his attentions when he finds something else to catch his interest.

I was enraged to read in your letter that Benedict forced Jasper to go out with him in a small boat in rough seas. Jasper is not a boy who needs 'toughening up'. He is strong in his own way and it does him no discredit that he resisted his father's demands with such force. It is very wrong of me but I do wish I had seen Benedict's black eye! I thank God the fishermen were able to bring them both safely back to shore after the boat sank and, uncharitably, I hope Benedict suffered a bad cold after his unexpected swim. I miss the children a great deal.

Will you pass a message to Jasper for me? Tell him I hope he still visits our special painting place in Port Gaverne and that he will have some good work to show me when I return.

I am enjoying the heat of the Provençal sun in my bones again. My father demands to know when I shall find myself a bride and talks about a grandson to continue the Joubert name. I smile but, in my head, I am shouting that I have met the only woman I will ever love. I do not have enough words to tell you how much I miss you all day, every day. It is deeply painful to have to keep our love secret from my cherished parents.

I carry the ache of missing you like a stone in my chest and merely exist until I may hold you in my arms and begin to live again.

Forever yours,
Pascal

Edith held the letter to her heart. Their time apart had stretched like an eternity and now it seemed Édouard was failing and Pascal must stay even longer with his family. But she and the children needed him, too.

Surrounded by the perfume of the red roses that climbed over the gazebo, she let her gaze rest on the shining sea in the distance. The sound of the waves whispered on the onshore breeze, which brought the salty tang of the Atlantic with it. Pascal had sat beside her in the gazebo many times over the years, while they discussed their day and made plans for their future. They'd often talked about a time when her children would be grown and no longer need her. Perhaps then, if Benedict still remained at Spindrift House, they might journey around France and even go on to Spain or Italy. They would fill their sketchbooks as they travelled and then rent a studio where they would paint the wonders they'd seen.

Melancholy wrapped itself around Edith like a shroud. Such a time was far in the future since the twins were only eight years old. She slipped Pascal's letter into her pocket and felt the other one that the postman had brought. She opened it and saw it was from the Reverend Algernon Musgrave, the tenant of Woodland Cottage. He'd finished writing his epic poem and would not be renewing his tenancy at the end of the term. So her work would be interrupted again while she sought a replacement tenant. Meanwhile, she must shake off her sombre mood and find Jasper to give him Pascal's message. Sighing, she left the gazebo.

On the other side of the garden, Benedict was lying on a rug with the twins and the dogs. As Edith approached them, she saw he was blowing smoke rings into the air while the twins snorted with laughter. He passed Lucien his cigarette and the boy put it to his mouth, attempting to copy his father. Then he passed it to Nell, who drew on it until she coughed.

'Benedict!' yelled Edith. 'What are you *doing*?' She ran to Nell and snatched the cigarette away, grinding it into the grass. The sickly odour of Benedict's favourite Moroccan tobacco curled around them in a drift.

Benedict sat up, his shirt buttons undone and his expression indignant. 'For God's sake, Edith! I'm simply passing a few peaceful moments with my youngest children. Or I was until you came along and spoiled it.'

Lucien looked up at her with unfocused eyes. 'Go away, Mama. Papa is teaching us to blow smoke rings. It's a talent that will be useful to us in later life. Isn't that right, Papa?'

'Exactly, my boy.' Benedict pinched Lucien's cheek.

'It's made me feel sick,' wailed Nell.

'How *could* you, Benedict?' said Edith. 'Twins, you're far too young to smoke, especially those cigarettes. Please go and play somewhere else. And if I catch you smoking again you will be punished.'

'But, Mama . . . '

'Is that clear?'

The twins stood up, muttering under their breath.

'Go!' said Edith.

Nell took hold of Lucien's hand and they walked away with wavering steps, followed by the dogs.

Benedict took another cigarette out of his silver case and regarded her through heavy-lidded eyes as he lit it. 'You're such a spoilsport, Edith. The children never have any fun with you.'

'If that's the case,' she said tartly, 'it's because

I'm working hard to feed and clothe them. Which is more than I can say for you. Don't you dare encourage them to smoke again!'

Benedict sighed. 'You need to loosen your stays, Edith, or you'll make the children as narrow-minded as yourself. Like Jasper. Whatever is the matter with that boy? He looks as if he's been sucking lemons every time I speak to him. No manners, either. I asked him to sit with us and he didn't even answer.'

'Where did he go?' asked Edith, refraining from entering into any more arguments.

'Over there somewhere.' He waved towards the hydrangeas at the front of the shrubbery.

Still seething, Edith crossed the lawn to the shrubbery. Children's voices floated out from the bushes. 'Jasper,' she called.

The children's voices fell silent and the bushes rustled until he emerged.

'Whatever are you doing in there?' asked Edith.

'Making a camp.'

Edith removed a leaf from his hair. 'Uncle Pascal has sent you a message.'

Jasper caught his breath and looked up at her. 'What did he say?'

'He said to tell you he hopes you're still painting at your special place at Port Gaverne and that you'll have some good work to show him when he returns.'

'But did he say *when* he was coming home?'

Edith shook her head.

'I keep a chart and cross off each day,' said Jasper. 'It's been more than six months!'

'I know, sweetheart, and I miss him too.' She stroked his cheek. 'Off you go and finish making your camp.'

Whispers, murmurs and Pearl's distinctive giggle came from within the bushes.

'Who is in there with you?' said Edith.

'Pearl and Lily. And Tom came to play.'

'I thought I heard an older boy's voice. Is Will there, too?'

'Will doesn't play with us usually.' Jasper sucked his lower lip and a hint of pink crept into his cheeks. 'But he's here today.'

Edith returned to the house and called into the kitchen to speak to Mrs Rowe about the dinner.

Tamsyn slouched at the kitchen table with her chin propped on her hand, watching the cook scraping the carrots. The low-cut neckline of her dress exposed more of her swelling breasts than was decent above the growing mound of her stomach. She cast a glittering look of dislike at Edith. 'I saw you with Benedict,' she said.

Edith frowned at her hostile manner. 'What do you mean?'

'Fluttering your eyelashes and making up to him. You want him warming your bed again, don't you?'

'Utter nonsense!' said Edith. 'Nothing could be further from my mind. On the contrary, I was remonstrating with him for encouraging the twins to smoke.'

'Oh! *Remonstrating*, is it? What kind of la-di-da talk is that?'

Edith sighed. 'I don't have time for this,

191

Tamsyn.' She turned to Mrs Rowe. 'Miss Cox asked me to tell you there are plenty of runner beans for dinner. She'll bring them to you this afternoon.'

'Very good, Mrs Fairchild.'

Edith nodded and went into the kitchen passage. The door to one of the old storerooms was open and she glanced inside to see Will, reading a book. Dora had helped him to whitewash the walls and found him a bookshelf, a small table and an old armchair. She'd given him her rag rug and hung one of her paintings on the wall. The boy spent a great deal of his free time in his private den.

'I thought you were making a camp in the garden with Jasper?' she said.

He looked up from his book and pushed his spectacles more firmly onto his nose. 'I don't play with the children,' he said. 'I'm learning my Latin vocabulary.'

'Oh. Well done. Would you like me to test you?'

'No, thank you. Uncle Gilbert has promised to help me later on.'

'I shan't interrupt you then.' Edith backed out of the storeroom and went upstairs to fetch her sketchbook. She had no reason to doubt Will and that troubled her, giving her cause to believe Jasper had lied. Her son had never been a deceitful boy so what, or who, had prompted him to tell her an untruth?

18

Tamsyn heaved her bulk up the stairs and stood, panting, on the landing outside the studio. She'd never imagined climbing a flight of stairs could be so exhausting. Her ankles were swollen, there was another sharp twinge in her back and her dress was so tight she could see her belly button poking out like a boil on the mound of her stomach.

It had rained heavily for three days and still hammered down on the skylight above. The air was so humid it was almost too thick to breathe. On her way upstairs, she'd listened at the drawing-room door and heard Dora and Ursula moaning that their garden would be flattened by the torrents. Serve them right! Dora often made catty remarks to Tamsyn, telling her she should be ashamed of herself and ought to leave Spindrift. Well, she was blowed if she would!

Benedict's voice murmured behind the studio door, followed by Pearl's giggle.

Tamsyn didn't want him to see her sweating like a pig so she lifted the hem of her skirt and mopped her perspiring face. Pushing open the studio door, she went inside.

Pearl, wearing a white ruffled dress with a blue sash, lolled back on the chaise longue. It was the very same seat on which Tamsyn herself had posed countless times while Benedict painted her portrait. And, though it was very narrow for two, that wasn't all that had happened there . . .

Benedict looked up from his easel with a frown. 'Did you want something, Tamsyn?'

'I came to see what you were doing.'

'I'm working, as you see, and don't need to be disturbed.'

Tamsyn sank down onto a chair in the corner of the studio, trying not to feel too crushed by his comment. 'I'm bored of staying in the bedroom.' She tried, and failed, to find a comfortable way to sit on the hard chair because her back still ached like the very devil.

Benedict ignored her, as he so often did these days, and turned back to study his daughter through narrowed eyes. 'Lift your chin, Pearl, just a little bit.' He nodded approvingly. 'That's good. Now don't move.'

Pearl followed Benedict around and made him laugh with her cheeky comments. He puffed up his chest at her hero-worship and called her his 'little mascot'. Tamsyn sighed. Perhaps she ought to be grateful his interest in Pearl was keeping him out of mischief. She knew he still itched for Edith. It nettled him that she wasn't interested in him anymore. Whatever nasty thing he said to her seemed to be like water off a duck's back and she simply stared back at him with those cat-like green eyes. He wasn't the sort to do without a woman for very long. One thing was for sure, once she'd had the baby and got her waist back, Tamsyn would have to lure him into her arms again very quickly.

Benedict was concentrating on mixing a new colour when Pearl stuck out her tongue at Tamsyn.

'Why, you little . . .'

'Quiet, Tamsyn!' said Benedict. 'I need to concentrate.'

She had caught hold of Pearl in the garden the other day and warned her off from hanging around her dad all the time. The brat had squirmed out of her grip and run off, laughing.

Pearl stuck out her tongue again.

Tamsyn pretended not to notice. A trickle of sweat ran down between her breasts. The baby moved inside her, churning around and kicking, as if it couldn't wait to get out. The hard chair was torture. Restless, she padded across the floorboards and stood behind Benedict to look at Pearl's portrait.

'Tamsyn, stop breathing in my ear!' He dropped his palette and paintbrush on the work table with a clatter.

'I only wanted to see what . . .' Tamsyn caught her breath. Something inside her had popped. And then she felt a gush of fluid run down the inside of her thighs and pool around her feet.

Pearl squealed with a mixture of laughter and disgust. 'Look, Papa! Tamsyn's wet herself!'

'I did not!'

Benedict took a sharp step back, his nose wrinkled in disgust. 'For Christ's sake!'

Tamsyn bundled her skirt between her legs but the fluid continued to trickle down her legs. And then she felt it. A deep grinding pain inside her.

195

Pearl laughed and pointed at the puddle on the floor.

'Shut up, you little heller,' yelled Tamsyn. 'I haven't wet myself, I'm having a baby!'

'Are you sure?' said Benedict.

'Don't just stand there geeking at me like you was mazed,' said Tamsyn. 'Fetch the midwife!' She groaned and doubled over, kneading her back with her fists.

Benedict sighed and clumped off down the stairs.

'Does it hurt?' asked Pearl.

''Course it bleddy hurts! Now stop asking stupid questions and let me get downstairs to bed.' Tamsyn waited until the spasm had passed before making her way slowly down the stairs.

Pearl followed her into the bedroom.

The pain was mounting again and Tamsyn moaned and gripped the brass bedrail until it faded. When she opened her eyes, she was surprised to see that the girl had made the bed and turned it down for her.

'You'd better lie down until you feel better,' said Pearl. 'Can I stay with you? I've never seen a baby being born.'

'No, you can't,' said Tamsyn, easing herself into bed, 'but you can fetch me a drink of water.'

Pearl sucked her bottom lip. 'All right. But don't have the baby until I'm back.'

'Get along with 'ee!'

After the girl had gone, Tamsyn leaned back against the pillows and stared at the rain cascading down the windowpanes. Once she had the baby, she'd be well and truly trapped in this godforsaken house. Somehow she'd managed to avoid thinking about the child but she knew Benedict didn't really want it. When he'd first asked her to move into Spindrift, she'd been over the moon, imagining herself swanning about as mistress of the house. She'd never imagined Edith would stay, not after the way Benedict had insulted her. Now, the question was whether Benedict would keep her and the baby at Spindrift or if he'd already tired of her and would throw them out.

She lay for some time alternately fretting about how she could make Benedict love her again and cursing the cramps that gripped her like a mincer. And they were getting worse.

The door opened and Edith stood in the doorway.

'Come to gloat, have you?' said Tamsyn.

Edith placed a glass of water on the pot cupboard and sat down beside the bed. 'I thought you shouldn't be on your own until the midwife arrives. I saw Benedict rush out into the rain and then Pearl told me what was happening.'

Tamsyn didn't want Edith watching her in her misery but another pain gathered force in her belly and she couldn't speak. She felt a cool hand on her forehead brushing her hair away and, just for a heartbeat, it reminded her of her ma. When the contraction had gone, she lay back, tears seeping from under her eyelashes.

'It will be all right, you know,' said Edith. 'At the time, childbirth is frightening and painful but, when it's all over and you hold your baby in your arms, you'll forget the pain.'

'Will I?' she gasped. 'Another one!' She screwed her eyes shut and braced herself.

'You have to ride the waves,' said Edith, 'or it will be more painful. Try breathing in deeply and counting slowly when the contraction comes. I'll count with you. Ready? One, two, three . . .'

'It hurts!' Tamsyn cried.

'You mustn't panic,' said Edith, glancing at her watch. 'Count with me.'

Tamsyn echoed her. Strangely, it did help a little. She drifted into a waking nightmare where she dozed until the grinding pain jolted her awake again. Once or twice Edith went to look out of the window and frequently she looked at her watch.

Tamsyn drifted off again and woke when she heard Edith having a whispered conversation with someone outside the door. 'Benedict? Is that you?' she called.

Edith reappeared, carrying a pile of towels. 'He's not back yet. It's still raining and the path may be slippery. Or perhaps the midwife isn't home.'

'But she must be!' Panic rose up inside Tamsyn and she struggled to sit up.

Edith gently pushed her back against the pillows. 'If Benedict can't find her, he'll bring the doctor.'

A great ache of misery expanded inside Tamsyn. 'I want Benedict!' she wailed. But it wasn't really him she wanted, it was her ma. And then the torture began again. She shrieked and rolled her head on the pillow.

'Tamsyn!' Edith's voice was sharp. 'Stop that! You'll make it worse. Now breathe slowly and count with me until it's gone.'

Pain-hazed, Tamsyn submitted to the torment, falling into a doze between each fresh bout of agony. Voices whispered around her and she opened her eyes a slit to see Edith and Dora with their heads together.

'Benedict says the storm's caused another landslip on the coast path,' murmured Dora, 'so Augustus has driven him in the trap along the lanes to the village.'

'It may be too late for the midwife to arrive here in time,' whispered Edith.

Tamsyn's belly grew hard and the agony gripped her again. This time it felt different, as if a great pressure was building inside her. She heard herself groan as an irresistible force made her push down.

When the spasm had eased, Edith wiped Tamsyn's sweating face with a damp flannel and gave her cool water to sip.

Dora lifted Tamsyn's skirt and looked between her legs.

And then she closed her eyes and surrendered to the rhythm of agony followed by brief moments of rest, while Edith shouted at her to bear down or to stop pushing and pant. Intrusive fingers prodded her privates. The powerful downward pressure caused a burning, tearing sensation inside her that made her scream for her ma. And then the baby slid out of her and she fell back, sweaty and limp. 'Is it all right?'

Edith wiped the babe's face with a towel and it spluttered and yelled. 'A lusty little boy,' she said. 'Just a minute while Dora ties the cord and then you can hold him.' Moments later, she placed the baby, wrapped in a towel, in Tamsyn's arms.

She stared at her son. His head was strangely pointed, as if it had been squashed, and one ear was bent forward, but he had a good head of dark hair. She wiped a smear of blood off his cheek. He opened his eyes and squinted at her. 'Hello, my handsome,' she said, wonderingly. 'I'm your ma.'

Later, Tamsyn sat up in bed wearing a clean nightgown with her hair brushed free from tangles. Dora had given her a blanket bath and Tamsyn had allowed her attentions without protest, though being careful not to meet her eyes. Edith had helped her put the baby to her breast until he suckled and Tamsyn had made herself mutter a thank you. And she was truly grateful to Edith and Dora, even though that was the last thing she wanted to feel.

'Baby's asleep, Tamsyn,' said Dora. 'I'd catch a few minutes' rest while you can, if I were you. I'll go down and wait for Benedict.'

'I'll stay here,' said Edith.

Tamsyn glanced at the drawer placed beside the bed. Her son nestled inside, his eyes closed and his chest rising and falling in sleep. Her heart sang and she smiled. 'He's *beautiful*, isn't he?'

★ ★ ★

Later, Tamsyn awoke to the sound of voices. Benedict, Edith and Mrs Bolitho the midwife huddled together in the doorway.

'You must wait, Mr Fairchild, while I examine baby and mother,' said Mrs Bolitho. She pushed him firmly out of the way before going to look at the infant. She laid him on the bed, unfolding the towel to examine him. 'You've led us all a merry dance, haven't you?' The baby made a little whimper and she laughed. 'Go back to sleep and I'll look at your ma.'

When Mrs Bolitho had left, Edith returned. 'I'll tell Benedict he can visit you now,' she said.

Tamsyn sat up in bed with the baby in her arms and her hair carefully arranged over her shoulders. Taut with anxiety, she waited. Soon, she heard Benedict talking to Edith and then he came into the bedroom and dropped a kiss on her forehead. 'All right, Tamsyn?'

She nodded. She could hardly say she felt as if she'd been pushed through the mangle and ripped apart in places she'd never even seen, could she? 'Aren't you going to look at your son, then?' She held the baby out to his father.

Benedict hesitated slightly.

Tamsyn felt her smile falter but fixed him with a bold stare. 'Go on. He won't bite you. Not yet, anyway.'

Benedict took the child, laid him on his back and studied his face.

Tamsyn glanced at Benedict's expression. Everything depended on the next few minutes and it didn't look good so far. 'I thought we might call him Roland, after your dad. That's a gentleman's name, isn't it?' In desperation, she leaned over and stroked the baby's cheek with her finger. One side of his mouth curved up in a smile. Then he opened his eyes and stared at his father. 'Look, he's saying hello to you!'

Benedict lifted the baby up so their faces were level and they stared solemnly at each other. 'My son!' he said. 'Welcome to the world, Roland.' Then he kissed the baby's forehead and reached for Tamsyn's hand. 'I promise you,' he said, 'it's going to be different this time.'

Limp with relief, she sank back against the pillows.

★ ★ ★

Shaking from the aftershock of assisting Tamsyn to give birth, Edith escaped into the garden. The rain still fell in torrents and her shoes and hair were soaked by the time she'd hurtled across the lawn to the sanctuary of the gazebo. Rainwater trickled down inside her collar so she took off her mackintosh and draped it over the bench seat. The rain-drenched blooms of the climbing rose drooped from the trellis, dripping as if they wept.

Images of Tamsyn as she laboured raced through Edith's mind's eye, finishing with the picture of Benedict kissing his baby son and reaching for Tamsyn's hand. His new family. Edith's bitter resentment against her husband seethed to the surface again. If her relationship with Pascal became generally known she would be treated like a leper but, untroubled by any guilt or public censure, Benedict had made himself a new family, whilst Edith and her children were left in limbo.

As always, her gaze was drawn to the sea; leaden grey today with the waves crested with Chinese white where they slapped against the rocks. The horizon was hidden by mist that melded into a rain-bruised sky. Her knuckles were as white as pebbles where she gripped the wooden handrail. She'd made a huge effort to lock away her emotional turmoil and rancour against Tamsyn, doing her duty to help the other woman in her hour of need, but she couldn't rid herself of the thought that, if Tamsyn's baby had died before the midwife arrived, then she the discarded wife might have been accused of murdering it. It had all the makings of a sordid story in the worst kind of newspapers. *Wife murders husband's mistress's love child!*

Rain still pelted down onto the waterlogged lawn. Pascal's absence was a physical ache that drained her energy and sapped her *joie de vivre*. Please, God, she prayed, bring him home soon.

A moment later, something landed on her lap. She opened her eyes to see a red rose lying on her skirt, the velvety petals bejewelled with raindrops.

'Edith?'

She turned and caught her breath. 'Pascal! Oh, Pascal, it *is* you!' She flung herself into his waiting arms. Crying and laughing at the same time, they clung together while he covered her upturned face with kisses.

'Why didn't you let me know you were coming home?'

'It happened in a rush. Delphine hired a nurse to look after Édouard, so I wasn't needed any more,' he said. 'I caught a train the next morning. There was no time to write.' He shrugged in that typically French manner she loved. 'And here I am.'

'I was *praying* you would come soon. It's been such an eventful day.'

'I met Dora in the kitchen. She told me you had to be midwife to Tamsyn's child.' He shook his head. 'That must have been difficult for you.'

'I tried not to let it be,' said Edith. 'In truth, I pity Tamsyn, a little. She may have relished humiliating me but it's been a hollow victory. Benedict isn't kind to her and she has no friends amongst the community. She must feel very lonely. While she laboured, she kept calling for her dead mother.'

Pascal kissed her forehead. 'You are extraordinarily charitable, *mon amour*.'

'I can't like her but it's Benedict I blame for all this mess.'

'I'd hoped he would have left Spindrift but perhaps he will be too occupied now to follow us everywhere. Even so, I warn you, I shall pretend indifference to you when he is near. And you must do the same to me.'

'That will be difficult when happiness is glowing within me as bright as any lighthouse.'

He bent to kiss her, gently at first and then with passion. 'I want to undress you and kiss every part of you,' he murmured. 'You cannot

204

know how much I long to be alone with you, my Edith!'

'Oh, I think I do,' she whispered, and gave him a sideways smile. 'And I have an idea about how we might manage it.'

'Tell me!'

'I'm afraid you'll have to wait a little longer,' she teased.

'In that case, I shall brave the rain and return to the house to tell the children I am home.'

Edith put on her mackintosh and held out her hand to him.

They dashed across the lawn and bundled through the back door into the coat lobby, laughing and shaking raindrops from their hair.

Pascal came to a sudden stop, all traces of laughter wiped from his face.

Benedict, an unlit cigarette clamped between his lips, froze momentarily in the act of shrugging on his raincoat.

Edith tensed.

'So,' said Benedict, 'the Bad Penny has turned up again.' He shook his head. 'I really hoped I'd seen the last of you, Pascal.' He didn't wait for an answer. Barging past them, he went outside, slamming the door behind him.

Pascal wiped his face with his palm. 'And so it begins again.'

Their euphoria of only a few moments before vanished.

'Let's find the children,' said Edith.

They walked silently into the hall and then came the pounding of footsteps on the stairs and Jasper hurtled into view.

'Uncle Pascal!' He threw his arms around Pascal's waist and hugged him with all his might. 'Auntie Dora said you were back. You've been away so long I thought you might never come home.'

Edith knew it wasn't only raindrops that ran down Pascal's cheeks as he greeted Jasper. She watched the two of them delighting in their reunion and guilt over her long-held secret tainted her own joy at Pascal's return.

19

September 1903

Dora leaned on her rake and admired Ursula's energy as she turned over the second of their three large compost heaps. Her springy fair hair was tied up in a scarf fashioned into a turban. 'A garden is only as good as its compost,' she'd said last February. And so it had proved. Dora scanned the walled garden, pride swelling in her breast at how much she and Ursula had achieved, together with some help from the community.

The rain in July that had been so torrential it caused a landslip along the coastal path, had flattened and waterlogged the *potager*. At the time, it seemed like a disaster when the ruined plants and produce were washed away but, for Dora, none of that mattered when Ursula said it meant she would have to remain at Spindrift for another year to finish recording the gardening calendar. They'd laid out the paths and beds during the spring. Ursula thought that, by the second year, the hedges and landscaping plants would have matured a little and perhaps the cordons of apple and plum trees would fruit.

Another whole year! Dora hugged the thought to her, a smile spreading across her face. Another year with Ursula, who'd become her greatest friend and companion. Another year to illustrate the choicest plants and blooms and for Julian to take his wonderfully atmospheric photographs recording the monthly progress of the garden.

Dora finished raking the onion bed she'd dug over that morning and began to tread it down, ready for planting the autumn onion sets. Ursula said an onion bed was only as good as the heaviness of the gardener's boots.

Voices drifted on the air and Dora looked up to see Edith and Clarissa walking arm-in-arm towards her.

On the other side of the garden, Ursula thrust her garden fork into the manure heap and waved.

'I'm restless and uncomfortable today,' said Clarissa, 'so we've come to see how you're getting on.' In her ninth month, the mound of her abdomen looked too large to be supported by her slender frame.

'Come and sit over here,' said Dora. She led her friends to one of the curved seats that encompassed a circular gravelled area.

Ursula came to sit with them.

A rose with strongly fragrant, deep pink blooms climbed over the obelisk that was at the exact centrepoint of the garden.

'What a heavenly perfume!' said Edith.

'Isn't it glorious?' said Dora. 'It's an old Bourbon rose called Louise Odier. I wonder who Louise was? She must have been very beautiful to have a rose named after her.'

'Or perhaps she was a fearfully rich old dowager or a king's mistress,' said Clarissa.

'Nothing so interesting, I fear,' said Ursula, a

smile in her aquamarine eyes. 'Louise was the wife, or possibly daughter, of a Monsieur Odier who bred roses fifty or sixty years ago.'

'Well, I expect she was beautiful in her husband or father's eyes anyway,' said Dora.

Ursula laughed and patted her wrist. 'You are such a romantic, my dear.'

Dora's cheeks warmed. Perhaps it was true.

They basked in the September sunshine for a while, chatting about nothing in particular.

'Isn't Spindrift quiet once the children are back at school after the summer holiday?' said Edith. 'And now they're old enough to walk themselves to school.'

'They're all growing up,' said Dora, 'even the twins.'

Edith smiled. 'They'll have happy memories of their early days playing smugglers down in the cove, making dens in the shrubbery or playing in the Mellyns' barn. It's so very different from my own strictly regulated childhood.'

Clarissa sighed. 'I wish Will would join in with their adventures. He led a very quiet life with his grandmother and was tutored at home so has never learned to make friends. He's lonely but resists any show of affection from me. Julian says to give it time but I do worry. And I can't blame Lily for ignoring Will because he doesn't willingly engage in any conversation with her.'

'Perhaps the new baby will give them a common interest?' said Dora.

'I hope so,' said Clarissa, her expression doubtful.

'I can't say Pearl is very enamoured of her new half-brother,' said Edith. 'Surprisingly, Benedict has really taken to Roland and he's much less interested in Pearl now. Secretly, I'm relieved but I don't want her to feel abandoned.' Sighing, she said, 'Nell was upset the other day when one of her schoolfriends taunted her about Tamsyn and her baby.'

'The Penroses have always done everything they can to sully the reputation of the Spindrift community,' said Clarissa, her mouth curled in a wry smile. 'They must be thrilled this time that there are real grounds for blackening our name.' She stood up and stretched out her back. 'I ache,' she said. 'I'll go for a little walk to take my mind off it.'

'There's a lovely Damascus rose on the wall beside the gate,' said Ursula. 'If you're looking for a job, you can collect the petals to make pot pourri?'

Clarissa laughed. 'That sounds like a very ladylike occupation.'

'Perfect for you, then,' said Edith. 'I'll fetch a basket and help.'

'Back to the grindstone, Dora,' said Ursula. 'Shall we plant those onion sets now?'

★   ★   ★

That evening, an hour or so after supper, Dora and Ursula sat in companionable silence, working at the dining-room table. Ursula was compiling a list of tasks to complete in the *potager* during September, while Dora was lost

210

in writing her latest story, *The Mermaid and the Piskie*. She looked up and smiled when she saw Ursula was watching her.

Outside the room, footsteps clipped briskly across the hall. The drawing-room door opened, followed by a buzz of excited chatter. 'I'll go and see what's happening,' said Dora.

Augustus hurried out of the drawing room as she arrived. 'Clarissa's having her baby!' he said. 'I'm going to fetch the midwife.' He sprinted off along the corridor.

In the drawing room, Julian was talking to Edith and Pascal. Mabel and Maude had put down their embroidery to listen.

'Shall I fetch the children from the coach house?' asked Dora. 'Lily can sleep in her old bed and we'll put up a truckle bed in the boys' room for Will.'

'Thank you,' said Julian, a muscle working in his jaw. 'Clarissa will be all right, won't she?'

'I'm sure she will,' said Dora, squeezing his hand. She was a little anxious herself. At thirty-two, Clarissa was no spring chicken.

'I must go back to her.'

'Oh, no, dear!' said Maude. 'That wouldn't be at all suitable. This is women's work.'

'I'll sit with her until the midwife comes,' said Edith.

'Why don't you stay here with us to keep you company, Julian?' said Pascal.

He nodded, anxiety in his eyes.

'Don't worry,' said Mabel. 'Maude and I will go over to the coach house at intervals and bring you regular news of how she progresses.'

'And, for now,' said Pascal, 'shall we play a hand of cards to distract you?'

★ ★ ★

Rose Elizabeth Clemens was born as the sun appeared the following morning. Dora and Pascal had kept an all-night vigil with Julian in the drawing room. Dora had fallen asleep, curled up on the sofa, when Edith came to tell them the news.

Julian shot out of the armchair, his hair standing up in tufts. 'Is Clarissa all right?'

Edith patted his shoulder. 'She's perfectly well though rather tired. She wants to introduce you to your lovely daughter.'

'Thank God! I was so anxious.'

Dora guessed he was thinking about his first wife, Sarah, who'd died in a fire. It would have been unbearable for him if anything had happened to Clarissa.

Edith yawned. 'The midwife is about to leave but she says you can have a few minutes with Clarissa before she has a nap. I suggest you sleep in Will's bed so you'll be on hand if she needs you.'

'You must rest, too, Edith,' Pascal said to her. 'It has been a long night for you.'

Dora couldn't help noticing the loving look he gave to Edith. 'Julian, shall I bring Lily and Will to meet their new sister for a few minutes before they go to school?' she asked.

Julian nodded. 'Please.' He exhaled a great sigh of relief. 'Thank you all for your support

212

and now, if you'll excuse me, I'm going to see my wife and daughter.'

★   ★   ★

During breakfast, Lily could hardly sit still for excitement. 'Can we go and see Rose now?'

'Eat up your toast first,' said Dora.

'*Must* I go to school today?'

'Of course you must!'

Will stopped chewing and said, 'I don't know why you're making such a fuss. Rose is only a silly baby and won't be able to do anything but cry.'

'But she's my sister!' protested Lily.

'Mine too,' said Will. 'Unfortunately.'

'It's true, Lily,' said Pearl. 'Aunt Tamsyn won't let me play with Roland and all he does is drink his bottle, sleep and cry.'

Since when had Pearl called Benedict's fancy piece 'Aunt Tamsyn'? wondered Dora. 'You'll have to wait a while until both babies are old enough to play with you,' she said. 'Now drink your milk, Lily, and then we'll go and have a peep at Rose.'

Lily skipped along, holding Dora's hand as they went over to the coach house. Will trailed behind them, kicking at stones in the courtyard.

Clarissa, her flaxen hair loose around her shoulders, was sitting up in bed with Julian on a chair beside her. She held out her arms to Lily, who ran to hug her.

'Congratulations, Clarissa,' said Dora, kissing her cheek.

213

'Come and see your baby sister,' said Julian to Will. He led his son to the cradle beside the bed. 'Isn't she beautiful?'

Will wrinkled his nose. 'How can you say that? Her face is all squashed.'

'All babies, even you, were like that once,' said Julian, his expectant smile fading. 'It will change over the next few days.'

Lily leaned over the cradle and stroked the baby's cheek. 'Hello,' she said, 'I'm Lily, your big sister.'

Rose drew in a deep breath and began to cry.

'Lily!' said Clarissa. 'You've woken her! Bring her to me, Julian.'

Cautiously, he lifted the baby, supporting her wobbling head in the palm of his hand. She screamed and her face turned an alarming shade of puce.

'Give her to me, Julian!' Clarissa took the baby and rocked her protectively against her breast. 'Run along, children,' she said, 'I'll have to feed her.'

Will left the room without comment.

Julian watched him go, his face set in an unreadable mask.

'Come along, Lily,' said Dora, holding out her hand. 'You mustn't be late for school.'

Her mouth quivered. 'I didn't mean to wake Rose.'

'Of course you didn't,' said Dora. 'Mother's tired and Rose is very new and a bit sensitive, that's all.' Dora glanced at Clarissa. 'Say goodbye.'

''Bye,' muttered Lily.

But Clarissa and Julian were bent over the baby, attempting to soothe her, and didn't respond.

Lily's eyelashes glittered with tears.

'I tell you what,' said Dora, 'why don't I walk you to school today?'

Lily nodded, tears spilling down her cheeks.

Dora, her own heart aching at Lily's distress, took hold of the little girl's hand and led her away.

20

April 1904

Pearl sat with her chin propped on her hand, gazing out of the schoolroom window. The sky was as blue as in one of her mama's pictures and there were puffy white clouds floating across it, looking exactly like baby lambs. She sighed. What a waste of time it was to be inside when it was sunny, especially on her birthday! It was a special birthday, too, because she'd reached double figures. It was annoying that she wasn't the oldest of the Three Sisters as they called themselves. Lily had already turned ten a month ago. Still, Adela wouldn't reach that milestone until next month.

Miss Lansdale droned on and on while she wrote on the blackboard and Pearl yawned, without bothering to cover her mouth since the teacher's back was turned.

Lily and Adela were bent over their copy-books, writing as fast as they could.

Rolling up a small piece of blotting paper, Pearl threw it at the back of Adela's head.

Adela looked behind her, her suspicious frown melting into a suppressed giggle when she saw Pearl was the culprit.

Miss Lansdale turned around but Adela and Pearl were quick enough to gaze at her with rapt attention.

It was strange, thought Pearl, how friendly she and Lily had become with Adela Penrose. After that day she'd met Adela in the cove and they'd played with Star and Blue, they'd become best friends. Jasper and Tom Mellyn were pals of Adela's older brothers, Timmy and Noel, too. Since last summer, they all, even the twins, met up as often as they could to roam the countryside and made camps, climb the cliffs and play pirates on the beach. They'd cut their thumbs, mingled their blood and called themselves the Tregarrick Cove Gang.

The gang was a deadly secret, which made it all the more thrilling. None of the grown-ups must ever know that the Spindrift children and the Penrose children had anything to do with each other. Their friendship was forbidden because of some silly argument between Pearl's papa and Adela's parents, who would stop them playing together if they found out. Timmy said his father would thrash him with his belt, which made Pearl feel quite sick. None of the Spindrift children were ever beaten.

At last, the school bell rang and the girls filed out of the schoolroom and into the playground to stand by the gates. Nell waited with Pearl and Lily until the boys raced outside, whooping with the joy of freedom. Will followed more sedately, talking to Noel Penrose.

Pearl grabbed Jasper's arm as he ran past, chasing after Timmy. 'Have you seen Lucien?'

'He has to stay behind until he's written 'I must not bring worms into the classroom' one hundred times.'

217

'We'll have to wait for him or Mama will be cross.' Pearl sighed. 'I'll be late for my birthday tea now.'

'You go on home,' said Jasper. 'I'll bring him back.'

'I'll stay, too,' said Nell.

Pearl gave them a sunny smile. 'I won't cut the cake until you arrive.'

Arm-in-arm, Lily, Pearl and Adela set off along the street.

'I wish you were coming to my birthday tea, Adela,' said Pearl. 'Auntie Dora's making me a chocolate cake.'

'If there's any left over, you can bring me a slice down to the cove afterwards.'

The girls ambled up Roscarrock Hill and then along the cliff path above the sea. Despite the sunshine and blue sky, the sea was choppy. They came to the place where the land had slipped into the sea on the day Roland was born. It looked as if a giant had taken a greedy bite out of the cliff, exposing a raw scar of crumbly, reddish soil and rock. A new footpath had already been trodden in a semicircle around the landslip.

Pearl saw a cushion of beautiful pink sea thrift growing a little distance away. 'I'm going to pick some of those flowers for Auntie Dora,' she said.

'You'd better be careful,' warned Lily. 'They're very close to the landslip.'

The coarse grass was springy under Pearl's feet as she walked towards the clump of pink flowers. A deep crevice had formed near the cliff edge and Pearl jumped over it onto an area of flat ground that had dropped down by a couple of feet. It was still topped with grass and wildflowers and she wondered if the Hanging Gardens of Babylon had looked like this.

She peered down over the edge of the cliff at the waves crashing onto the rocks below and hurling spume high into the air. A gust of wind tugged sharply at her pinafore and, for a moment, she felt as if she were falling. The wind and the sea roared in her ears and the rocks far below seemed to spin. Catching her breath, she regained her balance and hastily stepped backwards.

Her heart pounding, she glanced behind her at her friends, wondering if they'd seen her falter. That would never do. Inching her way closer to the edge again, she reached out to pick the flowers. The stalks were tough and she yanked at them, pulling up small pieces of root and snapping off some of the flower heads. Anxious to return to the others, she rested one hand on the grass and stretched out with the other to pluck an especially pretty bloom. As she leaned forward, the ground shuddered and sank beneath her palm. Throwing herself backwards, she watched in horror as the cushion of sea thrift trembled and, together with the edge of the cliff, disappeared from view.

Lying on the grass, clutching the bunch of flowers to her chest with trembling hands, a wave of sickness churned in her stomach. What if she'd fallen onto the rocks below? Mewing with terror, she scrambled back over the deep crevice and ran to her friends.

'Are you all right?' asked Lily. 'I thought I saw

219

some more of the cliff slide away.'

'It did but I picked the flowers first,' said Pearl. She smiled with bravado, though she was shivering and a sweat had broken out on her forehead.

'Weren't you scared?' said Adele.

'I'm not scared of anything,' said Pearl. 'Come on, we'd better get home.'

★ ★ ★

Dora scolded Pearl when she saw the mud and grass stains on her pinafore but her face softened into a smile when the girl thrust the untidy bouquet into her hands.

'They're to thank you for making my birthday cake.'

'I'll put them in water and you, miss, can go upstairs and change.'

Pearl was on the landing when she saw Benedict come out of his bedroom carrying Roland in his arms. 'Hello, Papa,' she said. 'Did you remember it's my birthday?'

'Is it really?'

'I'm having a special tea today. Would you like to come?'

Roland chuckled as Benedict tickled him under his chin. 'Well now, I'm not sure your mother would like me to be there.'

'Roland is my brother and it's my birthday and I should be able to choose my party guests,' she said. Pearl wanted her papa to come. He'd be sure to make a fuss of her and that would make her day even more special. Roland reached out to pat her face. She caught his hand and pretended to bite his fingers, making him chuckle again. At eight months old, he was an endearingly sturdy baby with curly dark hair, his father's hazel eyes and dimples. 'There's chocolate cake,' she said.

Benedict's eyes gleamed with mischief. 'How could I possibly resist the lure of chocolate cake? Besides, Tamsyn's sleeping.'

'Five minutes, then,' said Pearl, 'and I'll see you in the dining room.'

She hurried to her room and put on her best dress. It had grown too tight but Mama had said there wasn't enough money for a new one until she'd sold another painting. Brushing her hair, Pearl wondered why it was that Papa rarely paid her any attention these days but carried Roland about in his arms all the time.

Downstairs, she stopped in the dining-room doorway. Lily was already there with Auntie Clarissa, who dandled baby Rose on her knee. Her mother and Auntie Dora were chatting to Uncle Pascal. Will sat at the other end of the table, his chin on his hand, looking bored. But it was the sight of the dining table that made Pearl's eyes widen. It was spread with delicious things: triangles of cucumber sandwiches, scones spread with strawberry jam, a blancmange shape, currant biscuits and a magnificent chocolate cake decorated with shiny glacé cherries and ten candles. The bunch of sea thrift was in a vase in the centre.

'Isn't it all lovely?' she breathed, and felt her cheeks turn pink with pleasure. The only thing that could have made her party any better was if Adela had been there.

Edith came to kiss her. 'Happy birthday, sweetheart. Come and sit here in the guest of honour's chair,' she said. There was a big pink bow tied to the back of it. Pearl sat down between her mother and Uncle Pascal.

'I thought you'd be working, Uncle Pascal,' she said.

'How could I miss such an important occasion?' His brown eyes had little creases at the corners when he smiled. 'You look very pretty in your best dress, *ma petite*.'

Pearl inclined her head graciously, exactly as she'd seen the Reverend George's wife acknowledge parishioners' greetings on a Sunday morning. 'Thank you.'

'Jasper and the twins are home,' said Edith, 'but I sent them to wash their hands.'

Hannah brought a plate of egg and cress sandwiches from the kitchen and then the twins rushed in, closely followed by Jasper.

They were eating their sandwiches when Benedict arrived with Roland sitting on his shoulders. 'Hello, hello!' he said. 'Shift further down the table, Pascal, will you?' He lifted a chair from the other end and pushed it into the narrow gap between Pearl and Pascal, forcing him to move his chair.

Benedict sat down, swinging Roland from his shoulders onto his knee. 'Any more tea in the pot, Edith?'

Pearl glanced at her mother, whose face was like a mask as she fetched another cup from the sideboard. Uncle Pascal's hands clenched into fists and Pearl wondered if she ought not to have invited Papa, after all.

Rose began to fuss and Clarissa rocked her and patted her back but the baby didn't stop crying.

'Shall I hold her?' asked Dora. 'You look exhausted.'

Clarissa shook her head. 'No one can settle her except me.'

Lily sighed loudly. 'Rose screams *all* the time,' she said, raising her eyes heavenwards, 'but Mother never lets me hold her. It's not as if I'd drop her or anything.'

'She has colic again,' said Clarissa. 'You should be sorry for your baby sister instead of complaining.'

Benedict smiled pityingly at Clarissa. 'Roland rarely cries,' he said. 'My youngest son has inherited his cheerful nature from me. It's such a pleasant change to enjoy fatherhood this time.'

Jasper ceased chewing his sandwich and looked at his father resentfully.

Edith put down her cup with a clatter.

'Let us all pray that it's the only characteristic he inherits from you,' said Clarissa tartly. 'It would be such a shame if this baby grew up to be a moral degenerate.'

'And sad indeed,' said Benedict, 'if your daughters turned out to have their mother's shrewish tongue.'

Rose, as if conscious of his fears for her future character, let out a series of ear-piercing shrieks.

'If you will excuse me,' said Clarissa, 'I shall

223

take Rose home and feed her. Something disagreeable here appears to have upset her.' She gathered Rose against her shoulder and swept from the room.

Lily thumped her glass of milk down onto the table. 'Why does Rose always spoil everything?' she wailed.

'She can't help it,' said Will. 'She's only a stupid baby. And a girl, at that.'

'But she might have stayed quiet for once,' said Pearl. 'It is my birthday, after all.'

'She's *always* crying for attention,' said Lily, 'and Mother never has time to talk to me anymore. Why doesn't Rose just shut up?'

'Children!' admonished Dora. 'If you can't say anything nice, don't say anything at all.'

Benedict laughed. 'Dora, ever the peace-keeper.'

Dora flushed.

'I think it's time to light the candles on the birthday cake, don't you?' said Edith. 'Pearl, now you're ten, I think you're quite grown up enough to do it yourself.'

Bustling with self-importance, Pearl fetched the box of matches from the sideboard and carefully lit the candles.

Everyone began to sing 'Happy Birthday' and Pearl's heart swelled. How lovely it was to be made a fuss of for once! She glanced at her papa and her smile faded. He wasn't singing. He wasn't even looking at her. He was supporting Roland around his pudgy middle while he bounced up and down, laughing. It was too bad! She'd invited Papa so that he'd notice *her*, and there he was with eyes only for Roland. Again. Nothing had been the same since that baby arrived. Roland had stolen her papa's love away from her. Pearl's eyes smarted and her lower lip trembled.

The singing stopped.

'Pearl?' said Edith. 'Aren't you going to blow out the candles?'

She shrugged, trying not to cry.

Uncle Pascal took her hand and squeezed it gently. 'Shall I help you, *chérie?*'

Together they blew out the candles and Dora cut the cake.

Pearl watched her papa feeding crumbs of chocolate cake to Roland and then hooting with laughter as the baby tried to grab the rest of the slice. Mama was chatting to Auntie Dora about her latest commissions and wasn't taking any notice of her either. Pearl picked disconsolately at her thumbnail.

When tea was finished and she had opened her presents, the others left, one by one.

Roland grew sleepy in his father's arms. 'I'd better take this little chap back to his mother,' said Benedict.

Pearl waited for him to wish her a happy birthday but he didn't even look at her when he left the dining room. She felt a lump in the back of her throat but she mustn't cry.

'And I have to return to the studio while the light is still good,' said Edith.

Pearl pouted. She'd waited all year for her birthday, her special day, and now it was nearly over. There was nothing left to look forward to until Christmas. 'Must you go, Mama?'

'You know I must work, sweetheart.'

At last, there was only Lily left. Sighing, Pearl said, 'Shall we go down to the cove?'

Lily nodded. 'I wonder if Adela is there?'

Hannah came to clear the plates.

'We're going to the cove for a while, Hannah,' said Pearl.

After the maid had loaded the tea tray and departed for the kitchen, Pearl snatched up the knife and hacked off a large piece of the birthday cake. Lily helped her to wrap it in a napkin and then they ran away with their prize.

Climbing down the cliff steps, Pearl saw Adela jumping up and down and waving at them with both arms. Her spirits lifted. Even if none of their parents bothered about them, the Three Sisters would always be best friends.

21

The following morning, Edith glanced over her shoulder as she sauntered across the courtyard, trying not to draw attention to herself. A regular tap, tap, tap interrupted by a gravelly cough came from the open door of Gilbert's studio as he worked on his statue of Artemis. Through the window of Clarissa's jewellery workshop, Edith glimpsed Augustus bent over his workbench.

Once Edith had passed the studios unnoticed, she darted towards the barn gallery, scattering the chickens, who set up an indignant squawking. Cursing under her breath, she snatched open the gallery door.

Inside, Pascal stood on a stepladder, hanging one of his seascapes on the wall in his display area. He turned at the sound of her footsteps and his face broke into a smile. 'This is a pleasant surprise, *chérie*! I am preparing my exhibition ready for the gallery opening in June.'

'I've barely started to think about mine,' she said. 'I've been so caught up lately with finishing my submissions for the Royal Academy and now the last of my commissions.'

'Was there something you have come to tell me?'

She nodded, anticipation of his delight making her smile. 'Are you busy this afternoon, Pascal?'

Descending the ladder, he shrugged. 'No more than usual. I shall go into the village with my

227

sketchbook. What are you planning? A picnic?'

'Would you wait for me up Port Gaverne Hill at, say, two o'clock? I'll drive Ned and the trap.'

'For you, I will wait until the end of time.' He caught her in his arms and kissed her.

She melted against his chest, starved of his touch, but a few moments later, she broke free. 'We must be careful,' she said, tucking a loose curl behind her ear. 'We never know when Benedict will creep up on us.'

Pascal sighed. 'Meanwhile, he struts around Spindrift with his mistress and their child, knowing you dare not risk even a glance at me in case he finds an excuse to punish you.'

'It is to my everlasting regret that I married him,' she said in a low voice. 'If I could only go back in time . . .'

'Hush,' said Pascal, stroking her cheek. 'Remember, we have agreed never to look back but always forward to our future. Now tell me why I must wait for you on the road to Port Gaverne this afternoon.' There was amusement in his eyes. 'It is most intriguing. Are we to become highwaymen?'

Laughing, she said, 'You will have to wait to find out. It's a secret.'

'In that case,' said Pascal, putting a finger to his lips, 'I shall say nothing.'

She kissed him, yearning to press herself against him but disciplined herself to step back. 'Until later, then.'

Hurrying back to the house, she smiled as she pictured Pascal's expression when she revealed her idea. It had come to her last week and, growing increasingly excited by it every day, she'd kept it to herself, planning how to make it work.

A short while later, she was in the studio standing before her easel working on *A Callybash Ride Down Rose Hill*. It was as she'd walked down the steep hill a few weeks ago that she'd heard excited shouts and a loud rumbling noise behind her. She'd barely had time to flatten herself against a wall before a makeshift trolley fashioned from an orange box and a set of perambulator wheels hurtled towards her, nearly knocking her off her feet. A boy sitting in the orange box, clung to the sides with grim determination. As she watched, the trolley ploughed into a wall further down the lane. Then another one with two screaming passengers crammed inside careened past and ran into the wreckage of the first, ejecting a small boy and girl. Fearing for their safety, Edith picked up her skirts and sprinted down the hill.

The children, filthy dirty and one with a bloody nose, were screeching with laughter when she reached them, eyes bright with excitement. They accepted her handkerchief to staunch the blood but assured her they'd never had as much fun in their lives as when they were riding their callybashes down the hill. Edith had left them to it with only a word of caution. She then hurried back to her studio to make rapid sketches capturing the children's faces in the grip of excited terror as they barrelled down the hill.

Now, she studied her painting with satisfaction. She'd really caught the impression of speed as the two callybashes raced towards their fate. The little girl's tangled hair and pinafore flew out behind her and the mixture of terror and elation on her brother's face was wonderful. She was adding a tiny spot of carmine to the girl's cheeks to heighten her flush of excitement when she heard Benedict and Tamsyn's voices coming up the stairs. Benedict often came to see what she was doing and to make snide remarks. Her concentration broken, she braced herself for more of his unpleasantness. It wasn't long in coming.

The footsteps paused outside the open door and Benedict, one arm wrapped around Tamsyn's waist, entered the studio. He glanced around and his gaze settled upon Pascal's empty easel. 'Where's your Frenchman, then?'

Edith, pretending to be absorbed in her work, waited a moment and then looked up. 'Yes,' she said, 'was there something?'

'I said, where is Pascal?' said Benedict.

'I've no idea. Why?'

Benedict frowned. 'Have you fallen out with him? You don't seem to be in each other's pockets all the time since he returned from France.'

She shrugged. 'Life moves on, doesn't it?'

Tamsyn chuckled. 'He's ditched you, hasn't he?'

'I have my work and the children to keep me occupied,' said Edith. 'Talking of children, where is Roland?'

'I'm going to paint Tamsyn's portrait,' said Benedict, 'so I gave Hannah a shilling to mind him for a while.'

230

Edith's mouth twitched in annoyance. 'It's not your place to ask Hannah to watch over Roland, shilling or no shilling. The community pays her wages, with an extra contribution from Clarissa and me for minding the children after school. She's busy enough already with the cleaning. If you want a nursemaid, you'll have to employ a girl from the village. Now, if you don't mind, I don't have time to stand here chatting.'

'For God's sake, Edith,' said Benedict, 'why must you be so contrary?'

'And why,' said Edith, 'must you continually goad me?' She caught sight of Tamsyn's gloating expression. Clearly she was enjoying the disagreement. 'What is it you want from me, Benedict?'

'You're my wife, dammit!' He jabbed his forefinger at her. 'Give up your aspirations to be an artist and put your efforts into being a proper mother to our children and wife to me, and then we can be happy together again.'

Tamsyn gasped and stepped away from him.

'The great tragedy of my life,' said Edith, 'is that I *am* your wife. To have given up my ambitions as a painter would have made the tragedy even greater. Now, why don't you take your fancy-piece away and stop pestering me so I can continue to earn enough to feed our children?'

Benedict huffed out his breath. 'Come on, Tamsyn, we won't waste any more of our time arguing with this infuriating woman.' He grabbed her arm, none too gently, and pulled her out of the room.

A moment later, the door to his studio slammed shut.

Edith turned back to her easel but couldn't quite wipe away the memory of Tamsyn's stricken expression when Benedict had asked Edith to give up her work and be his wife again.

She hadn't been working for long when Pearl pushed open the studio door and came to stand behind her, sniffing.

'Where's your handkerchief, Pearl?'

'Lost it. Haven't you finished that painting yet?'

Edith sighed and put down her brush. 'Unfortunately not. There have been too many interruptions.'

'I have a sore throat. Can you make me some lemon and honey?'

'Hannah will make it for you. I'm trying to finish this before I have to go out.'

'May I come with you?'

'Not today.'

Pearl scowled. 'You're *always* too busy to spend time with me.' She stamped across the floor and banged the door behind her.

Edith picked up her paintbrush and attempted to forget this accusation. It wasn't true. Was it?

A few moments later she heard raised voices in the studio next door and then Pearl shouted, 'I hate you!'

Exasperated, Edith went to investigate.

In Benedict's studio, Tamsyn, wearing nothing but a pink feather boa, reclined on the chaise longue. Benedict, his shirt untucked and unbuttoned, glowered at Pearl.

'What's going on here?' said Edith, though she had a very good idea what had been going on between Benedict and Tamsyn.

'Papa was painting *my* portrait,' yelled Pearl, 'and now he's not going to finish it because he's going to paint *hers*.' She pointed at Tamsyn, shaking with outrage. 'Papa *promised* me he'd finish my portrait and it would be in a famous gallery in London.'

'Don't be such a silly little girl!' snapped Benedict.

'I'm not! You said I was your best girl . . .' She burst into noisy sobs that quickly turned into a coughing fit.

Benedict rolled his eyes. 'I can't be bothered with all this. Can't you make her be quiet, Edith?'

She cast him a look of loathing and went to hug Pearl.

Her daughter slipped from her grasp. 'I hate you all! Papa tells lies and none of you ever has any time for me. I wish I'd never been born!' She ran out of the studio, her feet thundering down the stairs.

Edith froze, too shocked to speak.

'Spare the rod, spoil the child,' said Tamsyn.

'Well, that's really helpful, Tamsyn,' said Benedict, his voice dripping with sarcasm.

Edith went after Pearl but couldn't find her. She hurried outside and found Dora painting at the table on the terrace. 'Have you seen Pearl?

'She came running out of the house a few minutes ago,' said Dora. 'She was upset. I was having a heart-to-heart with Lily at the time. She was in tears because Clarissa had scolded her. The two girls ran off together, saying they'd look for the other children in the cove.'

'I'd better go after them.'

'Pearl is a child of tempestuous moods,' said Dora. 'It's sure to be a storm in a teacup. Why don't you leave her to calm down and speak to her later?'

'I have to go out shortly,' said Edith, 'but now I'm not sure if I should leave her.' She massaged her temples, weighing up the probability of Pearl having forgotten all about the disagreement if she gave up her longed-for meeting with Pascal and went in search of her daughter.

'It'll all blow over,' said Dora. 'You go on your errands and I'll look out for her in a little while.'

'You always did know how to manage her better,' said Edith, still hesitating.

Dora laughed. 'I've had plenty of practice.'

'Well then, thank you.'

Half an hour later, washed and changed, Edith guided Ned and the trap up Port Gaverne Hill until she saw Pascal waiting for her, his knapsack and folding easel on his back and wide-brimmed hat pulled down over his eyes.

'I nearly didn't come,' she said. 'Pearl had a fit of temper and ran off but Dora said she'd let her calm down and then look out for her.'

'What happened?' asked Pascal. He took off his knapsack and settled himself down on the seat beside her.

Edith related the tale.

'Pearl likes a drama. I expect she will have forgotten it by teatime,' said Pascal. 'Now, tell me where we are going.'

'You'll have to wait and see.'

He gave her a sideways glance, his lips twitching in amusement. 'It's certainly a beautiful day for a drive in the country.'

Ned trotted at a brisk pace along lanes banked by sweet-smelling, verdant grass crowded with herb robert, celandine, red campion and primroses. Edith shook off her unease over Pearl's outburst and enjoyed the spring sunshine. She glanced at Pascal and saw that his eyes were closed and his face turned up towards the sun. His chin was flecked with dark stubble and she remembered how it used to graze her skin when they lay together. A little shiver of desire ran through her. It had been so long.

Half an hour later, she drove the trap through a gateway into a copse. Light filtered through the delicate tracery of leaves above. Wild garlic, bluebells and dog violets carpeted the ground to either side of the narrow track. And there, in a sunlit clearing ahead, was a fairy-tale cottage with a thatched roof. Edith pulled the trap to a halt, excitement bubbling up inside her.

'How picturesque!' said Pascal. 'Have we come to visit someone?'

'You'll see,' said Edith. 'I'll tie Ned to the oak tree and fetch him some water from the well.'

'Let me,' said Pascal. He lowered the bucket into the well and filled the horse trough, while Edith retrieved a key from its hiding place in the log store.

'Come,' she said. He followed her and she unlocked the low front door. 'Welcome to

Woodland Cottage, Pascal.'

He gave her an enquiring look as they entered the beamed living room with its inglenook fireplace. 'What is this place?' he asked.

Edith slid her arms around his neck and tipped up her chin to kiss his beautiful mouth. 'It was Benedict's aunt Hester's secret love nest,' she said. 'For today, it's ours.'

'But how . . . '

She kissed him again, savouring the feel and taste of him without having to look over her shoulder or worry they might be interrupted.

He remained perfectly still for a moment then wrapped his arms around her waist and kissed her until, breathless and laughing, she had to come up for air.

She took his hand and led him up the creaking staircase to the low-ceilinged bedroom with its dormer window.

Pascal glanced at the brass bed made up with clean linen, the wildflowers in a jam jar on the windowsill and fresh towels on the washstand. 'You planned all this?'

'Sshh!' She touched a finger to his lips. She took a small tin containing a rubber sheath from her pocket. 'And I went into your bedroom and took this from your drawer.'

He nodded and placed it on the bedside table.

Edith slipped her hands under his paint-spattered jacket and eased it over his shoulders until it slid to the floor behind him. Slowly, her eyes never leaving his, she untied his neckerchief and unbuttoned his waistcoat. Removing his watch from the waistcoat pocket, she carefully

236

placed it on the bedside table. One by one, she undid his shirt buttons and then rested her cheek against his warm and naked chest, inhaling the scent of him: Coal Tar soap, fresh air and warm skin with a hint of linseed oil.

All the while he stood stock-still but, under her cheek, Edith felt the pounding of his heart.

'Oh, my Edith,' he whispered, 'how I have hungered for you!' He crushed her to him and they kissed again, while his hands caressed her back, her waist, her hips.

She clung to him, her knees weak with wanting him, and then he undid her dress and lifted it over her head. Her undergarments followed and she stood before him naked and unashamed.

His eyes were dark with longing as he scrambled out of his clothes and then swept her up in his arms and carried her to the bed.

She closed her eyes, every nerve vibrating at his tender touch, and lost herself in the delight of their passion.

Later, they dozed facing each other, foreheads touching and legs still entwined. When Edith awoke, she languidly traced the angles of Pascal's jaw and cheekbone, luxuriating in the afterglow of their loving. 'The magic we make between us is still there, isn't it?' she murmured.

'Did you doubt it?'

'Of course not,' she said. 'Though sometimes I wondered if we would ever have the chance to experience it again.'

Stroking her hair, he sighed. 'I cannot feel that our love is sinful, not when it is so beautiful and hurts no one. *Au contraire*, it is only the view of others that renders it immoral.'

So relaxed that their bones felt liquid, they watched the leafy pattern of shadows dancing on the whitewashed wall, cast by the oak tree outside the window.

Shivering slightly as her skin cooled, Edith pulled the patchwork quilt up over their shoulders. 'I never want to leave Woodland Cottage.'

'Here, it would be possible to forget time and the outside world entirely,' said Pascal. He picked up his watch from the bedside table, glanced at it and sighed. 'But I suppose we must return before we are missed.' Kissing her forehead, he said, 'Thank you for your beautiful secret. I shall treasure the memory of this afternoon forever.'

Edith stretched and smiled. 'It needn't be our last visit,' she said. 'The tenant left last week and I haven't yet found a replacement. Since I arrange the lets, Benedict would never know who rents the property, as long as the money appears in his bank account. The rent is very low because the cottage is remote and old-fashioned.'

Abruptly, Pascal sat up in bed. 'You plan for us to rent the cottage?'

'As our private place. Is it very shameful of me?'

He laughed and pulled her into his arms. 'Utterly and I adore you for it.'

'Meanwhile,' she said, 'I suppose we'd better return to Spindrift.'

They dressed hurriedly, made the bed and

locked the door behind them.

Edith drove along the lanes, her happiness suffused with melancholy at returning to the real world. She glanced at Pascal, who appeared lost in thought.

'Edith,' he said, slipping his arm around her, 'it has been a sublime afternoon and to visit the cottage together whenever possible will be a precious thing, but I want more than that.'

'I know,' she said, 'but I can't . . .'

'Not now,' he said. 'In the future. I can bear our difficulties if I know we have a future together. When the children are grown up and Benedict can no longer threaten to take them from you, will you then come to France with me, where we will live as man and wife?'

'Leave Spindrift?'

'Yes.' He studied her face, his jaw clenched.

She thought of all he had given up for her, the unborn children and the years he'd spent, and would spend, away from his homeland so that he could be with her. The decision was simple. 'Yes,' she said. 'So long as we are together, I shall be happy.'

He let out his breath in a contented sigh.

Before they reached Port Isaac, Edith pulled the trap to a halt.

Pascal gathered up his knapsack and sprang down to the ground. He looked up at her and said, 'I love you, Edith,' then slapped Ned on the rump to send him on his way back to Spindrift.

Edith smiled to herself all the way home, remembering Pascal's arms around her nakedness and his soft kisses on her throat and breasts.

She drove into the courtyard, still daydreaming of their love-making, and unhitched Ned from the cart. Rapid footsteps came from behind her and she turned to see Clarissa, her hair escaping from its pins and her eyes swollen from weeping.

'What is it?' Edith asked, suddenly alarmed.

'Edith! Oh, Edith, I can't bear it. Everyone is out looking for them but it's going to be dark soon and they're all alone!' Clarissa's mouth twisted and her knees buckled.

Edith caught her friend in her arms. 'What's happened?' But already, like a knife in her heart, she knew.

Clarissa looked up, her face a mask of grief and terror. 'It's Lily and Pearl. Edith, they're gone!'

22

It was past one o'clock in the morning and Dora, Edith and Clarissa sat around the kitchen table, holding hands. So tight was their grip that Dora's fingers were numb but there was no question of breaking the circle. Together, they had weathered many crises, always drawing strength from their deep friendship.

The kitchen clock ticked into the tense silence, marking the growing number of hours since Lily and Pearl had disappeared. The whole Spindrift community, except for Edith and Pascal, had gone to look for the children when they didn't arrive for tea. Pearl was never late for her tea.

What worried Dora was that they hadn't stolen food from the larder so, unless it had been a spur-of-the-moment decision, it seemed unlikely they'd planned to run away. As soon as she'd discovered that, she'd run, helter-skelter, down to the cove, wondering if there'd been an accident. Jasper, the twins and Tom Mellyn had been on the beach but they shook their heads when asked if they knew of the girls' whereabouts. Nevertheless, she'd searched behind the rocks and glanced inside the cave, calling their names, just in case, before returning to the house.

A gust of wind rattled the kitchen window and spat raindrops onto the glass.

Abruptly, Edith shook her hands free and stood up. 'I can't sit here waiting.' She paced up

241

and down, her face ashen.

'The men are out looking for them,' said Dora, 'so we must remain here in case they come home.'

'How can they possibly find the girls in the dark?' said Clarissa. 'They could be anywhere. Are they hiding or have they been taken?' Her voice was shrill with distress.

Dora put her arm around Clarissa's shoulders. 'Both of them were upset and they probably encouraged each other in their grievances and decided to hide. I'll bet they've fallen asleep in a barn or some other hidey-hole.' Dora forced herself to sound calm but, inside, she was terrified. She loved the girls as much as if she'd given birth to them herself. She was the one who'd been there to change their napkins, soothe their grazes and amuse them while Edith and Clarissa had concentrated on their careers.

Mute with misery, Clarissa nodded. Unable to sit still, she went to check on Rose, asleep in her Moses basket in the corner.

Dora stared at her hands, reliving her last conversation with the girls. Lily, in tears, had come to her first, saying her mother didn't love her anymore. Rose suffered terribly with colic, sometimes screaming for hours on end. Clarissa had become permanently anxious, fussing over the infant and refusing to let anyone else attempt to soothe her. It was this that had upset Lily so much. She'd offered to rock Rose in her arms while Clarissa rested but her mother had spoken sharply to her and wouldn't even let her try.

Edith filled the kettle and put it on the range.

'Hot water bottles,' she said. 'We need to warm their beds for when they return.'

If nothing else, Dora thought, it gave Edith something useful to do.

The door burst open and the oil lamp suspended over the table flickered in the sudden draught.

Clarissa gasped and clutched her hands to her chest.

Edith and Dora flew to the door, where Julian, Pascal, Wilfred and Augustus were taking off their wet mackintoshes and wiping their shoes on the mat.

'Did you find them?' The naked hope in Edith's voice made Dora's heart bleed.

Pascal shook his head. 'We have searched the outbuildings here and also at the Mellyns' since the children so often play there.'

'We walked along the coast path into the village,' said Julian. 'Benedict was in the Golden Lion earlier on, asking everyone there to look out for the girls.'

'He came home when the inn closed,' said Dora. 'He's gone to bed but he hadn't any news.'

Augustus put his lantern on the table. 'We reported the girls missing to the police constable. If they haven't turned up by morning, he'll organise the villagers into a search party.'

'I promise you,' said Wilfred, 'no outhouse, shed or barn in the area will remain unsearched.' He sighed. 'We can't do any more tonight. There's no moon and it's too dark to be thorough. I suggest we all get some sleep and start looking again at first light.'

'How can we sleep while the children are still missing?' wailed Clarissa.

'You must conserve your strength for the morning,' said Julian. 'And Rose needs you to be strong enough to feed her.' As he spoke, the baby whimpered and began to cry. 'There you are!' he said. 'I'll carry her home and you can feed her and then sleep.'

'But . . . ' protested Clarissa.

'No buts.' Julian picked up the Moses basket. 'We're going home.'

Dora hugged Clarissa. 'I'll come and tell you straight away if there's any news.'

'Promise?'

'Cross my heart and hope to die.' Dora felt her reassuring smile crumple as she said the words the children so often used.

After they'd gone, Wilfred said, 'Augustus and I will wait here for a couple of hours. If we stay awake in shifts then we can all have a little time to rest.'

'We sent Gilbert off to bed earlier,' said Augustus, 'so we'll wake him first.'

'Call me then, too,' said Pascal.

'I'm Pearl's *mother*,' said Edith, 'and I wasn't here when she ran off. I must wait up for her.' She covered her face with her hands. 'I should have been here!' she wept.

Dora took her hand. 'You're not to blame and you must rest so you'll be fit to start searching again at first light. Come with me now.' She glanced over her shoulder as she led Edith away and saw her distress reflected in Pascal's eyes as he watched them go.

244

Upstairs, the twins had crawled into Edith's bed and the dogs were curled up together on the mat.

Dora waited until her friend had slipped under the covers beside the twins before going to peep into Jasper's room.

He was sitting up in bed, reading a book.

'Whatever are you doing?' said Dora. 'Blow out the candle! It's nearly two in the morning and you have school tomorrow.'

The candlelight emphasised the shadows under his eyes. 'I keep thinking how frightened Pearl and Lily must be, out there in the dark.'

'I know,' said Dora, smoothing a lock of dark hair off his forehead. 'I expect they were just being silly and decided to hide for a while because they were cross with their mothers. I can imagine Pearl saying, 'We'll make them sorry!' '

Jasper smiled briefly and then chewed at his lip.

Dora sighed. 'Your mother and Auntie Clarissa are terribly frightened and upset. If you think of anywhere Pearl and Lily might have hidden themselves, you will tell me, won't you?'

Jasper closed his book and lay down, his expression troubled.

'Try not to worry,' said Dora. She turned out the lamp. 'Perhaps they found a nice, sheltered place to hide and they'll come home in the morning, starving hungry. Night-night, Jasper.'

He sighed deeply. 'Mind the bugs don't bite,' he murmured.

Dora closed his door and tiptoed along the corridor to her own room.

Ursula sat in bed, writing in her notebook. 'Any news?'

Dora shook her head.

'I'm so sorry.' Ursula closed her notebook. 'As soon as it's light, we'll go together to look for the children.'

Dora undressed and put on her nightgown, her whole body feeling as heavy as lead. 'Lily and Pearl were my babies. I ought to know all their hiding places but I don't know where else to look.' Her voice thickened as her throat closed up with the effort of not weeping.

'My dear!' Ursula sprang out of bed and caught Dora in her arms.

She laid her head on her friend's shoulder and sobbed until she had no tears left. At last, embarrassed, she stepped back. 'I'm sorry. It doesn't help to cry. I'm so tired but I can't stop thinking about my girls out there in the dark.'

Ursula unpinned Dora's hair and brushed it for her. 'My mother used to brush my hair when I was unhappy,' she said.

Dora tipped her head back, feeling the soothing strokes of the hairbrush massaging away some of the tightness in her scalp.

'Come now,' said Ursula. 'Lie down and you will sleep.'

Obediently, Dora climbed into bed and Ursula pulled the eiderdown up to her chin for her, just as if she were a child again.

'Good night, my dear.'

Against all her expectations, Dora was asleep within two breaths.

The following morning, Dora hurried downstairs. As soon as she saw Edith, waiting in a chair by the drawing-room window, her heart plummeted and she knew there was still no sign of Pearl and Lily.

Benedict, carelessly dressed and with his hair uncombed as if he'd just woken up, came to find Edith as the community were having an early breakfast. 'Any news?' he asked.

She shook her head. 'We're going into the village to start a search party.'

He rubbed at his eyes. 'I wish I hadn't shouted at Pearl.'

Slowly, as if it hurt her to move her head, Edith looked up at him. 'I wish I'd spent less time working. At least you took her out and about and showed an interest in her.'

'Until Roland came along. I didn't think . . .'

Edith sighed. 'Will you help with the search?'

'Of course.'

Dora, astonished by his remorse, poured him a cup of coffee.

He sat down at the table and sipped it in silence.

Leaving Clarissa, Mabel and Maude at home to search again through all Spindrift's cupboards, storerooms and outbuildings while they waited for news, the rest of the community, except for Tamsyn, turned out in force. They hurried through the rain into the village, escorting the Spindrift children to school before starting their search. The local police constable

247

had already raised the alarm and a crowd of villagers had gathered outside the school, waiting to help.

Tamara Mellyn ran up to Dora and Edith and hugged them, tears running down her cheeks. 'I can't begin to imagine how frightened you must be,' she said.

Since the rain was still falling in torrents and it was too rough to put out to sea, several of the fishermen had offered their help. The police constable divided the party into groups. The men were sent to scour the coastline and outlying areas of countryside. The women knocked on every door in the village enquiring if the girls had been seen and if they might look in any outbuildings.

It was a long and exhausting day and growing dark again when Dora and the others returned to Spindrift. Rain still lashed at the windows and the sea roared as it crashed against the rocks. Hannah had lit the drawing-room fire and Mabel and Maude had helped Mrs Rowe make soup and sandwiches for the search party. Clarissa, baby Rose held tightly against her chest, let out a sob when she heard there had been no sign of the girls. Julian, grey-faced, put his arms around her and she buried her face in his shoulder.

'I can't believe we haven't found them,' Dora said to Wilfred as they dried themselves before the fire. Despair weighed her down like a lead overcoat. 'Not a single stone has been left unturned,' she said, 'and it makes me wonder if they've left the area. But where would they go?'

'The station master said they couldn't have got on a train without him knowing. It's not yet the season for holiday visitors so the station is quiet, unlike in the summer.' Wilfred glanced at Edith, who sat silently on the sofa, staring into the fire. 'I can't imagine what she is going through,' he whispered.

Dora could. Lily and Pearl may not have been her blood kin but she'd been another mother to them all their lives. She saw Benedict glance at Pascal, who was talking to Augustus. Benedict hunkered down beside Edith and they exchanged a few words. Listlessly, Edith nodded and Benedict fetched her a sandwich. For all his faults, he appeared to be comforting Edith.

Unable to face any food, Dora asked Hannah if the children had eaten their tea.

Hannah nodded, her narrow features tight with anxiety. 'They're in Jasper's room.'

'I'll go and see them,' said Dora.

A few minutes later, she knocked on the bedroom door and went in. Jasper and Will were sitting on the bed, reading, while the twins lay on the floor doing a jigsaw puzzle.

Jasper looked up with an enquiry in his eyes. When Dora shook her head, he blurted out, 'Why won't they come home? Everyone is so upset.' He sounded angry.

'Your hair is wet, Jasper,' said Dora. 'Where have you been?'

He shrugged. 'I went to look in the cave. Sometimes we play there.'

'We've already searched it twice,' said Dora. 'It seemed an obvious place for the girls to hide, safely out of the rain.' She sighed. 'Perhaps too obvious.'

'The cave floods at high tide,' said Jasper. 'It's very dark and it smells of dead fish.' He shuddered.

'Pascal will go to Wadebridge tomorrow and put up notices,' said Dora, forcing herself to sound hopeful. 'Someone is sure to have seen the girls.'

She closed the door quietly behind her and went downstairs again. As she passed Tamsyn and Benedict's sitting room, she heard Roland screaming through the half-open door.

Tamsyn snatched the door open and stood there with her hands on her hips and her black eyes snapping with resentment. 'Is Benedict in the drawing room with the others?' she asked. 'He's left me and Roland alone all day with never a word to let me know what's been happening. Downright selfish, I call it.'

Dora raised her eyebrows. 'You call it selfish for him to spend a day in the teeming rain searching for his lost daughter? I noticed *you* never bothered to join the search.'

'There are plenty of others to worry about his precious Pearl,' said Tamsyn. 'He's completely forgotten about Roland who's crying his eyes out for his dad.'

'Pearl was Benedict's daughter long before Roland came along,' said Dora. 'Edith is beside herself with worry and Benedict is trying to comfort her.' She rubbed her temples, hoping to rid herself of the headache that pressed behind her eyes.

Tamsyn scowled. 'Weaselling her way into his good books again, no doubt. Why doesn't she bleddy well leave him alone? She plays a clever game with Benedict, pretending she isn't interested in him. It only makes him want her more.' Tamsyn pushed in front of Dora so that she couldn't pass. 'You can go and tell her to remember Benedict loves *me* now.'

The simmering anger and distress in Dora's chest seethed up and boiled over. 'The last thing I need when I'm frantic with worry for Pearl and Lily is a squabble with a self-centred barmaid! *Of course* Benedict doesn't love you; he only moved you into this house to annoy Edith. He returned to Spindrift expecting she'd welcome him back into her bed but she wasn't having any of it and he can't bear it.'

Tamsyn gasped as if Dora had slapped her. 'That's not true!'

'Isn't it? He may be stuck here with you but, if Edith *was* ever stupid enough to want Benedict back, she could have him in a jiffy. Then you'd be out on your ear with your little bastard in your arms. Now get out of my way!' Dora pushed Tamsyn aside and ran back upstairs to her room. That selfish girl had no thoughts for anyone else but herself and, meanwhile, precious Lily and Pearl were nowhere to be found. Dora threw herself face down on her bed and wept as if her heart was broken.

23

During the second night the girls were missing, Edith slept very little. When it was her turn to keep watch with Pascal, she stood by the drawing-room window, staring out into the dark, waiting and praying. The storm still raged and the sky was rent by thunder. Once, a jagged flash of lightning made her gasp when she imagined she saw the girls illuminated in the garden outside.

Pascal came to stand behind her, resting his chin on her head.

She turned, clutching at him convulsively. 'I feel so guilty,' she whispered. 'It's tearing me apart that I abandoned Pearl when I knew she was unhappy. All the time we were together at Woodland Cottage, she was so miserable that she ran away.'

'Our guilt will not bring the girls back,' said Pascal. 'For now, we must concentrate on thinking where they might have hidden themselves.'

'Do you suppose I haven't racked my brains about that? But *did* they hide somewhere or were they taken? Surely they'd have come home by now if they could, if only to escape the storm? I'm worried that either someone stole them away or they're lying hurt somewhere. What if they've fallen into some old mine workings?' And Edith buried her face against Pascal's chest, her shoulders heaving as she wept.

Once it was light, Edith, Pascal, Julian and Clarissa assembled for an early breakfast with the remaining children. It was a subdued affair with few words exchanged. Edith forced herself to nibble at a piece of dry toast.

Pascal murmured to Jasper, absent-mindedly crumbling his toast into crumbs. The boy shook his head at Pascal's comment, his expression troubled.

Clarissa made sure Rose was still sleeping in her Moses basket in the corner before taking her place at the table. She lifted her cup to her lips with a shaking hand and spilled coffee onto the tablecloth. Covering her face with her hands, she burst into sobs.

Julian took her in his arms, patting her back.

Will rolled his eyes heavenwards. 'Why does Clarissa have to make such a dreadful to-do about it all?' he snapped. 'Lily's sure to have done this on purpose. She'll be hiding somewhere, hoping to get even more attention than usual, instead of the whipping she deserves.'

'Will!' barked his father. 'That's a dreadful thing to say. Now apologise to your stepmother and address her properly as Mother.'

'I shan't!' Will's face flushed an angry red and his eyes glittered. 'She isn't my mother. How *could* you have stopped loving my mama to marry *her*? You make such a fuss of Clarissa and Lily and the new baby but you wouldn't care a jot if I disappeared, would you? All I am is a terrible nuisance to you all.'

Clarissa gasped and Julian's expression was thunderstruck. 'That's simply not true, Will!' he said.

'It is and you know it!' shouted his son. 'No one here wants me. I doubt you'd have noticed if I'd been the one who'd gone missing. I'm so miserable I might as well be dead!' He pushed back his chair so suddenly it fell over backwards and crashed to the floor.

Julian leaped to his feet and caught hold of his son before he reached the door. 'Never, ever think I don't, or didn't, want you, Will. I only left you with Grandma because she could give you a stable home. I wanted you at my side every single day for every one of those years. And if you think I wouldn't care if you ran away . . . ' Julian's voice cracked and he hid his face in Will's hair. 'I don't know how I could go on if anything ever happened to you.'

Will stopped struggling in his father's grip and grew very still.

Julian cupped his son's face in his hands, forcing the boy to meet his gaze. 'I was very ill after your mother died in that fire, not only because I was burned too, but because nothing could ever be the same again. I'd lost the woman I loved and was in no fit state to bring up a two-year-old child. When Grandma offered you a home, I did what I thought was best for you, though it nearly broke my heart.'

Clarissa, tears still staining her cheeks, came to stand beside them. 'It's true, Will,' she said. Her mouth trembled. 'Your father told me years ago, when he first came to Spindrift, how desperately he wanted you to live with him.'

'Did he?'

'He loved your mother very much,' she said. 'And it's right and proper that he'll always keep a special place in his heart for her. I won't even attempt to take your mother's place; that would be impossible, wouldn't it? But, if you'll let me, I want so much to be your friend and for us all to feel like a proper family.'

Will stared at the floor. 'I can't call you Mother,' he muttered. 'It wouldn't be right.'

'No, I can see that,' said Clarissa. 'You're growing up now, so perhaps just Clarissa would be more suitable?'

His shoulders dropped and he gave a barely perceptible nod.

Edith's heart ached for Will, Julian and Clarissa. She'd thought Will was simply an awkward boy by nature. She had discovered herself how easy it was for a parent to be guilty of failing to understand what was going on in a child's mind.

Julian squeezed his son's shoulder. 'We'll talk more about this after school.'

'Meanwhile,' said Edith, 'you children must hurry up and finish getting ready.' She sighed. 'And we shall continue the search, though I hardly know where else to look.'

Jasper and the twins went to clean their teeth but Will hung back in the doorway. 'Clarissa,' he said, 'I've seen Lily and Pearl playing with the Penrose children down in the cove sometimes. They were with them on the afternoon they went missing.'

255

'The Penrose children?' Clarissa frowned. 'I thought the girls didn't like them?'

Will shrugged. 'I saw them together.'

'Thank you for telling me, Will.'

He dropped his gaze and hurried away.

Julian ran his fingers through his hair. 'I wish to God he'd told us that before.'

Edith rose to her feet abruptly. 'We must speak to the Penrose children, Clarissa. If we hurry, we'll catch them before they leave Cliff House for school.'

'I can't,' said Clarissa, glancing at Julian. 'Every time I've spoken to Hugh or Jenifry Penrose in the past there's always been a dreadful quarrel. I doubt either of them would even speak to me.'

'Surely Pearl and Lily's disappearance transcends any previous petty squabble we've had with our neighbours?' said Edith.

'Nevertheless,' said Clarissa, 'it would be more productive if you went without me.'

'But Clarissa . . . '

'I agree. It wouldn't help,' said Julian.

Clarissa reached for his hand.

'We shall go together, Edith,' said Pascal.

They hurried to don gum boots and mackintoshes. Splashing through the puddles along the lane, they soon reached neighbouring Cliff House.

Edith rang the doorbell, refusing to allow herself any time to lose her courage.

A maid let them in and they waited, dripping on the polished hall floor, while she went to inform her mistress. The scent of bacon drifted

256

on the air, making Edith feel queasy.

A door opened and Hugh Penrose, frowning and blotting his lips with a napkin, came out of the dining room. 'What do you want?' he asked brusquely.

Edith forced herself to remain polite. 'I'm sure you've heard that two of our children, Pearl and Lily, have been missing for more than two nights?'

'Hardly surprising if the moral depravity and general laxity of discipline amongst the Spindrift community has resulted in your children running off. They've been seen roaming wild all over the countryside with never a nursemaid to mind they don't get into mischief.'

Edith swallowed her anger. This wasn't the time to defend herself or to argue with him. 'I'd like to ask your children if they have any ideas on where the girls might have gone or if they saw someone taking them away. They were seen playing with Pearl and Lily on the afternoon they disappeared.'

'Whoever imagined they saw that was mistaken,' snapped Hugh. 'My children have been expressly forbidden from any contact with yours.'

'They were definitely all together in the cove,' said Edith. 'Surely, as a parent, you can understand our desperation to find Pearl and Lily?'

'I can't help you.' Hugh turned abruptly to the maid, hovering beside the stairs. 'Sarah, show these people the door.'

'You *won't* help us, you mean.' Edith pinched

her lips together, then took a deep breath. 'Whatever may have caused difficulties between our houses in the past, those little girls have been missing for two nights. For the love of God,' she pleaded, 'have some pity! It's such a small thing we ask.'

'Leave my house at once!' Without another word, Hugh returned to his breakfast, slamming the door behind him.

Edith stepped forward to follow him but Pascal took hold of her arm.

Outside, on the doorstep, she said, 'What an unmitigated beast that man is! I don't know how he can live with himself.'

Pascal lifted her hand to his lips. 'His whole life is tainted by bitterness but he will never be content unless he lets it go.'

When they arrived back at Spindrift, the children were buttoning their mackintoshes before setting off for school.

'Mr Penrose wouldn't let us ask his children if they'd seen Pearl and Lily,' said Edith. 'Please, please, at school today, children, will you ask the Penroses if they have any idea where the girls might be?'

'We will, Mama,' said Lucien.

'Do I have to go today?' asked Jasper.

'Yes, you do,' said Edith. 'I know you're worried but it's better to keep busy. Besides, you might discover something about the girls' whereabouts from your school friends.'

'But . . .'

'No arguments, please, Jasper.' Edith kissed him and the twins goodbye and tucked Nell's plaits inside her coat to keep them dry. 'Take care not to slip along the coast path,' she said, opening the back door. 'It'll be muddy after the rain.'

Julian hugged Will and the boy clung to him for a moment.

Clarissa wished him a good day at school. He nodded briefly and trudged off across the lawn with the others.

Julian went to his studio, where he'd been developing photographs of the missing girls to pin up in the village.

'I'd no idea Will was so unhappy,' said Clarissa to Edith, her expression troubled. 'He's not been easy to talk to and rebuffed me every time I tried, but I thought he was rude rather than distressed. I should have made more of an effort.'

'It's easy to be wise after the event, isn't it?' said Edith. 'And Rose has needed so much of your time.'

'Even so, how could I have neglected my darling Lily?' Clarissa dabbed her eyes with a handkerchief. 'All I want is to have our girls back safe, Edith! If they ran away to give us a fright, surely they'd have come back by now?'

'I've been worrying about that all night,' said Edith, 'but I refuse to allow myself to sink into despair. I'm going to put up posters in Wadebridge this morning.'

Edith, Pascal and Clarissa returned to the hall, discussing the day's plans to continue their search.

Pascal picked up an envelope from the

doormat. 'A letter for you, Edith.'

She took it from him and scanned the contents. She gave a mirthless laugh and handed the letter back to him. '*Children Flying Kites* and *A Callybash Ride Down Rose Hill* have both been accepted by the Royal Academy for their Summer Exhibition.'

'But that's excellent news,' said Clarissa. 'I'm so pleased for you.'

'Congratulations, Edith. It is a very great achievement,' said Pascal.

Edith's face crumpled and she pressed her knuckles against her mouth. 'I've dreamed of this for so long, I should feel triumphant to be recognised in my own right. But artistic success means nothing while Pearl and Lily are missing. How can I celebrate until we find the girls safe and sound?'

Footsteps thundered along the passage from the kitchen and Jasper rushed towards them. 'Mama!'

'Have you forgotten something?' asked Edith.

He flung himself against her, his hands clutching her waist.

Alarmed, Edith held him at arm's length to look at him. 'Whatever is it?'

'Pearl and Lily!' he sobbed.

She gripped his upper arms, hope soaring. 'Have you seen them? Where are they?'

Jasper lifted his tear-stained face. 'I was going to take them some breakfast but then I saw what had happened!'

'Breakfast?' said Edith.

Clarissa gasped. 'You know where they are?'

Pascal crouched down before him. 'Tell us. Where are Pearl and Lily?'

Jasper's eyes were wide with shock. 'I begged them to come home. I didn't want to keep their secret but we're blood brothers and they made me promise . . . ' His voice rose to a wail. 'And now it's too late!'

24

Will and the twins ran towards them, shouting Jasper's name.

'What's happened?' said Edith.

'Is Jasper all right?' asked Will, panting. 'He screamed when he saw the landslide and then bolted back here.'

'A landslide?' echoed Edith.

'Pearl and Lily are in the cave,' sobbed Jasper, 'and now there are rocks and earth over the entrance and they can't get out!'

'We searched that cave more than once,' said Edith. 'They weren't there.'

'But they were!' insisted Jasper. 'They were in a secret cavern reached from an entrance at the back of the cave. There's a rock in front of it and you can't see it unless you know it's there. Timmy Penrose told us about it.'

'God in heaven,' whispered Clarissa. 'Why didn't I remember that before now? Someone once told me that there was a place there where the smugglers used to hide their contraband.'

Edith shivered, suddenly deathly cold. 'And the girls are trapped in the cave?' Black spots danced across her vision and she swayed.

Pascal caught hold of her and guided her to the hall chair. 'Jasper,' he said, 'when did you last see Pearl and Lily?'

'Last night, after tea. I took them my cake, more candles and dry shoes. The sea was so rough that it went into the cavern at high tide and their feet were wet. Noel and Adela brought them extra blankets and some apples. Pearl was coughing and coughing and I *begged* her to come home but she said she wasn't afraid. She and Lily said they'd never speak to me again if I told anyone where they were.'

'So the Penrose children knew where the girls were hiding?' said Clarissa.

'It was Adela's idea for Pearl and Lily to hide,' said Jasper. 'She said it would make Mama and Auntie Clarissa sorry that they hadn't taken any notice of them.'

Clarissa buried her face in her hands.

'I shall run to the cove and see the landslide,' said Pascal. 'If Lily and Pearl are in a cavern behind the cave they should be safe but we'll need help to clear the entrance.'

Edith drew a deep breath and stood up. 'Jasper and Will, go and tell everyone what has happened. Ask the men to take all the spades, pickaxes and the garden forks down to the cove. And the wheelbarrow! I'll tell Dora and Benedict and then send to the village for help.' She ran upstairs and knocked on Dora and Ursula's door.

Dora appeared in her nightgown, her hair in a tangle. She rubbed her eyes. 'Sorry, I must have overslept. I didn't fall asleep until dawn.'

'The girls are in the cave on the beach,' said Edith.

'Thank God!' Dora pressed her fingers to her mouth.

'But there's been a landslide and they're trapped.'

Dora gave a mew of terror.

Ursula, already dressed, came to the door.

'Would you go to the village and raise the alarm, Ursula?' said Edith. 'We need more men to help.'

'Perhaps the fishermen will come?' said Ursula.

Dora rapidly undid the buttons of her nightgown with shaking fingers. 'I'll get dressed and come and help, too. Poor little mites, they must be terrified.'

Edith left them and hurried along the corridor to bang on Benedict's door.

He burst out of the room. 'Have you found Pearl?'

'There's been a landslide,' said Edith. 'The girls are trapped in the smugglers' cave.'

Benedict paled. 'Christ Almighty! Are they hurt?'

'I don't know. We're going to clear the entrance. Will you come and help? Please?'

He frowned. 'Did you really imagine I might not?'

Without answering, Edith ran downstairs to put on her coat and boots.

When she hurried outside, it was still raining heavily and she slipped on the wet grass on the clifftop. Pulling herself to her feet, she saw where the landslide had occurred, carrying away another section of the coast path. Clinging tightly to the handrail, she climbed down the steps to the cove.

The sight that met her eyes there made her falter. A great chunk of the cliff had fallen away and the entrance to the cave was buried beneath a vast mound of boulders, stones and soil. It seemed an impossible task to move it all and the two girls were trapped inside. Please God, Pearl and Lily had stayed in the cavern, but what if they'd been near the cave mouth during the landslide?

Pascal, Gilbert, Julian, Augustus and Wilfred had already made a start with shovels and were filling the wheelbarrow with soil.

Pascal emptied the barrowload of earth down by the water's edge and came to stand beside Edith, his hair soaked and his face smudged with mud. 'We're trying to dig a tunnel through the rubble so we can climb down into the cave,' he said, 'but we can't see where the entrance is.' He shook rain out of his eyes. 'I must go back.'

'I'm coming, too,' said Edith.

'Stay here!' said Pascal. 'The earth keeps slipping down between the rocks. It's dangerous.'

'If it were your child that was trapped, would you stay here to watch?'

Pascal sighed. 'Be careful, then.' He pushed the empty barrow up over the mound of fallen soil and rock.

Lifting her skirts so she wouldn't trip over them, Edith scrambled up the steep slope. Gilbert was working about three yards away from the others, levering a boulder out of the soil with a crowbar. Suddenly, it came free and he yelled a warning.

Edith leaped to one side as it rolled away, gathering speed and bouncing as it went, before crashing onto the sand below. Her heart hammered but she continued up the slope on all fours, slithering backwards several times as mud shifted and loose stones rocked under her feet. Finally, she made it to where Augustus was wielding a pickaxe to lever rocks from the soil. Using her bare hands, she scrabbled to get a purchase on the already loosened boulders and then rolled them down the incline towards the beach.

A short while later, Dora clambered up beside her and handed her a spade. Side by side, they dug out mud, hurling it as far as they could down the slope. Rain battered down continually upon them. The pins fell out of Edith's hair and it hung in rats' tails around her shoulders. Dora slipped and fell face down on the slippery mud.

Then Wilfred yelled out. 'Over here! I think I've found the mouth of the cave!'

They all swarmed over the landslip like so many ants returning to their nest. Wilfred had excavated soil away from part of the cliff face, revealing a small cavity under a fissure in the rock.

Edith's spirits rose. If only they could clear away enough soil to climb through into the cave, perhaps they'd be able to reach the girls.

And then the cliff face above the fissure began to tremble.

Someone shouted and, out of the corner of her eye, Edith saw Pascal hurtling towards her with his hands held out. She felt a hard thud to her chest and the breath was expelled from her lungs with a whoosh. Tumbling backwards, she slithered down the slope while her face was showered with a hailstorm of gravel and soil. Coming to an ungainly halt against a boulder, she heaved in her breath. Coughing, she pulled her skirt down over her knees and wiped mud from her eyes.

The second landslip had caught Pascal and carried him all the way down to the beach.

Edith held her breath until she saw him sit up and shake his head.

Wilfred had also been swept away and blood was dripping from a wound on his head. Dora slid on her bottom down the slope towards him, pulling a handkerchief from her pocket.

Hindered by her sodden, mud-caked skirt, Edith dragged herself to her feet, scanning the scene for the others. Benedict and Julian had been knocked over by the rush of soil but were pulling themselves to their feet. Augustus and Gilbert had been far enough away from the slip to escape any more than a splattering of mud. Thankfully, no one was missing.

Edith heard a shout and saw Ursula leading a dozen or so men down the cliff steps. They carried picks, shovels and long planks of wood.

'This is Mr Bates,' said Ursula when Edith greeted them at the foot of the steps. 'His grandfather worked in the tin mines so he has some knowledge of tunnelling.'

A miner's Davy lamp swing from Mr Bates' fingers. His black hair was streaked with silver and his complexion weather-beaten. He smiled when he caught sight of Edith's bedraggled appearance, the skin around his eyes wrinkling like well-worn leather. 'You'm look like a bal-maiden in times of old, missus,' he said. 'But you can't dig hell-for-leather through loose earth like that without shoring up the tunnel or you'll be in deep mire.'

'I can't thank you all enough for coming to help,' said Edith.

Mr Bates sighed. ''Tis a hard thing to fear for a child. I shall get this crew organised.' He called all the Spindrift men to join him and they gathered together to form a plan of action. The women were firmly told to keep out of the way and, as if God was smiling down upon the men, the rain ceased.

Dora and Ursula were sitting on a nearby rock and Edith went to join them.

The members of the rescue party were all assigned different tasks and then set about methodically clearing away the soil and rocks. The second landslip had turned out to be their good fortune since much of the overhanging cliff had ended up on the beach, reducing the need to shore it up.

Edith watched the men as they worked. All the time memories of Pearl as a newborn baby and then as a toddler learning to walk flitted through her mind. Every time Pearl fell over, she'd struggled back onto her feet with a determined expression. That same stubbornness and refusal to give up hadn't always made her an easy child to live with and it wasn't unusual for mother and daughter to be at odds. Nevertheless, Edith was eaten up by guilt that Pearl hadn't felt secure, despite the deep love Edith felt for her. It hadn't helped, of course, that Benedict, after making a pet of her, had grown bored by his daughter's company after Roland was born.

Jasper came down to the cove and offered to help the men but was turned away. Grief and guilt were clearly visible on his face and Edith called out to him.

He came to sit with beside her. 'Will has taken the twins to school but I couldn't bear to go, not until I know Pearl and Lily are safe.' His hand crept into hers. 'I'm sorry, Mama,' he said. 'I know now I should've told you before where they were hiding. What if . . . ' He broke off, unable to speak.

Edith squeezed his hand. 'You didn't know there was going to be a landslide and I admire your loyalty. Pearl can be very persuasive when she wants something.'

'I really thought they'd have come home before now,' said Jasper. 'Pearl has a cold and it's horrible in the cave, though they pretended they liked it.'

'It's my fault, not yours,' said Edith bleakly. 'I should have told her, told all of you, every single day how very much I love you; that you mean everything to me and are my whole reason for being. I'm more proud of my beautiful children than of any other thing in the world.'

'Don't cry, Mama!'

She hugged him fiercely, burying her face in his hair.

An hour or so later, Pascal came to let them know what progress was being made, before hurrying back to the cliff face.

The waiting was torture and Edith was glad to

have Jasper's hand to hold. She tried hard not to think of the terror Pearl and Lily must be suffering. The cave would be cold and, once their candles burned out, pitch dark. Pearl had never liked the dark.

Edith turned her face into the wind, inhaling its briny smell. The sullen sky was still pregnant with rain and the storm had churned up the sea so that the waves breaking on the sand had a dirty, yellowish cast.

Clarissa climbed down the cliff steps carrying a basket. Her eyes were red and swollen with weeping. 'Any news?' she asked.

'We'd have let you know straight away,' said Dora.

'Whatever happened to you both?' she said. 'You're covered in mud!'

The wind teased a damp curl across Edith's face and she brushed it away impatiently. 'We were caught up in a second landslide.'

'I've left Hannah minding Rose and brought beer and sandwiches for the men,' said Clarissa. 'Mabel and Maude are bringing flasks of tea and a sponge cake.'

It was mid-afternoon when a cheer broke out from the tunnellers.

Augustus slithered down the slope and ran towards them. 'We've shored up the tunnel and broken through to the top of the entrance to the cave!' he said. 'I'm going to fetch a rope from the stable and then we'll lower ourselves down to find the children.'

Clarissa let out a sob. 'Thank God!'

Edith squeezed Jasper against her side and he

threw his arms around her waist and hugged her. 'They'll be all right now, won't they?' He looked up at her with such hope in his eyes that she pushed away her lingering fears and nodded.

A short while later Mr Bates secured the rope around his waist and crawled into the tunnel, pushing his grandfather's Davy lamp before him. The men braced themselves and paid out the rope as he let himself down into the cave, cheering as he disappeared from view.

Mabel and Maude held hands and stared steadfastly at the tunnel opening.

'What's keeping him?' said Clarissa some time later.

The tension was unbearable as Edith watched and waited for a sign that Mr Bates had found the girls. The men called out to each other but she couldn't hear what they were saying. Frightened again, she scrambled up the slope with Jasper following close behind. 'What's happening?' she asked Pascal.

'Mr Bates has reached the cave floor,' said Pascal, 'but the children aren't there. He's looking for the way through to the cavern behind.'

'I could show him,' said Jasper, eager to help. 'There's a big rock in front of it. You have to climb up some stone steps behind it to reach the opening. It's narrow, only wide enough for small kegs of brandy or a smuggler to go through it sideways.'

'You are a brave boy,' said Pascal, ruffling Jasper's hair, 'but it's too dangerous.'

Involuntarily, Edith shivered. She didn't like at

271

all the thought of being under the weight of the cliff above.

A shout echoed from inside the cave and the men braced themselves to pull on the rope.

Edith's pulse skipped. Would she hold Pearl in her arms again in only a minute?

The men heaved on the rope and Mr Bates hove into view. He shook his head. 'They're not there,' he said.

Edith caught her breath, suddenly icy cold.

'They were there,' said Mr Bates, 'because I saw the candle ends and a crust of bread but no sign of the little girls. Perhaps they left before the landslide?'

'But where are they then?' said Edith, panic nearly choking her.

Mr Bates shrugged. 'Not in the cave.'

Edith's knees began to tremble so much that Pascal had to catch hold of her.

Benedict came and took Edith's arm, pulling her away from Pascal. 'Those little minxes deserve a hiding for frightening us all,' he said, grim-faced.

Edith drew a deep breath and shook herself free from his grip. 'We'll return to the house and make tea for the men after all their hard work.'

Julian hurried down the slope to tell Clarissa that the children hadn't been found and Edith heard her wail of distress.

Despondent, the search party climbed the cliff steps. It was as they walked across the headland that Edith saw a small figure emerge from a thicket of gorse bushes. She blinked, barely able to believe her eyes. Speechless, she caught hold of Clarissa's sleeve and then pointed.

Clarissa stared at the child and then screamed, 'Lily!' She ran to her daughter and caught her up in her arms.

Edith raced to the gorse thicket. She forced her way between the bushes, oblivious to the sharp thorns tearing at her skin and clothes. 'Pearl! Pearl, where are you?' The wind snatched her words away.

But Pearl wasn't there.

25

It was pitch-black when Pearl woke up. It was so very dark that even when she touched her nose, she couldn't see her hand. The terrifying blackness and absolute silence suffocated her like a thick blanket tucked in too tightly over her face. Where was she? She was lying on something cold and hard. Sudden panic made her shout but her throat was on fire and it came out as a tiny whimper. She attempted to sit up but her body was too heavy and she was tired, so tired. Closing her eyes, she counted inside her head until she fell asleep again.

★　★　★

She dreamed she was in a rock pool, floating in limpid water. A gigantic shrimp with protuberant black eyes skittered out from a crevice and waved its feelers menacingly at her. Alarmed, she backed away but sinuous strands of seaweed twined around her legs, dragging her down and down into the depths of the deep, dark pool where the monsters lurked.

Underwater sounds boomed in her ears and it seemed for a moment that someone called her name. Gasping for air, she surfaced back to consciousness. Her head pounded and the cold seeping up from the rocky ledge beneath her, made her bones ache. It was still inky black and when she touched her face it was damp. Had it been a dream or had she been dragged into an underwater world? It hurt to breathe and the sound of her rasping breaths echoed around her. She didn't want to be in this dark and frightening place.

'Mama?' she whispered into the blackness.

But there was no answer, only the irregular whistling of her breath.

A long time later, a light startled her. It was so bright it hurt her eyes and she moaned and turned away. That small movement set off an outburst of coughing that made her fight for breath. Exhausted, she fell back against her rocky bed, each breath wheezing in and out. Strong hands lifted her up and she flopped against a comfortingly warm chest, her eyes tightly closed against the dazzling light. She sighed and slept again.

* * *

Something cool and damp dabbed at Pearl's burning forehead and cheeks. Turning her head, she whimpered in pain. Something bad had happened but she couldn't remember what it was. She didn't want to remember. Puzzled, she concentrated on a small grunting noise, as regular as a ticking clock, before realising it matched the laboured rise and fall of her own chest.

Later, Pearl heard the gasping and sobbing of someone weeping. Her eyelids fluttered and opened. Staring straight ahead in the dim light, it took a while for her to make out the painting on the wall before her. Pirates in a boat sailing towards a treasure island. She frowned; she knew that picture.

'Pearl? Are you awake, sweetheart?'

A hand stroked her cheek. 'Mama?'

'Yes, my darling. I'm right here beside you.'

'Don't leave me!' A great cough rose up in Pearl's lungs, racking her body and almost choking her. After the paroxysm subsided, she sank back against the heap of pillows, exhausted. She slept again.

The next time Pearl awoke, it was daylight. She stared at the painting on the opposite wall. Her own bedroom wall. She remembered now. Auntie Dora had painted the picture. Theodora, Queen of the Pirates was standing up in the rowing boat, wearing a black eye patch and with her green parrot on her shoulder. And there were Jasper, Lily and the twins sitting in the boat while Pearl's painted self leaned over the side, holding out her hand to a mermaid sitting on a rock in the sea. She was back at home in her own bed. A sob of relief escaped her.

Edith, dozing in an armchair beside the bed, sat bolt upright. 'Pearl, it's all right. I'm here!'

'Mama!' Pearl held out her hand and Edith gathered her against her bosom, rocking her and murmuring words of love. She stroked Pearl's sweat-soaked curls off her face. 'You've been very ill, my darling,' she said. 'You'll need to stay in bed for a while until that nasty cough is better but your fever has gone.'

'Is Lily all right?' asked Pearl when her mother

finally released her.

Edith nodded, dabbing at her eyes with her handkerchief. 'She's well, though still shocked. She's worried about you, too. How much do you remember of what happened?'

Pearl screwed up her face while she thought. 'Lily and I were very upset and we ran away. We hid in the secret cavern behind the cave for a night. It was an adventure but then we were frightened to come back in case we got into trouble. So we stayed another night. I didn't feel well and we decided we'd better come home, even if everyone was cross. We had to wait until the tide went out because the cave floor was flooded with seawater. But when it was low enough for us to wade through it, there was a horrible noise like thunder. Rocks and earth fell down and then it was very dark.'

Edith squeezed Pearl's hand. 'You must have been terrified.'

Pearl nodded, her throat closing up at the memory of it. 'We had some candles left and a lantern so we went back into the cavern. Lily was screaming and I had to slap her face to make her stop.' She closed her eyes, trying not to think about how brave she'd had to be because she'd wanted to scream, too. 'Then I remembered . . . ' She bit her lip; she mustn't mention Adela. 'I remembered a friend had told me once that smugglers had a secret passage going from the cavern up to the cliffs. So we searched all around the walls until we found it.' She squeezed her eyes shut for a moment. 'It was scary in the passage because it was so narrow and our

277

candles were running out and I couldn't stop coughing. There were places where the rock had been hollowed out so I lay down for a while. Lily was shouting at me to wake up but I couldn't.'

'Lily didn't want to leave you in the passage,' said Edith, 'but the candle was burning low so she carried on alone until she came to some steps. The candle went out but then she saw a glimmer of light ahead. She scrambled out into a thicket of gorse up on the headland. Once we found her, we sent someone into the passage to bring you home.'

Pearl coughed and her mother gave her some sips of water. 'Can I see Lily now?'

'She went back to school today. If you have a rest now, she can come and see you later.'

Sighing, Pearl leaned back against the pillows again. 'Mama,' she murmured, 'are you very angry with me?'

Her mother didn't answer straight away. 'We shall have to talk about it when you're completely well but I couldn't survive the terror of the past week again, thinking I might have lost you.'

'So you did miss me, then?'

'I don't have the words to tell you how much.' Edith kissed her forehead. 'One day, when you have a little girl of your own, then you'll really know how very much I love you. You mean *everything* to me.'

Pearl's lips curved into a smile. So her mama did love her after all.

★ ★ ★

Later, Dora brought her a tray with a bowl of chicken soup and some bread and butter cut very thinly with the crusts removed.

'Mrs Rowe's even put a lace cloth on the tray for you,' said Dora. 'It's ever so posh, isn't it?'

Pearl sat up, delighted to be treated as if she were a lady.

Star and Blue, always on the lookout for scraps, nosed their way into the bedroom and sat beside the bed, staring at her adoringly while she ate her soup.

Lily peeked around the door. 'Can I come in?'

Auntie Dora beckoned to her. 'It's your partner in crime, Pearl. I shall leave you two troublemakers to have a little chat.' She carried the tray off to the kitchen.

Pearl slipped a piece of bread and butter to the dogs.

Lily sat gingerly on the edge of the bed. 'I thought you were dead,' she said.

'I thought I was too.'

Lily's bottom lip quivered. 'I was so frightened when you wouldn't wake up. It was cold and dark and I didn't know what to do,' she whispered.

Pearl gripped her hand, remembering the terror of that narrow passageway and how she couldn't breathe properly.

'I'm never going to run away again,' said Lily.

'Me neither.'

'Mother cries every time she looks at me and won't stop hugging me. She says I'm old enough to help her look after Rose now.' Lily smiled. 'She's quite a sweet baby, actually. Her colic is a bit better and she doesn't cry as much as she used to. She smiles when I sing to her.'

'Uncle Pascal came to see me this afternoon,' said Pearl. 'He had tears in his eyes when he saw I was getting better and Lucien brought me a pet earwig in a matchbox but I made him keep it. And then Papa came, too.'

'Was he cross?'

Pearl shook her head. 'He said he was sorry he'd upset me by spending so much time with Roland. He said the three of us could have a picnic on the beach together.' She thought about that for a while and decided she liked the idea, as long as it wasn't too near the cave. 'Did you get told off?'

Lily made a face. 'Mother is making me write thank you letters to every single one of the people who helped to look for us and she's told me never to play with the Penrose children again.' She sighed. 'We did cause a lot of trouble for a lot of people. Timmy and Noel's father thrashed them for bringing us food and blankets and says he's going to send them away to boarding school.'

'What about Adela?' said Pearl.

'Mother told me not to play with her again. I don't know why she was so cross about it. And Adela isn't allowed out for the next month, except to go to school and then the maid has to take her to make sure she doesn't speak to us.' Lily smiled. 'We can talk in the playground, of course.'

'I haven't had my lecture yet,' said Pearl. 'Mama says we'll talk about it when I'm properly better but I don't think she'll punish me too much.'

'In the end,' said Lily, 'it all worked out quite well, didn't it? It made our mothers take notice of us and now they know how much they'd miss us if we weren't here.'

'Mmm,' said Pearl, 'but I'm still never going to run away again.'

26

July 1905

There had been a continual flow of summer visitors to the Spindrift Gallery all day. Edith's feet ached and she shifted from foot to foot while she wrapped one of Clarissa's sea-glass pendants in tissue paper. 'I hope your daughter likes it,' she said, handing it to the waiting purchaser with a smile.

After he'd gone, Edith locked up the display cabinet. Dora was chatting to a potential customer about one of Gilbert's stone carvings and two visitors were looking at a vast embroidered collage made by Mabel and Maude. The couple, a woman in a city-smart straw hat and silk frock and a man in a pale linen suit, seemed perfectly content to browse without assistance.

Edith took a feather duster from beneath the sales counter and went to tidy her display. The focal point of her exhibition was her canvas entitled *Children Flying Kites*. The painting was precious not only because it had been accepted for the Royal Academy's Summer Exhibition the previous year, along with *A Callybash Ride Down Rose Hill*, but because it was a constant reminder of that happy afternoon playing with her children.

After the terrible time when Pearl and Lily had

run away, Edith had taken a hard look at what was important in her life. Whilst she still had to earn her living, she'd made the decision to temper her artistic ambitions and spend more time with her children. They were growing up so fast, Pearl and Lily eleven by now, and as Pascal said, Edith would still be young enough to build her career after they'd gone out into the world.

As she dusted the canvas, she knocked it sideways. Stepping back to check she'd realigned it perfectly, she almost trod on the toes of the man in the linen suit.

'I'm so sorry!' she said.

'My fault entirely.' He gave a small bow. 'My wife and I have been bowled over by the exceptional quality of the work we've seen in this gallery. It's so unexpected in the wilds of the country.'

'We're a small community,' said Edith, 'but we're all dedicated to art in our various fields.'

He studied *Children Flying Kites*. 'Most unexpected,' he said. 'This wouldn't be out of place in the Royal Academy's Summer Exhibition.'

Edith laughed. 'In fact, this painting along with another one of mine, was exhibited at the Royal Academy last year.'

He peered at a small card tucked into the corner of the frame. 'Oh!' he said. 'So it isn't for sale?'

'My children and their friends are the ones flying their kites in the painting. I'm too fond of it to sell it.'

'What a pity!' He stepped closer to examine

283

the canvas at some length and then called to his wife. 'Lavinia, come and look at this!'

The visitor's wife came to stand beside him. 'Oh, isn't that charming? I can almost feel the sea breeze in my hair. Perhaps . . . '

'It's not for sale,' he said.

His wife made a *moue* of disappointment.

Taking a silver case from his pocket, he handed Edith his card. 'Should you change your mind, do let me know. Or perhaps you take commissions?'

'I certainly do . . . ' She glanced at the card. 'Mr Cavendish.'

Much later the Cavendishes left, promising to return before the end of their holiday to see the sketches Edith was going to prepare for them.

The gallery was empty now, except for Dora. 'We can close in half an hour,' said Edith.

'Was that another commission for you?' asked Dora.

'That depends on whether they like my sketches,' said Edith.

She glanced through the window to the courtyard where Pearl and Lily were minding Roland and Rose. Good had come out of that dreadful experience last year. Clarissa, Julian, Lily, Rose and Will had, after a difficult start, grown into a close family. As for Pearl, she still liked to be the centre of attention but was learning to consider the results of her actions. Unexpectedly, Benedict had done the same. He still doted on Roland but made more of an effort to show a fatherly interest in Pearl. That didn't extend to Jasper and the twins, though. Now that she didn't feel excluded, Pearl had become fond of her little half-brother, though still didn't care for Tamsyn.

'I doubt we'll have any more visitors today,' said Dora. 'Shall we count the takings?'

Edith was checking the sales ledger when Dora let out a sigh. 'Bother! Two more visitors,' she said. 'I was hoping to finish promptly today and help Ursula in the garden.'

'I'll deal with them, if you like,' murmured Edith, making the final entry.

'Oh!' said Dora.

'What is it?' Edith glanced up from the ledger. In the courtyard an expensively dressed woman, her pompadour hairstyle topped by a hat trimmed with bird of paradise feathers, had stopped to talk to the children. She twirled a lace-trimmed parasol and held the hand of a dark-haired girl. Edith frowned as something tugged at her memory.

'I don't believe it!' said Dora. 'Isn't that Pascal's sister Delphine? Whatever is *she* doing here?'

For a split second, Edith forgot to breathe. It had been thirteen years since, on their honeymoon, Benedict had betrayed her with Delphine. Edith hadn't thought she'd ever have to face her again. Or her daughter, Benedict's child.

'Edith?' said Dora.

'Pascal told me Delphine's husband died six months ago,' said Edith.

Dora made a face. 'I remember Édouard. Stout and rather full of himself, wasn't he? It

285

wasn't surprising Delphine was bored with him and flirted so disgracefully with Benedict.'

Rather more than flirted, thought Edith, though Dora, unlike Clarissa, hadn't realised the truth of it. 'Pascal never mentioned she was coming,' she said. 'And I suppose that must be her daughter, Gabrielle.' She sighed again. 'Oh, Lord, she's coming to see us!'

The bell on the gallery door jangled and Delphine swept in. She looked them both up and down. 'You 'ave not changed,' she said, 'except that you are older and still pay no attention to fashion.' She smoothed down her exquisitely embroidered skirt of arsenic-green silk and preened her dark hair.

Edith noticed that, although Delphine's tendency to plumpness had been firmly subjugated by an excellent corset beneath the expensive frills and lace of her bodice, her sulky pout had hardened into lines of discontent around her mouth. 'We have all grown older,' said Edith, allowing her gaze to rest on the other woman's jowls.

Delphine lifted her chin. 'I 'ave come to visit my brother and my Cousin Wilfred.'

'Is Pascal expecting you?' asked Edith. 'He went out with his sketchbook this morning.'

'Wilfred?'

'He'll be working in his studio, I expect.'

'Edith,' said Dora, 'shall I take Delphine to the drawing room for some tea, while you close the gallery?'

'A splendid idea,' said Edith, sending her a grateful smile. 'I'll fetch Wilfred.' Turning away, she finished writing in the ledger, holding her breath until the doorbell jangled as they left. She slammed the ledger shut, irritated that Delphine had seen her when her fingernails were ingrained with oil paint. If she'd had any notice of the visit, she'd have changed out of her faded skirt and plain cotton blouse, too. Edith turned the sign on the door to CLOSED and locked up.

Outside, Lily and Pearl were galloping around the courtyard on their hobbyhorses while Roland and Rose toddled after them, laughing so much they kept falling over.

'Mama,' said Pearl. 'That lady said she's Uncle Pascal's sister.'

Edith nodded. 'Her name is Madame Caron.' Roland ran towards her and gripped her skirt in his grubby little fists. She bent down to say hello to him. Laughing, he looked up at her, his eyes the same hazel as Pearl's and their father's.

'Papa gave me sixpence to mind Roland while he paints Tamsyn's portrait again,' said Pearl.

'And Mother promised to take me shopping for new shoes if I looked after Rose while she's working.'

'Why isn't Hannah keeping an eye on the little ones?' asked Edith.

'She's making strawberry jam with Mrs Rowe.'

'I've finished for today,' said Edith.

'Perhaps there'll be strawberry jam for tea,' said Pearl.

★ ★ ★

Later, Edith was sitting with the children in the dining room when she heard Pascal and Jasper's voices in the kitchen passage. She hurried to catch them.

'Did you two have a good day's sketching?' she asked.

Jasper's cheeks were rosy from the sun. 'We went to our favourite place near Port Gaverne. I'll need a new sketchbook soon, Mama,' he said. 'Uncle Pascal has been teaching me about perspective.'

'An essential skill for any artist,' she said.

Pascal tousled the boy's dark hair. 'And there is no doubt that this one will be an artist one day.'

Jasper smiled up at him, beaming at the compliment.

It was no wonder, thought Edith, that Benedict had little time for Jasper when his temperament was so similar to Pascal's, the man Benedict most loathed. She sighed. 'Go and wash your hands for tea, Jasper,' she said.

'Yes, Mama.' He hurried away.

'What is it, Edith?' murmured Pascal.

'You always know when something is troubling me, don't you?'

He caressed her cheek. 'Tell me.'

'Your sister and her daughter are with Wilfred in the drawing room.'

'Delphine? Here?' He pinched the bridge of his nose. '*Mon Dieu!* How could she come when she knows how angry I am with her?'

'It's insensitive of her,' murmured Edith, spirits plummeting even further. 'But you'd better go and see her.'

'I hope she will not make trouble,' muttered

Pascal as he hurried away.

Edith returned to the dining room to supervise the children. Benedict had joined them and was offering Roland the jam spoon to lick. She hesitated, wondering if she should tell him about Delphine, but Pearl pre-empted her.

'Papa,' she said. 'Uncle Pascal's sister and her daughter have come to visit. They're having tea with Uncle Wilfred.'

Benedict dropped the jam spoon. 'Delphine is here? Well, well! I'd better go and say hello.' He hefted Roland up onto his shoulders.

After he'd gone, the children left the table and Hannah took Rose off for her bath.

Edith hurried to tell Clarissa the latest news.

'Good God! Delphine's not staying at Spindrift, is she?'

'Not if I can help it.'

'Let's go and find out.' Clarissa linked her arm through Edith's and led her into the hall.

Tamsyn was lurking at the bottom of the stairs. 'Where's Roland?' she asked.

'Benedict has him in there,' said Edith. She glanced at the drawing-room door and they heard voices raised in discord emanating from inside.

Clarissa threw open the door and went straight in, followed by Edith.

The heated conversation stopped abruptly.

Pascal was standing looking out of the window, his back rigid, and Delphine, her cheeks flushed, sat with her arm around her daughter.

'Ah, Edith!' said Benedict, not quite looking at her.

289

At that moment, Delphine's daughter looked up and studied Edith with a clear direct gaze.

She caught her breath. Gabrielle's eyes were the exact same colour and shape as Pearl's. The same colour as Roland's eyes. And their father's.

'It seems,' said Benedict, measuring his words, 'that Delphine brings me the gift of . . . '

'Another daughter,' said Edith.

'*Six* children, Benedict?' said Clarissa. She glanced at Roland who was toddling around the room. 'My,' she said, 'you have been busy! Or are there still more little by-blows that you might have forgotten about, due to appear out of the woodwork?'

Benedict's jaw tensed but he ignored her. He stood up, legs planted apart and hands on his hips. 'I'm proud to own Gabrielle as my daughter,' he said, 'and that's an end to it. She's a pretty girl, isn't she?'

Tamsyn erupted into the room and stood before Benedict, mirroring his pose. 'Is it true?'

He turned his palms up and shrugged. 'We're all one big happy family here at Spindrift.'

'Benedict, you may fancy yourself as some powerful Eastern potentate with a harem of wives and concubines,' snapped Edith, her voice glacial, 'but the truth is very far from that. Your irresponsibility is breathtaking.'

'You oughta be ashamed of yourself, Benedict!' yelled Tamsyn.

'Now I am a widow, Benedict,' said Delphine, paying no heed to this outburst, 'and since you acknowledge Gabrielle is your daughter, there should be no difficulty when I demand you contribute to her upkeep.'

Edith's sudden outburst of laughter had a wild, sharp edge to it. 'You're a better woman than I, Delphine, if you can make Benedict do that. He's too lazy to work and hasn't yet supported his legitimate children, never mind any he's fathered out of wedlock. I am the one who largely funds his excesses. Even his mistress,' she glanced at Tamsyn, 'is obliged to continue her work as a barmaid to support her child.'

'For God's sake!' Benedict cracked his knuckles. 'I'll be damned if I'm going to stay here and listen to you harpies nagging me!' He strode across the room and slammed the door behind him so hard that flakes of plaster drifted to the floor.

The ensuing silence was profound but Edith's ears still rang with the echoes of discord.

'Papa?' Roland burst into tears, ran to the door and rattled the handle. Fat tears rolled down his cheeks and there was a note of panic in his voice. 'Papa?' he shrieked.

27

Tamsyn lay face down on the bed, sobbing. She let out a loud moan and Roland, busy pulling all her clothes out of the chest of drawers, went to investigate.

He climbed onto the bed and pulled her hair away from her face. 'Ma?'

Sniffing, she turned over and caught him in her arms. 'Whatever shall we do, my 'andsome?'

Solemnly, he touched the tear that rolled down her cheek.

Tamsyn couldn't put out of her mind the memory of how Benedict had run away like a coward when she, Edith and that Frenchwoman had confronted him. Edith had accused him of being lazy and not supporting his children and it was true. He'd told Tamsyn to carry on at the Golden Lion for the company but she was the one who had to pay Hannah to look in on Roland while she was working. She'd begun to wonder if he wanted her to work only so he could keep 'borrowing' her earnings to spend on beer and that Moroccan tobacco that made him so sleepy and lazy.

He'd bamfoozled her all along, lying about why his marriage to Edith had gone wrong, saying it was because she'd cheated on him with Pascal. He'd lied when he promised Tamsyn she would be the mistress of Spindrift House, in all but name. He'd lied when he'd said he loved her.

She'd heard he'd been seen drinking in the Dolphin with another woman. And Dora had told her he still loved Edith and that he'd only brought Tamsyn to live at Spindrift to make his wife jealous. It hurt Tamsyn to believe it but now she was painfully sure it was true.

The grandfather clock on the landing struck the hour and she sighed. It was time to wipe her tears and put Roland to bed so she could get off to work. Once he was down in his cot, she stroked his dark curls, watching him fall asleep. Nothing about her life with Benedict was how she'd thought it would be. The thing that made her most ashamed was the way she'd humiliated Edith. Despite that, she'd helped when Roland was born. She'd even given him some of Lucien's hand-me-downs. Without those, Tamsyn's son would be running about barefoot with his arse hanging out of the tatters in his breeches.

One thing was certain, though. Benedict was weak and he was never going to change. Just like Edith, his mistress was going to have to look out for herself and her child. But how could she? She began to weep again, realising she was trapped in this Godforsaken house with nowhere else to go. She had no friends and everyone at Spindrift wanted her gone.

★ ★ ★

The Golden Lion was heaving with summer visitors that evening and Tamsyn's head ached as she fetched and carried. The holidaymakers gave

293

good tips, though, so it paid to pretend to be cheerful and friendly. Naturally she wouldn't tell Benedict about these tips, neither. She had to build up a rainy day fund.

There was a visitor sitting on his own at the corner table who'd been there for the past five evenings. He watched her all the time, though he pretended not to, and when she took him his beer, he made excuses to chat. She didn't mind. He was youngish with mid-brown hair and quite nice-looking, sort of solid and comfortable.

She sauntered over to him to collect his empty glass. 'Another one?'

He nodded. 'And have one for yourself.'

Polite and generous. 'You're not from these parts then?' she said.

'London.'

'That explains the accent and the smart suit.' She smiled, allowing her gaze to linger on him until the tips of his ears turned pink.

She brought him another glass of beer and leaned against the corner of his table. 'I've never bin upcountry to London,' she said. 'Is it true the streets are paved with gold?'

He laughed, shaking his head. 'Sadly, not.'

'What a shame that is! Still fancy a visit there, though. P'raps I'd see the King out and about in his fancy carriage?'

'You might.' The man's eyes twinkled. They were a silvery grey, like dawn light on the sea. 'Or you might visit a music hall and walk in Hyde Park.'

'The shops are what I yearn to see.'

'Most ladies like the shops. I own a draper's

shop in Camberwell. We sell high-class fabrics, haberdashery and hats.'

'We?' She wondered if he was married, not that it made any difference to her, of course.

'I inherited the shop from my father but Mother assists me with the customers.'

Tamsyn was impressed. He was a man of substance and not full of flim-flam, like Benedict. Out of the corner of her eye she saw Old Curnow beckoning to her from behind the crowded bar.

'I don't know anyone here and it's pleasant to chat,' the customer said. 'Perhaps I could tell you more about London after you finish your shift?'

She examined her fingernails. 'What's your name?' It felt important to her that he didn't think she was the kind of girl who might walk out with just any man.

'Albert Fisher.' His forehead furrowed. 'Look, my intentions are perfectly honourable.'

Mr Curnow yelled at her. 'Get yourself over here, Tamsyn! Customers waiting!'

'Tamsyn.' Mr Fisher smiled. 'A pretty name.'

He seemed decent and she wasn't in any hurry to get back to continue her quarrel with Benedict. 'All right, then,' she said. 'I'll meet you by the harbour wall after closing time. Better go, Old Curnow's getting teasy.'

Later on, she was wiping glasses when she glanced up to see the Frenchwoman and her girl sidling through the bar to the private dining room. Earlier, when she'd had that fight with Benedict, Tamsyn hadn't really looked at the girl. It gave her quite a turn to see that she was the dead spit of Pearl, except older and her dark hair was straight, not curly. No chance then that the Frenchwoman was lying about Benedict being the girl's dad.

'Are they staying here?' she asked the landlord.

He nodded. 'Summer blow-ins. Foreigners, too. They're late for dinner. You can tell them the stargazy pie's all gone but there's still some mutton stew.'

Tamsyn pursed her lips. 'Can't you see to them?'

'What do I pay 'ee for, Tamsyn Pengelly? Get 'ee in there now!'

Muttering under her breath, she made her way through the throng to the private dining room.

Benedict's French tart was chattering away to her daughter and didn't notice Tamsyn straight away. Or perhaps she only pretended not to see her.

After a moment, Tamsyn tapped her foot and said, 'There's mutton stew for your dinner.'

'What is this mutton stew?'

'Sheep stew,' said Tamsyn.

Delphine pulled a face. 'Is there another choice?'

'No.'

Delphine spoke in her own tongue to the girl and then nodded. Tamsyn turned to leave but the other woman caught her sleeve. 'Do not look at me as if I am nothing! Benedict was mine first.'

'Benedict don't belong to no one but his self.' Tamsyn pulled her sleeve free from the other woman's grasping fingers. Despite herself, she said, 'If he belongs to anyone, it's Edith.'

Delphine raised her finely plucked eyebrows. 'I do not understand why you live together in one house. In your place, I would 'ave made her leave.'

Tamsyn glared at her. 'You didn't manage to get rid of her when you had Benedict in your bed.'

'I was married then.' Delphine pouted. 'Now I am a widow, I came seeking the so 'andsome and charming Benedict I gave my heart to. I am shocked to find him older and fatter and his complexion puffy from drinking. And what of 'is artistic talent? *Pouf!* It is gone!' She shrugged. '*Tant pis.* So much the worse. Now we 'ave a different situation.'

'We?'

'But of course! You and I must work together.' Delphine narrowed her eyes. 'Or 'ave you already made safe your son's future?'

'What do you mean?'

'Do you want Edith's children to 'ave all Benedict's money when he dies?'

Tamsyn plucked at her apron. She'd never thought about what'd happen if Benedict weren't around. She swallowed back a sudden wave of nausea. 'He's too young to die.'

'My 'usband, he died young,' said Delphine. 'Fortunately, I 'ad already made certain he would leave me and Gabrielle his money.'

'Did he know she wasn't his child?'

Delphine shrugged again. 'He never asked. What is Benedict's situation? Does he 'ave money?'

297

Tamsyn shook her head. 'There's the house but Edith and the community own nearly half of it. They pay him rent but I've never seen any of it. He disappears for a week or so sometimes and comes back with new clothes and cases of wine or some such. He likes the horses, too.'

'You must stop 'im, or he will leave nothing for the children.'

'It ain't that easy! Why don't *you* try stopping him?' Tamsyn turned on her heel and hurried to the kitchen, muttering to herself, 'Bleddy interfering Frenchwoman!'

Ten minutes later, she banged down two plates of congealing stew and potatoes onto the table in front of Delphine and her daughter. The girl looked up at her with a hard stare, as if weighing her up and finding her wanting.

Tamsyn whisked herself away before either of them rubbed her up the wrong way again and she gave them a slap to teach them a lesson.

She was kept busy behind the bar for the rest of the evening. That Hugh Penrose was in again, looking down in the mouth and drinking steadily. For all the ale she brought him, he never once left her a tip. She didn't see the Frenchies leave the dining room but, all the time she was working, kept thinking about what Delphine had said. She *must* make a plan for the future.

★　★　★

The following morning, Roland woke Tamsyn by rattling the bars of his cot and shouting, 'Ma! Get up, Ma!'

Benedict sighed and pulled the covers over his head.

Tamsyn put her fingers to her lips and gave Roland a stern look. 'Shush!'

He smiled at this new game and yelled, 'Shush, shush!'

Reluctantly, Tamsyn climbed out of bed and lifted him from his cot. 'You can come into bed with me, you little heller,' she murmured, 'but you'd better be quiet or your pa will tan your backside.'

Roland snuggled down into Tamsyn's arms, whispering and patting her face while she pretended to sleep.

Tamsyn didn't want to open her eyes and face the day. She thought back to the previous night when she'd met Albert Fisher after closing time. He'd behaved like a perfect gent. When he'd asked her where she lived, she hadn't the heart to tell him about Benedict and Roland but waved her hand vaguely at the village and said she lodged with her aunt, then changed the subject by asking him about his shop, or his 'little emporium', as he called it.

'One wall is lined with glass-fronted mahogany drawers filled with fancy ribbons in a rainbow of colours,' he'd said. 'We stock every kind of haberdashery imaginable — silk handkerchiefs, ladies' petticoats . . . ' he'd actually blushed when he'd said that, making Tamsyn giggle ' . . . and silk and woollen hosiery. Another wall displays bolts of cloth, from plain and embellished muslins to special silk damasks. There's a large mahogany counter and several chairs for the customers.' He'd laughed. 'Often, the ladies arrange to meet their friends and have a good old chinwag while they do their shopping.'

He'd spoken kindly of his ma, too. 'A God-fearing Methodist,' he'd said, 'but kind and hard-working.'

Tamsyn liked the way Albert was so enthusiastic about his shop and had promised to meet him again the next evening to hear more about his plans for expanding the business. It was interesting and she imagined his shop to be like an Aladdin's cave, full of rich materials in a rainbow of colours, twinkling pearl buttons and rolls and rolls of silk ribbon. She couldn't help but compare Albert's industry to Benedict's laziness. He rarely settled to anything and never made plans beyond his next beer or smoke. The only thing in Benedict's favour was that he loved Roland. He'd been a rotten father to the rest of his children even though he was fond of Pearl. He didn't care at all for Jasper, who was far too serious for his liking. And the twins, well, they didn't need anyone but themselves.

Over the past months, she'd had sleepless nights thinking about what might happen if Benedict found another woman. She'd have to leave Spindrift and her meagre earnings wouldn't be enough to support her and Roland if she had to rent a room. It wasn't as if she could find a husband, either, not with Roland hanging onto her skirts. And now Delphine had opened her eyes to the uncertainty of Roland's future if his father should die. However angry it made Benedict, she was going to have to make him write a will and include something for Roland. Meanwhile, she must save every penny she could for her rainy day fund.

28

Dora was taking a bottle of lemonade to the kitchen garden to share with Ursula when she met Edith coming through the gate with a trug full of beans. 'You look as if you've lost a shilling and found a sixpence,' she said when she saw her friend's expression.

'Delphine is returning to France,' said Edith, 'but she's leaving Gabrielle at Spindrift for the rest of the summer.'

Dora stared her friend. 'But why?'

Edith scuffed her toe through the gravel on the path. 'She's persuaded Benedict to write a will, leaving everything to his children, both legitimate and illegitimate.'

'She hasn't!'

Edith nodded, her expression tightly controlled. 'Delphine and Tamsyn ganged up on him, insisting that all his children should have an equal share. You missed the screaming match going on in the sitting room.' A bitter smile flickered across her lips. 'I'm afraid I hung around in the hall and eavesdropped.'

'I'd have done the same.'

'Dear Dora! You're always so loyal.'

Heat rose up Dora's throat and warmed her cheeks. 'Of course I am.' She shook her head in disbelief. 'But this! It makes me so angry. I'd like to batter that smug smile off Delphine's fat face. As for Benedict . . . words fail me. I can hardly believe *anyone* could be so wicked and dishonourable as to commit adultery on their *honeymoon*. And as if the adultery wasn't bad enough, father an illegitimate child as a result.' Sighing, she shook her head. 'He's not fit for decent society.'

Edith paled and looked away, her chin trembling.

Dora reached out to squeeze her hand. 'I knew you were upset because Delphine flirted with Benedict back then. I remember how unhappy you were after that terrible quarrel you had, but I never imagined he'd gone that far.'

'It's all in the past,' said Edith, her voice quivering. 'Benedict has agreed to Delphine's suggestion that Gabrielle shall stay here until the end of the summer to improve her English.'

'To learn English, my elbow!' said Dora. 'I'll bet it's so the girl can keep her foot firmly in the door and watch over her future inheritance.'

'Quite possibly,' said Edith. 'But Pascal has promised to keep an eye on her and he and Wilfred will help her with her English, too.'

'But where will she sleep? She can't stay alone at the Golden Lion.'

'Benedict persuaded Pearl and Nell to share their room with her. There's Lily's old bed there so I suppose it makes practical sense.'

'Did Pascal know his niece was Benedict's daughter?' asked Dora.

'Delphine wrote and told him three years ago. He was very distressed and angry about it.' Edith sighed. 'I'd better take the beans to Mrs Rowe. I've been distracted by this latest upset but I have those sketches to finish for the Cavendishes. I can't afford to miss the opportunity of a good commission.'

'We'll meet at supper, then.'

Edith nodded and set off to the house.

Dora ambled into the walled garden and found Gilbert watering the rows of beans. He wiped his forehead on his cuff. 'Warm, isn't it? If you're looking for Ursula, she was thinning the parsley seedlings in the herb garden last time I saw her.'

Dora had dreaded the time when Ursula would move on after she'd finished writing *A Year in the Potager*. The thought of her leaving had made Dora feel quite sick, but then she'd gone away for a few days on a mysterious errand to London. When she returned, she caught Dora in a bear hug and danced her around the drawing room. Laughing, she'd said, 'Mr Pettigrew has agreed to publish my new book, *The Illustrated Herb Garden*. And you're to do the illustrations, if you'd like.'

Dora had liked. She was glad of the work but, most of all, the new book meant Ursula would stay at Spindrift for another year.

Ursula was on her hands and knees and so intent on her task that she didn't see Dora approaching until her shadow fell across the ground. She looked up and smiled. 'There you are, my dear! Look how beautifully our parsley seedlings are coming along.'

'I brought some lemonade,' said Dora. She pinched the leaves of a mint plant to release the fresh, sharp scent, and held her fingers to her nose. 'Heavenly!' she said. 'In fact, this garden is my idea of how Heaven should be.'

They sat on the wrought-iron bench to drink the lemonade. The herb garden had been laid out in one corner of the *potager* and Gilbert had made them a sundial to stand at the intersection of the brick paths that formed the herb beds. Bees hummed on the rosemary and purple-headed chives.

It had been a revelation to Dora how many different varieties of herbs there were and she loved their pungent perfumes. Growing up in a small terraced house in London, the ground in the shady back yard was too sour for any plants to flourish. Her ma had come home from the market sometimes with a small bunch of parsley but, if she'd had even a quarter of the herbs grown in this small patch, the plain fare of Dora's childhood would have been far more appetising.

'Poor Edith,' said Dora. She sipped from the lemonade bottle and then passed it to Ursula. 'As if it wasn't enough that another of Benedict's by-blows has come to light, Delphine has foisted her girl on us for the summer.' She explained how it had come about.

Ursula shuddered. 'I could never marry and be subject to such a man's selfishness. Still, we must remember that none of this is the child's fault. She's recently lost the man she thought was her father and now, to be left with strangers when she speaks little of the language, must be difficult for her.'

Dora twiddled a lock of hair around her finger

305

while she thought about that. 'I was so incensed on Edith's behalf that I forgot about Gabrielle's feelings.' She let her gaze drift over the garden and wondered how she might make the next few weeks easier for the girl.

'Gardening is a peaceful pursuit and allows my mind to wander,' said Ursula, 'and I was thinking how much Lucien and Nell enjoy pottering in the garden with us. Nell is a quiet little girl but she takes such pleasure in making things grow and Lucien, watching the butterflies on the buddleia bush for hours, asked me what other plants we could grow to encourage butterflies and bees.'

'He's always been fascinated by insects and animals,' said Dora.

'I had the most marvellous idea,' said Ursula, her pale eyes alight with enthusiasm. 'Why don't we write a book on gardening for children? You could illustrate it with piskies climbing up the delphiniums and fairies peeking out from behind the roses. Perhaps there could be a hidden fairy on every page and directions on how to grow easy flowers like nasturtiums and sunflowers?'

'And sweet peas and marigolds,' said Dora. 'There might be garden birds and insects in the illustrations, too.' She laughed and hugged her friend. 'It's a wonderful idea and combines the very best of our talents!'

'We need to finish *The Illustrated Herb Garden* first,' said Ursula, 'but I thought you might want to think about a couple of sample illustrations. If I write an introduction and the first chapter, then we could go and see Mr

Pettigrew together. We might spend a few days looking at the sights in London and take in a matinee performance, perhaps?'

'It would be a little holiday!' said Dora. And that would be lovely but, best of all, writing another book together would ensure that Ursula would remain at Spindrift for yet another year.

29

May 1906

Edith and Pascal lay naked on the bed in Woodland Cottage, foreheads touching and fingers interlaced while their racing heartbeats slowed.

Pascal's breath was warm on Edith's cheek and he smiled as she kissed his mouth.

'*Mon amour*,' he murmured.

Lazily, Edith pulled the sheet over their shoulders. 'Whatever would we do without Woodland Cottage?' she said. 'But when the children are grown, we shall live as man and wife. We'll spend our days painting and our nights in each other's arms.'

'And meanwhile,' said Pascal, 'we have our first exhibition together to prepare for.'

The previous summer, Mr and Mrs Cavendish had commissioned Edith to paint a view of Port Isaac harbour. One of their acquaintances, a Mr Walworth, had seen the painting in their dining room. Upon hearing about the Spindrift Gallery, he'd come to visit the following spring and been impressed by what he saw. To Edith and Pascal's great delight, he'd told them he had a gallery in Knightsbridge and that he would like to hold a joint exhibition of their work in the autumn.

Pascal rolled onto his back and folded his

hands behind his head. 'I shall fulfil my obligation to paint Cornish seascapes for Mr Walworth, but afterwards I intend to try something more experimental.'

'I thought you loved painting seascapes?' said Edith.

'I do but they have become too easy for me. Painting them no longer makes me feel as if a fire burns within me. I need the excitement of a new challenge.'

Edith frowned, wondering if she had become too complacent about her own work. She'd developed her style and always strived to make each of her paintings better than the last but she hadn't attempted anything experimental for a while.

'Do you remember when we first met in Provence,' said Pascal, 'how my paintings were vivid with colour and the canvases were born out of the sun-scorched landscape?'

'There was one in particular that I loved,' said Edith. 'An explosion of colour. It depicted a gnarled olive tree silhouetted against a field of yellow wheat under a fiery sun. A peasant girl trudged across in the near distance and the brooding sky above was a deep purplish colour, as if there was going to be a flash of lightning and a crack of thunder at any moment.'

'If I had never left Provence, perhaps I might have developed that strong use of colour,' said Pascal. 'Cornwall has a softer palette and that guided me in a different direction.'

'And it has proved successful.'

'When I visited Paris three years ago, I was

309

uplifted by what I saw in the ateliers.' Pascal's voice was alive with enthusiasm. 'Colour and more colour! It was so bright sometimes it hurt my eyes but, used in that way, colour becomes an emotional force. The artists were using the pigment to express themselves, rather than concentrating on perfect form.'

'I wonder if the British public will be open-minded and willing to buy such unconventional work?'

Pascal shrugged. 'This idea rekindles the fire within me and I am driven to experiment, even if I must still earn my bread and butter with Cornish seascapes.'

'You must go where your heart leads you,' said Edith.

Pascal turned to face her again, pulled back the sheet and ran his hands down her flanks. '*You* are where my heart leads me. And when I see you naked like this, you take my breath away. I find it astonishing you have borne four children.' He sighed. 'My only regret is that none of them are mine.'

The warmth of their lovemaking drained from Edith's body, sending a shiver down her spine. She had a sudden, desperate need to tell Pascal that Jasper was his son but he'd been so unyielding in his contempt for Delphine's deceit that she feared his reaction to her own.

And then there had been Dora's disgust with Benedict when it came to light the previous summer that Gabrielle was his daughter. '*I can hardly believe anyone could be so wicked and dishonourable as to commit adultery on their* honeymoon,' she'd said. '*And, as if adultery wasn't bad enough, there was a child.*'

Edith had always told herself it was imperative to keep her secret in case Benedict took the children from her. In her innermost heart, though, she admitted there was another reason. Shame and wretchedness engulfed her at the thought of her friends' disdain if they learned of her deception. She couldn't begin to imagine how Delphine, despite being a widow, had been brazen enough to confess, not only to her adultery but also an illegitimate child, with no apparent qualms. How was it that she felt no shame?

'Edith?' Pascal cupped her chin with his palms. 'I'm sorry, I shouldn't have said that. You know I love you and your children without reservation. Nothing will change that. I had the choice once to marry another woman and perhaps have children with her, but I could not do it. She wasn't you.'

Tell him! The words reverberated through Edith's mind. But her courage failed her and the moment passed. Unable to meet his eyes, she turned her head to kiss his palm. 'You're too good for me,' she murmured. Heavy-hearted, she stepped out of bed and began to dress.

★ ★ ★

The kitchen was warm and smelled comfortingly of vanilla as Dora sipped a cup of tea and enjoyed the peace and quiet. It was Jasper's birthday. Although he was thirteen now, his face

311

had still lit up when she'd offered to make him a cake.

Mrs Rowe pottered about by the stove, adding vegetables and seasoning to the stew.

Dora sighed contentedly to herself as she spread raspberry jam onto two of the layers of sponge cake.

The kitchen door burst open and Tamsyn entered with Roland trailing behind her. 'I smell cake,' she said. 'Can we have some?'

'It's for Master Jasper's birthday,' said Mrs Rowe, wiping her hands on her apron. 'There's fresh bread in the larder, if you're hungry.'

Tamsyn sighed heavily and rolled her eyes to the ceiling as she went to fetch the bread.

Dora noticed a letter fall out of Tamsyn's pocket and drift to the floor. She picked it up and saw it was postmarked from London. The envelope had already been opened and a corner of the letter protruded from it. Her fingers twitched but she stopped herself from sneaking a look at the contents. Curious as to why anyone from London should write to Tamsyn, she reluctantly put it on the table. On several mornings she'd found Tamsyn loitering in the hall at the time the postman was due. With any luck, she might have applied for a housemaid's position in London, though how she thought she'd get a reference, Dora couldn't imagine.

Roland climbed up onto a chair and watched Dora intently while she sandwiched the layers of cake together. He reached out to pick up some crumbs and she frowned at him. 'Don't touch!' she said. 'Your hands are grubby.'

Tamsyn clattered about fetching the bread-board, dropping the knife and slamming the dresser drawers.

Dora sighed at the shattering of her peace and collected butter and sugar from the pantry to make the icing. When she returned, Tamsyn was frowning at her, the letter in her hand.

'Did you put this on the table?' Her eyes were accusing.

'I saw it fall out of your pocket.'

'You had no right to touch my letter!'

'Oh, I do beg your pardon,' said Dora, her voice dripping with sarcasm. 'Next time I'll tread it underfoot.' She was distracted from Tamsyn's hostile stare because Roland dipped his little hand inside the jam jar and then licked his fingers. 'Hey!' she shouted.

He stuck his tongue out at her and rammed his fist back into the jar.

'Don't do that, you naughty boy!'

He snatched his hand out of the jar and it flew onto the floor and smashed into smithereens. Alarmed, he burst into tears.

'For Heaven's sake, Tamsyn!' said Dora. 'Can't you keep an eye on your child for one minute?'

'Don't you get teasy with me!' snapped Tamsyn, her mouth full of bread.

'Roland has filthy fingernails and he had them in the pot of jam.'

'Well, that don't matter no more 'cos it's broke now.' She turned her back on Dora and hunkered down before Roland. 'Stop your squalling or I'll give you a slap! Can't hear myself think.'

Roland howled and Tamsyn slapped his legs. Shrieking, he shrank away from her.

Tamsyn grabbed his arm and shook him. 'I said, stop it, you little heller, or you'll get another one!'

Roland cowered and wrapped his arms over his head. 'Don't hit me again, Ma!'

Dora gasped when Tamsyn raised her hand. 'What kind of mother are you? It's your fault he's being brought up to behave like a little savage.'

Tamsyn whirled around and thrust her face into Dora's. 'Don't you tell me how to raise my child! You don't know what it's like to be a mother, nor never likely to. Dried up old spinster!' She yanked at Roland's arm and dragged him out of the kitchen.

Shaking, Dora held her breath, listening to the child's shrieks fade into the distance.

Mrs Rowe stood stock-still before the range, still grasping the oven cloth against her narrow chest. She glanced at Dora and then turned away to lift the soup, bubbling and spitting, off the heat.

Dora, muttering under her breath, went to the cupboard and fetched the broom to clear up the broken glass and spattered jam.

'Let me do that,' said Mrs Rowe.

'I've nearly finished,' said Dora, tight-lipped.

Mrs Rowe hesitated, her eyes anxious, and then turned away.

Silently, Dora mixed the butter cream and iced the cake.

★ ★ ★

314

Dora spent the afternoon sitting at the garden table, working on an illustration for *Flower Gardening for Girls and Boys*, while Ursula sat opposite her, writing a chapter on sowing seeds. Birdsong, the happy cries of the children playing in the rhododendrons and the regular ebb and flow of the sea, aided concentration.

Dora rinsed her paintbrush in the pot of water at her side and glanced at Ursula. Absorbed in her writing, her friend had pushed her sleeves up to enjoy the warm touch of May sunshine on her forearms. Her springy curls had escaped from their confining hairpins and were backlit by the sun into a blonde halo.

A wave of pure happiness washed over Dora and she sighed contentedly.

Ursula looked up at her, tiny creases forming beside her pale eyes when she smiled. 'What are you thinking?'

'About how happy I am.'

Ursula rested her hand on Dora's wrist. 'What more could we wish for? The sea, the sun, our work and good friends. Especially good friends.' Her thumb described tiny circles around the delicate skin on the inside of Dora's wrist.

Her light touch made Dora's skin tingle. She dropped her gaze and stared down at Ursula's strong and capable hand. Her fingernails were cut short for gardening but had perfect white half-moons.

'Dora?' Ursula's voice was soft.

There was a slight shifting feeling inside Dora's chest, a pang of . . . She didn't know what it was she felt. Something pleasurable but at the same time uncomfortable.

A loud halloo came from the French windows and Dora saw Wilfred waving at them. 'Wilfred is back from Gloucestershire, then,' she said. Slightly against his better judgement, he'd accepted a commission to decorate a Georgian manor house owned by a man who'd made his fortune manufacturing pickled onions.

'I'll go and say hello,' said Dora. She collected up her painting equipment and set off for the house.

As she went through the French doors, she glanced over her shoulder and smiled when she saw Ursula was still watching her.

30

The older children were considered grown up enough to dine with the adults now and, since it was Jasper's birthday, Edith invited him to sit at the head of the table for the evening.

'I can remember the day you were born as clearly as if it were yesterday,' said Dora. 'I sat by your mama's bedside and saw you even before she did. A big, lusty baby, you were. You squinted suspiciously at us both as if you didn't much like what you saw.'

'I'm sure I didn't do that,' said Jasper, a flush of embarrassment creeping up his cheeks.

Pascal picked up his glass. 'A birthday toast to Jasper!'

The assembled company raised their glasses and then Hannah served the soup.

'Wilfred,' said Gilbert, 'tell us about your stay in Gloucestershire. How was the manor house?'

'My dears,' he said, 'you have no conception of the utter ghastliness of the place when I arrived. Mr Bagshawe, the Onion Pickler, had inherited a houseful of furniture from his dear departed mama and refused, simply refused, to throw the lot on the bonfire. Every wall was painted ox-blood red or waiting-room green, the furniture was overstuffed to the point of corpulence, the piano legs draped with red velvet to avoid over-stimulating the gentlemen's imaginations and every surface cluttered with dusty

317

ferns and collections of *objets d'art* in questionable taste.' He grimaced and lowered his voice. 'Can you imagine? Some had been prizes from a hoopla stall in a fairground!'

Augustus widened his eyes in mock horror. 'How utterly sickening!' he said.

'So did you persuade him to change his mind about his mother's furniture?' asked Dora.

Wilfred's eyes gleamed with suppressed mirth. 'I enlisted Mrs Bagshawe's aid. I flirted with her quite *outrageously*.' He glanced at Augustus, who smiled and rolled his eyes. 'I suggested we made a start by making a clean sweep in her bedroom since her husband could find no fault with that. I began by emptying her wardrobe and making her give most of the dreadful contents to her maid. Then I took her to the dressmaker and selected garments to flatter her figure. She really looked quite presentable by the time we'd dressed her hair more fashionably.'

'I don't see how that led to redecorating the house,' said Dora.

'Well, by that time, Fanny Bagshawe was eating out of my hand,' said Wilfred. 'So she gave me absolute free rein to decorate her boudoir. I concealed the hideous mustard walls beneath a pretty paper patterned with sweet peas climbing over a beribboned trellis. I confiscated the vulgar red and blue Persian carpet, gave it to the cook and replaced it with a new rug in sugared almond pastels.'

'That does sound rather lovely,' said Clarissa.

'It was.' Wilfred's expression was smug.

'I want to make houses look pretty and elegant

318

when I'm grown up,' said Lily.

'Then I shall teach you, my sweet.' Wilfred patted her flaxen head and resumed his story. 'Fanny was so entranced she refused to allow her husband into her boudoir, or her bed, until he gave permission for me to make improvements of my choice throughout the house.'

Dora frowned. 'Hush,' she whispered, glancing at Lily and Pearl, 'the children!' Ursula, she noticed, was trying not to laugh at Wilfred's scandalous comment.

'Suffice it to say,' he continued, 'in the end, Mr Bagshawe was as delighted with his refurbished house as he was with his refurbished wife.'

'You always were marvellously persuasive,' said Augustus, stroking his auburn moustache.

Wilfred's lips curved in a smile as he gave his friend a sideways glance. 'Anyway, that's enough about me,' he said. 'Tell me, Jasper, are you having a good birthday?'

He nodded his head vigorously. 'I had a whole day out with Uncle Pascal. We went to Port Gaverne with a picnic. I used the folding easel from Mama and the set of oil paints.' His eyes glowed with enthusiasm. 'They're the best birthday presents I've ever had.'

'We thought you'd appreciate them,' said Maude.

'And you've inherited your mother's talent,' said Mabel.

'Uncle Pascal is an *excellent* teacher.' Jasper smiled at him with what Dora could only describe as hero worship.

319

'In Africa,' said Gilbert, 'they say it takes a whole village to raise a child. Here we have an artists' community influencing seven children,' he shrugged, 'eight if you include Roland, and it will be interesting to see how many turn out to be professional artists.'

'I've wanted that for as long as I can remember,' said Jasper. He nodded at his younger brother. 'And Lucien is excellent at drawing, too.' He smiled. 'As long as it's an insect, a bird or an animal.'

'I like to see a creature's details,' said Lucien. 'If you look at a fly or a caterpillar with a magnifying glass, they're very beautiful.'

'I don't want to spend every day standing in front of an easel,' said Pearl. 'But I might like to write stories, like Auntie Dora does.'

'But Nell', said Ursula thoughtfully, 'has a gift for making things grow. She might be a gardener.'

'It's the most exciting thing ever, watching a seed sprout and flower,' said Nell. Her cheeks flushed pink at being singled out and she hid her embarrassment by twisting her plait around her finger.

'And Will is learning from Julian how to take excellent photographs,' said Clarissa.

He shot his stepmother a shy smile.

'It won't be long,' said Gilbert, 'before we'll have to make additional display space in the Spindrift Gallery for the talented younger members of our community.'

Jasper's eyes widened with delight at the suggestion.

After the ceremony of the birthday cake, Hannah came to clear the dishes. Edith, Pascal, Clarissa and Julian went down to the cove with the children for a game of rounders before it grew dark. Wilfred and Augustus retired to the drawing room with coffee.

Dora and Ursula opted to stay behind to water the vegetable garden. When they entered the courtyard to take the short cut to the walled garden, they saw Tamsyn with her hands on her hips, arguing with Benedict. Roland was sitting on the dusty cobbles watching his parents with wide eyes.

Dora sighed. 'Tamsyn was in a nasty mood this morning. She was dreadfully rude to me.'

'Perhaps she's lonely?' said Ursula. 'She's entirely out of place here at Spindrift.'

'That's hardly surprising if you remember how she weaselled her way in. And for her to remain here with her child and continue flaunting herself as Benedict's mistress is unforgivable. Poor Edith!'

'Benedict is as much to blame for the situation as Tamsyn.'

'Benedict is to blame for a lot of things,' said Dora. 'He hasn't even wished his own son a happy birthday.'

On the other side of the courtyard, Tamsyn suddenly flew at him and battered at his chest with her fists. 'You lying bastard!' she shrieked. 'Don't you dare see her again or . . .'

Benedict held her at arm's length and laughed in her face. 'Or you'll what?'

Roland wailed, 'Stop it, Ma!'

'He shouldn't have to see his parents fighting,' said Dora.

Ursula sighed. 'But they won't thank us if we interfere and it might make it worse for the boy. Shall we retreat?'

But before they could leave, Tamsyn saw them. 'What you looking at, you pair of old witches?' she yelled.

Dora tensed and angry heat pulsed through her body.

Ursula gripped her arm. 'Don't!' she said.

Dora fumed as they walked arm-in-arm the long way round to the walled garden. 'If Benedict is sniffing around another woman, why doesn't Tamsyn just go away!' she burst out.

'Perhaps she has no financial option but to stay,' said Ursula. 'Come now, my dear, don't let her have the satisfaction of upsetting you. We shall water the garden and find peace in nurturing our seedlings.'

Dora sighed heavily. 'You're right, of course. But it hurts me because I've seen Edith suffer for so long at Benedict's hands.'

'Perhaps he has less power to hurt her now? She no longer loves him and, perhaps, her friendship with Pascal compensates her for . . .'

'Edith would *never* do anything immoral with Pascal,' said Dora.

Ursula was silent for a moment and then said, 'You have loved Edith for many years.'

'Of course I love her!' snapped Dora. 'She's been my best friend since we were at the Slade together.'

'But if she cares for Pascal, does she not

deserve some happiness?'

Dora tightened her lips. 'Should she have any impure thoughts, she buries them in her love for her children and her work.'

'Perhaps,' murmured Ursula. She pushed open the door to the walled garden and they went inside.

The early-evening sun slanted over the walls, rendering the bricks a glowing russet. The plants and seedlings grew neatly in regimented rows, giving a sense of tranquil order.

'I love the garden in the early summer,' said Ursula. 'Everything is so tidy and controlled. Later in the year our little seedlings will grow exuberantly, reaching for the sun until they flop over, stretch out their tendrils and finally go to seed. A metaphor to remind us to grasp at whatever chances life offers, I always think.'

Still agitated by their recent discussion of things she didn't want to think about, Dora went to fill her watering can and then walked slowly up and down the rows. After a while, the tranquillity and the gently repetitive exercise had cast its usual spell over her and her thoughts were serene again. She glanced at Ursula, thinning out the lettuces at the other end of the row, and bit her lip, hoping she hadn't upset her.

The sun was sinking towards the horizon when Dora went to put her watering can away in the potting shed. She saw Ursula ambling towards her and regretted being so sharp with her earlier. The thought of any coolness between them was unbearable. Of course, she'd always value Edith's friendship but the closeness she had with Ursula had given her life new meaning. She knew, without question, that she really mattered to Ursula.

'A peace offering,' said Ursula. 'I've brought you the first sweet peas of the year.' She held out a small bunch of exquisitely scented blooms.

Dora lifted them to her nose and inhaled their sweet perfume. 'So very beautiful,' she said.

'Yes,' said Ursula.

Dora glanced up from the flowers and saw her friend's gaze was fixed upon her. Ursula's turquoise blue eyes were so light it was as if Dora was looking into a clear stream. So mesmerised was she that she didn't move when Ursula caressed her cheek.

'My dearest Dora.' She leaned forward and pressed a soft and lingering kiss on Dora's mouth.

Still frozen to the spot, Dora experienced a sudden twinge deep within her. A tremor ran down her legs and, light-headed for a moment, her eyes closed and she swayed towards her friend. There was a rushing noise in her ears. When Ursula's mouth moved against hers, she involuntarily parted her lips.

And then Ursula's arms were around her and Dora was clinging to her, quivering with pleasure.

'My dearest,' whispered Ursula, 'I've waited so long to hold you like this. I knew from the first day we met that we were meant for each other.'

Dora's eyes were still tightly closed. She couldn't think, didn't want to think, for the pounding of her heart.

And then came a voice behind them. 'Ho-ho! I always knew there was something unnatural about you two!'

Dora's eyes snapped open.

Tamsyn, her cheeks flushed with prurient glee, stood nearby.

Dora let out a cry of horror and stepped back.

Tamsyn pointed a finger at her. 'Now I know what you really are, you sanctimonious bitch! And don't think that once I've found out your nasty little secret, I won't tell everyone how you've been carrying on all these years.'

'I haven't,' stammered Dora. 'We never . . . '

'Yes, you did! I *saw* you so don't try lying your way out of it.'

'Tamsyn,' said Ursula, 'you don't understand.'

'Oh, yes, I do. And now you can both suffer for it as much as you've made me suffer.' Tamsyn gave a harsh bark of laughter. 'How you had the bare-faced cheek, Dora Cox, to be nasty to me with your holier-than-thou accusations when you've been doing *that* with a woman beats me. You shouldn't be allowed near the children in case you corrupt them with your ungodly ways.'

Tamsyn's harsh laughter grated on Dora's nerves like a fingernail down a blackboard. 'Get out of our garden! Get out!' She flew at Tamsyn, raking her fingernails down her cheek.

'Dora!' shouted Ursula.

Tamsyn yanked Dora's hair so sharply she screamed.

Strong hands pulled Dora back. 'Stop it, both of you!' commanded Ursula.

Tamsyn spat on the ground by Dora's feet.

'You're *really* going to cop it now!' she taunted. 'That's assault, that is.' She wiped blood from her cheek and sprinted out of the garden.

Ursula pulled Dora into her arms. 'It's all right, dearest,' she soothed.

Dora recoiled and pushed her away, her chest heaving. 'Don't!' She scrubbed violently at her mouth as if to erase the soft touch of Ursula's lips. 'You disgust me!' Her pulse boomed in her ears as if her heart might burst.

Ursula's face blanched. She folded her arms tightly across her chest. 'Dora?'

'You make me feel sick!' Dora's voice was low and vicious. 'Get out of my sight!' There was a bitter tang in her mouth.

There was a long moment when neither of them moved, the air between them thick with tension.

Then Ursula bowed her head and walked swiftly away.

After she'd gone, Dora bent to pick up the bunch of sweet peas that lay crushed upon the ground. Their sweet scent turned her stomach now and she flung them on the compost heap. Then she began to shiver uncontrollably. Barely able to walk upright, she dragged herself into the potting shed where she hunkered down on a pile of old sacks and wept.

It was dark when she unfolded herself from the floor. Her eyes were gritty and swollen and her heart aching and empty. Cautiously, she crept back to the house and slipped up the stairs without anyone seeing her. She waited for a second in the corridor outside her bedroom, determining to get into bed without acknowledging Ursula. The lamp was lit when she opened the door.

Ursula's bed was empty. It had been stripped and the blankets neatly folded.

Dora caught her breath in a sudden panic. She flung open the wardrobe doors but every single one of Ursula's possessions had disappeared.

31

Tamsyn held her hand mirror up to the bedroom window and examined her cheek. The scratch marks were fading rapidly. Scowling, she dropped the mirror onto the dressing table. She'd been jubilant at the clear evidence of Dora's attack but when she told Benedict she was going straight away to tell the police constable, he'd said she was to pack her bags and not come back to Spindrift.

'The police won't be interested in your little cat fight,' he'd said. 'No one will believe you. Dora's such a quiet little mouse and Ursula's so personable, it's impossible to imagine either of them taking part in lewd practices.' He'd shuddered at the thought.

'But I saw them!'

Benedict had raised one eyebrow in that annoying way of his and turned his back on her.

'Look at me when I'm talking to you!' She'd stamped her foot. 'You're using this as an excuse because you want to get rid of me!'

He'd sighed heavily and turned to face her. 'Why do women have to nag?'

'Because men are so bleddy useless, thass why.' Tamsyn had lifted her chin defiantly. 'You're slipperier than a fresh-caught mackerel, you are, Benedict Fairchild. You thought I was gawky enough not to know you've been seeing that woman. Even if you hadn't come home tight

328

and smelling of her scent, you musta known someone would tell me they'd seen you with her in the Dolphin. It's disrespectful to me, that's what it is.'

'Mrs Plumridge is a wealthy woman, a widow, and I'm buttering her up so she'll commission me to paint her portrait.' He'd sighed. 'I'm going to take Roland for a walk in the cove and I'm not discussing the matter anymore.'

A week later, Tamsyn was still fuming. She'd tried to tell Edith what she'd seen but Edith had frowned at her as if she didn't understand before hurrying upstairs to the studio.

Tamsyn's only satisfaction was that Ursula had left Spindrift, as clear a sign of guilt as any, and Dora was moping about looking more miserable than a sack of drowning kittens. That'd teach her a lesson!

★ ★ ★

Later that evening, Tamsyn began her shift at the Golden Lion. It was still early in the summer season and not too busy. She was wiping down the bar when Hugh Penrose came in and ordered a pint of ale.

Stocky, with thinning fair hair, he perched on a stool at the bar and slouched morosely over his pint pot.

Tamsyn stood on the other side of the bar, drying glasses and eyeing him covertly. Usually, she barely said a word to him, mindful that he and Benedict had fallen out years ago. Perhaps now she might turn that to her advantage. She sidled up to him and smiled. 'What's going on with you then? Gotta face like a wet Sunday.'

He lifted his head and frowned at her. 'You're Benedict Fairchild's woman, aren't you?'

She lifted her head, a glint in her eye. 'I'm no one's woman but my own,' she said.

'You've left Spindrift, then?'

'Not yet but I will.' She glanced away, knowing she was on rocky ground. 'There's such dirty goings on there, you wouldn't believe it.'

Hugh Penrose's eyes gleamed. 'Whatever do you mean?'

Tamsyn touched the fading scratch marks on her cheek. 'You see these?' She leaned closer. 'Well,' she murmured, 'you'll never guess what I saw the other day.'

A little while later, Hugh Penrose stood up to leave. 'I enjoyed our little talk, Tamsyn.' He placed a few coins on the bar. 'Buy yourself a drink on me.'

'Thank you kindly, sir!' She gave a self-satisfied smile as she watched him leave. Well, she thought, if he didn't spread some tales about Dora, she'd be very surprised.

Old Curnow had rung for last orders when she heard someone call her name. She turned around and saw a smartly dressed man with smiling grey eyes.

'As I do live and breathe!' she said, smiling widely.

Albert Fisher's face lit up.

'You said in your letter you wasn't coming down for your holiday until July.'

'I couldn't wait so long to see you again. Ma

330

said she'd mind the shop and I arrived this evening.' He looked down at his feet and then said, 'You're just as lovely as I remembered you.'

Tamsyn laughed. Customers often made up to her but she had a feeling that Mr Fisher really meant it. Cornwall was a long way from London so, when he'd asked her last summer if he could write to her, she'd risked giving him her address at Spindrift. He'd sent a letter at least once a month ever since and they did her heart good after all the unpleasantness she'd endured recently. She smiled as she fetched him half a pint of beer and agreed to meet him after closing.

There was a full moon when she left the Golden Lion and trotted down to the Platt. Mr Fisher was sitting on the rocks beneath the cliff, waiting for her.

He stood up when he saw her and laid his coat upon the rocks for her to sit down in comfort.

Flattered that he treated her like a lady, she arranged her skirts and folded her hands in her lap. 'So how's life treating you, Mr Fisher?'

'Very well,' he said. 'Very well indeed. But call me Bert, won't you? Business has been brisk, so when the opportunity presented itself last month, I bought the adjacent premises to my shop.' He grinned at her. 'I couldn't wait to tell you. I take possession of it next month and I'll be able to offer a much wider range of goods.'

'What a successful businessman you are!' said Tamsyn. He really was quite good-looking but what she liked best was that he seemed so kind and steady. Not like some she could mention.

'My goods are sold at fair prices and I make sure my customers are happy.' He picked up a small parcel from his side. 'I brought you this,' he said. 'I hope you don't think it forward of me but, as soon as I saw it, I thought of you.'

'A present? For me?' Her eyes widened. No one ever gave her presents. She took the parcel from him and undid the ribbon — a *silk* ribbon, mind you! Inside was a lace shawl. Holding her breath, she lifted it up and, even by moonlight, could see how delicately and intricately it was made. She pressed it against her cheek and tried not to cry.

'Nottingham lace,' he said. 'Do you like it?'

'Oh, Bert! It's the most beautiful thing I've ever seen,' she whispered.

His face split into a wide smile. 'Shall you put it on and then we could take a little promenade along the beach?'

Tamsyn draped the shawl around her shoulders and, as they walked sedately along the water's edge, she felt as elegant as any high-society lady.

32

June 1906

Of late when Dora awoke, the first thing she always did was to glance at Ursula. But now the bed was stripped and her friend's curly head no longer rested on the pillow. A sob rose up in her throat and she buried her face in her hands.

In the month since Ursula ran away, Dora had drifted about Spindrift like a wraith, weeping and wringing her hands, unable to settle to anything. When the others asked her why Ursula had left without saying a word to anyone, she could only shake her head and say they'd had an argument. And then she'd panicked because the book they'd been working on together, *Flower Gardening for Girls and Boys*, couldn't be delivered to Mr Pettigrew. Until now, she'd never failed to complete work by the agreed date.

Everywhere she looked were memories she and Ursula had made together. It was a torture to take her turn weeding and watering the vegetable garden, when almost every plant reminded her of their happy discussions about which varieties of seeds to grow and then of how they'd nurtured the seedlings together and taken delight in harvesting the crop. Nothing would ever be the same again. Dora blew her nose and forced herself out of bed to face yet another miserable day.

After breakfast, the postman called with a letter from Mr Pettigrew. She remained rooted to the hall floor while she hurriedly slit open the envelope with trembling fingers.

Dear Miss Cox

Thank you for your letter with reference to Flower Gardening for Girls and Boys. Please, be anxious no longer that I shall sue you for breach of contract as nothing is further from my mind. Miss Hoffman wrote to tell me she has been called to Germany to assist her elderly grandmother during her final illness and I would not wish to add to any distress by demanding the manuscript and illustrations at this time.

I would remind you, Miss Cox, that your books for children are greatly loved by many and urge you to begin something new with all haste. Do let me know soonest what you have in mind.

Yours,

J. Pettigrew

Dora closed her eyes with a sigh of relief. Although she had savings, it would have put her in an awkward position if Mr Pettigrew had been angry that he'd been let down and then refused to publish her future work. Nevertheless, the letter struck her another blow by ramming home that the dreadful end of her friendship with Ursula wasn't merely a nightmare, their separation was real. Ursula wasn't coming back.

Dora sank down on the hall chair, her face in her hands. She had no idea where Ursula was. One thing she did know was that she wasn't nursing a terminally ill German grandmother since her beloved *Oma* had died years ago. Her letter to Mr Pettigrew was nothing more than an excuse.

Quick footsteps came along the passage from the kitchen and Dora's stomach turned over when she saw it was Tamsyn.

'Blubbing, are you?' she jeered. 'Missing your lady friend now with no one to warm your bed at night?'

'You're disgusting!' Dora turned tail and fled.

Tamsyn yelled after her: 'You're the disgusting one. And now everyone knows it!'

After that Dora hid in her room, shaking and sick. *Did* everyone know what had happened or was she imagining that the rest of the community were avoiding her? The huge knot inside her chest grew tighter and tighter until she could hardly breathe. Panicky, she ran out of the house. She didn't stop when Wilfred waved at her from the terrace but raced across the lawn and through the gate into the field. In the distance, Edith and Pascal had set up their easels on the headland so she turned in the other direction.

Leaning against the Bronze Age standing stone on the top of the cliff, she turned her face into the breeze and gulped in the sea air. After a while she felt calmer. Unable to bear the thought of returning home and having another confrontation with Tamsyn, she set off instead to Polcarrow Farm.

Tamara was in the farmyard, scattering grain for the chickens. She glanced up and became still when she saw Dora open the gate. She didn't give her usual cheerful smile and dumped the remaining grain in a heap on the ground. She glanced around and then said, 'I was going to come and see you this afternoon. You'd best come inside.'

Uneasily, Dora followed her into the kitchen.

'I'm sorry, Dora,' said Tamara, 'but we need to talk.' She peered through the window into the yard. 'I don't want Walter to interrupt us.'

'What is it?' asked Dora. Inside her was a cold, sinking feeling.

Tamara twisted the hem of her apron between her fingers. 'I went into the village yesterday,' she said. 'I saw Mrs Penrose come out of Parsons the bakers and when I went in, three or four customers were huddled together. Mrs Parsons saw me and whispered to one of the other women. Then she said to me, 'You're Dora Cox's friend, aren't you?' Of course, I said yes but then . . . ' Tamara pressed her fingers to her mouth. 'They asked if I was your *special* friend. There was something quite unpleasant about the way they said it.' She drew a deep breath. 'Mrs Parsons told me they'd heard Ursula had left Spindrift after you'd both been caught kissing and dancing *naked* in the garden. Please tell me it isn't true, Dora!'

'Of course it isn't true! We weren't naked or dancing.'

'Were you,' Tamara lowered her voice, 'kissing?'

336

'No! Well, yes, but it wasn't like that.' Dora swallowed. 'I had no idea that . . . ' She drew a deep breath. 'Ursula kissed me. It was completely unexpected and I was so shocked, I froze like a statue. It was bad luck that Tamsyn Pengelly was spying on us. You see, we'd had a bit of an up-and-downer earlier that day and she was cock-a-hoop she had a way to get back at me.'

'That's dreadful!'

'It was.' Dora swallowed. 'I was fond of Ursula and what happened came as a dreadful shock.' She pushed away a memory of the softness of Ursula's kiss. 'I was sickened by what happened and made sure she knew it. She ran away from Spindrift that day and I haven't heard from her since.'

'I see.'

'You do believe me, don't you?'

'I've never known you lie. It's too bad of Mrs Penrose to have spread her poison in so many of the village shops. I heard the same story everywhere I went.' Tamara sighed. 'There have been rumours about unseemly behaviour at Spindrift for years but you do see, don't you, that for the sake of my husband and son, I daren't be tarred with the same brush by any close association with the Spindrift community or I'll never sell our butter, cheese and eggs.'

'But . . . '

'I'm really sorry, Dora,' said Tamara firmly, 'especially if it wasn't your fault, but I promised Walter I'd stay away from you.'

Dora stumbled out of the farmhouse and

made her way back over the fields. Ursula and Tamsyn between them had blighted her life and the terrible injustice of it was that she had never nursed unnatural feelings for Ursula. She'd loved her as a dear friend but there had never been any suggestion of anything indecent. But then the memory of Ursula's thumb making tiny circles on the inside of Dora's wrist, and how it had made her tremble, flashed into her mind before she could thrust it away.

The aching loneliness swept over her again. Blinded by sudden tears, she tripped and fell heavily to the ground. Utterly wretched, she curled into a ball on the grass and sobbed.

33

It was a splendid June day and Edith set up her easel in the garden under the shade of the beech tree. *Washing Day* was the last but one canvas she had to complete for the exhibition she and Pascal were to share at the Walworth Gallery in November. She'd been inspired to paint it when she'd seen Hannah struggling to unpeg a line of billowing sheets before the wind snatched them out of her hands. It was bright and sunny weather and the maid's cap was awry and wisps of hair fluttered around her laughing face.

Poised to add a highlight to Hannah's painted cheek, Edith saw Dora crossing the lawn to the gate at the end of the garden. A picture of despondency, her head was bowed and her arms folded tightly across her chest. Edith waved and called out but either Dora didn't notice her or she chose not to.

It was six weeks since Ursula had left Spindrift. She'd sent a note to Edith, apologising for her abrupt departure due to 'personal circumstances', and enclosed a postal order for a month's rent. Since then, Edith had tried several times to discover from Dora why they'd quarrelled but she refused to discuss it and became tearful if pressed.

There were footsteps on the gravel behind her and she turned to see Pascal with Star and Blue beside him.

339

'You look troubled,' he said. 'Is your work not going well?'

'I was worrying about Dora,' said Edith. 'She's so unhappy. Whatever can she and Ursula have argued about that was so terrible Ursula felt she must leave Spindrift? I didn't tell you before but Tamsyn came to speak to me that evening. She had such a spiteful gleam in her eyes and told me some garbled tale about Dora and Ursula's friendship being 'unnatural', whatever that means.'

'I heard some unpleasant gossip in the village,' said Pascal. 'Dora is an innocent . . . ' He frowned. 'Perhaps that is why Ursula left so suddenly.'

'I haven't been to the village lately. What do you mean?'

He shrugged. 'Do you remember when Oscar Wilde was imprisoned some years ago for acts of indecency? It was well known in their social circle that Wilde and Lord Alfred Douglas were lovers.'

'I read about that in the papers,' said Edith. 'It was very shocking. I'd never realised before then that a man might have such feelings for another man.'

'But imagine for a moment that such behaviour wasn't considered, in law or by society, to be degenerate. Perhaps, for a certain type of man, to love another man feels natural and right?' said Pascal. 'If such love, illegal or not, is discreet and not flaunted in an obvious or sordid way, should these men not be allowed to live quietly and happily together?'

'Well, when you put it that way, it isn't so very different from our own case, is it?'

'*Exactement!*' Absent-mindedly, he covered Edith's palette with a turpentine-soaked rag. 'Don't let your paint dry out,' he said. Then he looked directly at her. 'You must know Wilfred and Augustus are very close friends?'

'Yes, of course,' said Edith. 'Oh!' She clapped a hand to her mouth. 'You don't mean . . .'

Pascal nodded. 'But what harm do they do to others?'

'None that I can see.'

'So now we consider Dora and Ursula.'

'But women don't have such feelings for other women.'

Pascal laughed. 'You, too, are an innocent *chérie*. When I lived in Montmartre, I saw with my own eyes women who loved each other in that way.'

'But,' she hesitated, 'I can't imagine how . . .'

'You don't need to imagine. Believe me when I tell you, some women are made this way. I wonder about Ursula. Suppose she made an advance to her dear friend Dora?'

'Dora would have been terribly shocked.'

'And perhaps even more shocked,' said Pascal slowly, 'if she realised, for the very first time, that she felt the same?'

'There's never been any indication . . .' Edith rested her palm on her breast. 'I could never ask Dora about such a private thing.'

'You have no need to ask but, if this is so, it is no surprise she is confused and miserable.'

'All I want is for her to be happy.'

'And what about me?' Pascal's tone was teasing.

'I want you to have your every heart's desire.' Edith dropped her gaze from his smiling eyes. The bitter knowledge that she'd deprived him of his heart's desire, a child, gnawed at her again.

'You are my heart's desire.' His finger traced her bare forearm. 'I've finished my final canvas for the exhibition,' he said, 'and am taking the dogs for a walk. Come with me? We have been working so hard we haven't visited Woodland Cottage for weeks. I hoped we might talk, away from prying eyes.'

'I'd love that,' she said.

'Shall we slip away right now?' There was a mischievous glint in his eye.

'Why not? The children won't be home from school yet.' Hurriedly, she cleaned her brushes and put on her straw sunhat. 'Now I'm all yours!'

They went through the garden gate, with Star and Blue trotting along beside them, and set off along the coast path in the opposite direction to the village. The sun was warm on their backs, though the heavy rain of the preceding week had left the path very muddy in places.

Edith gathered her skirt up above her ankles and leaped across a large puddle, then skidded across the wet grass when she landed.

Pascal caught and steadied her. He glanced around and, seeing no one was in sight, pulled her into his arms and kissed her.

Afterwards, Edith straightened her hat. 'We must visit Woodland Cottage before the school

342

holidays begin, or we'll have to wait until the autumn.'

'And Delphine is bringing Gabrielle to see Benedict again for the summer.' Pascal gave a wry smile. 'No doubt he will be busy doing nothing and it will be left to Wilfred and me to keep an eye on her, like last year.'

'Apart from a few squabbles, Pearl enjoyed her company,' said Edith. 'I expect she'll keep her amused.'

'Nevertheless,' said Pascal, 'I must take responsibility for Gabrielle if Benedict neglects her. Besides, it interests me to see a child's character unfold as they grow.' He sighed. 'My niece is contrary at times. It may be she will share many character traits with Benedict.'

'I sincerely hope not!'

His voice softened. 'Jasper is so different and I take much pleasure in encouraging his artistic talent.'

They walked hand-in-hand along the path above the sea while Pascal recounted anecdotes of Jasper's developing skills and Edith brooded upon her guilty secret.

Pascal glanced at her. 'What is it, *mon amour?*'

She sighed. 'I'm so weary of being obliged to conceal our love. I can't help feeling jealous every time I see the happiness in Clarissa and Julian's eyes. And then there's Benedict and Tamsyn.'

'You are jealous of *them?*' He shrugged. 'They no longer find delight in each other.'

'No,' said Edith, 'but I'm resentful they live

343

openly together and we can't.'

'We have known for a long time we cannot risk Benedict finding a reason to deprive you of your children. He and Tamsyn have forfeited all respectability by their actions and that reflects upon our community. We shall not do the same.' Pascal squeezed her hand. 'Let us not spoil the time we do have together with jealous thoughts of others.' He looked up at the blue sky. 'It's a beautiful day and I have a present for you.'

'A present?'

'Come, we shall sit on the rocks over there.'

The land sloped steeply downwards and they rested on a stony outcrop near the edge of the cliff, where they could admire the wild and rocky foreshore below. The dogs wandered off to investigate some gorse bushes.

The breeze teased wisps from the thick knot of hair at the nape of Edith's neck and tickled her cheeks. 'Isn't this sublime?' she said, looking out at the sea and imagining how she would paint it. The Atlantic was a deep ultramarine blue at the horizon but the surf swirled and foamed around the rocks at the foot of the cliff in a glorious palette of cobalt turquoise, viridian and manganese blue.

Pascal turned his face to the sun and breathed in the salty air. 'I love Cornwall quite as much as my native Provence.'

'I can't imagine living without the sound of the waves to lull me to sleep,' said Edith. 'I'll always want to live by the sea. Once the children are grown, we shall travel the world until we find the perfect place to settle.'

Pascal lifted her hand to his lips. 'We shall live where no one will ever imagine we aren't a long-married couple.' He thrust his hand in his pocket and then held out a tiny leather box. 'This is for you, Edith.' His gaze never left her face as she opened the box.

She caught her breath. Inside was an intricately chased gold ring formed from two hands clasping an emerald. 'Oh!' she breathed. 'It's so beautiful!'

The tension left his face. 'I designed it and had it made for you,' he said. 'The emerald is to match your lovely eyes. I cannot give you a wedding ring but this is to affirm my enduring love for you.'

The wave of love she felt for him was almost painful in its intensity. 'I shall treasure it forever,' she whispered.

He took the ring from her and slipped it on the third finger of her left hand.

She bit her lip. 'But, Pascal . . . '

He pressed a finger to her mouth. 'I know. You are going to say you cannot wear it for everyone to see. That is why I didn't ask Clarissa and Augustus to make it for you.' He pulled a fine gold chain from his pocket and clasped it around her neck. 'But you can thread the ring on here and wear it beneath your clothes.' He smiled. 'Then I shall always be close to your heart.'

'You already are.' Her mouth trembled. She loved him so much that she ached inside. He was loving and unselfish and she trusted him yet, still, she was frightened to reveal the truth.

'Edith?' He wrapped his arms around her. 'I

hoped the ring would make you happy.'

'It does!' A sob burst through the sudden thickness in her throat and she hid her face in his shoulder. 'I'm sorry!'

Blue lifted his head to see what was happening. Star settled down beside Edith and leaned against her leg.

'What are you sorry for?' Pascal asked. Gently, he caressed her cheek.

She made a tiny mew of distress. There was a stone-cold mass of dread in her chest but she knew the time had come to be honest with him. She lifted her head, even though she couldn't meet his eyes. 'I'm deeply sorry, Pascal. I've lied to you.'

'Lied?' A muscle flickered in his jaw. 'You love someone else?'

'Of course not! But I concealed something. I hope you'll understand my reasons.' More than that, she prayed he'd be so thrilled he'd forgive her.

He frowned.

Now. She swallowed and looked directly up at him. 'Many years ago, you asked me if Jasper was your son. I told you he was Benedict's but . . . ' she licked her lips ' . . . that wasn't true.'

Pascal became as still as the rock they sat upon. After a moment, he said, 'Jasper is *my* son?'

She nodded.

'Are you sure?'

'Absolutely.'

Joyous realisation dawned on his face. 'My son,' he murmured. 'The child of my heart is

346

also the child of my blood?' He smothered a sob with his hand. 'But why didn't you tell me?'

'I was married to Benedict and I was too ashamed.'

'But all this time, you have kept the knowledge from me,' he whispered. His olive complexion blanched. 'You *lied* to me! About *this*?'

'It happened long before we fell in love . . . '

'Before you loved me, perhaps, but you know I have loved you since the first moment I set eyes upon you.'

Edith leaned towards him, pleading with him to understand. 'Pascal, I was young, pregnant and married to a man who would have cast me into the street if he'd known my baby wasn't his. My family would have disowned me if I'd brought such disgrace upon them. I was terrified and didn't know where to turn. I had no choice but to pretend my baby was Benedict's.'

'Did you think I would have abandoned you, like Benedict?' His voice rose. 'Did you imagine I was so dishonourable I would not have taken care of you?'

His hurt and anger cut her to the quick. 'I barely knew you then, Pascal, and I was the one left to face stark choices after what happened between us. And then, when you left Spindrift, I didn't think you'd ever come back, so I kept my secret.'

'I left because I loved you. It was too painful to stay when I believed you had healed your marriage.'

She sighed. 'I tried to make it work with Benedict but it was useless. And after he'd deserted me, when you returned to Spindrift, I already had Pearl and was about to give birth to the twins. I was distraught, expecting Benedict to sell the house and leave me destitute. I worked night and day with Clarissa and Dora to found the community and save Spindrift.' She closed her eyes, remembering those dark days. 'My friends despised Benedict for being an adulterer and I was terrified they'd despise me if they knew I was one too.'

'But why did you not tell me later, when we became lovers?' Pascal rose abruptly to his feet and paced jerkily back and forth across the grass.

'The longer I left the lie between us, the bigger it became,' she said. 'After the suffering Benedict inflicted on me, it took me so long to learn to trust again.'

A seagull screamed overhead and swooped away over the sea.

'You could have trusted *me* enough to tell me Jasper was my son.'

'Four years ago, I'd grown completely secure in your love and I did pluck up the courage to come and tell you.' She twisted her fingers together. 'But it was the day you had a letter from Delphine and discovered she'd concealed from Édouard that Gabrielle was Benedict's daughter. You were so blazingly angry. You said it was an unforgivable betrayal, that Delphine was deceitful and you would disown her — your own sister! I tried to explain that, probably, she didn't have any alternative but to pretend the baby was Édouard's. You wouldn't listen and were so unyielding in your opinion, I was far too terrified then of losing your love by telling you about Jasper.'

'But Delphine *deliberately* and wantonly continued her affair with Benedict over several weeks,' said Pascal. 'She knew it was possible she risked having his child. Our situation was different. You were in a state of shock and distress and it happened only once.' He wiped his palm over his face. 'Afterwards, I was tormented by guilt because of my weakness in taking advantage of you.'

Edith stared at him. 'But you didn't! It takes two.'

'Am I such a monster that you should be so frightened of me?'

'I wanted to tell you!' Edith's mouth trembled. 'But you were bitterly angry with Delphine and I couldn't bear to have that rage turned on me. I know you love Jasper and I'd hoped that, now, you would forgive me and rejoice in discovering he is your son.'

'Forgive you?' Pascal raked his hand wildly through his hair. 'All those lost years! The worst thing, the *very* worst thing, is that you, the woman I have loved for so long, deceived me.'

Star stood up, his hackles raised at Pascal's angry tone.

'Pascal, I'm sorry . . . '

'How shall I ever trust you again?'

Her heartbeat pounded so loudly in her ears that it drowned out the sound of the waves. 'I've never lied to you about anything else.'

'You knew how desperately I wanted a child,' he said. 'You could not risk having a baby with me because of Benedict so, for your sake, I always took precautions. Each time, I was *tourmonté*. But I did it for you because I loved you. And all that time I suffered, you hid the truth from me.'

Edith reared to her feet, reaching out to him, but he recoiled. 'Please, Pascal, listen to me!' She snatched at his sleeve.

He shook her hand off his arm. 'Don't touch me!' he shouted.

Blue gave a sharp, warning bark and Star growled.

Abruptly, Pascal turned away, catching his foot on a half-concealed rock. He tripped and tried to right himself but his shoes skidded on the wet grass and he staggered backwards.

The wind snatched away Edith's scream as she threw herself towards him while he teetered on the cliff edge.

Waves crashed onto the rocks below sending up a fountain of spray.

Pascal's mouth was open in a silent scream, his eyes wide with terror.

Edith reached out for him but all she grasped was air.

34

July 1906

Pearl helped Dora put clean sheets on the spare bed in Pearl and Nell's bedroom, ready for Gabrielle's visit.

'You'd better clear some space for her clothes,' said Dora.

Pearl pulled open one of the drawers and shoved her nightgowns and vests to one side. She lifted out a painted wooden box and frowned. 'Auntie Dora, would you look after my treasure chest while Gabrielle is here?'

'Can't you put it under your bed?'

'I'd rather you looked after it. Last summer, when Gabrielle shared my room, my sea-glass pendant disappeared. I think she took it.'

'Not the one Auntie Clarissa made for you?' Dora straightened the eiderdown. 'Are you sure? You aren't always very careful where you leave things and it's wrong to accuse Gabrielle of taking it, if you aren't sure.'

'I loved my pendant and I was careful with it!' Pearl's expression was indignant. 'Besides, I had those pretty origami birds in my treasure chest, the ones Uncle Wilfred folded for me, and they were all crumpled up, too. Gabrielle had asked me the day before if she could take them home but I'd said she couldn't.'

Dora sighed. It was bad enough to have one of

351

Benedict's by-blows come to stay for the summer without having to worry if she was going to pinch the silver teaspoons. 'Put it on the chest and I'll take it to my room when I've finished the dusting.'

Pearl put the box down. 'If Mama wants to know where I am when she returns from the hospital, I'll be in the cove with Lily.'

'I'll tell her.'

'Auntie Dora?' Pearl's face was troubled. 'Uncle Pascal will get better, won't he? He's been in hospital three weeks now. Mama weeps all the time and Jasper stays in his bedroom and won't come out. I think he's been crying, too.'

Dora busied herself dusting the bookshelf. She couldn't tell the child that Pascal's life hung in the balance and, even if he recovered, it was unlikely he'd walk again. 'It'll take a long time for him to feel better, I'm afraid.'

Pearl's mouth trembled.

Dora dropped the duster. 'Come here!' She enfolded Pearl in her arms and kissed the top of her head. 'The most helpful thing you can do is to be kind to your mama. You might brush her hair or bring her a cup of tea when she returns from the hospital.'

'I just want everything to be how it was before.'

'I know, sweetheart. We all want that.' Dora sighed and thought of Ursula. 'Go and play with Lily, then. And remember to take off your sandshoes before you come back into the house. There was sand everywhere yesterday.'

'I will!' sang Pearl as she escaped.

Dora finished the dusting and carried the treasure chest back to her room. Hesitating a moment, she placed it in one of the empty drawers that Ursula had used. She sat down on the stripped bed and, lifting up the pillow, held it to her face and sniffed. There was the faintest hint of the Castile soap Ursula had used to wash her hair, bringing back memories of sitting in the sun together, drying their hair and laughingly calling themselves mermaids. Like Pearl, Dora wished beyond anything that things were just as they had been before.

She hugged the pillow tight to her chest but nothing could make the ache inside her go away. She and Ursula had been so close and had rarely had any sharp words in their four years together. Dora had never been so happy in all her life. Why, oh, why, did Ursula have to go and spoil it all?

★ ★ ★

Promptly at two o'clock, the ward doors opened and Matron's eagle eyes scanned the visitors as they shuffled in bearing bags of grapes and bunches of flowers. The beds were placed a regimented distance apart and the patients tucked in firmly enough to restrict movement or undesirable displays of affection to their loved ones.

Edith entered the ward, hoping she might see some small improvement in Pascal's condition today. He always lay so pale and still, never speaking, and she was desperately afraid for him.

353

She reached his bed and stopped in confusion. The cage that was used over his legs and pelvis to prevent the weight of the blankets pressing on his injuries had disappeared. The mattress was bare. She stared at it, catching her breath in shock and disbelief. A wave of faintness washed over her and she swayed and clutched at the iron bedstead.

'All right, my bird?'

She swallowed and saw an elderly man with a fuzz of white hair watching her from the neighbouring bed. 'What happened?' she whispered.

'Don't 'ee worry! He's moved over there.' He nodded his head towards the far corner of the ward.

She pressed a palm to her heart. 'Thank God!'

The old man smiled in sympathy. 'Gave you a turn, did it?'

She nodded and forced a smile before walking unsteadily down the ward to sit at Pascal's bedside. His eyes were closed and his face turned away from her. Was he unconscious or merely pretending to sleep, to avoid speaking to her?

She held his hand, just as she had every day since she'd first been allowed to visit him, but it remained unresponsive in her palm. Sitting straight-backed on the hard chair, she felt as if she was existing in a living nightmare. Unable to sleep, she'd walked the floor every night since the lifeboat men had stretchered Pascal off the rocks and into their boat. Her pulse raced as she relived that terrible scene before he had plummeted backwards over the cliff. *My fault, my fault*, echoed through her thoughts night and day. The memory of his eyes, wide with horror, and his mouth open in a silent scream would be for evermore imprinted upon her memory. Her fingers touched the front of her blouse, seeking the ring he'd given her, suspended on the fine chain beneath her clothes.

The bell rang, signifying the end of visiting time, and Edith kissed Pascal's forehead. 'I love you, my darling,' she whispered.

His eyelids flickered but he turned his head away as if he couldn't bear her touch.

★　★　★

The following afternoon, after visiting an unresponsive Pascal again, Edith walked the three miles back from Port Isaac station to Spindrift House in hot sunshine. Dispirited and bone-weary, she unlatched the garden gate, intending to lie in a darkened room for half an hour before Delphine and Gabrielle arrived later on. She heard the clip-clop of horses' hooves coming along the lane and a hired carriage drew up beside the gate.

Delphine descended from the carriage in a rustle of silk skirts and imperiously ordered the driver to unload Gabrielle's baggage.

Edith's heart sank. The very picture of cool elegance, Delphine and Gabrielle had arrived much earlier than expected. Her own dress clung to her, damp with perspiration, as she ushered them into the hall. She asked Hannah to request

355

Wilfred, Benedict and Pearl join them for tea in the drawing room.

A peal of childish laughter came from upstairs and Edith looked up to see Tamsyn and Roland sitting on the stairs and peering down at them through the banisters. Tamsyn jerked back out of sight but not before Edith had seen her sullen expression.

'Shall we go into the drawing room, Delphine?' said Edith.

'And how is my brother?' she enquired, sitting down on the sofa.

'Pascal sleeps a great deal. Since I am not a relative, the doctor is disinclined to give me much information. As I wrote to you in my letters, your brother has suffered a broken leg and ribs. More worrying are the injuries to his pelvis and back. The lacerations will heal but he will require a long period of convalescence.'

'But will he walk again?'

'The doctors don't seem to know.' Edith swallowed back the tears that were never very far away. 'They say it's very uncertain.'

Delphine waved a hand dismissively. 'The doctor will speak to me tomorrow when I visit him.'

The door opened and Pearl and Benedict entered. He acknowledged Delphine and enquired about the sea crossing before making a fuss of Gabrielle, complimenting her on how she'd become quite the young lady.

Wilfred sauntered in, followed by Hannah who placed the tea tray on the table before Edith.

Delphine offered her cousin Wilfred her

cheeks to be kissed and accepted his expressions of sympathy for Pascal's unfortunate accident.

'Will you pass around the cups, please, Pearl?' murmured Edith, pouring the tea.

Her daughter rested a hand on her mother's shoulder. 'You look tired, Mama,' she whispered.

Edith swallowed back the lump in her throat. 'I am a little, sweetheart.'

Pearl kissed her cheek and carried a cup of tea to Delphine.

'I planned to return to France once Gabrielle had been handed into Benedict's care but now,' Delphine puffed out her breath, 'now I 'ave to see what to do for Pascal. If necessary, I shall move from the Golden Lion to an inn near to the hospital until it is time for Gabrielle to return home.'

'She is welcome to stay as long as she likes,' said Benedict, smiling expansively.

'She will speak English all the time and will return to France with me before her school opens,' said Delphine.

The French girl sipped her tea with eyes lowered.

Pearl eyed her half-sister covertly. 'I can help you unpack, if you like?'

Gabrielle shrugged.

Edith sat very still allowing the subdued conversation to fade into the distance while she pictured Pascal lying silently in his hospital bed.

'Edith?'

She blinked. 'Yes, Delphine?'

'Will you give the address of the hospital to the driver of my carriage?'

'I take the train to Camelford every day to see Pascal,' said Edith. 'Perhaps you'd care to accompany me?'

Delphine's fincly plucked eyebrows rose. 'There is no need for you to visit my brother now I am here.'

'Nevertheless,' said Edith, 'I shall continue to do so.'

'I prefer the comfort of a private carriage to another dirty train.' Delphine sighed. 'If you wish,' she said, reluctance written plainly across her face, 'you may come to the Golden Lion tomorrow and travel in the carriage with me.'

Edith couldn't imagine anything she'd like less but it would have been churlish to refuse.

★   ★   ★

The following afternoon, Edith presented herself at the Golden Lion, where the hired carriage was already waiting outside. Since there was no sign of Delphine in the parlour, Edith asked the landlord to send a message to her room.

Ten minutes later, Edith glanced at her watch. She drummed her fingers on the arm of the chair. It would be difficult to arrive at the hospital on time now and the visiting hour was strictly observed.

Another five minutes passed before Delphine appeared in the parlour doorway, her lips pursed. 'Do come now, Edith,' she said, 'or we shall be late.'

Silently, Edith followed the trail of Parisian perfume that clouded the air around Delphine's

358

person, nettled that the other woman had implied she was to blame for the lateness of the hour.

In a short while, they were ensconced in the carriage and Edith was relieved that her travelling companion showed no inclination to make small talk. The journey passed in almost total silence, leaving Edith free to dwell once more on what she might have done to avert the catastrophe that had befallen Pascal.

The carriage rolled to a stop outside the hospital and Edith led the way to the ward. They had missed fifteen precious minutes of visiting time.

Outside the door, Delphine put a restraining hand on Edith's arm. 'I wish to see my brother alone for a few moments.'

'Then I shall wait over there,' said Edith.

Delphine nodded and went into the ward.

Edith sat on a bench. After twenty minutes of fidgeting, she decided she'd given Delphine sufficient private time with her brother and made her way into the ward. As she approached Pascal's bed, she was surprised to see his upper body slightly raised on pillows. He was talking to Delphine.

'Pascal!' Edith said. 'You're awake.' Her fatigue left her in a surge of elation. 'How are you feeling?' She sat down beside him, longing to kiss him but unable to do so while Delphine was watching.

Slowly, Pascal turned his head on the pillow. His eyes were dull, as if someone had turned out a light within him. 'How do you expect me to

359

feel, Edith?' His voice was hoarse. 'How would
you feel if, at one stroke, you had been crippled
for life and everything that mattered to you had
been snatched away?'

Edith's joy turned to misery again. 'You *will*
get better, Pascal. It may take time but, before
you know it, you'll be painting again.'

'I will be nothing but an inconvenience, being
pushed from place to place in a wheeled chair.
What life is that?' He closed his eyes and tears
seeped out from under his dark eyelashes. 'I wish
I had died on those rocks.'

'Don't say that, Pascal!' She took his hand and
smothered it with kisses. 'Everyone at Spindrift
loves you and we'll all help you along the road to
recovery.'

'Don't!' he croaked, pulling his hand free.

'Pascal?' She felt as if he'd slapped her face.

'I will not be pitied. Please do not visit me
again. You remind me too much of everything I
have lost.' He closed his eyes, the corners of his
mouth turned down. 'Go home.'

'Wait for me in the carriage, Edith,' said
Delphine.

She reared to her feet. 'No! Pascal, you can't
send me away like this.'

A nurse bustled towards them. 'I must ask you
to leave,' she said, gripping Edith's arm. 'I
cannot allow my patient to be distressed. Come
with me now.'

There was a tightness in Edith's chest and a
rushing in her ears but she was powerless to
resist.

35

September 1906

Dora turned around the CLOSED sign and locked the gallery door behind her. Clarissa and Rose were on the other side of the courtyard and she went to say hello.

'Busy day?' asked Clarissa.

'It's quietening down now the summer season is almost over,' said Dora. 'Though I sold those silver and pebble bracelets of yours.'

Ned stretched his neck over the stable door and Clarissa lifted Rose up to pat his head. The pony whickered and three-year-old Rose squealed and snatched back her hand. She wriggled in her mother's arms until set down on the cobbles. 'Julian went to visit Pascal again today,' she said, her brow troubled.

'How was he?'

'Out of bed and in a wheelchair. Julian made the mistake of saying he was pleased to see him up and about. Pascal was upset and asked him to leave. He said he didn't want anyone's pity.' Clarissa's chin quivered. 'But how can you *not* pity him?'

'Pascal was always so calm and good-natured,' said Dora.

Clarissa sighed. 'Julian asked if Edith could visit again but Pascal became angry. Told Julian, in no uncertain terms, to go away. He won't see anyone from Spindrift.'

'Poor Edith!' said Dora. 'She keeps his room dusted and aired, hoping he'll feel more like himself again when he's back in his own bed.'

Rose pulled at her mother's skirt. 'Can we find Lily now?'

'We'll see if she's in the garden,' said Clarissa.

'I saw her walking through the courtyard with Pearl and Gabrielle earlier,' said Dora.

Clarissa sighed. 'I'll be glad when the children return to school. They've roamed around the countryside all summer and often I don't see Lily for hours at a time.'

'But children need some freedom, don't you think?' said Dora. 'And they're old enough to look after themselves most of the time.'

'That's true,' said Clarissa. 'The autumn will be here before we know it and it'll be a relief to have Spindrift to ourselves again after the holidaymakers have gone. I can't say I'll be sorry to see Gabrielle return to France, though. Her English may have improved in leaps and bounds but she's a little too pert for my liking.'

'Benedict sloped off again this morning to Heaven knows where,' said Dora, 'leaving Gabrielle to amuse herself and she's not very good at that. What she is good at is sulking and making mischief.'

'Don't I know it!' Clarissa shook her head. 'She's unbecomingly forward and knowing for thirteen. Will is completely dazzled. The poor boy flushes scarlet every time she speaks to him. He's at that awkward age when his voice breaks when he least expects it.'

'I don't think Will is the only boy she's interested in, either,' said Dora. 'I was walking along the headland yesterday, thinking about my new book. Down in the cove, Pearl and Lily were chatting with Adela Penrose but Gabrielle was larking about with the Penrose boys. They were chasing through the waves and splashing each other. If they'd all been older, I'd have said they were flirting.'

'Lily was with Adela Penrose and her brothers?' Clarissa's eyebrows drew together. 'Are you sure?'

'Well, yes.'

The colour drained from Clarissa's cheeks. 'I must put a stop to that!'

'Does it matter? I know Hugh Penrose kicked up a fuss after he found his children had brought food to the cave when Pearl and Lily ran away but . . .'

'Hugh Penrose is poisonous,' said Clarissa, 'and I won't have his boys anywhere near Lily. I shall utterly forbid her to meet them again.'

Dora stared at her, surprised she spoke so vehemently. 'But Hugh hasn't caused us any trouble in an age, Clarissa.'

She hesitated and then replied, 'I'm afraid you're wrong, Dora. He'll always be delighted to do anything he can to cause trouble for the Spindrift community. Didn't you know that he and his wife were the ones who spread those unpleasant rumours around the village about you and Ursula? He must have heard it from that little hussy Tamsyn in the Golden Lion.'

363

Dora's cheeks blazed. She swallowed. 'You know about that?'

'My dearest girl,' Clarissa's voice was full of pity, 'the whole village knows about it.'

'What Tamsyn thought she saw was wrong! I didn't . . .'

'It's irrelevant whether it's true or false, the damage is done.' She patted Dora's arm. 'I know you and Ursula were the greatest of friends and that you had a dreadful quarrel with her. I don't need to know any more than that. I'm desperately sorry you're so unhappy but it wouldn't matter a jot to me even if there had been a special relationship between the two of you.'

'I loathe Tamsyn.' All the distress and anger Dora felt for the other woman seethed up before her like a red mist. She clenched her fists. 'I'm not a violent person but if she were here now I'd kick her to the other end of Cornwall.'

Clarissa put an arm around her friend. 'Tamsyn has sunk very low by spreading such vile gossip. Never apologise, never explain, that's my motto. It worked for me, as a fallen woman with a child, and now I'm a respectable wife. I promise you, in time, it'll all be forgotten.' She reached out for Rose's hand. 'I must find Lily.'

Dora watched them walk away. It was all very well for Clarissa to say the rumours would be forgotten but Dora would never be able to wipe from her memory that shocking moment when she'd fallen under the enchantment of Ursula's beautiful, mesmerising eyes. And then, when Ursula had pressed her mouth softly against hers, how she had clung to her, quivering with pleasure.

* * *

Edith was in her studio, staring blindly out of the window. The words *my fault, my fault,* churned endlessly through her mind. It had been two months since she'd seen Pascal and not a day had passed without her hoping he'd send for her. Twice, she'd made the journey to the hospital but both times been told firmly by the matron that the patient refused to see her.

'Mama!' Pearl came running up the stairs calling to her and burst through the studio door with Star and Blue at her heels. 'Gabrielle's mother is downstairs. She wants to speak to you urgently.'

Edith's stomach lurched in sudden fear.

'She's taking Gabrielle back to France,' said Pearl.

Edith let out her breath in a rush. Thank God Pascal hadn't taken a turn for the worse! 'We weren't expecting her to leave until next week,' she said. It was a relief she and Delphine were going. Perhaps now she'd be able to see Pascal. 'I'll come down.'

She heard Delphine scolding Gabrielle in voluble French, even before she entered the drawing room, followed by Pearl and the dogs. The girl stood before her mother, her chin raised in defiance.

'Delphine,' said Edith, 'we weren't expecting you.'

365

'So I see, since my daughter is wearing dirty clothes and her hair is unbrushed.'

'I believe the children have been playing on the beach.'

Delphine's dark eyes glittered. 'You *believe*? Has my daughter not been properly supervised?'

'Everyone in this community needs to work,' Edith said with some asperity, 'and the children, apart from the two smallest, are considered old enough to be self-sufficient and to amuse themselves.'

Delphine drew back her skirts and kicked out at Star as he sniffed at her shoes. 'Where is Benedict?'

'He said he had to go and meet a man about a dog at the Dolphin Inn again,' said Pearl.

Edith closed her eyes momentarily and prayed for patience. 'I'm afraid you have been misinformed, Delphine, if you imagined Benedict would devote his time to Gabrielle.'

'Is he good for nothing at all?'

Edith chose not to answer Delphine's question. 'Shall I call for some tea?'

'I 'ave no time. Pascal is discharged from hospital and awaits me at my hotel. We return to France tomorrow. We will pack Gabrielle and Pascal's possessions immediately.'

Edith's knees buckled and she sank down into an armchair. 'But — we all thought, we hoped, he would return to Spindrift.' She took a steadying breath. 'Surely, in his condition, he isn't able to undertake such an arduous journey? How can he possibly manage the boat, a train to Paris, crossing the city and then another long train journey south? I assure you, if he were to return here, he would receive the most attentive care.'

'It is most inconvenient for me but Pascal refuses to return here. I 'ave bought him a wheelchair and engaged a nurse and a male servant to lift him.' Delphine pouted. 'He writes you a note.' She snapped open the clasp on her handbag and withdrew a piece of folded paper. 'Take this to your *maman*,' she said to Pearl.

Edith smoothed the note flat and read it.

Edith
I am returning to my family at Belle Vue. I shall never paint again so Jasper may have my paints, brushes and sketch-books. Do what you will with my canvases, sell them at the exhibition in November and keep the proceeds for Jasper, or burn them. It is of no matter to me.
I will not inflict a crippled father upon Jasper or reveal your secret so you need not fear that shame will fall upon you.
Pascal

The note fell from her shaking fingers onto her lap. Rage and anguish burned within her. After all she and Pascal had meant to each other, he was leaving her without even a proper goodbye! 'I must speak to him,' she said.

Delphine shook her head. 'He will not see you and I will waste no time. Please pack Pascal's clothes, Edith. Two bags only, since there will be little room in the carriage. One pair of shoes will suffice since he will not walk again.'

Edith caught her breath in outrage. 'It's far too soon to condemn him to a life spent in a wheelchair! We must hope that, in time, he *will* walk again.'

Delphine shrugged. 'I do not believe in fairy tales, Edith.' She turned to her daughter. 'Gabrielle, take me to your room and we will pack your valise.'

Upstairs, Edith pulled open a drawer in Pascal's room. She lifted one of his folded shirts to her cheek and caught the merest hint of the scent of his skin. Closing her eyes, she pictured him laughing, with the sun on his face, the wind in his hair and love in his eyes. She knew she'd wronged him but, after what they'd shared, how could he have turned away from her so completely?

'Mama?' Jasper stood in the doorway. 'Is it true?' His face was pinched and ashen. 'Is Uncle Pascal really leaving Spindrift?'

Not trusting herself to speak without weeping, she merely held her arms open to him. Even at thirteen, he didn't hesitate but ran into her embrace.

'But *why*, Mama? And why won't he let us visit him?'

The anguish in his voice nearly broke her heart all over again. 'He's been very ill, my darling, and the hospital don't allow children to visit. Now he prefers to be with his family while he convalesces.'

'But *we* are his family! We could help him to

convalesce. I could read to him or support him while he learns to walk again. I want to see him. Please, let me see him!' There was a rising note of panic in his voice.

'I'm afraid he won't see any of us.' Edith struggled to keep her voice even. 'And he must rest before the journey tomorrow. We shall write to him and I hope, one day, we will see him again.' She forced a smile. 'He hasn't forgotten you because he asked me to give you his paints and sketchbooks.'

'For me?' Jasper's eyes opened wide. 'But he can't stop painting — he's too talented!'

'Perhaps he intends to buy new paints in France?' Edith swallowed back her tears. 'Will you help me to choose what to pack for him? There isn't room for everything.'

They worked together until the two bags were stuffed full.

'I'm going to put one of my paintings in Pascal's bag,' said Jasper. He hurried from the room and returned a moment later with a small roll of canvas. He slid it into one of the holdalls.

Defiantly, Edith pushed a second pair of shoes into the other.

'There are so many things that won't fit,' said Jasper, resting his hand on a pile of clothing left on the bed.

'We'll store them carefully.' Edith lifted up Pascal's battered painting hat, the brim smudged with paint. 'Would you like this?'

Jasper turned the hat round and round in his hands. 'Uncle Pascal always wore it.' His smile trembled. 'It kept off the sun and the rain when he was working *en plein air*.' He put on the hat and studied his reflection in the looking glass.

Edith's heart somersaulted at the sight of him. Wearing the hat, his silhouette reminded her so much of Pascal's.

Gabrielle appeared in the doorway. '*Maman*, she say to me you must hurry. We go now.'

Edith nodded at Jasper and they each carried one of the bags downstairs to where Delphine stood waiting in the hall. Gabrielle and Pearl whispered together in the corner.

'Delphine,' said Edith, 'please will you tell Pascal he is welcome to return to Spindrift as soon as he wishes?'

She shrugged. 'My brother is very stubborn and we do not always agree. My parents are growing too old to care for him and I tell him to stay here with his friends but he will not.'

'I shall write to him and try to change his mind.'

The whole party went outside. As the driver loaded the luggage into the carriage, Benedict sauntered up the lane.

'Not leaving us already, Gabrielle?' he asked.

'I shall bring your daughter to you next summer, Benedict,' said Delphine. 'Please be polite and respond to her letters in future.' She pushed Gabrielle forward. 'Kiss your father, *mon enfant*.'

Dutifully, Gabrielle stood on her tiptoes and pecked Benedict's cheeks.

He caught her in a bear hug. 'Come back soon.'

370

She gave him a coquettish smile and he handed her into the carriage just as if she were a fine lady.

'Why does Papa always make such a fuss of her?' Pearl muttered to her mother.

'Don't be jealous, sweetheart,' murmured Edith. 'She's only here for a few weeks a year and you have your father to yourself for the rest of the time.'

Pearl shrugged. 'If he isn't off somewhere with Roland.'

'Au revoir, Edith,' said Delphine.

There was a horrible hollow feeling inside her stomach. 'Bon voyage, Delphine. Please say goodbye to Pascal for me. Tell him . . . ' She shook her head, unable to say any more.

Delphine climbed into the carriage and Benedict gave her a cheerful wave.

Jasper moved closer to his mother, his face pale and set.

The driver flicked the reins and the carriage rolled off down the lane.

'I'm going to find Lily,' said Pearl. The dogs trotted off along the garden path behind her.

Jasper's expression was so woebegone Edith caught him in her arms and hugged him.

He remained still for a moment and then pulled away. Muttering something incomprehensible, he ran off, but not before Edith saw his face was contorted by tears. She thought of following but guessed he'd prefer to be alone.

'What's the matter with him?' asked Benedict as they returned to the hall.

'Delphine is taking Pascal back to Belle Vue,'

said Edith, her voice breaking. She didn't want to speak to Benedict. She wanted to hide in her room and sob her heart out.

'Pascal is leaving for good?' asked Benedict. He closed the front door.

She nodded and tried to edge around him but he blocked her way.

'Edith?'

Her face crumpled and she let out a mew of misery.

He sighed and pulled her into his arms. Taken aback, she tried to release herself but he held her so firmly she couldn't escape. His chest was broad and comfortingly warm so she gave up the struggle and laid her head on his shoulder and howled.

He patted her back until her sobs turned to sniffs. 'I'm sorry,' she said. Embarrassed, she fumbled for her handkerchief and blew her nose, even though he still imprisoned her in the circle of her arms.

'I'd thought you and Pascal were no more than friends these days but you still love him, don't you?' he murmured.

Another sob escaped her and she turned her face away. 'Let me go,' she said. *It was my fault he fell!* The words screamed in her head.

Benedict lifted her chin. 'You're still so lovely, Edith, even when you're weeping.'

She opened her mouth to protest but, before she could speak, he pressed his lips to hers in a passionate kiss. Shocked, she froze. And then, over his shoulder, she saw Tamsyn watching them from the staircase.

Edith pushed Benedict away. 'Don't!' she said. She glanced up at the staircase again, but Tamsyn had gone.

36

She glanced up at the staircase again, but
Edith pushed Benedict away. 'Don't' she said
the hall was empty.

November 1906

Dora and Clarissa waited in the hall to see Edith off on her visit to London. Dora tensed when she saw Tamsyn loitering there yet again, and guessed she was waiting for another letter. They came regularly and, if Dora got there first, she noticed they were always addressed in the same hand. She wondered if they were from an employment agency. If that were so, Tamsyn clearly hadn't had much luck in finding a position, probably due to the fact that she had Roland to accommodate, too.

Tamsyn gave them one of her sulky looks and sauntered off towards the kitchen, her hips swaying.

Dora gritted her teeth.

'Remember,' murmured Clarissa, 'never apologise, never explain.'

'I can't bear to be anywhere near her,' said Dora.

Clarissa glanced at her watch. 'Edith will miss her train, if she's not careful.'

Dora called up the staircase. 'Edith! Are you ready?'

A door closed above and Edith hurried down the stairs. She paused before the hall mirror to fiddle with the angle of her hat. 'Will I do? My coat is frightfully old-fashioned for Knightsbridge, isn't it?'

'You look beautiful, as always,' said Dora.

'Besides,' said Clarissa, 'when you deliver my parcel of jewellery to Madame Monette, she'll be sure to find you something lovely to wear for the first night of your exhibition.'

Edith's mouth trembled and her eyes glistened. 'I don't want to go. I can't bear to leave Jasper,' she said. 'He's still so upset. And it feels all wrong for me to be exhibiting at the Walworth Gallery without Pascal.'

'Of course it isn't!' Clarissa. 'You both worked extremely hard to produce such superb canvases and it would be unforgivable for them not to be displayed. Pascal is too unwell to attend, so it's your responsibility to represent him.'

'The exhibition will bring you new clients,' said Dora, 'and, Heaven knows, we all need more of those. Don't worry about the children. Clarissa and I will keep an eye on them, especially Jasper.'

'Kiss them all for me when they return from school, won't you?'

'Of course we will!' Dora gave her a hug.

'Julian is waiting for you in the courtyard,' said Clarissa. 'He's loaded your luggage.'

They hurried outside and Julian handed Edith into the trap.

Mabel and Maude came out of their studio to wish her a fruitful trip to London, soon followed by Gilbert, Augustus and Wilfred.

'See you in ten days!' called Clarissa.

They all waved goodbye and Julian drove out of the courtyard.

Dora caught a last glimpse of Edith's woebegone face as the trap turned into the lane. 'I hope her exhibition goes well,' she said. 'She needs something good to lift her out of the doldrums. I simply can't understand why Pascal refused to let her visit him or why he wouldn't return to Spindrift. It's almost as if he blames her for the accident in some way.'

'It's hardly surprising he needs time to adjust,' said Clarissa. 'Perhaps he doesn't want Edith to see him while he's in such a weakened condition.'

Dora dawdled back to the house, worrying about Edith. Her wretchedness after Pascal's recent departure had made her accept that Edith loved him and that they'd probably loved each other for years, until his dreadful accident changed his feelings. But could their love have been so very wicked when they'd always seemed so right together; two halves of a perfect circle? That was exactly how she and Ursula had complemented each other, bringing a sense of completeness to their lives. At least until that shocking kiss arrived out of the blue and destroyed their friendship forever.

★ ★ ★

Tamsyn sat by the hall window again, waiting for the postman. She'd waited every day for a week and was beginning to fear the hoped-for letter wouldn't come. Roland was playing in the sitting room but his frequent shrieks of glee as he kicked over his towers of bricks were getting on her nerves. To tell the truth, everything had got on her nerves for ages but especially since she'd seen Benedict kissing Edith in the hall a couple of months before. That had been the last straw and she'd known then that, however painful, things had to change.

'Stop that, Roland!' she yelled. She held her breath, ready to go and larrup him if he did it again. Mercifully, all went quiet.

Benedict didn't know she'd seen him with Edith and she hadn't picked a fight with him. It was different from the times he'd had a dalliance with other women; that Mrs Plumridge, for instance. He always tired of them in the end but Edith was another kettle of fish entirely. Tamsyn had always suspected Benedict still loved his wife, even though he'd laughed in her face when she accused him of it. But now she had proof. With her own eyes, right here in the hall, she'd seen them kissing.

She heard the click of the gate latch outside and glimpsed the postman's blue uniform as he walked up the path. The moment the post fell through the letterbox and onto the mat, she snatched it up and sifted through it. There was one for Dora, too, and she shoved it down behind Gilbert's statue of some Greek woman with no arms that stood on the hall table. And there was the letter she'd been waiting for! She hurried into the sitting room and plumped down on an armchair.

'Ma?' Roland tried to climb on her lap but she pushed him off.

'Not now!' she said. She tore the envelope

open and knew it was going to be all right as soon as she saw the train ticket inside.

My dearest Tamsyn

My heart was filled with joy when I had your letter. I had almost given up hope that you would accept my proposal, even though Mother said to bide my time. She reminded me how difficult it must be for you to consider leaving the beautiful place where you grew up, to come to a city you have never seen. Remember, I shall be waiting for you at the station, eager to show you your future home.

We have set aside several yards of the best quality white silk satin for you and some exquisitely embroidered net. Once you arrive, you shall instruct Mother's dressmaker on the style you would like for your wedding dress and we shall be married in time for Christmas.

My dear, I dream of you every night, hardly able to believe I shall soon hold you in my arms.

Forever yours,
Bert

Tamsyn kissed the letter and held it to her heart. She'd refused his proposal the night before he'd returned to London in the summer. He'd been terribly downcast but had written to say his offer remained open. Later, seeing Benedict and Edith kissing had made her reconsider. She'd known there was no future for her at Spindrift but there

378

was a dreadful price to pay for her escape.

Roland sidled up to her and, seeing she wasn't about to scold him this time, climbed onto her lap.

Tamsyn rested her chin on his curly head. She'd have to find him a nice Christmas present; some toy soldiers, perhaps. 'Who's Ma's lovely boy then?' she whispered.

He laughed up at her with Benedict's hazel eyes and pressed a sticky kiss on her cheek.

* * *

One morning a week later, Tamsyn wrote a note to Benedict and placed it on the chest of drawers. The previous night, he'd pushed himself up against her in bed but she'd turned away. It wouldn't have felt right, not even for old time's sake. He'd still been in a huff with her this morning when he took Roland down to the cove.

The grandfather clock on the landing struck nine. Time to go. Hastily, Tamsyn pulled on her best petticoat and least-mended dress and stockings. Once she'd pinned up her hair, she decorated it with a bit of ribbon she'd pinched from Dora's sewing box. Soon, she'd be able to have all the ribbon she wanted, even silk, from Bert's shop. She rolled up the beautiful lace shawl he had given her and placed it in her holdall. One of Roland's vests lay on the floor and, sighing, she tucked it into her bag. Putting on her hat, she glanced around the bedroom and then went downstairs. Thankfully, she met no one. Edith was still up in London at her exhibition and Dora had gone to the studio earlier that morning.

In the kitchen, Aunt Nessa was making Christmas mincemeat. 'Where are you off to in your best dress then, my girl?' she said. She glanced at Tamsyn's holdall and raised her eyebrows.

'Just into the village,' said Tamsyn, making her eyes wide and innocent. She collected her coat from the back lobby and buttoned it up.

Aunt Nessa gave her a sharp look. 'Where's Roland?'

'On the beach with Benedict. I'm going to see him now.'

'So, you've come to your senses, at last? You must know there's no future for you here.'

Tamsyn stilled.

Aunt Nessa smiled. 'I hoped you'd find yourself a position where you could make a fresh start. Told them you're a widow with a little 'un, have you?'

Tamsyn hesitated and then nodded. She'd made sure never to mention Bert to her aunt.

'Come and give me a hug then.' She held out her arms and Tamsyn kissed her cheek. 'Write to me when you're both settled.' She turned back to her mincemeat.

Tamsyn swallowed the lump that had risen in her throat and slipped out of the back door.

She walked through the back garden gate and onto the headland. The November wind sliced through her thin coat like a knife. She hurried towards the cliff steps and stood at the top watching Benedict and Roland spinning clumps of seaweed into the waves. Star and Blue danced around them, the sound of their excited barks carrying on the wind. Benedict crouched down beside Roland and they dug in the sand with pieces of driftwood.

Tamsyn stared at them, fixing in her mind a picture of the two of them, heads together. Bert knew nothing about Roland or Benedict, and his mother was a God-fearing Methodist. It had still been a terrible hard decision to make but Tamsyn could hardly turn up on their doorstep with her love child in tow, could she? But Benedict really loved Roland so he'd be all right.

Running along the coast path towards her new future, she wasn't sure if the tears streaming down her cheeks were caused by sorrow or the bitter wind.

★　★　★

Edith caught the morning train back from London. Darkness was falling when she found Gilbert waiting for her with the trap outside Port Isaac Road station.

'Thank you for coming to meet me,' she said, shivering in the cold wind.

'Happy to be of service, my dear.' He took her case and parcels and loaded them into the trap.

'So how was it?' he asked as they drove away.

'Almost all the canvases sold,' said Edith, 'and I'm expecting three new commissions.' She massaged her temples to relieve her headache.

Gilbert glanced at her. 'You don't sound particularly happy about it.'

381

'The journey is tiring,' she said. 'And . . . ' she hesitated ' . . . it was heartbreaking Pascal wasn't with me. His work was so much admired and he'd have had several commissions, if only he'd been there.' She sighed. 'I'll let him know the details of the interested parties but,' she shrugged her shoulders helplessly, 'I've written to him every week since he returned to France and, so far, there's been no reply.'

'You need to give him time, my dear,' said Gilbert. 'I expect he's finding it hard to face up to his new circumstances. Anyone would.' He patted Edith's hand. 'Knowing Pascal, eventually he'll climb out of the pit of despair and start anew.'

Edith forced a smile. She still had to live with the fact that it was her deception that had almost destroyed Pascal.

The lamps were lit when they arrived at Spindrift. Edith wanted nothing more than a cup of tea and to go early to bed, but as she climbed down from the trap, Clarissa came running out of the coach house.

'Edith, I wanted to catch you before you go indoors,' she said. 'Benedict's on the rampage. Tamsyn's done a flit.'

'Tamsyn's gone?'

'To London. Left him a note on the dresser telling him she's engaged to be married.' Clarissa shook her head. 'That's the good news. The bad news is that she's left Roland behind. Said she wanted a fresh start.'

'No!' Edith pressed her fingers to her mouth. 'How *could* she abandon her child?'

382

'As easily as Benedict deserted his children, it would seem,' said Gilbert. 'Edith, you'd better go inside and get warm.'

She heard Roland wailing and Benedict shouting somewhere in the house as soon as she opened the kitchen door.

Mrs Rowe, her narrow back rigid, was chopping carrots for the soup in sharp, staccato bursts.

'I hear Tamsyn has gone,' said Edith.

The cook wheeled around, bright spots of scarlet on her cheeks and her nostrils flaring. 'How could she?' She shook the raised knife with a jerky movement. 'I can understand her wanting to leave Spindrift but how could she leave her own child! Especially with *him*. It's not right, I tell you. I always knew she was flighty but this . . . ' She let the knife fall to the table with a clatter and dabbed her eyes with the corner of her apron. 'Begging your pardon, Mrs Fairchild.'

'Poor little Roland!' said Edith. 'Tamsyn spent quite a bit of time with you here in the kitchen, didn't she? Did she say anything about where she was going?'

Mrs Rowe blew her nose and shook her head.

'I can see you're upset. Shall I make you some tea?'

'Best get on,' said the cook. She drew a deep breath. 'The dinner needs cooking.'

'I'll go and see what's happening.'

Edith hurried into the hall and found Benedict pacing the floor, yelling curses and kicking at the walls. Roland sat on the stairs, howling.

Edith glimpsed Pearl peering at her father

383

from behind the drawing-room door. 'For goodness' sake, Benedict!' said Edith. 'Calm down, you're upsetting Roland!'

He rounded on her. 'And what about me? That little witch has pinched money out of my wallet and scarpered off into the wide blue yonder to deceive some other poor bugger!'

'Perhaps you should have treated her better then?'

'I'm not staying here to listen to you nagging at me!' He pushed past her and strode towards the front door.

'Benedict!' shrieked Edith. 'You can't just walk off and leave Roland!'

'Watch me!' The door slammed behind him.

There was a momentary silence and then the child began to howl again.

Pearl appeared from behind the door. 'Well,' she said, 'I'm glad Tamsyn has gone.'

Edith pinched the bridge of her nose. Her head ached and she couldn't stand the noise. Sighing, she went to soothe Roland.

★　★　★

It was after lunch the following day when Benedict came upstairs looking for Edith in her studio. He carried two cups of coffee and put them down on her work table with shaking hands before drawing up a chair beside her easel.

Edith raised her eyebrows. 'You look as if you slept in a hedgerow last night.'

He rasped at the stubble on his jaw. 'I came to apologise for shouting at you.'

She stepped back to avoid his beer-laden breath. 'Where's Roland?'

'Making scones with Mrs Rowe.' He scowled. 'I can't believe Tamsyn's gone. The scheming vixen must have been planning this for a while. Turns out she'd been sneaking a few of her things out of our bedroom every day for the past week and storing them at the Golden Lion so I wouldn't rumble her.' He sipped his black coffee and grimaced. 'The landlord told me she'd been particularly friendly with one of the summer visitors and she'd been seen walking with him down by the harbour. I'd no idea she'd found someone new.'

'Why would you?' said Edith. 'You've paid her very little attention for years.'

Benedict shifted uneasily on his chair. 'After you wouldn't have me back, I wanted to hurt you for not wanting me anymore. Bringing Tamsyn to Spindrift was a means of retaliating.' He scratched at his scalp. 'If she hadn't found herself pregnant, I'd have booted her out years ago.'

'Tamsyn didn't get pregnant all by herself!'

'But then, when Roland was born, straight away I knew I loved him.' He shrugged. 'So I let Tamsyn stay.'

Edith folded her arms tightly across her chest. 'Have you any idea how painful it is to me that you never felt the same about the children we had together?'

'I suppose I was too young to be a father then.'

'Certainly you were too irresponsible,' said Edith, through gritted teeth.

'I've made such a mess of it all.' Benedict looked up at her with a wavering smile. 'Why did it all go so wrong?'

'Because you only think of yourself. You have to give as much, or more, than you take in life,' murmured Edith.

'You always did that, didn't you? I never appreciated it before.' He wiped his hand over his face. 'I've made many mistakes but losing you was the very worst and I didn't even know it. I regret it every day now. Love is such a complicated thing, isn't it? It hits you like the seventh wave and knocks you senseless but then, after a while, it washes away and leaves you icy cold and shivering.'

'You've always wanted so much more than you had, Benedict.'

'It took me a long time to understand what I'd lost.' His hazel eyes were filled with remorse. 'I still love you, Edith. You do know that, don't you?'

Discomfited, she looked away. 'It's too late, Benedict.'

'I thought you might say that. I've been hoping, now Pascal has gone . . . '

'It's too late,' she repeated.

'Can we at least be friends again?' He stared down at his fingers, clasped in his lap. 'I'm lonely and so tired of always being on the outside of the community. I want to learn how to fit in. And, perhaps, in time, you might learn to love me again?'

Extreme weariness made Edith want to cry. She stifled the tug of pity she felt for him with a

386

tart rejoinder. 'You can start with the children, then. Roland needs you. And Pearl loves you but in the past you've made a fuss of her and then pushed her aside. Can't you see how hurtful that is, especially for a child?'

'I hadn't thought . . .'

'That's exactly your problem, Benedict! If you are ever to be truly happy, you must learn how to put yourself in other people's shoes and understand how much pain you cause by your selfishness.'

Slowly, he nodded. 'I want to earn your love again, so I'll try, Edith. I'll try, for you.'

Exasperated, she let out a sigh. 'Not for me. Do it for yourself and for your children. Start by making arrangements for Roland. Hannah is too busy to look after him all the time so, unless you're going to do it, he'll need a nursemaid.'

'Can't you . . .'

'No! Since you don't support our four children, I have to work, remember?'

'There's no need to . . .'

'Yes, there is!' She buried her face in her hands. 'Please go away now, Benedict. I have work to do.' She held her breath until she heard his shuffling footsteps leave the room.

Afterwards, too unsettled to paint, she sat by the studio window. Once, she'd loved Benedict with all her heart. If only he'd become the man she'd thought he was, perhaps she might have learned to forget Pascal and they could have recaptured the love they once shared.

37

In the weeks before Christmas it appeared to Dora that Benedict had turned over a new leaf. He was subdued and appeared to take pleasure in Roland and Pearl's company. Jasper still avoided him and the twins were always lost in their own little world. On the occasions that Hannah was free to mind the little boy, Benedict began to paint again.

'I can hardly believe it but he seems to have mended his ways,' Dora said to Edith.

'Let's hope he doesn't become bored with playing nursemaid to Roland,' said Edith. She sighed. 'I wondered if we ought to invite him and Roland to join us for the Christmas festivities? I heard Roland asking Benedict yet again when his ma was coming back. I don't care to see a child punished for his parents' failings.'

'I agree, if only in the spirit of Christian duty,' said Dora.

'Then I'll ask the others at supper tonight,' said Edith.

★ ★ ★

The whole community gathered for Christmas lunch but afterwards, Jasper, still silent and grieving for Pascal, retreated to his room again, straight after he'd finished his Christmas pudding. The others, replete and outwardly full of good cheer, retired to the drawing room. The dogs stretched out on the hearthrug and dozed before the fire. Several of the older children sprawled on the carpet beside the Christmas tree, working on a jigsaw puzzle, while Wilfred, resplendent in a velvet smoking jacket, poured a glass of port for Augustus. Clarissa and Julian held hands on the sofa.

Benedict crouched on the floor with Pearl, helping Roland to set up the track for his toy train. Every now and again, he glanced up at Edith, who chatted desultorily with Mabel and Maude. Edith's face was drawn and tired and Dora was worried she'd grown too thin. Edith didn't talk of her private feelings but it was obvious she missed Pascal dreadfully. It appeared both she and Edith had secrets they were unable to discuss, even with their closest friends.

Curling up in an armchair, Dora stared into the flames, recalling her warm glow of happiness at Christmas the previous year. Ursula had sat beside her then and they'd chatted about her cousins in Germany and their different Christmas traditions. 'Perhaps next year we will visit them and enjoy the warmth of German hospitality together,' Ursula had said.

But now that would never happen because Ursula had disappeared from Dora's life as completely as if she'd vanished from the face of the earth. There'd been no word from her and Dora didn't know how to contact her, even if she'd wanted to.

'Dora,' said Gilbert, breaking into her reverie.

389

'Won't you play us some carols?'

She gave a mechanical smile and went to sit at the piano. Perhaps a sing-song would make her forget the ache in her heart for a while. She lifted the lid and started to play 'Once in Royal David's City'.

Half an hour later, she was giving a second rendition of 'Silent Night', or *Stille Nachte* as Ursula had called it, when the door opened and Jasper came in.

When Dora finished the carol, he sidled up to her. 'I was coming downstairs when I accidentally knocked a bunch of holly off the garland on the banister,' he said. 'It fell behind Gilbert's statue of Aphrodite and, when I went to pick it up, I found this letter.'

Dora took it from him and a sudden coldness tingled through her. Ursula's writing! Staring at the postmark, she saw it was dated over a month before. She ripped open the envelope and took out the letter.

My very dear Dora

I regret beyond anything that I allowed my intense feelings for you to frighten you. Causing you distress was the last thing I ever wanted and I apologise unreservedly.

For that one magical moment in the garden when I believed you returned my affections, I was in Heaven. But then Tamsyn saw us there and everything changed in a heartbeat. In that foolishly unguarded second, I lost you forever. I was in such a state of despair that I fled from

Spindrift without attempting to explain my feelings to you.

I have returned to Stansfield Hall in Surrey and Lady Violet Stansfield is happy to allow me to stay here for another month or so. I have no wish to reopen old wounds, and I expect you have quite put out of your mind the friendship we once shared, but I cannot let matters rest without opening my heart to you.

I confess I fell in love with you the first time we met. I accepted you were unlikely to feel that same passion and resolved to be grateful for the wonderful friendship you bestowed upon me. I vowed never to tell you my true feelings. But, oh, my dear, how hard it was!

You have made it clear you do not care for me in the way I might have hoped for but I will never forgive myself if I don't at least ask if you might continue to be my valued friend? Of course it goes without saying that, in such a case, I would promise never to mention what happened between us and never again to make any unwelcome advance to you. I bitterly regret any distress I may have caused you.

If you do not reply I shall have my answer.

With the warmest of friendship,
Ursula

Dora let the letter fall to her lap. Her legs shook and her mind felt fogged.

'Are you all right?' asked Clarissa. 'You look as if you've seen a ghost!'

'It's from Ursula,' Dora said. 'She's at Stansfield Hall in Surrey. If you will excuse me — ' She stumbled from the room and ran upstairs, where she climbed into bed and pulled the eiderdown over her head.

★ ★ ★

The following morning at breakfast, Dora silently sipped a cup of tea, allowing the general chatter to fade into the background. Aching all over from a sleepless night, the words of Ursula's letter still went round and around in her head. She missed Ursula so much but was it possible they could be friends again, without the spectre of what had happened driving them apart? Could she ever be easy in her mind, knowing that Ursula loved her in such an unnatural way?

Wilfred sat down beside her with his plate of toast and marmalade. 'You're not looking top notch this morning, Dora,' he said.

She shook her head.

'Tell you what, why don't we take a walk by the sea? The breeze will blow the cobwebs away.'

Sighing, she said, 'Perhaps that's a good idea.'

Twenty minutes later, wrapped up in warm scarves and gloves, they went down to the cove. The wind had whipped up white horses on the sea and waves pounded against the rocks shooting explosive sprays of spume into the air.

Wilfred drew in a lungful of sea air and laughed. 'Go on, Dora, take a deep breath!

There! Doesn't that make you feel better?'

'A bit.'

'Do you want to talk about Ursula's letter?' he asked.

She considered confiding in him but how could she discuss something so shocking? 'Not really,' she muttered.

'In that case,' he said, 'I'm going to tell you a story.' He tucked his arm through hers and led her along the strand. 'It's about a boy who felt he never quite fitted in,' he began. 'He knew he was different from his friends but he wasn't sure how. The boy didn't much like rough and tumble games and preferred drawing. He didn't care to be dirty or untidy like other boys so they often teased him and called him a sissy. Reluctantly, he learned to box so that, when they bullied him, he could stop them. Once he'd knocked down the most vicious of the bullies, the others never troubled him again. After that, the boy learned to turn aside cruel comments by responding with a rapier-sharp put-down. Have you guessed yet, Dora, that the boy was me?'

'I wondered,' she said.

'I wasted so many years hiding my true nature, even from myself,' Wilfred said. He came to a stop and looked out at the churning sea. 'There's a second part to my story. When my father died, an old friend of his took me under his wing. He was a cultured man and we visited art galleries and museums together. We dined in the best restaurants and went to the theatre and he was the most amusing company.'

A large wave raced towards them, foaming

around their feet before they could step back.

'And then,' said Wilfred, shaking water off his boots, 'after some years, my friend introduced me to love.'

Dora felt herself sway as the water receded, sucking the sand from beneath her.

Wilfred steadied her. 'Do you understand what I'm saying, Dora?'

'Yes.' She shook her head. 'No.' She didn't want to know.

'I think you do. I was deeply shocked at first but my friend was kind and gentle and it wasn't long before I understood that I'd found the final piece of the jigsaw puzzle that made me complete.'

Dora couldn't look at him. 'And now?'

'Eventually my friend and I parted but, by then, I knew who and what I was. I'll always be grateful to him for that. I was very lonely for a long while afterwards. And then I met Augustus. You see, Dora, when you meet your soulmate, it doesn't matter if they're the same gender as you are. It's still love.'

'I can't — '

'All I would say to you is that, for such as you and me, the chances of meeting another soulmate are few and far between.' He caught hold of Dora by her upper arms and looked into her eyes with an intensity she longed to evade. 'I know how happy you were with Ursula, even if you didn't know you loved her. Don't risk losing that!'

A sob burst out of her. 'I miss her so terribly!'

Wilfred hugged her until she stopped weeping.

'Don't waste any more time agonising over it. Go and find her!'

★ ★ ★

Two days later, Dora stood outside the imposing wrought-iron gates to Stansfield Hall. The stone lions on top of the gateposts looked down upon her with a disapproving glare. A long tree-lined drive stretched ahead, leading to a vast mansion about half a mile away.

An old man came out of the gatehouse and shuffled towards her.

'I believe Miss Hoffman is staying here,' stammered Dora.

The old man dragged up the great bolts that secured the gates, unlocked the padlock and chain and opened one gate sufficiently wide to allow Dora through.

The walk up the long drive seemed endless and she couldn't rid herself of the idea that there were eyes watching her from behind the rows and rows of windows. All the while, she wondered if she was making a dreadful mistake in coming to talk to Ursula. Even if she promised they could just be friends, could Ursula be trusted? And what would Dora do if Ursula had already left Stansfield Hall?

Finally, she reached the stone steps that led up to the imposing portico over the front door. She hesitated before ringing the bell. If she ran away now, before anyone saw her, she would avoid any upsetting scenes. But before she could scuttle away, the door opened.

A butler greeted her and she gave her name and asked to see Miss Hoffman. She stepped over the threshold onto a marble floor and glanced up at the ceiling soaring above her. There was no place for someone like herself amongst such grandeur.

The butler took her coat and handed it to a liveried footman, who had mysteriously appeared out of nowhere. 'Please, follow me,' said the butler.

Dora's pulse raced but it was too late to run away.

The butler opened a door. 'Lady Stansfield, Miss Cox, to call upon Miss Hoffman.'

Confused, Dora hovered in the doorway. The enormous drawing room had a ceiling decorated like a wedding cake and a soft Persian carpet underfoot. A huge fire danced in the marble fireplace and there were fresh flowers, fresh flowers in *winter* mind you, in crystal vases set upon delicate gilded tables.

'Miss Cox, how delightful to meet you.' An elegant lady of middle years smiled up at her from one of the silken sofas. 'Ursula has told me all about you.' She turned to the butler. 'Wharton, will you show Miss Cox to the winter garden? I believe Miss Hoffman is tending to the orchids.'

A moment later, Wharton opened a glazed door to an enormous conservatory and ushered Dora inside before closing the door quietly behind her.

She remained motionless, her mouth suddenly dry. The air was hot and humid and numerous specimen palm trees reached up to a domed glass roof high above. Comfortable wicker chairs were set in groups and marble statues were displayed in stone niches. There was no sound except for a fountain splashing into a pool edged with ferns and the rapid beat of her own heart in her ears.

Then she caught her breath at the sound of light footsteps across the stone floor.

Ursula, holding a watering can, stepped into view from behind a small forest of broad-leaved shrubs. Her hand flew to her mouth and she came to an abrupt halt. 'You came?' she whispered.

'As you see.' Dora's lips were so numb it was hard to form the words. 'I only found your letter a few days ago.' She drew back when Ursula took a step closer.

Her face twisted in momentary pain and she looked away. 'I hoped you'd come but I had no real expectation of it.'

'I think, perhaps,' Dora said, measuring her words, 'I might not have done, if I'd received your letter before. Now I've had time to think and appreciate exactly how much our friendship meant to me.'

'If only our friendship could be restored,' said Ursula, 'I'd promise never, ever, to distress you in such a way again.'

There was such desperation in her tone it made Dora want to cry. 'I've missed you more than you will ever know,' she murmured. Her gaze fixed on a pulse beating wildly in Ursula's throat. White mist swirled through her thoughts, making it impossible to think clearly.

'If we could only return to that state of tranquil happiness we once shared,' said Ursula, her head bowed, 'I would be more than content.'

'But,' said Dora, the fog in her mind suddenly melting away, 'I'm afraid I couldn't be content with that. Not anymore.' She stepped forward and caressed Ursula's cheek with her forefinger. 'You see, I never knew a door to Paradise existed until you opened it and showed me a tiny glimpse of what was on the other side.'

Ursula looked up then, her marvellous clear eyes wide with hope.

'I wasn't prepared to go through the doorway then,' said Dora, 'but now, if you'll hold my hand and promise never to let it go, I'm ready to walk through it with you.'

Ursula let out a sob and took a tentative step forwards.

'Oh, my love!' said Dora, gathering her into her arms. And this time, her heart sang when they kissed.

38

March 1907

It was the last day of term and Adela and the Spindrift children cheered as they raced each other home from school. Hannah had their tea ready and sat with them to make sure Rose and Roland behaved themselves while they ate.

'I can't wait to go down to the cove!' said Pearl. Adela had told her that her brothers had returned the previous night from boarding school for the Easter holidays. It seemed ages since Christmas when the whole Tregarrick Cove Gang had last been together.

'Will and Jasper, are you coming with us?' asked Lily. 'Noel and Timmy will be home by now.'

Jasper sighed. 'I suppose I could bring my sketchbook with me.'

'I'll come, too,' said Will.

'I want to come,' said Roland, spitting out his sandwich crusts.

'Me too,' said Rose.

'Well, you can't,' said Pearl. 'You're both too little.'

'I'm three!' said Roland indignantly.

'Exactly,' said Pearl. 'Too little.'

Scowling, Roland banged his plate on the table. 'I want my ma!'

'That's enough of that, my lad!' said Hannah. 'And the rest of you can get down, if you've finished.'

Lucien and Nell raced off to find their shrimping nets. The dogs bounded along after them, yipping with excitement.

'Days and days with no school!' said Lily as they dashed through the garden towards the sound of the sea. At the edge of the cliff they peered down into the cove. 'Are Noel and Timmy there?' asked Lily.

'Yes! Do you see? They're sitting on the rocks with Adela,' said Pearl. She flew down the cliff steps, her palm growing hot as it rasped along the rope handrail.

'Wait for me!' cried Lily.

But Pearl, the wind in her hair and her soul full of the joy of freedom, hurtled across the sand towards the others. She came, panting, to a stop by the rocks, cheeks flushed and her hair ribbons slipping.

'Hello again,' said Timmy.

All at once, Pearl was tongue-tied. Timmy, now nearly sixteen, seemed to have grown taller since Christmas and his voice had deepened. 'Hello,' she said.

'Come and sit up here by me,' said Adela. 'Is Will coming?'

Pearl nodded.

'And here comes the little mermaid,' said Noel, watching Lily cross the sand, her long flaxen hair flying in the wind.

Soon Jasper and Will came down the steps and climbed up onto the rocks beside them. The twins and the dogs arrived and took themselves off to see what they could find in the rock pools.

Pearl glanced at the mound of tumbled rock

and earth that the landslip had carried down the cliff to bury the entrance to the smugglers' cave. She shuddered. Sometimes, the memory of being trapped inside still gave her nightmares.

'So, the Tregarrick Cove Gang meet again,' said Timmy. Before long they were all joking and exchanging news. Jasper sat a little apart, sketching them.

It was strange, thought Pearl, but something was different this time. She'd known the Penrose children for years, but now there was a peculiar tension, a fizzing sensation inside her, as if she were waiting for something exciting to happen.

Later, they grew quiet as they watched the sun sink into the sea in a wash of gold and pink. Timmy put his coat around Pearl's shoulders when she began to shiver.

Once the sun had dropped below the horizon, she said, 'We'd better go in, before anyone comes to look for us.'

'There's always tomorrow,' said Noel, smiling at Lily.

'Tomorrow,' she echoed, glancing at him from under her eyelashes.

Pearl called to the twins and the Penroses set off up the steps to Cliff House, turning to wave before they disappeared over the clifftop.

★ ★ ★

The following morning, Pearl was passing through the hall when a telegram arrived for Benedict. She went to find him in his sitting room, where he was trying to read a newspaper with Roland playing noisily with his toy train on the floor beside him.

Benedict sighed. 'Can't a chap have five minutes' peace and quiet! What is it, Pearl?'

'There's a telegram for you, Papa.' She held it out to him.

Frowning, he opened it. 'Dear God! Father's dead.' He thrust the newspaper aside and rose to his feet. 'I must go to London.'

'What about Roland?' asked Pearl.

Benedict ran his fingers distractedly through his hair. 'Where's your mother?'

Pearl shrugged. 'Working, I expect.' She followed him as he ran upstairs to the studio.

Edith was priming a new canvas and put down her brush with a sigh while Benedict explained what had happened.

'So will you look after Roland while I go to see Mother? My brother says she's collapsed with the shock and is asking for me,' he said. 'There'll be the funeral to arrange . . .'

'Benedict, you know I'm just starting my new commission. Time is tight enough already . . . '

'Please, Edith?' He pulled out a fistful of notes from his pocket and put them on the work table. 'Hannah can do some extra hours and perhaps there's a woman in the village who'd be glad of a bit extra?'

'It's really inconvenient. It's not as if Dora was here to give me a hand. She and Ursula won't be back from their walking holiday in Germany until the summer.'

'Please?' He caught her hands between his own. 'There's no one I'd trust more than you to look after Roland, especially while he's still so upset and missing his mother.'

Edith sighed. 'I suppose, since it's an emergency . . . '

Pearl watched in amazement as her papa dropped a smacking kiss on her mother's cheek.

'Darling Edith! I'd better run and pack if I'm going to catch the next train.' He thundered off down the stairs.

Pearl followed him and went to sit on the end of his bed to watch him throw clothes into a suitcase. 'When will you come back?' she asked.

'A few days after the funeral, I expect.' He held up two waistcoats. 'Which one?'

'You can't wear that yellow one if your father's just died,' said Pearl.

'No, I suppose not.'

'You will be back for my birthday, won't you?'

Benedict rummaged through his sock drawer. 'When is that, then?'

Pearl was hurt. 'The tenth of April. You should know when your daughter's birthday is.'

'I suppose I should. Sorry.' He sat down beside her on the bed. 'Tell you what. If you'll help to look after Roland while I'm away, I'll bring you back something nice from London for your birthday.'

Pearl nodded. 'You promise?'

'Absolutely!' Benedict snapped his suitcase shut. 'Right, I'm off then. I wonder if Julian will give me a lift to the station?'

'Don't forget to say goodbye to Roland,' said Pearl.

Benedict pursed his lips. 'He'll probably get

upset if I do. Why don't you tell him where I've gone?' He tugged one of Pearl's ringlets. 'Be a good girl and I'll see you soon.'

And then he was gone.

39

Edith drove the trap into the courtyard and came to a stop outside Ned's stable.

Clarissa lifted Rose and Roland down from the trap and picked up one of the baskets full of groceries.

'I'll see to Ned,' said Edith, 'if you'll take the shopping inside.'

Roland tugged at Edith's skirt. 'Auntie Edith, will my ma and papa be home now?'

'Not today, Roland,' said Edith, 'but I expect Papa will be back before long. Will you be a big boy and take this bag of flour to the kitchen?'

'Come with me!'

'In just a moment.'

The corners of the little boy's mouth turned down but he set off for the house carrying the flour.

'He's becoming too attached to me,' said Edith, with a worried frown. 'He called me Ma the other day and he follows me everywhere.'

'It's sad, isn't it?' said Clarissa, watching Rose hurry after him with a bag of sugar.

'I'm really annoyed with Benedict,' said Edith. 'He should have returned by now. His mother absolutely dotes on him and I daresay she doesn't want him to leave. Still, Pearl says he promised faithfully to come back for her

405

birthday tomorrow.'

Gilbert came out of his workshop, patting his clothes so that he raised a cloud of marble dust about his person. 'I'll put Ned away,' he said. 'You ladies are busy enough with the children and the shopping.'

'Thank you, Gilbert,' said Edith. 'I'm desperate to get back to work once Hannah is free to mind Roland this afternoon.'

They collected the baskets and followed the little ones into the house. 'Spindrift is so quiet now the children are back at school,' said Clarissa. 'And it feels empty with Dora, Ursula and Benedict away and Tamsyn and Pascal gone.'

Edith's stomach lurched as it always did when she thought about Pascal. 'At least there's less tension since Tamsyn left.'

'Except that Roland is so anxious,' said Clarissa.

'And I'm worried about Jasper,' said Edith. 'He still misses Pascal terribly and he's become so withdrawn.' Her voice cracked. 'It's awful not knowing how Pascal is. I can hardly bear it that in nine months he hasn't responded to a single one of my letters.'

Clarissa put down her baskets and hugged Edith. 'I don't understand it,' she said. 'I'd have imagined he'd turn to you for comfort at such a time.'

'I never told you but we had a terrible argument before he fell.' Edith's breath caught on a sob. 'We both said some unforgivable things.' The agony of that memory was seared into her mind.

406

'All lovers have tiffs,' said Clarissa. 'Pascal's accident had devastating consequences. Perhaps he can't face you now he's not the man he once was?'

'But that doesn't stop me loving him!' wept Edith. 'I wrote to Delphine and she sent me the briefest of notes telling me he barely speaks and sits in his wheelchair looking out of the window all day.'

'Why don't you go and see him, then?'

'In France?'

'Yes, of course in France! Have it out with him, face to face.'

'I can't travel there on my own,' said Edith.

'Perhaps Wilfred would escort you. I'm sure he'd be pleased to see his cousin.'

'But my children . . .'

'The rest of the community could manage for a while. After all, the twins are twelve now, hardly babies anymore.'

Edith swallowed. Perhaps she should go and see Pascal. As things were, she was in purgatory and at least then she'd know if there was ever any hope of a reconciliation. If not, she'd simply have to put him out of her mind. Though she didn't see how that would ever be possible.

'Come, Edith,' said Clarissa. 'Dry your eyes and we'll see what mischief the little ones are getting up to.'

★ ★ ★

The following morning was Pearl's birthday and she came down for breakfast late, wearing her

Sunday hair ribbons and a clean pinafore, even though it was a school day. A chorus of birthday wishes went up from the community gathered around the table.

'Papa will be here for my birthday tea this afternoon,' Pearl said, buttering her toast liberally. 'I wish Auntie Dora was here. She always makes me a chocolate cake.'

'I haven't yet received word from your father that he's returning today,' said Edith. She sincerely hoped he wouldn't let Pearl down.

'He promised he'd be here. He said he'll bring me a lovely present from London.'

'I'll make you a birthday cake,' said Edith. 'I can't promise it will be as good as Dora's, though.' She turned to Roland, sitting at her side. 'Would you like to help?'

He nodded vigorously.

'If you make it, Mama, it will be special to me,' said Pearl.

Mabel smiled at her. 'A pretty sentiment, my dear.'

'You're growing up to be quite the young lady,' said Maude.

'Thirteen is almost grown up,' said Pearl.

'Meanwhile,' said Edith, 'you'd better get along to school with your brothers and sisters. If you're late, your teacher won't make allowances because it's your birthday.'

After the older children had left for school, Edith took Roland into the kitchen. Mrs Rowe gave them space at one end of the table to mix the cake. Finally, the tins were in the oven but both Roland's face and the kitchen floor were liberally splattered with flour, eggs and choco-late. He scraped out the bowl with a teaspoon while Edith began to wipe up the mess.

Clarissa came into the kitchen, holding Rose by the hand. 'I saw the postman,' she said. 'There are two letters for you, Edith.'

Her heart somersaulted. 'Pascal?'

'I'm afraid not.'

She took the envelopes, her shoulders drooping. The first bore a London postmark and the writing was ill-formed and smudged.

Dear Edith

I did wrong to let Benedict bring me into your home and I'm sorry for that. I paid for it, too, with tears of misery because it was always you Benedict loved, even if he didn't know it. I had to leave Spindrift before the hopelessness shrivelled me up. I daresay you think badly of me for leaving Roland with his dad but I did it for the best. He is young enough to forget me and Benedict loves him and will give him a better life than I ever could have on my own. I'm married now to a decent man, something I could never have managed with Roly hanging onto my skirt. So I'm sorry for what I done to you because you are a good woman and I beg you, out of the kindness of your heart, to keep an eye on my lovely boy.

Tamsyn

Edith swallowed and glanced at Roland as he

and Rose squabbled good-naturedly over the last scrapings of chocolate cake in the bowl.

'What is it?' murmured Clarissa.

Silently, Edith handed her Tamsyn's letter and picked up the other envelope. 'Oh! It's Benedict's writing.' She smiled at Roland. 'Let's find out when your papa is coming home.'

My dear Edith

I am the bearer of good news! You may not be aware my father and I had a disagreement over my debts some years ago. He made it clear to me then that I would not be mentioned in his will. As I expected, the bulk of his estate goes to my brother, with an allowance for my mother to include the upkeep of the house.

Since I had no expectations, I am delighted to discover that Father had second thoughts regarding myself, as follows:

1. On my mother's death, the house in Berkeley Square will come to me, on condition that I live with and cherish her for the remainder of her life.

2. I may not have any person to live at the house with me, or to stay for any period longer than two weeks, without Mother's permission, excepting my wife and legitimate children.

3. If the above conditions are adhered to, Mother has the means to administer an allowance for the maintenance of myself, my wife and legitimate children.

Edith, you cannot imagine how happy I
am at this wonderful news! At last I can
make up to you for the sins of the past.
Here in Berkeley Square, as my wife, you
will no longer have to slave away scratching a living from your paintings but shall
enjoy dabbling with your paints as a pleasant hobby. The children will have my old
nursery and a full-time nanny so we will be
free to live our lives as we wish. You shall
enjoy yourself shopping, gossiping over the
teacups or accompanying Mother to the
theatre.

Mother's health is still delicate so I am
unable to return to Cornwall at present
but I trust to your usual good judgement
and capabilities to make the necessary
arrangements. Come as soon as may be
managed as I am impatient as a bridegroom
to begin a new and happier chapter in our
lives.

Yours in very good cheer,
Benedict.

P.S. My mother will assume Roland is our
son and therefore he will be able to join us
at Berkeley Square. If you are not prepared
to oblige me in this matter, please will you
find a suitable family for him in the village,
or a woman of good character to live at
Spindrift and care for him? I don't quite
like the prospect of an orphanage. The boy
misses his mother and I do not wish him
to be further upset by removing him from

familiar surroundings. I shall, of course,
make an allowance to his foster mother.

Edith closed her eyes for a moment while she resisted the urge to shout and curse like a fishwife. Carefully, she folded the letter in half, aware of Roland's gaze fixed upon her. 'I'm afraid your papa still has some business to attend to in London, Roland.'

'But he's coming home?'

'Not just yet.' She hated to see the sadness and disappointment in his face. 'Mrs Rowe, would you keep an eye on Roland and Rose for a short while? I'll be back in time to take the cake out of the oven.'

The cook gave her a sharp glance and nodded. 'Well, then, children,' she said, 'shall we have a look and see if I've any spare raisins in the pantry?'

Edith caught hold of Clarissa's arm and led her into the drawing room. She closed the door firmly behind them and pressed her fist to her mouth. She handed the letter to Clarissa with shaking fingers.

Clarissa read it and then looked at Edith, her face expressionless. 'How do you feel about reconciling with Benedict? It would make life much easier for you. Will you go to London?'

The pounding in Edith's ears grew unbearable. 'Go to London and become entirely subject to Benedict's whims again? Of course I won't! Can you *imagine* me giving up my painting to be an unpaid companion to his mother? And when did I ever want to gossip at tea parties?' Her

412

breath came in harsh gasps. 'But that pales into insignificance against the horror of how he could treat Roland as an afterthought to be conveniently disposed of. How could he even think of such a dreadful thing?'

Clarissa shrugged. 'The lure of easy money, I suppose.'

Edith paced across the drawing room. 'But not *Roland*! I thought Benedict loved him but he's effectively abdicating all responsibility for the child.'

'Exactly as he did with all his other children.'

'But I was there. Roland has no mother. You've seen Tamsyn's letter and she's not coming back for him. Now he's entirely alone.'

'If you're not careful, Edith, you'll end up being his adoptive mother.'

'Do you think I can't see that? The last thing in the world I want is to be responsible for the child of my husband's mistress.'

'What do you suggest?'

Edith rubbed at the tension in her neck. 'I don't know. Try and find a local foster family, I suppose. If Benedict offers a reasonable sum, I may find a kind family of good character to take him.'

'You'll need to ask a solicitor to draw up an agreement for the allowance,' said Clarissa. 'You can't trust Benedict to keep up the payments otherwise.'

'Do you think you might mind Roland for half an hour, while I ask Mrs Rowe if she knows of anyone in the village who might take him in?' Edith sighed. 'This isn't going to help our social standing in the locality, is it?'

'As to that,' said Clarissa with a wry smile, 'we already have a reputation for wildness and depravity to maintain.'

* * *

Pearl's birthday tea was all laid out on the table ready for when the children returned from school. They hurried to sit down and start on the ham sandwiches. Roland was very excited and proudly showed Pearl the cake he'd decorated with pink candles and hundreds and thousands.

'Are those thumbprints?' Pearl asked, squinting at the myriad dents in the icing.

'Only small ones,' said Edith, 'and I made sure his hands were clean, for a change.'

'But where is Papa?' asked Pearl. 'Shall I tell him tea's ready?'

The moment Edith had been dreading had arrived. 'Sweetheart, Papa sent me a letter. His mother is unwell and he must stay with her.'

Pearl's eager smile faded. 'He's not coming to my birthday tea?'

Edith shook her head.

'But he *promised*! When is he coming home?'

'Let's talk about this after you've had tea. Look, there are tiny little egg and cress sandwiches with the crusts cut off.'

'No,' Pearl said. 'I want to know now.'

Edith took a deep breath. 'As I said, your father must remain in London to look after your grandmother.'

Lucien, his cheek bulging with bread, said,

414

'When exactly is he coming home then?'

Edith held her breath.

'Well?' said Pearl.

'At present, he has no plans to return,' said Edith, a cold, empty feeling inside her. The last thing she'd wanted was to ruin Pearl's birthday tea.

Pearl drew in a sharp breath and her face crumpled. 'Papa's not coming home *at all*?'

Biting her lip, Edith wondered if she should tell a lie but the truth had to be faced some time. 'I'm afraid not.'

Jasper's lip curled. 'A leopard never changes his spots,' he murmured.

Roland looked at Pearl and then up at Edith. 'Papa isn't coming?' His eyes filled with tears. 'Is my ma coming, then?'

Edith was lost for words.

Roland's face turned scarlet and he began to shriek.

'Stop it, Roland!' yelled Pearl. 'It's not *your* birthday Papa has ruined.'

But Roland, his face growing more purple by the second, screamed and screamed.

Edith caught him up in her arms but he fought against her, arching his back and drumming his heels. After several minutes, he suddenly went limp. His head was heavy and hot against Edith's breast and his desperate sobs soaked her blouse.

Shocked, the other children were silent, their sandwiches untouched on their plates.

Pearl sniffed back her tears and came to stroke Roland's hair. 'Even though Papa has gone,' she

415

said, 'I'm still your sister and I will always look after you, Roly.'

Roland hiccoughed and said in a small voice, 'But who will be my ma?'

Tears ran down Edith's cheeks. 'It's all right, Roland,' she said. She kissed his hair and rocked his shuddering little body. 'From now on, I shall be your ma.'

40

'Are you nervous?' asked Ursula when Dora came to an abrupt halt outside the garden gate.

'A little,' said Dora, 'but it's not that.' She smiled at Spindrift House, the warm grey stone walls clad with Virginia creeper. Sunlight filtered through the leaves of the copper beech, making dancing shadows on the grass, and the sky above was the purest cerulean blue. 'I love this house,' she said, 'it's been my refuge, my home and my delight for fifteen years.'

'I love it, too,' said Ursula.

'Walking in the Black Forest together over the last months has been quite magical and,' Dora gave Ursula a mischievous smile, 'enlightening. But now I'm here, I'm so pleased to be home.'

Ursula brushed her finger down Dora's cheek. 'Then we shall not tarry.'

They strolled around the house to the back garden and Dora laughed. 'Listen!' she said.

At the end of the undulating lawn bordered by hydrangeas and rhododendrons, the field inclined steeply down towards a grassy headland with the sapphire sea beyond.

'How I've missed the sound of the sea!' said Dora.

'And tonight it will sing us a lullaby as we fall asleep in each other's arms,' murmured Ursula.

Lucien, waving a wooden sword and closely followed by Nell and the two dogs, raced out of the shrubbery and towards the gazebo.

'Do you see Edith and Clarissa?' said Ursula. 'They're sitting on a blanket with little Rose by the hydrangeas. Shall we join them?'

'It feels strange not to be holding hands,' said Dora as they walked towards the others.

'I know,' said Ursula, 'but we agreed it is wise to be discreet in our affection. Remember, though, hold up your head fearlessly. Our love is not illegal.'

'Whereas Wilfred and Augustus's love is against the law,' said Dora. 'That's the only instance I know of where the law regarding women is kinder than it is for men.'

Ursula chuckled. 'But only because men do not believe that a woman might ever find another woman's love more desirable than a man's sexual attentions.'

Edith glanced up.

Dora hesitated, suddenly nervous.

Edith rose swiftly to her feet and ran across the lawn towards them. She enfolded first Dora and then Ursula in a hug. 'How wonderful to have you both back!' she said, her eyes shining. 'You didn't let us know you were returning today or I'd have prepared your room. Come and tell us about your holiday.'

Dora felt a sudden release of the tension she'd carried all the while they'd journeyed back to Spindrift. It was going to be all right.

Clarissa stood up to hug them, too. 'Welcome home!' she said.

They sat on the tartan rug and Rose came running to kiss Dora.

Dora drew the little girl onto her knee and covertly studied Edith. Her muslin dress couldn't disguise how very thin she'd grown and there was a pale fragility about her that was worrying.

Roland, his face dirty, pushed his way out of the shrubbery and clambered onto Edith's knee.

Dora couldn't help but raise her eyebrows when Edith dropped a kiss on his head. 'I'm dying for some tea,' she said. She smiled teasingly at Ursula. 'You simply can't get a decent cup of tea in Germany, though the beer is very good.'

'Roland and Rose,' said Edith, 'will you please go to the kitchen and ask Hannah to bring out a fresh pot of tea? And perhaps some of the sponge cake?'

The two little children ran off towards the house.

'Before they return,' said Edith, 'I need to bring you up to date.'

'Has something happened?' asked Ursula.

Edith nodded. 'Benedict has left Spindrift.'

'But that's wonderful!' said Dora. She noticed the expression on Edith's face. 'Isn't it?'

'Well, it would have been, if he hadn't abandoned Roland.'

'Abandoned his son?' Ursula frowned. 'But why? I thought he was fond of the boy.'

Edith explained the terms of Benedict's inheritance and his instruction to her to find a foster family for Roland. 'The poor little mite

419

was so dreadfully distressed. Everyone he loved had deserted him.' She shrugged. 'I couldn't bear to see it. So I promised Roland I'd be his mother.'

'But he's Tamsyn and Benedict's child!' said Dora. 'Suppose he turns out like them?'

'He can't help his parentage and he's not four until August so he's still young enough for me to mould him.' Edith sighed. 'I hope. Generally, he's a cheerful and good-natured child but still, I'm furious with Benedict that he's left me, yet again, to pick up the pieces from the trail of emotional destruction he leaves in his wake. I wrote to him in the strongest of terms, begging him not to desert Roland.'

'With little effect, I imagine?' said Ursula.

Edith bowed her head. 'His response was that it was my fault Roland is deprived of his father's presence.'

Dora gasped. 'What?'

'He said, if I'd only pretended Roland was ours and resumed my proper role as a wife, then Roland could have lived with us and the rest of our children in London.'

Clarissa gave a half-smile at Dora's aghast expression. 'Breathtaking, isn't it?'

'You wouldn't ever go back to him, would you?' asked Dora.

'Not for all the tea in China.'

'What is the news of Pascal?' asked Ursula, changing the subject.

Edith looked into the distance, her face tight with pain. 'He hasn't replied to a single one of my letters.'

420

'But then you must go and see him!' said Dora. She no longer shied away from accepting Pascal and Edith's illicit love. How could she, now she herself lived outside the bounds of what society considered acceptable? She wasn't hurting anyone and was happier than she'd ever been in her life.

'That's what Clarissa thought,' said Edith, 'but now there's Roland. Hannah could look after him but he's grown to trust me and I can't desert him, too. I'd be frightened he'd suffer irreparable harm.'

Hannah arrived then with the tea tray and the two children trotting along at her side.

Roland ran straight to Edith and wriggled himself onto her knee. 'Look, Ma,' he said, pressing a kiss on her cheek, 'a present. It's a special biscuit I made for you today with Mrs Rowe. It's you! It's got currants for eyes and a cherry for your pretty mouth.'

Edith took the proffered biscuit from him. 'Aren't you a clever boy, Roly!' she said, hugging him.

Dora met Edith's eyes over the top of Roland's dark head. No more could be said in front of the children but, for Dora, the despair in Edith's expression had saddened her homecoming.

★ ★ ★

During supper, Dora and Ursula were heart-warmed by their welcome. The children were clamorous in their greetings while Wilfred gave

421

Dora a knowing smile. 'I'm so happy for you both,' he murmured when he hugged her.

'And I'll never thank you enough for making me see the truth,' she whispered back.

No one mentioned Dora and Ursula's argument or the rumours that had spread through the village six months before. They entertained the community with tales of their walking holiday through the Black Forest and the kindness of Ursula's cousin and his family who had invited them into their home.

Dora showed their friends her sketchbook and talked excitedly about the book of German fairy tales she intended to write. The sketchbook was filled with drawings of fantastical creatures that lived in the forest, of wolves, squirrels and owls. There were trees with faces, both benign and frightening, that reached out with twiggy fingers towards any hapless soul who wandered into the forest.

After supper Dora and Ursula excused themselves to take a stroll down in the deserted cove. They left their shoes at the foot of the cliff steps and revelled in the feel of the sand between their toes. Hand in hand, they wandered along the water's edge.

'The children have grown so much while we've been away,' said Ursula.

'Especially Jasper. I can hardly believe he's fourteen,' said Dora. 'Did you notice his voice is breaking? It doesn't seem five minutes since I held him in my arms as a newborn.'

Ursula sighed. 'And now Edith has yet another child to bring up.'

Dora bent to pick up a pearly shell. 'I loathed Tamsyn for what she did to Edith in coming here as Benedict's mistress. I hated her for spreading those rumours about us and I'm delighted she's gone.' She turned to face the sea. 'But life at Spindrift will be the better for it, even for Roland, once he's forgotten her.'

'Edith must be the most magnanimous person I've ever met,' said Ursula. 'Not many women would take on responsibility for her husband's natural child.'

'I'm worried about her.' Dora threw the shell into the waves. 'She looks ill, completely worn down with care. And she still grieves for Pascal. If it weren't for Roland, she'd go to him.'

'She might still find that Pascal doesn't want to return to Spindrift.'

'Perhaps, but, don't you see, Ursula — then she'd *know*? While you and I were apart, it wasn't just the anguish of our broken friendship that hurt me; the worst thing was not knowing if I'd ever see you again or whether there might be some way of reconciling.'

'Of course I remember,' said Ursula in a low voice. 'Every day of our separation was unbearable to me.'

Dora lifted Ursula's hand to her lips. 'But, after that dreadful time, we've been fortunate enough to find our happy ever after.'

They continued their walk, both of them in contemplative silence.

After a while, Ursula said, 'Do you recall Gilbert telling us once that, in Africa, it takes a whole village to raise a child?'

'I do.'

'What matters to Roland is that he is loved. Really loved. So you and I must gain his trust. We must learn to love this child as if he were our own. I'm sure the others will help. Then Edith can leave Roland in our care for the time she needs to visit Pascal.'

Tears sprang to Dora's eyes. 'My darling Ursula, I hoped so much you would guess what was in my mind.'

'I thought as much,' said Ursula, her eyes smiling.

41

July 1907

Provence

Colour-washed a soft pink with faded green
shutters and terracotta roof tiles, Belle Vue was
exactly as Edith remembered it. The sun-
warmed courtyard remained shaded by chestnut
trees and the path to the front door was still
lined with billowing clouds of lavender, hum-
ming with bees.

Jasper touched her arm. 'Shall we go in,
Mama?'

'I was remembering the last time I was here,'
said Edith.

The fierce heat of the sun pressed down on
them as they descended from the hired carriage.
Jasper tucked his parcel under one arm and
offered his other to Edith.

Bless him, she thought. He'd insisted on
accompanying her, anxious about her safety if
she travelled alone, and desperate for a chance to
see Pascal. Her firstborn had grown up so much
in the last year and been a perfect travelling
companion on the long and fatiguing train
journey south, keeping silent while she struggled
with her doubts or planned what she would say
to Pascal, solicitous when she was tired and
always attentive to her comfort.

They walked arm-in-arm along the path, Edith's skirt brushing the lavender and releasing its glorious fragrance.

Jasper tugged the pull of the doorbell and they listened to the faint ringing in the depths of the house.

Edith swallowed, her heart skittering in her chest. She'd waited so long to see Pascal again but what if he refused her?

A moment later, a maid opened the door and Edith asked if Madame Joubert or Madame Caron was at home to Mrs Fairchild.

Pascal's mother, Madame Joubert, a frosting of silver in her dark hair, received them in the salon and welcomed them in lightly accented English.

'I've come from Spindrift House in Cornwall,' said Edith. 'I wish to enquire after Pascal's health.'

Madame Joubert nodded. 'In the past, he spoke of you many times and you have written to him every week since his accident.' Her dark eyes widened as she scrutinised Jasper. 'And who is this young gentleman?'

'May I present my son Jasper?'

He came forward to shake Madame Joubert's hand.

'I have heard much about you and of your artistic talent,' she said, still studying his face.

Jasper flushed and mumbled that Uncle Pascal had been an excellent teacher.

'I'm very concerned for Pascal,' said Edith, 'because he has never replied to my letters.'

'There has been an improvement in his

426

physical condition,' said Madame Joubert, 'but his spirits remain so melancholy I fear for him.' Worry lines were etched around her eyes. 'He has lost the desire to live. I bought him paints but he has not touched them. He rarely speaks. He doesn't want to eat. He refuses to attend church or to receive visitors. I do not know how to help him.'

Edith closed her eyes in pain. *It was her fault!* 'May I speak to him?' she asked.

Madame Joubert shrugged, her palms turned up. 'I warn you, he has changed. I will not ask him if he wants to see you because he will say no. He is in the loggia, as usual. I believe you know where that is?'

'Thank you,' said Edith, rising to her feet.

'May I come, too, Mama?' asked Jasper.

Madame Joubert smiled sadly at him. 'Perhaps in a little while. For now, will you stay and tell me about yourself? I shall send for some lemonade.' She rang the brass bell on her side table. 'It is a shame Gabrielle is not here to see you but now she lives with her mother and new stepfather in Nice.'

Edith was relieved that she wouldn't have to see Delphine.

'Will you give this to Uncle Pascal?' Jasper handed Edith his parcel. There was desperation in his expression. 'Tell him I painted it especially for him.'

Edith took it from him and let herself out of the French doors into the garden. The heady perfume of jasmine scented the air and heat radiated up from the flagstones. The song of the cicadas vibrated all around. It was exactly as she remembered it that hot summer afternoon long ago, when she'd been a blissfully happy new bride. Before Benedict ruined it all.

There was the cottage in the garden where Delphine had lived then and where Edith had seen her with Benedict *in flagrante delicto*, setting off a chain of events that had changed the future irrevocably for them all. She remembered her agonised, heart-pounding flight from the shock of what she'd seen. And there was the shrubbery where she'd hidden and where Pascal had found her. That hot afternoon had led to her shame and the secret that had ultimately been the cause of Pascal's terrible accident.

Guilt and sorrow weighed her down as she turned away and walked around the house towards the loggia.

And then she saw him.

Pascal sat hunched over in a bentwood wheelchair, a book lying unheeded upon the table beside him. Unmoving, he stared over the garden wall towards the terracotta roofs and the cypress trees on the land that sloped steeply down towards Nice.

Edith stilled, her fingers pressed to her mouth and her heart breaking all over again. Shivering, despite the heat, she took a few faltering steps towards him.

He shifted slightly in his chair, as if he'd heard her footsteps.

Her mouth was dust-dry. 'Pascal,' she murmured, 'it's Edith.'

He turned his head abruptly, his eyes momentarily widening with joy, but then the light went out of them and he looked away again.

Edith moved a garden chair to place it facing him, a few inches away. She sat down on it so he had little choice but to look at her.

'What do you want?' he said, his voice hoarse, as if he rarely spoke. He was as thin as a reed and his clothes hung in loose folds around him.

'I want *you*, Pascal.' She stroked his hand but he jerked it away as if she'd burned him.

'Don't mock me!'

'How could I ever do that? You didn't reply to my letters and I've been beside myself with worry for you.'

'I did not want your letters. How could you imagine I would want to be reminded of the life I've lost?'

She trembled in the face of his bitterness. 'I've lost that life, too.'

He gave a bark of laughter. 'You aren't the one sitting in this chair. Now why don't you leave me to my misery?'

'Because I love you. I will always love you.'

'You cannot love this empty shell of the man you once knew.'

Edith blinked back tears. 'I'm the best judge of that, Pascal. You stood by me through thick and thin, always there to support me when I was at my lowest ebb, and now it's my turn.'

'Don't you understand? I don't *want* you to support me.' He raked his fingers through his hair. 'You lied and kept from me the knowledge that we have a son. You, the person I loved beyond all others, did that to me.' He looked up at her then, his eyes dark with pain. 'I would have died for you.'

Pascal's misery felt like cold steel slicing into Edith's chest. 'Not telling you the truth was a terrible misjudgement,' she whispered. 'Hindsight is a wonderful thing. I was wrong and you will never know how sorry I am for that. If you wanted to make me suffer for what I did, you have your wish,' she said, 'but we are not the only ones suffering.'

'I don't understand.'

'Jasper doesn't know he's your son,' said Edith, 'but he's always loved you, not from a sense of filial duty but because he respects you and enjoys your company above all others. He's mourned your absence every single day since your accident.' She pressed her handkerchief to her eyes. 'And that has changed him in ways that are not right for a fourteen-year-old boy.'

Pascal made a small noise of distress.

She drew a deep breath. 'He was always quiet and sensitive but now he's retreated within himself. He rarely laughs. He goes off day after day, wearing your painting hat and carrying your paints in that old canvas bag you always used, with your easel under his arm. You're not there and it's as if he wants to *be* you.' Her face crumpled and she broke down.

Pascal's breath rasped in his throat but he didn't move.

Edith blew her nose and lifted up the parcel Jasper had given her. 'He wants you to have this.' She pulled off the brown paper and

430

turned the canvas to face him.

Pascal stared at it, his face working as tears gathered in his eyes. 'It's our special place near Port Gaverne, where we used to go together,' he whispered.

'He's painted countless canvases there, each time striving to better the previous one. He said he'd keep going until he finished one that was good enough to give to you.'

Pascal took the canvas from her and studied it. He sighed. 'This could be the work of a professionally trained artist. I knew he had a gift but this . . .' He covered his eyes. 'I didn't want him to suffer by having a crippled father who could be nothing but a hindrance to him. Oh, Edith, what have I done? Jasper was the last person in the world I wanted to hurt.'

'I had to come and tell you how he grieves for you. Even if you no longer love me, please don't hurt Jasper anymore.'

He looked up at her then, his eyes full of sorrow. 'But of course I still love you! And it cuts me to the bone that I've lost you. I have nothing at all to offer you now.'

A tiny shaft of hope jolted through her body. 'You haven't lost me! How could you, when your name is engraved upon my very soul?' She leaned forward to gather him into her arms.

He resisted for a moment and then clung to her, weeping. 'I said such cruel things.'

'You had good reason.' She rocked him against her breast, breathing in the familiar smell of him.

'I've had so much time to do nothing but think,' he said, his face buried in her neck. 'I felt

431

so angry and betrayed at first. It has taken me until now to understand that, then, you had no choice but to pretend Jasper was Benedict's son.'

Cheek to cheek, their tears mingled.

'I should have told you later, though,' she said.

'Yes, you should have trusted me to keep your secret.'

'I'm sorry. I was so terrified of what Benedict might do.' She bit her lip. Now was the time to lay her soul bare before him. 'And I was also afraid for myself,' she whispered. 'The community looks up to me. For years, they've despised Benedict for his adultery and I couldn't face the shame if it was revealed that I was an adulterer, too.'

'We could not know what vengeance Benedict might wreak upon you,' said Pascal, 'but I cannot believe your friends would condemn you.'

'What will you do now, Pascal? Will you tell them all?' She held her breath while she waited for his answer.

'The sin of adultery was never yours alone,' said Pascal. Frowning, he winced and kneaded his knees and thighs. 'I desperately want Jasper to know I am his father but . . . ' He sighed heavily. 'Perhaps that is only for my own selfish gratification? If it became common knowledge in the village, it would make him unhappy. And, until all the children are twenty-one, there's still the risk of what Benedict might do.'

'Whether or not Jasper knows the truth, he will always think of you as his father by choice.' She looked down at her hands, twisting her handkerchief in her lap. 'Without you, the light

432

faded from his life,' she said quietly. 'As it did from mine.'

Pascal squeezed his kneecaps and rubbed hard at his thighs.

'Are your legs hurting?' she asked.

He shook his head. 'Pins and needles. They come every day now. I haven't dared to think about it but feeling is returning to my legs. Yesterday,' he looked up to meet Edith's gaze, 'I moved one of them, just a little.'

'Pascal!' Her breath stilled and hope flared.

'It may come to nothing,' he said.

'I will always love you,' she said, 'and, whatever the future holds, I want to face it with you. Now and forever.' She reached for his hand.

This time, he did not pull away but gripped her fingers fiercely. 'If you will have me, Edith, I want to come home to Spindrift House.'

She cried out with joy and then held his face tenderly between her hands. 'I love you with all my heart,' she whispered. And then she kissed him.

Afterwards, Pascal let out a long sigh. 'Still, there is the old magic, *n'est-ce pas?*'

'Always,' she said. 'There is something else you should know. Benedict has returned to London.'

Pascal closed his eyes for a moment. 'So he will trouble us no longer?'

She shook her head. 'I'll tell you all about that later but now there is another piece of magic I must perform. I shan't be long.' She left him there and hurried back to the house, her heart singing.

She went through the French doors into the drawing room and Jasper rose abruptly to his feet. Both he and Madame Joubert's faces were taut with fear and hope.

'Jasper,' said Edith, 'you may go and see Uncle Pascal now. I haven't told him you are here so your visit will be a lovely surprise.' She smiled, close to tears again. 'He told me your painting is as good as that of a professionally trained artist.'

The pallor of Jasper's cheeks became suffused with pink and tears glittered on his lashes.

'Go around the side of the house to the loggia, Jasper,' said Madame Joubert. 'We shall come in a moment.'

He wasted no time and sprinted out of the French doors.

'I think,' said Edith carefully, 'that Pascal has taken a step towards whatever recovery is possible for him. I believe you will find his spirits considerably improved.'

Madame Joubert dabbed her eyes with a lace handkerchief. 'I often wondered why my son never wished to marry but now I have met you, finally I understand. I do not know what occurred between you last year,' she said, 'but I thank Our Lady for bringing you here today. Shall we go together to see him?'

They walked slowly around the house until the loggia came into view.

Madame Joubert pressed a hand to her mouth as the sound of Pascal and Jasper's laughter drifted towards them on the warm air. 'I haven't heard my son laugh once in the past year,' she said.

'Nor I,' said Edith. 'It's a beautiful sound, isn't it?'

They stood side by side, watching Pascal and Jasper talking, their dark heads close together as they studied Jasper's canvas.

'Will you be taking Pascal back to Cornwall with you?' asked Madame Joubert.

Edith nodded. 'I shall make him a bedroom and a studio downstairs and I hope he will rediscover his love of painting. I shall look after him with the greatest of care and you and your family will be made very welcome whenever you wish to visit him.'

'I would like that,' said Madame Joubert. She gave Edith a sideways look. 'Now that I have met Jasper, I must make up for lost time and grasp every opportunity to be with my grandson, don't you think?'

Edith caught her breath but saw no condemnation, only happiness, in Madame Joubert's eyes. 'That is an excellent plan,' she said.

Madame Joubert smiled, reached out for Edith's hand and lifted it to her cheek.

Hand in hand, they went to join Pascal and Jasper.

Historical Note

One of the exciting things for me about writing historical fiction is the opportunity to delve into the chocolate box of the past to choose all the champagne truffles, while leaving behind the strawberry creams. I didn't enjoy dry-as-dust history lessons at school but what did fascinate me was how real people lived in days gone by. It was only with the passing of the years that I made the connection as to how much politics impacted on peoples' day-to-day lives throughout history. As an author, there are countless factual and imaginary human stories to be told arising from historical social and political issues.

The Light Within Us, the first of the Spindrift trilogy, is set in the late Victorian period from 1891 to 1897. *The Fading of the Light* takes place only a few years later from 1902 to 1907 but it was interesting to discover through my research the change in ambience. The story opens during the summer of Edward VII's coronation and the social atmosphere, following Queen Victoria's death, is generally more liberal. While widowed Queen Victoria became more reclusive towards the end of her life, King Edward VII was a patron of the arts, and enjoyed meeting people and travelling. He engaged in international politics, earning himself the name of Edward the Peacemaker.

In homes, the cluttered, dark and heavily

patterned interiors of the Victorian era were swept away and replaced with pastel colours, elegant and timeless furniture designs and lightweight draperies. Fashion reflected this change and evolved into more pared-down styles, too. Skirts became narrower, often in a tulip shape and dresses were made of lighter weight fabrics. The Edwardian era was the last in which women were tightly corseted.

The Edwardian era is often referred to as 'the golden age' before the Great War, basking in the sun that was never expected to set on the Empire. The quality of the housing stock was improved and infant mortality dropped. Emmeline and Christabel Pankhurst founded The Women's Social and Political Union. There was, however, still a long way to go before women would receive the vote. The rich enjoyed extravagant country house weekends, balls and shooting parties, their lifestyle facilitated by the low wages of the poor, who remained in the grip of grinding poverty. Further education became more widely available, even for girls, and the middle classes prospered with more opportunity to 'better themselves'.

The Light Within Us explores the lives, loves and female friendships of the fictional Spindrift artists' community on the rugged north coast of Cornwall. *The Fading of the Light* continues the story with emphasis on marriage and infidelity and the effect upon a woman and her children if it all went horribly wrong. I'd never thought of myself as a feminist until I began to discover how few rights women had in the past and it made me boil with the injustice of it all. In an unhappy marriage, divorce wasn't an option at this time, except perhaps for the very rich and even then, only about ten private acts for divorce were passed in Parliament each year.

One of the great inequities was that a husband was able to sue for divorce if his wife had been unfaithful to him only once. Repeated acts of adultery or violence on his part weren't sufficient grounds for a wife to divorce her husband and, in addition, she had to prove cruelty, desertion, incest or bestiality. If she left her husband, she lost custody of her children as well as any property she'd brought to the marriage. *The Infants Custody Act 1839*, known as the 'tender years doctrine', did allow a mother to have custody of children under seven, provided she could prove herself of unblemished reputation. Of course, a husband's word as to his wife's reputation was far more likely to be accepted than that of her own.

After a divorce or separation, even an innocent woman would afterwards be shunned by society and the slur passed on to her children. If a marital breakdown became unbearable, the couple often found it preferable to make quiet arrangements to live apart. Or the husband might lock his wife in a lunatic asylum if she displeased him.

Thankfully, women have a great deal more say in their lives these days. Marriage has evolved over the centuries and expectations of the married state have shifted and changed, too. According to an old English proverb, marriages are made in Heaven. Many warring couples will surely agree that an unhappy marriage must be made in Hell? Nevertheless, hope springs eternal and for many second marriages, love will triumph. Hopefully.

Acknowledgements

I'm grateful to my lovely agent, Heather Holden-Brown and equally lovely editor, Eleanor Russell and the team at Piatkus for their continuing encouragement and support. My thanks also go to Lynn Curtis, who copy-edited the manuscript in her usual sensitive and careful way.

Beta readers are incredibly important to an author. My fantastic writing group, Wordwatchers, read the first draft and were generous with their constructive criticism and cheered me on when I was flagging. Author friend Liz Harris also brought her sharp eye for detail to the manuscript and discussed the plot with me when I had lost it. Thank you to all of you.

Thanks and love to my husband, Simon, who regularly discovers that, although I'm present in body, my mind is often lost somewhere in another century and I'm not always home in time for tea.

Last but definitely not least, I'd like to thank all those readers who bought the first book of the Spindrift trilogy, *The Light Within Us*, and whose enthusiastic response encouraged me to write the second, *The Fading of the Light*. Without you, dear Readers, there would be no more books!

THE LIGHT WITHIN US

Charlotte Betts

Cornwall, 1891. Talented painter Edith Fairchild is poised to begin a life of newlywed bliss and artistic creation in the inspiring setting of Spindrift House, freshly inherited by her charming husband, Benedict, and overlooking the stunning harbour of Port Isaac. But when her honeymoon turns sour, her dreams are all but dashed and after a moment of madness and desire she finds herself pregnant with another man's child.

Edith swears never to tell her secret and devotes herself to her art. Joined at Spindrit Holuse by her friends — Clarissa, Dora and the secret father of her child, Pascal — together they turn the house into a budding artists' community. But despite their dreams of an idyllic way of life creating beauty by the sea, it becomes clear that all is not perfect within their tight-knit community . . .